L.J. SHEN

Midnight Blue
Cover Designer: Letitia Hasser, RBA Designs
Interior Formatting: Stacey Blake, Champagne Book Design

Playlist

"Gimme Shelter" – The Rolling Stones
"Daddy Issues" – The Neighborhood
"Love Song" – The Cure
"Young God" – Halsey
"An Honest Mistake" – The Bravery
"Cigarette Daydreams" – Cage the Elephant
"One" – U2
"Shake the Disease" – Depeche Mode
"What You Know" – Two Doors Cinema Club
"Do Re Mi" – Blackbear
"April" – Deep Purple
"London Calling" – The Clash
"Handsome Devil" – The Smiths
"Brianstorm" – Arctic Monkeys

How is your soul feeling today?

"And now here is my secret, a very simple secret: It is only with the heart that one can see rightly; what is essential is invisible to the eye."

—*Antoine de Saint-Exupéry, The Little Prince*

For Amanda Soderlund and Lin Tahel Cohen

Prologue

Alex Winslow in another meltdown: arrested for DUI and possession of cocaine.

By Beth Stevenson, The Daily Gossip

British singer Alex Winslow was arrested again Tuesday night for driving under the influence and for possession of cocaine. The twenty-seven-year-old singer had been released from California's Lost Hill Sheriff's Station after a night in jail. A night during which, it is alleged, he swung on the bars of his cell and wrote the lyrics to his song "Wild Heaven" on the walls using a blue Sharpie given to him by a smitten station employee (a Sharpie he later used to sign her breasts).

As well as getting caught with three grams of cocaine in the glove compartment of his azure vintage Cadillac, the heart-throb is also accused of trying to seduce his way out of trouble when he got pulled over in the early hours on the Pacific Coast Highway cradling a nearly-empty bottle of whiskey.

The twelve-time Grammy winner allegedly unleashed his famous, one-hundred-million-dollar smile at the officer on the scene, a forty-three-year-old mother of three, saying, "You really are f***** arresting, love, but I reckon I'll be the one doing the cuffing tonight."

The "Man Meets Moon" singer infamously got arrested eight weeks ago for punching Steven Delton, owner of the website Simply Steven, and for stealing a Grammy statuette. Winslow stormed onto the stage at the Grammys mid-speech when fellow British singer William Bushell received the Best Album award, plucked the statue from Bushell's hand, lit a cigarette, and launched into a rant:

"Are you having a laugh? Raise your hands if you actually voted for this wanker without getting bribed with a complimentary handjob. Come on. Come. The. Fuck. On. His whole album sounds like background music at McDonald's. No offense. To McDonald's, not to Bushell. There wasn't even one creative track in the entire album. In fact, if creativity met this bloke in a dark alley, it would run the other way, screaming bloody murder. I'm taking this home. Doesn't feel too good when someone steals what's yours, eh, mate? Well, boo-fucking-hoo. It's called life, and it's a lesson you taught me."

Previously close friends and former London roommates, Bushell and Winslow had a falling out two years ago over model/socialite sensation, Fallon Lankford, and have been labeled enemies since. Both Brits slammed reports concerning bad blood between them. It has been alleged that Winslow's latest album, Cock My Suck—which peaked at number nine on Billboard and disappeared from the charts soon after, the worst in his career—had driven him into the arms of alcohol and cocaine.

Shortly after word got out of Winslow's arrest, Simply Steven ran an article titled, "Alex Winslow: The End of an Era." It is believed that Mr. Delton is now looking to sue Winslow, after the latter assaulted him with a jab to the face when asked about Fallon Lankford's new love interest, Will Bushell.

Within hours of his second release, Winslow offered an apology through his long-time agent, Jenna Holden:

"Alex Winslow is deeply sorry for doing a number of things that were very wrong and for which he is ashamed. He would like to apologize to the officer who arrested him, stretching the apology to her husband, children, and the local church in which she volunteers. Winslow acknowledges his out-of-control behavior can no longer be overlooked, and for the sake of his loved ones, his fans, and himself, has decided to check himself into a rehabilitation facility in the state of Nevada. We kindly ask you to respect his privacy as he fights this very personal battle against his demons."

Winslow's former publicist, Benedict Cowen, who parted ways with the singer days after his Grammy meltdown, was not available for comment.

Comments (1,937)

xxLaurenxx
He is off-the-rails crazy. Also: off-the-rails hot.

Pixie_girl
Dude, McDonald's background music? Richhhh. Winslow's last album was so bad my ears bled for two weeks after listening to it.

Cody1984
#LeaveAlexAlone
(just kidding, he'll probably shove a finger into an outlet or something if we don't keep an eye on him.)

James2938

Guy's a sociopath. You can very clearly see it in his art.

BellaChikaYass

I echo that thought…but I'd still do him. ;)

xxLaurenxx

Me too! Lol

Pixie_girl

Sadly, me three.

James2938

Good, because he's not the kind
Of guy who can offer you more
than a quickie. He is bad news.
LITERALLY.

Chapter One

Indie

Six months later.

*T*ap. Tap. Tap, tap, tap, tap, tap.

The soles of my shoes slapped against the granite floor like a persistent canary. I had to dig my fingernails into my thighs to make my legs stop bouncing to the rhythm of my restless, foolish heart.

Shut up, heart.

Chill out, heart.

Stop fussing, heart.

There was no need to panic. Not even a little. Not even at all.

I was going to get the job.

I elevated my head, flashing the woman sitting across from me my biggest, most enthusiastic smile.

"When we advertised the job for a PA position, we kind of, sort of, what's the word I'm looking for…? *Lied.*" Slamming her chrome MacBook shut, she splayed her bony, manicured fingers on top of it, showcasing a ring that must've cost enough to buy the better half of my up-and-coming neighborhood.

My throat bobbed, and I smoothed down my tattered pencil skirt. Actually, it wasn't even mine. It was Natasha's, my brother's wife, and two sizes too large at the waist. I only ever got called back from food chain restaurants that didn't require a suit, so I'd had to improvise. I tucked my knotted ankles under my chair, sparing my interviewer my silver Oxford shoes, a hint of my personality I'd forgotten to disguise.

Everything in the woman's office screamed excess. Her desk, white and sleek; the seats made of alabaster leather; and the bronze chandelier dripping down between us like liquid gold. The Hollywood Sign poured from her floor-to-ceiling window in all its promising, beautiful, broken promises glory. So close you could see the dirt clinging to the white letters. Her workplace was the size of a ballroom. There wasn't a drop of color or personality in this office, and not by accident.

Jenna Holden. Powerhouse agent to the biggest Hollywood stars. Owner of JHE Group. She didn't have time to get personal. Least of all with the likes of me.

"You're not looking for a PA?" The forced smile on my face crumbled. I needed this job like Mark Wahlberg needed to show his real junk in *Boogie Nights*. Really, *really* bad. Case in point: I was living with my brother, his wife, and kid, and as much as they loved me, I'm sure they loved not having to share their one-bedroom apartment with a twenty-one-year-old avant-garde slob slightly more. My only source of transportation was my bicycle, which in L.A. was the equivalent of getting from A to Z on a dead turtle's back.

"I'm looking for...*something*." Jenna tipped her chin down, bowing a thinly plucked eyebrow. "And it does involve some assisting."

My patience was hanging by a thread, ready to jump ship. I was hungry, thirsty, and desperate for the job. *Any job*. Summer had kicked my ass, and all the blue-collar positions had been filled by acne-ridden teenagers. This was the third time I'd come into JHE for this vague job this month. First, I'd gone through the HR girl who'd left me waiting for forty minutes because her pedicure appointment ran late. Then, Jenna's personal assistant had grilled me like I was fresh back from an ISIS training camp. Finally, I'd met with the mega agent herself, and now she was telling me I'd been misled this whole time?

"Tell me, Indigo, how carefully did you read the job description?" She sat back in her chair and laced her fingers together. She wore a crisp, buttoned shirt tucked into black velvet pants, and a smug smile. Her champagne-blonde hair was pulled into a painful looking bun, and my skull burned just from looking at the way her skin pulled around her hairline.

"Careful enough to repeat it by heart."

"Is that so? In that case, please do."

My nostrils flared. I decided to humor her one last time before collecting my bag and remainder of self-esteem and walking away.

*"PA needed: resilient, responsible, patient, and thick-skinned. Non-drinker, **NO DRUGS**, with a flair for arts and life. If you're twirling on the sidelines of mainstream, have great attention for detail, and don't mind long hours and endless nights, we're looking for you. *NDA needed, criminal record will be checked."*

I pushed a copy of my job application, tapping it with my finger. "This is me. Sans the twirling part. I'm prone to migraines. Now, can you tell me why I'm here?"

"What I'm looking for is a savior. A nanny. A friend. You're the closest thing to perfect I've found, but frankly, this whole thing is going to be a lot like an organ transplant. We won't know if you're a match until we put you two together."

I blinked, studying her like she was a mythological creature. If this was a joke, I'd officially lost my sense of humor.

She stood up and began to pace, her arms folded behind her back. "I have a client. No, not a client. *The* client. One of the hottest names in the industry this decade. He got himself into hot water recently and now he needs a big bucket of ice to cool his name off. Drugs, women, ego the size of China—you name it, he's suffering from it. Your job is not to book flights and make coffee. He's got an arsenal of people doing that for him. But you will be there when he goes on tour. You'll cater to his emotional needs. You'll make sure he doesn't snort cocaine backstage, or stay out late, or miss a show. You'll be there to grab his hand and pull him away when he gets into an argument with a journalist or a paparazzo. Your job, in short, is to keep him healthy and alive for three months. Think you're up for the challenge?"

Her words were so sincere and sharp, they sank into my skin like teeth.

A savior. A nanny. A friend.

"That's…a lot of responsibility. Sounds like that someone is in big trouble."

"Trouble is his middle name, a part of his charm, and the reason why I have a Xanax tab in my purse at all times." She cracked a bitter smile.

TMI, TMI, TMI.

"If he's in no shape to go on tour, why is he doing it?"

"He was supposed to leave six months ago and canceled for personal reasons. If he cancels again, he'll have to pay thirty million dollars to the production companies. The insurance will never pay up, considering the cause of termination was him swimming in enough cocaine to bake a five-tier wedding cake."

I tapped my toes against the shiny floor some more, gnawing at my lower lip. Jenna stopped moving around. She was now standing in front of me, her thin, golden Prada belt twinkling like a sad eclipse.

"Three months on the road. Private jet. Best hotels in the world. If you've somehow managed to hang onto the leftovers of your innocence in this city and want to keep it, I'd advise against taking the job. But if you have a thick skin and a taste for adventure, know this—this job will change your bank account, your path, and your life."

She sounded serious. Concerned. Every word had a weight and it sat heavy on my chest. "You'll sign a non-disclosure agreement. You'll take what you see to your grave. And you'll get paid mad bank."

Mad bank? Who talked like that? L.A. showbiz people. That's who.

"Mad bank?" I asked.

"A hundred thousand dollars for every month of your employment."

Beat.

Beat.

Beat.

Three beats had passed before I sucked in air, remembering I needed to breathe.

Somewhere in the distance, I heard office folk snort-laughing next to the vending machine. A printer spitting out papers. A spoon clinking in a mug. My gnawing intensified, as it did when my nerves got the best of me, and the metallic taste of blood spread inside my mouth.

Three hundred thousand dollars.

Three months.

All my financial problems—gone.

"Who is he?" I looked up, my voice cracking like an egg. Did it matter? Not really. At this point, he could be Lucifer himself, and I'd still accompany him on a lengthy tour in hell. Natasha and Craig's bills were piling up. Ziggy needed tubes in his ears—every winter my nephew cried and screamed himself to sleep. We had to tie socks around his little fists to keep him from clawing at his ears until they bled. We couldn't even afford a new bed for him, and his chubby legs constantly got stuck between the bars of his cradle. This offer was a no-brainer. The only issue would be parting ways with my family, but even that came with a big chunk of relief. My brother wasn't the best person to hang out with right now.

Besides, I'd been babysitting two-year-old Ziggy since the day he was born. This person was supposedly a grown-ass man. How hard could it be?

"It's Alex Winslow," Jenna supplied.

Evidently, the answer to my question is 'next to impossible.'

Winslow was huge. His songs were shoved down your throat by every radio station like he was the only person on the continent with vocal cords. But what truly worried me was that he seemed unapologetically arrogant. Alex Winslow looked through people like it was an Olympic sport and he wanted to make the queen proud, which was just one of the reasons why he'd managed to create beef with every person with a pulse in Hollywood. That was common knowledge, even if you tried to avoid gossip like the plague, which I did. Wherever he went, a string of reporters and palpitating fangirls followed. I'd get heat the minute his fans spotted me. The paparazzi shadowed him everywhere but to the bathroom. I once read in a gossip magazine—dentist appointment—that some girl had to shut down her Instagram account after partying with Winslow because a dark net website put a bounty on her head. Twenty grand was collected to predict her death date—*"fulfilling your prediction is entirely optional,"* they said.

Last but not least, Winslow was the most antiauthority mainstreamist in Hollywood. Not too long ago, he was arrested for DUI, and I hated, despised, *loathed* drugs and alcohol. Which basically meant that our "organ transplant," as Jenna had referred to it, would likely result in two casualties and one epic failure.

I cradled my face in my hands, letting out a breath.

"This is the part where you say something." Jenna's cherry red lips twitched.

I cleared my throat and straightened my posture.

Time to put on your big girl panties and make sure they stay dry for three months, despite him looking like Sean O'Pry's hottest brother.

"I promise to keep him safe and sound, Ms. Holden."

"Good. Oh, and I'm going to say this once to keep my conscience clear: don't fall in love with the guy. He's not the white picket fence type." Jenna waved a hand and scrolled her phone, pressing her thumb onto it and making a call.

"I'll try my best." My jaw muscles twitched as I swallowed a sneer. Alex Winslow was beautiful in a way storms were—only from afar. Just like them, he had the power to sweep and ruin you, two things I was too busy surviving to entertain.

"If your best is good enough, then you should survive this. I'll have my assistant print out the paperwork. Any questions?" She fired some instructions on the other line to said assistant, then ambled toward the door.

"When are we leaving for his tour?" I peeked over my shoulder, my fingernails burrowing into the armrest.

"Wednesday."

"That's two days away."

"Good at math." She sneered. "That's an unexpected plus. I'll get the paperwork. The tour is called 'Letters from the Dead' and is supposed to revive his career. Be right back."

I remembered that song. It was the soundtrack to my senior year, when everything looked so final and wrong.

Love is just a fraud,

Excuse me for being goddamn bold,

You asked me to believe,

As if I had some fucks to give.

With the door closing behind her, I sat back and blew a lock of blue hair away from my face. Crazy laughter bubbled in my throat, eager to pour out.

I was going to make three hundred thousand dollars and hang out with the biggest rock star in the world for three months. I looked up, and the chandelier winked at me mischievously.

I thought it was a sign.

Chapter Two

Alex

My soul was dying.

It wasn't an exaggeration.

It bled the last of my hopes and dreams onto the sticky floor, smeared in cigarette ash and pussy juice. My mobile chimed with a text message, forcing me to peel my gaze from the ceiling.

Unknown
Hey, Alex!

Me
Arse pic/ tit pic/ face pic.

Unknown
???

Me
You got my number. That means whoever gave it to you told you I don't sext without checking the assets beforehand.

Unknown
This is Elsa from The Brentwood Club. You are supposed to make an appearance tonight for the fundraising evening event for children with ASD. I contacted you directly to

extend my gratitude…

I was doing something for free tonight. Why was I doing something for free tonight? Most nights, I didn't even do stuff for money. In fact, it'd been a long time since I'd done shite. At all.

Fuck my manager, Blake, and my agent, Jenna, and my life, sideways scissors-style, for making me leave my room, my sanctuary, my personal space. And fuck Elsa, who now knew my true colors—fifty shades of dick.

"Oi, Waitrose. A new charity case." I threw my mobile at Lucas, who caught it in the air, groaning. Technically speaking, Lucas was my drummer, so covering my arse was not part of his jurisdiction. But Lucas—dubbed Waitrose after the fancy supermarket chain he grew up posh enough to afford—was notoriously nice to Suits. Me, I hated Suits. Loathed them. Because when you're a rock star and make a crap ton of money, everyone wants a piece of the pie. A pie *you* baked. With ingredients *you* bought. None of the Suits had given a shit about me when I sat, day in and day out, outside King's Cross tube station with Tania, my acoustic Tatay, and played, and begged, and shoved demos into people's hands just to watch them slam-dunking them to the nearest bin. None of the Suits were there when I knocked on doors in the pouring rain, and pleaded in the bitter snow, and bargained, and argued, to get myself heard. They also weren't there when I got booed in Glastonbury three years in a row opening for bigger bands, or when mostly-empty beer cans were thrown my way for a good laugh, or when a drunk girl puked on my only pair of shoes trying to tell me I sounded like a Morrissey knockoff.

They weren't there when I sold my soul to some other Suits, who thought I was really talented but wanted, *"poppy, short, catchy, with a flare!"*, and I caved in and gave it to them. Told you my soul was dying. Or maybe it simply belonged to other people. Either way, I needed a new one. Unfortunately, it was one of the rare things my money couldn't buy.

I hated everyone I worked with. Record companies, executives, producers, PR staff, marketing mavericks, big corporations using me as their spokesperson, and basically every single cunt who'd ever asked for a raise because they thought they were oh-so vital to the Alex Winslow brand. Newsflash: I *was* the brand.

I'd bought the ingredients.

I'd baked the pie.

I was going to eat the fucking pie.

All of it. Every single crumb and lick of filling. *Mine.*

My reluctance to share was, among other reasons, what branded me as a disreputable arsehole in the media. To say I didn't give two shits was an insult to said shits. The tabloids weren't my friends, and the day I'd invite a paparazzo to take a picture of me was the day hell froze over and Katy Perry released a decent song. I was still voted Nicest Celebrity to Fans three consecutive years, and that was genuine, and real, and *true*. I loved my fans. Harder than I loved the money or fame or pussy that came along with them.

"*Mate.* I can't believe you tried to sext a fifty-year-old chairwoman of a non-profit organization. Have you no shame?" Lucas nudged my shoulder with his foot, his thumbs already flying across my touch screen furiously, offering a profound apology in my name. I didn't even know why. At this point, my image was as wholesome as a Serbian war zone. Waitrose huffed but still cleaned up after my shit. It was partly why I kept him on my payroll.

I didn't like him. I barely even tolerated him after everything that had gone down two years ago.

We were all sprawled on my auburn velvet sofa. I'm saying 'mine,' but really, it belonged to the Chateau Marmont. I stayed at the cottage-styled room whenever I was in L.A. Which, granted, was seven months out of the year, but I refused to call this place my home. Los Angeles was like a B-Grade prostitute. She let anyone in, looked less than average, and once inside, you realized there was too much traffic and that whoever'd been there before you had left a mess. Add to this the pollution and white-toothed starlets who wanted to ride your anything—be it your knob, reputation, or black American Express card—and what did you get? My very own definition of hell.

I lit another cigarette and flipped through the channels. Reality show. Cooking show. Makeover show. TMZ. A bunch of people renovating a house and crying about it. A fake-tanned bird having a meltdown over her wedding invitations, which were sent in the wrong shade of pink. I threw the remote across the room. It crashed against the flat screen, cracking it into a spiderweb impression. No one batted an eyelash.

Alfie, my bass guitarist, farted. Then he said, "I need to scratch my arse, but I'm too knackered to move."

"I need to fuck, but I'm too knackered to go to the hotel bar," Blake countered, lying. He only had eyes for one girl, and she was the *wrong* girl.

"I'm sure Lucas is a willing candidate. Getting fucked over is his national sport." Alfie snorted, to which Blake responded by flicking his ear.

Why they were tired, I had no clue. At this point, we were collecting sleeping hours like they were antique typewriters. Dutifully. Indulgently. The next three months were gonna be rough.

I grabbed my mobile, since Lucas was done successfully extinguishing another fire I'd created, and scrolled down my contacts list. I'd had a few dozen regular bells in L.A., but I didn't want to wine and dine any of them, and that was a problem. They all nurtured some kind of a celebrity career, and they all wanted me to walk hand in hand with them at The Grove or stroke their cheeks adoringly at The Ivy. Unfortunately, I'd rather ram my cock into a roughly-opened tin than humor their millennial dreams, which made my sex life about as exciting as a beige painted wall. I didn't do groupies—respected my fans too much—and didn't do romance—ex-girlfriend from hell, more about that later—and that meant I'd normally settled on what I called 'Compromise Pussy.' Lonely stewardesses, mid-thirties career women sitting at the Chateau's bar, and the passing tourist who didn't care who I was. They weren't always the best looking, but at least they didn't make me feel like the plastic product my record company had shaped me into.

The doorbell rang. Maybe God had heard me and sent a bodiless cunt. Another thing I'd pay good money for and wasn't for sale—note to self: Google pocket pussy. Apparently, it *is* a thing.

"Expecting anyone?" Alfie gathered phlegm in his throat and spat it into an ashtray on the coffee table. Wanker had the manners of a used tampon.

I continued scrolling my mobile, ignoring him.

"Mate." Lucas shoved his foot into my chest—*again*—lying across from me, using one of his drumsticks to scratch his back under his tee. "Are you too famous to answer people's questions now? Who's at the door?"

"The Grim Reaper. Or Jenna. Same difference." I took a swig of my Coke—the drink, not the drug—regrettably—my finger halting over a name on my phone.

Fallon.

Fuck you, Fallon.

And I was. Going to fuck her, that is. Again. But this time on all fours, after she had my name tattooed across her ankle like a shackle, a punishment for what she'd done. I had a book-long list of things I wanted from Fallon Lankford, and she was going to give them to me, because deep down, she still loved me. It was etched on her face. The face that kept transitioning with the years to fit Hollywood's standards: puffier lips, smaller nose, longer eyelashes. I remembered the girl behind the mask, and she was crazy about me. Problem was, she was crazier about fame.

Blake stood up, stalking to the door. He looked like he was going to war, every muscle in his body tight with frayed nerves. Blake and Jenna never saw eye to eye, and I never saw the point in making them play nicely. I heard murmurs from the entrance. Growls, huffs, and then the metallic chuckle Jenna produced when she wanted to spit in your face. A few seconds later, they both marched in, a third person trailing behind them.

A girl.

A girl I didn't know.

Another bloody babysitter.

She floated into the apartment, on the shiny dark wood, the blond hue of the many lamps in the room illuminating her teardrop-shaped face, and all I could think about was how fast I was going to get rid of her arse. She looked...*fine.* Not my taste. Jenna went for the ones who weren't quite so pretty as to make me want to bang them harder than the bottom of a ketchup bottle, but still pretty enough for me to tolerate. This one was significantly smaller than a normal human being. Thumbelina-tiny, with olive skin, flat chest, and pointy little nose. Long icy-blue hair—if I wanted a hipster, I'd pluck one from the thousands of screaming fans trying to smuggle their way backstage—and I wasn't entirely sure what she was wearing, but I found it senseless to believe she actually paid for it. A vintage orange dress with flared cuffs and floral embroidery barely covered her knobby knees. Why the fuck did I know what any of these terms meant, you might wonder? Because my soulless arse did Armani and Balmain campaigns to support a cocaine habit that made Charlie Sheen look like a Boy Scout.

Welcome to my mess, New Girl. It's a bumpy ride from here on out.

I took another swig of my Coke, then ground my teeth. New Girl was going to be Old News in a week, max, just like the rest of the sitters who'd accepted the position before her. I'd make sure of it. My thumb almost pressed Fallon's name—*almost*—before I tucked the phone into my back pocket with a frown.

Not now.

Not here.

Not in front of all these wankers.

Jenna, the number one ballbuster in North America, folded her arms over her chest and awarded me with a look that could freeze hell and its neighboring sections. "Hello, Al. Are you going to continue the fart-fest on the sofa or come say hello to your new employee?"

I respected Jenna. She was the one Suit who'd never ask for a sexual favor or for a photo-op or for a fucking pony for her birthday. Which was why I'd agreed to her attaching a nanny for "Letters from the Dead" in the first place. The position was supposed to have been filled two months ago when I initially left rehab, but of course, I had to make the first nine quit in tears, and one moved to another state in a bid to put some space between us. I'd hoped that by the eighth, Jenna would give up on the idea altogether, but Jenna wasn't much of a quitter.

Thing was, I was a stubborn bastard, too.

Reluctantly, I scraped my arse from the settee, ambling in their direction.

"For the record"—I puffed my cigarette, shotgunning it from my nostrils like an angry bull—"Alfie is the one in charge of the questionable aroma. He can't stay away from Mexican food when in L.A."

"Damn right, I can't." Alfie cackled from the sofa, peppering the sentence with a burp. "Tacos for World Peace! I should start a non-profit organization."

I offered New Girl my hand. I was six something. She was five nothing. She was practically at eye level with my crotch, which would have been very convenient if it wasn't for the fact I wanted nothing to do with her. She dragged her head up to meet my gaze. Her eyes, a different shade of blue from her hair, were dark. And wild. Deep like a well-written riff.

Not completely bland. Good for you, love.

"Alex Winslow."

"Indie Bellamy."

"Your name is Indie?" My eyes ran her length from the floor up. Her tiny, sweaty palm tried to squeeze my big, cold one.

"Indigo. After the color."

"Hardly making it better," I quipped. She'd officially lost my attention, though, and I tossed the still-lit fag out the open window and propped my forearm against the wall, mentally rummaging my mind to find what I wanted to ask Jenna about. Something about a commercial I was shooting mid-year. Versace? Pepsi? Like it made any difference.

"Glad you think so. I've been anxiously waiting to hear what you think of my name," Indie said.

She was still here.

She was still here, and she'd answered back.

What the fuck?

Jenna shifted in my peripheral, scooping her mobile from her Hermès bag and pointing between us with the device. "You two, get to know each other, but not too well, and definitely with your clothes still on. I have a phone call to make. Be right back." Her heels punctuated the floor with noisy *thwacks!* all the way to the patio.

Indigo's gaze clung to my face, not unlike a puppy. I glared back, because I was a petty fuck, and because staring competitions were apparently my forte, along with sexually harassing middle-aged charity chairwomen in text messages.

"Hey." I leaned down, my lips finding the shell of New Girl's ear. She didn't shiver, and most nannies did. It caught me slightly off-guard, but not enough to deter me from my mission. "Wanna know a secret?"

New Girl didn't answer, so I took it as a sign to continue, "I wet my bed at night. Every. Single. Night. But with the tour jitters and all, I properly piss all over the place. Sometimes it mixes with the spunk from the last girl I rolled between the sheets. Sometimes her juices are a package deal, too. I always ask my assistants to make my bed because, unlike the hotel staff, they actually sign a non-disclosure. Think you can manage that, little one?"

I straightened, examining her face. This was the point where their eyes widened, their mouths fell open, and their faces paled. Not with this one. No. New Girl's smile was sun-bright and type-two-diabetes sugary.

"Mr. Winslow, I'd be more than happy to purchase a pack of adult diapers for you. In fact, I think they'd suit you just fine, considering your behavior."

Where had Jenna found this girl, and how could I send her back to whatever hellhole she'd come from before she boarded the plane with us on Wednesday? I smirked, my elbow still against the wall, raking my callused fingers through my long hair.

"Do you have any idea what you're getting yourself into?" I dropped the bemused tone. Playtime was over the minute she got cheeky.

"Actually, I do." She took a step forward. "I'm getting myself out of a really bad financial situation, which means your antics mean nothing to me. I need the money. I'll see these three months through and keep you sober, no matter what."

"You don't know what 'what' entails, so I wouldn't go around making promises if I were you."

Her eyes flashed theatrically, and I was beginning to really lose my patience with this one. "Here I am, making a promise. Sue me, Mr. Winslow."

Don't fucking tempt me, New Girl.

I took a wide step, erasing the space between us, and now her small tits brushed against my stomach. Her eyes were kindled with enough determination to burn down the hotel. I was on the verge of tossing her out to the balcony with my very own hands when Saint Lucas, AKA Waitrose, appeared from behind my shoulder, stretching his arm toward her and saving her day.

"Lucas Rafferty. Drummer." He flashed his megawatt, Brad-Pitt's-Nicer-Brother grin. Her guarded expression liquefied into a smile instantly, and she released her hand from mine, taking his. That was when I noticed we'd been shaking hands for three minutes. So, New Girl was a creep, too.

Nice touch, Jenna. You're getting a bin bag and a tabloid scandal for Christmas.

"Indie."

"Hippie parents?" Waitrose's soft chuckle probably melted her insides into marshmallow. Lucas had the ability to charm the knickers off of a fucking stapler, and although he kept his love life unusually private, women had the tendency to throw themselves at him. The irony was, Lucas didn't deserve these girls.

She shrugged. "Just literal. They called me Indigo because of my eye color."

A blush crept up her neck, crawling to her cheeks and resting on her hairline, like a crown. I shook my head and sauntered to the dining table, leaning a hip against it and shoving a handful of crackers into my mouth.

"Babies' eye color can change until they're four," Lucas pointed out from behind my back. Were they vying for The Most Boring Conversation in the World award? Because they sure as hell had my vote.

"I guess they were risk-takers, too." Her throaty laugh filled the room.

"Were?"

"They died." Pause. "Car accident."

"So sorry to hear." His posh, public school accent rang in my ears and jam-packed me with fresh, red rage.

He sounded gutted. I wasn't particularly happy to learn New Girl was an orphan, either. But the thing about Lucas was, he *literally* was hurting for her, the way children do before they grow up and get hardened by life. He was the most obnoxiously earnest human being I'd ever met. As far as my knowledge went, I was the only person in the world he'd fucked over. Which, one could argue, said a lot about my level of arseholery or likeability. Or lack thereof.

Jenna resurfaced from the terrace, shoving her phone into her bag. Her smile told me if I tried to say no to hiring New Girl, she was going to dump my sorry arse to the nearest curb. There were other agents, big and powerful as she was, but there was only one agent to bail my eejit self from jail at three in the morning when I'd decided to play a one-sided game of chicken with a police patrol car on the Pacific Highway and finish the night doodling on a booker's tit. I couldn't rely on my drummer, manager, and bass guitarist to flush the toilet, let alone be there when I fucked up in spectacular fashion. I loved my friends the way you love your pet. Fiercely, but with no expectations of reciprocation. My family...well, that was an entirely different story I didn't want to delve into.

"Hello," Jenna said.

I offered half a nod.

"This one talks, Jenna." I jerked my chin to the girl.

"The last one didn't and didn't survive four days on the job. I needed to try something different." My agent shrugged, and I puffed on my millionth cigarette that day and disregarded her, and the rest of the universe, my favorite pastime since I'd gotten out of rehab.

"Can I tell you something?" Jenna reapplied her blood-shaded lipstick in front of a pocket mirror she held up to her face.

"Manners don't suit you." Rhetorical questions channeled my inner bully.

"You need to start thinking about your next album, Alex. *Cock My Suck* did poorly, and you've taken the needed time off to focus on your wellbeing. I was surprised to learn you didn't write anything while you were in rehab."

I cocked my head sideways, arching an eyebrow. "Ever been to rehab, Jenna?"

"No." She clamped the mirror shut.

"I might've had a shit-ton of dead time on my hands, but I was too busy crawling up the walls Trainspotting-style and trying not to tear the flesh from my bones."

"Cocaine doesn't lead to physical dependency," she stated, unblinking.

"Ever done coke, Jenna?" I asked her in the exact same tone I'd asked the first question.

"No."

"Same answer."

The doorbell chimed again. Blake opened it, *again*, bypassing a chatting Lucas and New Girl. My band members and manager had already acknowledged she was a part of our landscape. At least they had the decency to ignore her, like she was an ugly vase no one had the balls to move. Other than Waitrose, of course, who made pissing on my parade a form of art.

"Who ordered Mexican?" Blake yelled.

"Stupid question, mate!" Alfie shouted from the sofa.

"Oh, shit. Literally," Lucas drawled in slow-motion, referring to Alfie's stomach, which didn't share his infatuation with the cuisine.

I turned around, moving my attention back to Jenna.

"So. Where did you find the little fighter?" I massaged the velvety part of her earlobe. Women melted under my hands like butter, and my agent was no different, with the exception that she'd never sleep with me because she had enough brain cells to know the outcome.

Jenna examined her nails while she talked. "Does it really matter? All you need to know is I don't trust you to stay sober on your own. You're volatile, angry, and bitter at the world. And she—she has too much to gain and a lot to lose if this doesn't pan out the way I want it to. Sorry, Al. This one's ready to go to war."

"Jenna." I *tsked*, brushing my thumb along my lower lip. "She's not a war. She's barely a fucking sport."

"If that's the case, promise me you'll play clean. She may have sass, but she's really young."

"Clean is not in my dictionary." It wasn't even a joke.

"Say that to one of your endless strings of one-night stands. I'm sure they'd still hop into bed with you." Jenna's eyes rolled so hard they almost hopped to another dimension. She brushed her shoulder along my chest as she waltzed to the door. Indigo shadowed her, her back ramrod-straight.

My agent turned around a second before leaving. "Write me an album, Al. Make it spectacular, settling the score between you and Will Bushell."

A kill switch clicked in my brain the minute she said his name.

There was no score to be settled. I'd released *one* bad album. Everyone had one. Even Bad Religion. But of course, I wasn't going to defend myself, not to her, not at all, and definitely not in front of my entourage and the little smurf she'd dragged into my den.

"It's on." I winked and finger-gunned her, turning around so she couldn't see the anger clouding my face.

The door closed.

I grabbed Alfie's Mexican food and threw it against the wall, watching the black beans crawling down and making a mess. The guacamole clung to the wall like concrete, fighting gravity. I was restless, and I wasn't even sure why.

New album?

New tour?

New *Girl*?

Will Bushell?

Things were about to change, and this time, there was no magic powder to take the edge off.

Chapter Three

Indie

"Soooo. Spill it, girl. What's he like?"

Disgusting. Gorgeous. Rude. Sexy. Screwed-up. Witty. Broody. Unbearable. Trouble. *Trouble.* **Trouble.** Alex Winslow was all those things and more, but my family didn't need to know any of this. Natasha was already crazy worried at the prospect of me leaving for three months. I turned off the faucet and wiped my hands with a kitchen towel, turning around to lean against the counter. We lived in an old Pico Blvd one-bedroom apartment, where the fridge made more noise than the highway outside, and the yellow walls were more naked and depressing than the strippers at the club right below the condo.

"Fine, I guess. Your average rock star. A chain-smoking, crazy-in-love-with-himself, conceited dude." I sucked my teeth, my eyes traveling anywhere but their gazes.

Natasha looked up from her bowl of plain pasta, while Craig flipped through the want ads in the daily paper and took a swig of his beer. He was already to the point where he'd sent applications to anything even remotely relevant on Craigslist, which he joked was named after him, and Monster, which he joked he'd become if he didn't find a job soon, and was a step away from knocking on people's doors begging for them to hire him to do anything—walk their dogs, water their plants, or sell them a kidney. It pained me to see my bright and proud brother groveling. Especially considering how he'd given up his college scholarship to raise his baby sister because one day his parents walked home from their twentieth wedding anniversary date and never made it back home.

"Cut the bullshit, Indie. You never badmouth people. He's probably a world-class prick, which doesn't surprise me. Show me a celebrity who isn't a jerk." He sat back in his seat, a black cloud of anger hanging over his light-brown mane. The chair squeaked under his weight. Utensils clinked together in Nat's bowl. Craig finished his beer and placed it next to the two other cans he'd already drunk.

"Another serving?" I jutted my chin to the bowl, ignoring my brother's vast consumption of alcohol when we couldn't even afford a bottle of Tylenol for Ziggy.

Nat shook her head. "There's enough for tomorrow. Better keep it."

"Counting pasta. Not very rock 'n' roll. Guess you're too good for us now, Indie," Craig said, and we both ignored him.

I washed the dishes. The kitchen was small and full—pans, containers, framed pictures catalogued all the good, sad, and funny memories of the four of us. Ziggy lay sleeping in his cradle in the living room. His ear infections were under control, but we all knew that come winter, that was going to change.

Nat slid behind me, hugging my midsection and resting her head against my shoulder. "You don't have to do this. You've never been on an airplane before. Never even left the States. We can still work this out on our own. I have some temp work on Venice Beach at least until October. And Craig will find something soon…"

I turned around and grabbed her shoulders, smiling.

"Three hundred thousand dollars to hang out with a rock star. Are you kidding me? Does that sound like something any twenty-one-year-old girl would say no to?"

"Yes," she deadpanned, flattening her palm over my antique orange dress. "If the girl in question is you. I know you. All you want to do is sew and play with Ziggy. You're the mother of all introverts. When we watched *Bubble Boy* together—you *envied* the poor kid for living in solitude."

Touché.

I didn't need the reminder I was a reclusive loser. But maybe that was a part of the charm of taking the job. Getting out of my shell was exactly what I needed. Plus, I'd come back with a suitcase full of unique and precious adventures. New smells, sights, and tastes on my tongue from all the wonderful places I'd always dreamed of visiting.

"Nat, I promise you, I couldn't be more excited if I tried."

"Would you tell us if you really didn't want to go?" she probed, and I wondered if she could see the terror I masked with my smile.

"Yeah, Indie." Craig stood up from his seat and walked toward the living room, still in the same PJ's from last night. "Don't feel like you have to do this. We're doing fine. Other than the fact we're behind on rent, the electricity payment, and Ziggy's pediatric bills. Oh, and, you know, life."

"*Craig,*" Natasha hissed, her eyes two narrow slits of anger.

He left, his bitter chuckle bouncing off the walls. A minute later, the bedroom door slammed shut. Ziggy protested the sudden noise with a moan. Time stood still as Nat and I waited to hear Ziggy's soft snores again.

I could see why my brother had very little success with finding a job, but it was important to remember he wasn't always sarcastic, rude, and borderline incoherent. Once upon a time, Craig was the lovable wide receiver who won Natasha Brockheimer's heart by serenading her an Alex Winslow song outside her window. She had the blondest hair and the tannest legs, and the richest daddy in Beverlywood. Natasha didn't care that Craig had dropped out of college to take care of me. But her parents did. And when she got pregnant at twenty-two, said parents then decided they wanted nothing to do with Nat, Craig, Ziggy, or me.

For a while, Craig remained positive. He worked two jobs, helped with Ziggy, and gave Natasha foot massages every evening, talking to us about how we were all going to make it. But then he got fired, and started drinking, and the pep talks, foot massages, and hope evaporated from our lives, replaced with a suffocating cloud of bleakness.

"I think I'm going to head to bed. Thanks for everything." I twirled one of Nat's fair locks. I slept on the couch next to Ziggy's cradle. It was convenient, because he woke up thirsty several times a night.

Who's going to give Ziggy his sippy when I'm gone? I shoved the question to the back of my head, allowing my legs to carry me past the couch, to my white bicycle, the only expensive thing I'd ever owned. My mom got the bike for me when I was fourteen. It was made in Paris, my favorite city in the world, though I'd never been.

I glanced at the big suitcase sitting next to the entrance door, glaring back at me, taunting me, reminding me of what was to come. There was no way I could sleep with so much weighing on my chest, my mind, my *heart*. I needed more air than was in the whole apartment building.

I went for a ride.

Outside, I swung one leg over the bike, pushed off the asphalt, and darted down the darkened street. The breeze was crisp and salty, the wind dancing across my face. Lights from convenient stores and old-school diners zinged by, and for the first time that day, I managed to inhale deeply.

A tingle ran down my spine when I remembered the first time I saw Alex Winslow's eyes up close. Whiskey brown. Bottomless and tawny like rich wood, full, expressive, and misleadingly warm. Straight nose, square jaw seemingly made of stone, and too-full lips that softened his appearance, despite his best efforts. His tousled hair was dirty brown, silk and cashmere, and he smelled of old leather and a new obsession. He may have looked beautiful, but it was important to remember that Alex Winslow was not, in fact, boyfriend material. Or anything-material. What he definitely *was* was: rude, impatient, a bully, and a recovering drug addict.

I pedaled faster, a mist of sweat forming on my brow. Winslow had worn army boots—unlaced—a pair of cheap-looking torn jeans, and a black tank top with raw-edge armholes, exposing his lean torso and tatted ribs. He was skinny—lithe but strong—and had several wristbands and rings on his hands, and was the very definition of sex on legs.

And I hated him.

Hated the way he walked, the way he talked, the way he'd undermined me. Hated that he held so much power over me, and the way he was going to use that power against me.

I rode my bike for almost two hours before making a U-turn and heading back home, then decided to skip the shower because I didn't want to wake anyone up. I tossed and turned until dawn, thankful when Ziggy woke up twice and cried for his sippy cup. And when the sun emerged and the clouds hung low and fat over my city, I stood up, grabbed the suitcase, and walked over to his cradle.

"I'm getting us out of this mess," I swore, leaning to kiss his forehead, reminding myself this temporary goodbye would later on grant us a steady future. He murmured to himself and waved his chubby little fist goodbye, blowing me kisses like I'd taught him.

That's when I knew this was a promise I was going to keep.

Alex

"*Dafuq?*"

I jolted awake at a sharp elbow slamming into my ribs. It dug through my black hoodie *and* my leather jacket, so it had to be that long-limbed tosser, Alfie.

I sat up, growling. The dead hum of industrial engines buzzed in my ears. You'd think I would've gotten used to it by now. Spoiler alert: I hadn't.

Alfie pouted like a groupie and slapped his forehead with the back of his hand. "Oh, Alexander, why don't you love me?"

"Because you have a cock, no tits, fart like you've consumed every rotten egg in America, and think Russell Brand is funny. The latter, by the way, is borderline criminal."

Alfie laughed and threw something at me—a blue guitar pick.

I picked it up from my crotch and slid it in my back pocket. "What do you want?"

"We're almost at the airport."

"I thought we were *on* the plane."

"Are you still using? We're in a traffic jam from hell moving at a snail's pace to LAX."

"So what's that annoying noise?" My head swiveled toward the window.

"That would be L.A., Lord McCuntson," Blake quipped, his eyes hard on his phone, always in work mode.

Forty minutes later, we were at the airport. Blake scrolled through our schedule on his iPad. We always started at the farthest point and worked our way back up to the States. Australia first—Sydney and Melbourne—then we'd do Asia, then Europe before we hit the land of the free—with a week-long break in England, to see our families.

"Letters from the Dead" was supposed to be a piece of cake. Best of. Songs I knew by heart. I had no new product to push. I was going to kiss my fans' arses and hope to fuck the sights, smells, and cultures were going to get my creative juices flowing.

This time, the record company had asked for, *"catchy, fun, bubbly, with a hint of rock 'n' roll."* So of course my inner rebel wanted to dump a bunch of fourteen-minute tracks about politics and global warming onto their table. I didn't even like politics, but I hated my record company more.

At the airport, we breezed past security and into the VIP lounge. The private jet was ready, and this was the part I despised the least about being Alex Winslow. I had access to the most ridiculous shite ever to be invented. Seven years ago, I'd drooled from the prospect of getting on a plane—any plane, fuck the destination or class—and now I was literally grousing about having one all to myself.

"Well, if it isn't the mother of dragons." Blake *oomphed* as I unloaded Tania, resting her guitar case against one of the tables. Blake often claimed Jenna had the ability to burn people alive if they disobeyed.

I wormed out of my leather jacket, looking around me to make sure my few valuable possessions—mobile, Tania, and wallet—were with me. "And you're telling me this because...?"

"Because she ain't alone."

I looked up, watching my agent striding in her snug three-grand dress toward me. She'd brought sitter number eleven. New Girl was now standing in front of me, wearing a *Mad Men* type yellow dress. Tight and completely ridiculous for a daylong plane ride. Her blue hair was braided into an embellished chignon, and she looked like a color-blind fairy.

"New Girl," I exclaimed with false enthusiasm, so that Jenna would think I at least tried before I gave her the boot. I refused to call her Indie because A) her name was silly, and B) that would be acknowledging she was a person and not an obstacle. I opened my arms and walked toward her, all swagger and easy smirk. "We're thrilled to have you on board."

New Girl's smile transformed from timid to irritated. When my arms wrapped around her shoulders, I heard her wheezing out the remainder of her hope that this was going to resemble something civilized. Jenna was standing beside us, and I took the opportunity—again—to loom over New Girl and whisper into her ear, "Run, darlin'. One last chance to do so."

Her body turned to ice, but she didn't cower, and for that, I sort of didn't hate her all the way. At least she had some backbone. So far, I'd treated her even worse than the rest. Because—unlike the rest—she hadn't budged.

"Glad you guys are getting along." Jenna eyed me, suspicion leaking from every syllable rolling between her lips. She knew something was fishy. But, like the majority of people around me, she didn't want to open that can of worms.

I leaned back and threw an arm over New Girl's shoulders, squeezing her into an embrace.

"Like, *legit,* we're gonna be best buds," I mimicked the whiniest, most valley-girl American accent I could scrape.

Jenna stubbed a manicured fingernail to my chest. "Write me an album, Al. One where you don't throw shade at half the industry. Make it good. Behave. And just a heads-up—Bushell is doing a similar tour. Your European dates parallel. Stay away from him."

My ears perked, possibly literally.

I wondered if Fucking Fallon—dubbed as such for ruining my life—accompanied him. Bushell, I never wanted to see again. Fallon? Now, that was a different story. Jenna saw the question on my face, because she was quick to answer it.

"Let me put you out of your misery—Fallon is coming with him. Listen carefully one more time—with. *Him.* Not with *you.* It's over, in case you needed any more clarification."

"Don't tell me—" I started, which prompted her to bang her open palm against my torso. I was ninety-nine percent sure that most agents didn't spend the better part of their time continuously smacking their clients in the chest.

"She nearly ruined your goddamned career! You almost snorted yourself to death. If you want to kill yourself over a girl, one who jumped from your bed to your ex-best friend's without batting a pretty eyelash—be my guest. But if you pull any funny business on 'Letters from the Dead,' I swear to God, your tour title will become literal, because I will *kill* you." She paused, took a deep breath, and then slapped on a Botoxed smile. "Metaphorically, of course. My lawyer said no more death threats to rock star clients until the Malibu house is fully paid off."

I tipped my head back and laughed. A hearty, big, that's-why-I-hired-your-crazy-arse laugh. Sure, I needed Jenna, but she needed me just as much. I was still the hottest shit since sliced bread in Hollywood, and even after *Cock My Suck,* which, admittedly, was a sugarcoated, mass-produced,

Maroon-5-meets-Ed-Sheeran-in-a-Catholic-school-prom   inspired
album, I had enough star power in me to light up Vegas. If my next
album flopped, maybe, just maybe, I'd be subject to that kind of threat.
For now, I needed to make an effort, but definitely not to submit to
Jenna's every whim.

"You're going to miss me." I winked at my purse-lipped agent,
who didn't even bother rolling her eyes anymore.

Jenna shoved New Girl in my direction. "Help her when you land
in Australia. She's never been on a plane before. We had to issue her a
quickie passport."

New Girl's face turned ruddy so fast I thought her head was going
to detonate. She tilted her chin up and tightened the grip on her duffel
bag. She needn't worry. I was a cunt, but I'd never make fun of someone because they didn't have the same opportunities I had. It wasn't
long ago I'd had to count every penny and sneak into the tube when I
needed to get places. But, just to be clear, I was still going to make her
life hell. I didn't do positive discrimination. Or a negative one. Call me
a saint.

"Anything else?" I plucked a cigarette from my Camel soft pack.

"There's a manual listing Indigo's job. Read it carefully and don't
argue. It's a process, Al." She slapped a folder onto my chest, her raised
eyebrow daring me to argue.

"And you"—she tossed something into Indie's hands—"this
phone has two contact numbers—mine and Hudson's, Alex's PA. No
Internet connection. No apps. It's only good for one thing, and that's
reporting back to me. You'll give me daily updates, got it?"

Then Jenna turned around and walked away, not even sparing her
new employee a goodbye. New Girl stood in front of me, her face a
mixture of defiance and determination.

"What the fuck are you looking at?" I lit up. Maybe I wanted to
get arrested. Jail time meant alone time, and alone time wasn't the
worst thing in the world.

"I'm looking at my worst nightmare." She blinked, almost willing
herself to un-see me.

If nothing else, she was bloody honest. Taking a step in her direction, I made sure we were toe-to-toe, my cigarette dripping ash down to her hair when I whispered the words, "I'm not your nightmare, sweetheart. Nightmares, you wake up from. With me, I'll keep going until you're out of my hair. We clear?"

Not allowing her to gather her wits—Arsehole Behavior 101, I trademarked that shit—I turned around, dumping the thick file with her job description into the bin on my way to the leather seats by the huge window.

I hoped, for her sake, she wasn't too frightened of flights, because she'd need to board one alone after I sacked her curious little bum.

From there on, it was same old shite, different day. We got on the plane. The takeoff was bumpy. Turbulence made New Girl's face ashen, and I was certain everything in her body clenched, cunt included. Fifteen minutes into the flight, a stewardess strolled into the room with the blond wooded cabinets and asked if we'd like something.

"Ginger ale on the rocks and a loaded gun." I waved her off, staring at a blank page I needed to fill with inspiring, thought-provoking prose.

"He means for himself, not for you," Lucas, who was sitting on a white L-shaped sofa next to New Girl, clarified. He was the only one who'd deigned to talk to her, probably to piss me off. "And if it wasn't for his treating alcohol and cocaine as a recreational hobby, you wouldn't have to be here."

I made a mental note to tell Lucas to kindly withdraw his tongue from New Girl's anus, because his arse kissing was getting on my last nerve.

I didn't want him to mess around with the girl who was hired for me.

I didn't want to see how easy life was for him while I was being dragged through a mud of depression every minute of the day, my old friends, alcohol and coke, the only ones able to pick me up from the dirt.

Mostly, I didn't need to watch them both making out on airplane sofas and backs of vans while I nurtured a breakup fiasco that left my ego bruised. Especially seeing as he was part of the reason I was in this situation in the first place.

"Careful, Lucas. My toys are mine, so keep your hands out of my toy box," I warned, taking a sip of my ginger ale, my eyes still on the blank sheet.

He didn't ask what I meant.

He knew.

Chapter Four

Indie

Sydney, Australia

"You aren't stupid," Lucas repeated for the ten-thousandth time.

My hands kept disappearing in the big holes of his stylish jacket, which he'd loaned me because I'd forgotten it was winter in Australia when it was summer in the States. I realized my mistake the hard way, when we poured out of the jet into the bitter wind and overcast sky. Even the short trip to the glitzy black Mercedes van left me shivering.

"You couldn't have known." Lucas' voice was so tender you could barely hear the pity it harbored.

"Yeah." Alex sniffed, walking ahead of us, not even turning around to spare us a glance. His guitar was strapped to his shoulder, hanging over his back like a turtle's shell. "How could you have known it's winter in the southern hemisphere when it's summer in the northern hemisphere? It's just one of those best kept secrets on *the fucking planet.*"

Everybody's chatter died down. Blake, Alex's manager—the guy with the stringy black hair, beefy figure, and sharp suit, frowned. Alfie, the tall one with the golden curls, shook his head and kicked little rocks on our way to the SUV. Lucas' sapphire eyes apologized on Alex's behalf, and he squeezed my arm.

"Don't mind him. You all right?"

I nodded. "Other than feeling like an idiot? Fantastic, thanks for asking."

We climbed into the van, where I successfully didn't squeak about the right-hand steering wheel, and continued my mute streak. I flipped through the schedule of the tour Blake had handed each of us before we boarded the plane. Alfie had used the edges of the paper as dental floss. I wanted to look out the window and watch Sydney for the first time, but the truth was, I didn't trust myself not to gush, and I wasn't in the mood for another round of being Winslow's punching bag. I figured I had to lie low, at least until I graduated from New Girl to Indie in his eyes. Nonetheless, I hated him for making me feel this way. I also knew I was not going to be Little Miss Doormat for the next three months. I'd find my footing and fight back.

We were staying at a fancy hotel that kissed the ocean of Darling Harbour. I'd been to hotels before, but they were the kind that sat on busy highways and referred to their eighties décor as 'charming' in their wrinkled brochures. This one was different. A monstrous building with arrows and arches for miles. *Holy crap* described the hotel pretty accurately, although *Jesus H* came in a close second. We had to drive around the place for ten minutes, waiting for security to block the sidewalk with metal barricades so the rock star could check into the hotel, but when we finally pulled over, I realized I had a bigger problem than trying to decide whether Sydney reminded me more of a clean, new Miami or an urban Palm Springs.

"What in the…" I gasped, too taken aback to finish the sentence. There were hundreds of fans lining up beyond the barriers, screaming and waving signs and posters in the air. Sobbing girls were clawing at their faces as they shouted Alex's name so loud I wondered if their eardrums could spontaneously burst as a result. The SUV rolled to a stop. The Brits stared at each other, contemplative grins playing on their faces. Alex's face remained emotionless.

"It's a lot to absorb." Lucas shuffled in his seat beside me, his palm finding mine then squeezing once for assurance. His touch was warm and sweet. He was attractive, in a soft, romantic way.

"Yeah, New Girl," Alex surprised me by saying, reaching out to me as well, squeezing my thigh. My heart tailspun to my lower stomach at *his* touch, prompting goose bumps to spread along my scalp. "This whole thing is about *you*, so please tell us how *you* feel about hundreds of people waiting for someone who is not, in fact, *you*."

My patience. My sweet, tender patience urged me not to throw a punch straight into his face. True, I needed the job. But Alex Winslow was starting to look like a tight draw next to my financial worries.

"Can I breathe without your nasty commentary?" I peeled his hand from my thigh and dumped it at his side. I wished he didn't look like an angry god and write like a tortured poet. It would have made hating him so much easier.

"Only if you do it silently and not in my direction," Alex was just as quick to respond.

"Congratulations, Winslow. You somehow managed to snag The Rudest Person in the World award," Blake grumbled, still typing on his phone.

"I accept, but probably won't be able to attend the ceremony."

"Good idea, you'd probably burst onto stage and steal statues that aren't even yours..." I muttered, my eyes widening in horror as the words left my mouth. The world paused for one second.

Alfie broke the beat, snorting from the back seat and exhaling, long and loud. "Oi! I'm getting a hard-on by proxy. If you two are gonna hate-fuck each other, I'm buying a front-row ticket."

"Alfie!" Lucas swiveled his head around with a scolding look.

"What? Front row's got several seats. You'll get to see them, too."

"Enough," Blake grumbled, tucking his phone into his pocket and sliding the door open. "Everyone—out! Indie, please try to keep a low profile. Our lad here can be a little touchy when it comes to Jenna appointing nannies to him. Understand that he's a twenty-seven-year-old and one of the most influential celebrities in the universe. You being here is hard to swallow."

Alfie raised his hand as if to ask for permission to speak. "But if you're good at that—at swallowing—maybe you could soften the blow after all."

Alex turned around and punched his shoulder so hard the thump filled everyone's ears. "That's enough of your smart mouth. Let's get going."

We emptied out of the SUV. I stumbled forward, blinded by the flashes of dozens of cameras and shouting paparazzi. I kept staring ahead, hoping I'd make it through the revolving door without a spectacular fall or an embarrassing period stain. I wasn't even on my period; it just seemed like something that could happen to me. The noise, the light, the laughter all mingled in my head like a lethal cocktail. My limbs liquefied and claustrophobia took over me.

A hand reached from my side, enveloping my arm firmly. "I've got you."

I galloped to the entrance, being led by whoever ushered me. I only took a breath when a thick glass wall divided me and the people behind the barrier. I turned around to thank whoever was still holding me, and my heart dropped at the sight of Lucas giving me his good-boy smile.

"Thank you." My mouth felt like it was full of cotton.

"Our rooms are ready. The perks of being in Alex Winslow's entourage." He tucked his hands into his front pockets, staring at his shoes.

Shit. "Where *is* Alex?" Jenna had specifically warned me about not letting him slip out of my sight. We'd be staying in separate rooms, with Blake rooming with Alex to make sure he wasn't doing anything stupid. All other times, I had to be by his side. Alfie was leaning against the reception counter and flirting with one of the concierges. Blake was on his cell phone and kept repeating the sentence, "I don't care that it's the best hotel in Paris, in Europe, or on the Milky Way. If Alex sees him, he'll kill him."

"Outside, as per usual." Lucas' eyes wandered to the rock star, following his movements. "Giving his fans what they want. Why do you think there are so many of them? They're his number one priority."

My gaze followed Lucas' line of sight. Alex was leaning over the barrier signing posters, backpacks, and breasts, while also taking time to snap selfies with hyperventilating fans. There were two security guards beside him, each of them the size of The Hulk, staring helplessly at the eccentric superstar and wishing he'd stop flirting with teenage girls and danger. The fans were seriously close to pulling him into the mob and swallowing him whole like a pack of zombies.

"I need to go get him," I said, to myself more than to Lucas.

"It's not like they can slip him some drugs. He's in plain sight."

"I can't believe he's actually nice to someone." I turned to Lucas. I also couldn't believe I chose to say this to his drummer and friend.

Lucas leaned into my space, but somehow, it didn't make me feel uncomfortable. "I know it sounds like a cliché, but really, life made him a massive jerk. He wasn't always like this. I think you'll find he's a great bloke. He's just…angry."

He sounds like my brother, I thought.

We both watched Alex before Blake reappeared, stepping too close to me, making me shift toward Lucas.

"Rooms are ready. Whose turn is it to pull Alex out of the sex claws?"

I pretended not to hear the question, doubting he even considered me an option. Other than Lucas, all the guys acted like they'd rather fight a hungry lion in a closed ring than have a civilized conversation with me.

"Alfie's turn. Who were you talking to, mate?" Lucas asked.

"Jace, Will's agent." Blake exhaled, his chest deflating. "There'll be an overlap in England and Paris. England I'm not worried about— Bushell will be staying at his Gram's cottage in Sheffield. But in Paris, we have that Halloween event at the Chateau De Malmaison. It's charity." Blake gave Lucas a pointed look.

"We can fake an emergency." Lucas shrugged, switching into business mode. "Though I guess it would raise some questions, especially this soon after rehab."

Blake nodded, rubbing his neck. "It gets worse. Word is that Will and Fallon are engaged. Nice of him not to mention it to us when we…" He never finished his sentence, and I knew better than to probe.

All eyes darted to Alex again. For the first time since I'd met him, he actually looked happy as he took a selfie with two girls with braces.

"Alex will use it as an excuse to binge-snort." Lucas tapped his closed fist against his thigh.

Blake shouldered out of his pea coat. "Yeah, well, I didn't give Jace the pleasure of asking about it, but if that's the case, he'll be out on a bender by tonight. Jenna's talking to her contact in TMZ now, buying time before publication."

Fallon was obviously a sore spot for Alex. I didn't know who she was—I never followed celebrity gossip—but I did know that for the past two years, Will Bushell had been Winslow's archenemy.

"We need to keep him offline and away from the tabloids," Lucas said, adding, "and make sure there are no paparazzi or journalists anywhere near him."

"The second part is a piece of cake. Alex is known for being a cagey motherfucker. But how do you tell a bloody grown-up not to go online?"

"You give him a reason he can't argue with." Lucas' voice flirted with panic, and I tried desperately to connect all the dots in the conversation.

Blake let out an exaggerated sigh. "Sometimes it feels like I'm raising a goddamn baby. Remember the Tamagotchis? Alex is like having a hundred of them chained to your neck."

Five minutes later, the British Tamagotchi walked inside, and Blake handed me my electronic room key, instructing me to be at the lobby at 6:00 p.m. Normally, he'd explained, there were a lot of rehearsals involved, but this tour required a sound check and a mostly-sober singer. When I walked into my suite—the whole floor had been reserved for Alex Winslow and his crew—the first thing I did was fall headfirst onto the queen-sized mattress and make a bed angel with a squeak. I choked the creamy satin sheets between my fingers and moaned. Every muscle in my body was tense from the long flight, and I didn't even have the strength to admire the marble floors or golden-framed murals of the desert hanging on the walls. All I wanted was to fall asleep and wake up three months from now.

My phone buzzed in my hand. I stared at it through narrow eyes, as if it were a living thing and we were having a heated argument. Lucas had helped connect me to a network and the Internet. Not that it mattered. The screen on my personal phone was cracked and I couldn't see anything, including who was calling. I pressed my phone to my ear and inwardly prayed it wasn't my credit company.

"Hello?"

"Indie, it's Nat! I just wanted to know everything's okay," she sang from the other line. What was the time in Los Angeles? The middle of the night was my educated guess. I rolled to my back, staring at the high, arched ceiling and wondering how come all the beautiful things in the world came with a hefty price tag.

This hotel.

The money I was going to get paid.

Alex's seemingly miserable life.

"Everything's awesome." My voice pitched high, and I mustered a smile just so she could hear it. My family didn't need to know I was being semi-bullied by a rock legend. They had bigger issues to deal with.

"Are they treating you well?"

"The best," I confirmed. *Liar, liar, pants on fire.* But if there ever was a white, pretty, hurts-nobody lie, it was this one.

"Did you hear about Winslow? Well, I guess they were talking about it the whole flight…" Nat fished. I wrinkled my nose, eyeing the mini bar from across the room. Life was too short not to eat minibar food on a billionaire rock star's dime.

"Nope. He's not much of a talker. I doubt he'd address it even if people claimed he was an alien who came here to suck the life out of nuns. Why? What's up?"

"The thing that's up is his dong, girl. A Hollywood starlet had her phone hacked—hell, if I can even remember who—and of course, she just *happened* to have saved pictures of Winslow's cock. Apparently, horses have nothing on this dude. They showed some pixelated images on TMZ, but it could have been his arm for all I know."

I chuckled into my fist, feeling my cheeks staining red. *Classic Nat.* Before she became a mother and a wife, she'd been a funny, happy-go-lucky cheerleader who was always down for a good dick pic.

"So, seeing as you're single and he's single and you're both hot and you're about to spend three months together on the road, I'd love a confirmation of that rumor."

"Don't hold your breath," I muttered.

"Why not, Indie? At least think about it. If you love riding your bike so much, just imagine what riding a celebrity would feel like."

"Hardly the same thing."

"How do you know? You've never ridden a celebrity."

I'd never ridden *anyone,* and hell if I was going to start with Mr. Cocky Rock Star. Not that I was a virgin. I'd slept with my one and only boyfriend junior year before…*before* I'd lost my libido. Men had been low on my priority list since my family had crumbled.

I glanced at the time on the overhead clock. Half past five. I needed to take a shower and make it to the lobby in time for the pickup to the arena. How the hell Alex and the guys were supposed to do a show after a long flight, I didn't know. Then again, they were professionals, even if they never acted like it.

"Gotta go. Send the boys my love. Also, please email me pictures of Ziggy. I'll find a laptop sooner or later. I miss him already."

"He misses you, too. Have fun and take pictures."

"I will."

"Of his dick."

"I won't," I deadpanned.

"'Least I tried. Love you. Go forth and prosper."

"All the love, Miss Horny O'rgasm. Ciao."

The big irony was that the opportunity to see Alex Winslow's privates presented itself an hour and a half after I hung up with my sister-in-law.

We were hanging out backstage before the first gig of the tour. To my surprise, Alex didn't ask for a lot of riders. The dressing rooms were spacious and clean, platters of fruit and bottled water lined over rows of white-clothed tables, but that was the extent of it. No alcohol. No fancy food. No Jacuzzis. No strippers swinging on wrought iron chandeliers. Winslow was humble by nature. He only hired people who were considered close childhood friends, which was probably the only positive attribute to his otherwise tyrannical personality.

I was shadowing his every move in the Sydney arena and he, in return, played a game called let's-tell-everyone-Indie-is-my-psycho-fan. Every time we passed by a colleague, an assistant, or a technician, he pointed at me with a serious expression and said, "Can someone please call security to escort her out? This bird's been following me everywhere and she isn't exactly my taste." I ignored him, knowing full well that by not answering back, I was brewing a mini heart attack or developing multiple ulcers.

Don't feed the troll, Indie.

The rest of his band was in their dressing rooms, drinking pop and warming up.

"Why do I play for the only rock star in the world who actually tries to stay sober?" Alfie moaned from his room at some point, loud enough for all of us to hear.

Blake was talking on the phone and pacing back and forth in the hallway next to us, and Alex looked like he was patiently waiting for the world to end. He was perched on a loveseat, frowning at his guitar like it let him down by not producing fresh, original tunes for him to use. At some point, he got up and walked aimlessly down the hall. The warm-up band on the other end of the blackened curtain was well into their fourth song, and Alex winced every time the lead singer referred to the crowd as "babes." Other than that, his cool demeanor never once cracked or wavered, at least not until he took a sharp right to a smaller, narrower hallway and I stood up silently, following him to the restroom.

"And where do you think you're going?" Alex sneered.

Alex turned on his heel, staring me down like I was a rancid cloud he couldn't get rid of. To him, it probably wasn't that far from the truth, which made my physical reaction toward him even more pathetic. Every time he looked at me, I felt warmer. Like his eyes were sunrays, caressing, kissing, and melting my logic and inhibitions away. Don't get me wrong, I still hated him with passion I usually reserved for political villains who started world wars, but those rich amber irises weren't even bedroom eyes. They were *everywhere* eyes. I bet girls let him bend them over in every single room in the house, be it the kitchen, bathroom, or the garage. And let's admit it, maybe even the front yard for the whole world to watch.

"You can't go to the bathroom alone, especially before a show. I'm required to accompany you to make sure you don't do drugs. You'd know that if you bothered to read the manual." I squared my shoulders, bracing myself for another argument. The sound technicians were walking back and forth between us. They skipped the heaps of cables snaking on the floor and nodded at Alex nervously like he was the principal of their strict, Catholic school.

"What if I have to take a shit?" Alex jerked his chin up, watching me through the length of his nose. His droopy, everywhere eyes shone with amusement.

I crossed my arms, jutting one hip out. "Then I'll have to remind myself of how much I need the money and hope to God you don't share the love for spicy food with Alfie."

He chuckled, shaking his head, and resumed walking. I followed him. He walked fast. Maybe it was because he was skyscraper tall. Or maybe because he'd found another way to make my life less easy. Either way, my ragged breath made him smirk as I tried to catch up with him.

"You'll have to see my cock," he said mid-stride, his back to me.

I was practically running at this point. "I'll close my eyes."

"That'd beat the purpose of making sure I don't snort a line or two."

"I've seen penises before. Yours is nothing special."

Did I just say the word 'penises'? I did. Why? I'm not seventy. Or a prude. Though I can see why he'd think that.

"*Wrong.* So wrong. Probably the wrongest thing you've ever said. How many?"

"Excuse me?"

He stopped by the restroom door, which was only a few feet from the VIP ring. The scent of cigarettes, beer, and hot dogs crept into my nostrils and settled there, and I wondered how he must feel, smelling liquor and not being able to take a sip.

Crap. He probably feels like crap. And you're only making it worse.

"How many cocks have you seen in your life?" His neutral gaze swept over my body. "I mean, you're, what? Eighteen? Nineteen? And you also look like a lot of work, so I'm guessing between two to four."

"Firstly"—I lifted my thumb—"I'm twenty-one, old enough to drink in every country in the world that serves alcohol, which is good, because working with you, I'll surely need it. Secondly"—I lifted my index finger, even though I'd lied through my teeth—I wasn't gonna drink. Not tonight and not ever—"it's none of your business how many penises I've seen, or how many men I've slept with. If I like to be hung by my nipples from the ceiling or spooned by a gentle lover while cuddling a teddy bear, it's not for you to know. Last but not least"—I offered him my middle finger on a sweet smile—"I really can't stress this enough, but I'll try—your little mind games are not going to work. I'm keeping this job. Get used to me."

We stared at each other for a long moment before Alex slammed his balled fist to the door behind me. The door swung open with a bang, and we slipped in. I pressed my back against it, staying as far away from him as I physically could, while he coolly unzipped his low-hanging jeans and took his cock out over the toilet seat. My eyes were hard on the wall. The sound of his urine pouring into the water filled my ears and my throat bobbed with a swallow.

Nat's words came back and haunted me like a bad haircut from the eighties. An irrational need to check the goods took over me. It wasn't like he minded. According to the rumors, his dick had seen more cameras than Kendall Jenner. Slowly—so painfully slowly—my eyes drifted down his sinewy body. I just wanted to see what all the fuss was about. Whatever I had in mind, though, didn't come close to the real thing. Thick, long but not atrocious. With thin veins running through its length.

"Nice view?" he groaned, tucking his junk back into his briefs. His profile was glorious. Strong jaw, pouty lips, eyes like sex…

My eyes snapped up when I realized he was talking to me. "I wasn't…"

"Looking? Yes, you were. Next time take a picture. It lasts longer." He rolled his zipper upward and flushed the toilet with the toe of his boot. He turned around and squirted soap into his palm, washing his hands almost violently—rubbing between each finger and scratching his knuckles like he wanted to shed his own skin. When he was done, he looked around for a towel.

I cleared my throat, scrambling to regain my wits. "Longer than the glimpse or longer than your performance?"

Casually—so unbearably casually—he wiped his wet hands over my purple dress. I gasped, moving sideways. It looked like he was about to open the door and get out, but before I had the chance to yell at him for using me as a human towel, he slammed me against the wall, bracing both his arms above my head and pinning me to my spot. I let out a shriek of surprise at the sudden proximity.

Alex Winslow is touching me. Willingly, my surprisingly pitiful brain squealed.

Heat rolled off his body, making my back arch and my breath catch in my throat.

"Let's make one thing clear—I could fuck you to a point of numbness without even breaking a sweat if I wanted to. Now, careful, New Girl. If you don't keep your distance from me, I think I just might."

I looked up and smiled, ignoring how pale I must've been. Inside, my heart thrust against my ribcage, wounded but defiant. It'd never been this way before. So…wild. Like an entity of its own. My heart wanted to rebel, and I wanted to fight back, which could only result in trouble.

Slow down, heart.

Relax, heart.

Take a deep breath, heart.

"Are you done?" I hissed.

"Are *you*?"

Why did he want me gone so badly? The idea of asking him had occurred to me more than once, but I always came to the same conclusion. No one would want someone shadowing their every step and watching them take a piss before a show.

"No," I said.

"Then neither am I." He pushed off the wall, giving me his back while lacing his fingers through his hair. And it was true, what they wrote in all the romance novels Nat read in dangerous quantities. Because when he walked away, I felt the loss of him everywhere.

My body.

My skin.

The pit of my stomach where lust resided, dormant and napping.

"Aren't you going to wish me luck?" He grabbed the handle and opened the door, his shoulder bumping into someone else's. He didn't slow down. Alex Winslow was a tornado, impacting everything and everyone on his way to destruction.

"Break a leg," I croaked. The light seeped through the black curtain of the stage, making his hair shimmer gold. Jesus' pinnacle. I closed my eyes and glued my forehead to the wall, inhaling.

I told my heart to stop beating so fast one last time. It didn't listen.

Twenty minutes after Alex took the stage, I headed into his dressing room, intending to catch up on some sleep. The jet lag was kicking my ass all the way back to North America, and I knew I needed to ride it out, but surely, a power nap wouldn't be the end of the world. Blake was there, with his back to me, talking on the phone. He couldn't see me from his position, which was probably why he was yelling and flinging his arms around. I took a deep breath, intending on making myself known, but Blake's voice boomed in the empty room.

"Yeah, Jenna. Yeah. For the hundredth time, it's under control. We leaked the photos and now he thinks we don't want him anywhere near the Internet because of that. All interviews and media access will be denied for the duration of the tour. He doesn't suspect a thing. He doesn't even remember the girl who took them." He paused, listening to Alex's agent on the other end of the line.

My blood froze in my veins. *They* were the ones leaking those pictures?

Then I remembered the conversation with Lucas. The talk about diversion...about keeping Alex offline. About meeting with Will Bushell...*oh, my God.*

"Listen. Listen...*listen!* Bloody hell, woman. You've got balls the size of watermelons. Do you realize it's quite unattractive? And before you say anything, yes, I am aware your sole purpose in life is not, in fact, to attract me. We bought enough time to recalculate. He won't check, because he doesn't give a flying fuck. Or a driving one, for that matter. No fucks at all, by any means of transportation. His knob could be on the cover of *Vogue* wearing a beret with a cigarette sticking from the tip and he would probably not even recognize it as he passed by a newsstand. He's a rock star, Jenna. Not a has-been reality TV loser. No one knows." Blake rubbed his face, then he turned around and stared right back at me. His phone was still cemented to his ear when he said, "Well, scratch no one. The sitter knows. I'll deal with her now. Sext me later?"

The other line went dead by the way Blake groaned. The need to slap him across the face actually made my fingertips tingle, and I didn't even know why. I didn't like Alex, but that didn't mean I was okay with his team wronging him. Hell, I didn't even *want* to be a part of said team, and I still thought this was bullshit. The people he trusted were betraying him. Why would they sell him out? Were they trying to sabotage his recovery?

"It's not what it looks like." He held his palms up, his face creasing into a grimace.

"You sound like a cheating husband, so I'm going to say what any cheated wife would answer: it is exactly what it looks like." I found my words somewhere in the back of my throat. They came out thick and angry. "Wow. You're…ungrateful."

"You don't understand how much is at stake here. Alex is obsessed with Fallon. If he finds out she's engaged to his archenemy, he will go through the mother of all downward spirals. You'll fail at your job. The tour will be canceled before it even begins. His career will probably be over, not to mention he'll have to pay millions of dollars for the damages and loss. We can't just ask him to swear off the Internet for two and a half months without any explanation. We're doing what we can to help him. Everyone who cares about him is involved. His family, friends, bandmates. Everyone. You fuck it up, and I swear, Indie, you're going to make a lot of enemies in Hollywood." He pointed at me with the hand that held his phone.

I blinked, incredulous, wondering if he was for real.

"Blake"—I took a step deeper into the room—"no matter how you spin this, you're lying to your client. To your ex-roommate. *To your friend.* You can justify it from now until your last day on this earth, but at the end of the day, you leaked pictures of his privates to keep him from logging onto the Internet, and that's shitty."

"*I* didn't. One of his one-night stands did. We paid her, and part of the money goes to charity, so don't slam it all the way."

"You shamed your friend, and the fact that he doesn't feel violated doesn't change the fact that he *was* violated."

"Don't act like a saint, Indigo. Part of your job is to slip into bathrooms with him. You're on this gravy train, too, doll. Just because your conscience is less stained, doesn't mean it's clean."

I narrowed my eyes.

"I'm telling him." I stomped down on an imaginary cockroach.

"Then you're out," Blake deadpanned, his face switching from wary and anxious to harsh in the blink of an eye. He took a step closer to me, eliminating the distance between us. I could smell his breath, cinnamon and a fruity gum. A fresh and light scent Alex was too carnally male to possess.

"The minute he knows the truth he'll drop everything and run to his precious coke. In which case, we will no longer need your services, Ziggy will no longer get his tubes, and Craig would still be a miserable, drunk sod. Think before you do something stupid, Indie. Because you can very easily steer your life onto a very bumpy road."

I stared at Blake.

He lifted his chin, returning a look just as firm.

He knew. Knew about my family, about our financial situation, even about the tubes we were planning to get Ziggy with the money.

How the hell does he know?

I'd gone through a personality assessment with the HR person who'd hired me. The girl with the pedicure asked me two hundred questions, all of which I'd answered with brutal honesty. She must've paid it forward. Now Jenna and Blake had leverage over me. Maybe Alex, too. Hell, for all I knew the whole tour knew how much debt I was in and my nephew's health problems.

Feeling my blood bubbling with the kind of anger that makes you want to puke, I turned around and stormed from Alex's dressing room. I was no longer sleepy and jet-lagged.

I was wide-awake.

Vibrating, like my stammering, rebellious heart.

Burning like bonfire and completely alive.

Chapter Five

Alex

"One is the loneliest number.
So you said we should be two.
But in the end, baby, it was all about you.
The worst part is, I'd still take you back.
Though this time, I'd be sure to be the one to break your heart."
— *"Poison and Poetry," Alex Winslow.*

Everybody wants to be a rock star. It's the closest thing to being a god, but what people often forget is that God has a hectic job. God creates. Twenty-four-fucking-seven.

God is worshipped.

God is expected to answer, to deliver, to reassure.

And when God is sent to earth to deal with humans? Well, God is bound to disappoint.

See, when you're a rock star, your fans feed you expectations.

And you almost always swallow them down greedily and ask for seconds.

Because *you* want to believe you're a genius, whose lyrics are immortal, whose tunes run chills down people's spines. *You* want to be unforgettable, irresistible, and unique. You don't want to believe there's nothing more after this—because there isn't, you might be a hotshot millionaire motherfucker with a different model in your bed every night—but at the end of the day, you're human.

So, terribly human. A human who is expected to be much more than a human. Which was how I'd gotten here. To where I was today. The very laughable cliché I'd taken the piss out of when I was younger. A washed-up, alcoholic, druggie rocker who is never alone but always feels so desperately lonely.

The first time I found true intimacy wasn't when I shoved my cock into Laura, the lorry driver's daughter, on a bench at age fourteen at Cassiobury Park. It was when I stood in front of thousands of strangers and sang to them. Asked them to love me. To believe in me. To support me. And. They. Did.

You feel stark naked on the stage.

Even with Waitrose behind me on the drum set and Alfie walking around with his bass guitar, it was mostly just me. And them. And the lights. And the fame.

The sweat dripping down on the guitar. *Sex.*

My muscles flexing, straining to produce that perfect harmony. *Climax.*

They see me, feel me. They hear me. *Bliss.*

But having sex with ten thousand people every night was not what you called a laid-back job. Which was why I'd needed a little pick-me-up to ensure my performance was up to par with my own unreachable standards. I used to get on stage with more coke in my bloodstream than platelets. I was high, and when you're high, you can't see how fucking low you've reached. Ninety days of rehab, and I'm clean now. Physically, mostly.

I gave my audience an encore. "Poison Poetry" was inspired by Fallon, who'd torn my heart out and fed it to the tabloid wolves. It was also one of the last decent songs I'd written before becoming too dependent and fogged by narcotics to produce anything real and substantial. Now that I was sober again, I wondered if my creative side hadn't washed out along with the drugs.

I got off the stage, and the first face I saw was New Girl's. She and her big eyes and narrow, Cupid's bow lips and purple flared dress that made her look like she'd stepped out of a film noir straight into the imperfect arms of this industrial arena. Her clothes felt like a statement. One that made my cock stiffen in my jeggings, and I wondered if wanting to fuck my chaperone was my way of trying to get rid of her, or claiming her by making sure Lucas didn't do it before me.

She wore her usual expression of annoyance, so I bypassed her, heading for my dressing room. Adrenaline simmered beneath my skin, making me roll my neck and cup the back of my head. The gig had been solid. No, fuck solid. It had been grand. I knew that, because I had been there—really there, not like when I was coked up, riding an invisible cloud of fake confidence.

I wanted to write.

I needed to write.

Alone.

Blake, New Girl, two groupies who'd sneaked in, and the local PR bloke all trailed behind me to the dressing room, but I slammed the door in their faces, not bothering to stop and explain. When the muse hits you in the nut sack, you crawl back and ask her to hit harder, faster, stronger.

Make me bleed. Make me gasp for it, live for it, then die for it. Make me lose my mind and find my soul. Do your magic, Muse. But don't leave me hanging like you did before. Howling for you to come rescue me in an empty room. Waiting for you to show up unannounced like an indecisive lover.

"Winslow." New Girl knocked on the door several times, and not gently. "Open the door or I'll have to call Ms. Holden." It didn't escape me that she'd dropped the word 'please.' Shame she was starting to adapt to her new environment, because I wasn't keeping her. I tipped my head back and squeezed my eyes shut. I needed solitude to write. My best words were usually found in silence.

"Go away," I barked.

"Trust me, spending time with you is very low on my to-do list. Unfortunately, it's part of my job description to be around you. You're not allowed to be alone with the door locked."

"Can you be any more annoying?"

"Can you be any more of a *jerk*?" She slapped her palm against the door. "Open. Up!"

"Oh, you're using periods between words. Now I'm really in trouble," I roared from the other side, kicking the coffee table to the other end of the room and watching it crash and lose a leg against the opposite wall.

Fuck, okay. I didn't need any more shit with Jenna.

I sighed, pushing to my feet and swinging the door open. The groupies, Blake, and a few sound technicians were standing behind New Girl, curiously peeking over her shoulder. I stepped sideways, giving her a sliver of space to come into the room, but she had to fucking work for it.

"She's addicted to the D. I need to accommodate that shit twenty-four-seven." I smirked tauntingly as she rolled her eyes and squeezed past my body. "Don't touch anything. Don't look at anything. If possible, don't even breathe. Actually, that'd be ideal."

I signed albums, posters, and tits, then slammed the door in Blake's face after the fans and technicians were gone. He'd mumbled something about not checking the Internet and dick pictures, but I tuned him out. I appreciated the concern, but who the hell cared? My knob was community property at this point. Every willing body that wasn't a fan or underage got a free ride and a complimentary selfie.

I walked back to the sofa, picked up the notepad and pen, and frowned at the blank page. New Girl was standing by the window overlooking the harbor, her back to me. I tried to remember the last time I'd been in a room with a bird who wasn't my mum or sister without having my cock shoved so deep down her throat she had to heave, and couldn't. I scowled some more. Stared at the paper. Mentally paced the room and punched the walls.

The muse was gone.

New Girl had fucking killed it.

Bollocks.

I sat back, watching her blue-silver hair, no longer in a braid, cascading all the way down to her small, round bum. Way I saw it, if I wasn't going to get any writing done, might as well burn the time re-loading my spank bank. Though I knew I could go to one of the many after parties my bandmates were probably hitting, this was a big, fat no. A) New Girl was going to accompany me, and that'd be entirely too embarrassing to endure, and B) I recognized that in order to rein in my desire to get all coked up and drink myself into a stupor, I had to stay in. My agent was going to cut my balls off, drain them, and use them as mini purses if I got anywhere near alcohol or cocaine.

"Take a picture. It lasts longer." New Girl threw my words back at me from her spot by the window. The sharp-edged crescent moon winked behind her shoulder. "I can see your reflection through the glass," she explained as an afterthought, a sad lilt in her voice.

Our eyes met in said reflection. Time stood still.

I still hated her.

I still wanted her gone.

But for the first time since she tagged along, I was starting to sus-pect she might not be as useless as I'd originally viewed her. It was that curve between her neck and her shoulder that did it. I wanted to bite that spot, produce blood, and write the lyrics of my next song with it. And the fucked-up thing about it was that this was my train of thought when I *wasn't* using.

"You chased my muse away." My tone was low, lazy, and sort of psychotic. Even to my own ears.

"And?" She didn't bother turning around.

"And now you owe me. So it's a good thing you're in my possession."

"Your possession?" she echoed, incredulous. "I'm not your any-thing, Winslow."

"You are. For three months. I have a signed contract to prove it, and now I'm going to take what's inside you and put it in my note-book, because I'm empty and you're full."

It was weird. To say the truth out loud. The truth was meant to be whispered, not shouted, but I didn't care what she thought of me, so I stood up and grabbed my leather jacket, not bothering to offer it to her.

"Meet me outside your hotel room at midnight," I said.

She opened her mouth. I didn't stay long enough to listen to what she had to say.

I was going to get my muse back and write that album.

Take over Billboard with every single I released and make it my bitch.

Reclaim my title as king of alternative music from that wanker, Will Bushell.

And claim what was mine. What had always been mine. *Fallon.*

Even if I had to cheat my way or bulldoze through everyone else to get it.

Legs stretched and crossed at the ankles, Tania in hand, my fingers flew over the fret board as I tried to come up with a melody. My back was pressed against my door, so I had a direct view to New Girl's door. Our rooms were in front of one another. Jenna had asked Hudson, my PA, to make sure New Girl was always ten feet or closer in all the hotels we'd stayed in.

At five past midnight, her door opened and she stepped out.

She was wearing red plaid PJ shorts and a gray hoodie with the name of a college she couldn't possibly afford plastered on it. I motioned to her with my chin to sit down, and she did. Her face, clean of makeup and pretense, was rapt. She slid down her door, tucking her knees under her chin, blinking at me. I couldn't decide if she had no personality at all, or too much of it. I was about to find out.

I continued moving the pick over the strings of the acoustic guitar, ignoring the red, lush carpet and impersonal hallway, and imagined we were someplace real. A house or a beach or a cobblestoned London street with the bite of rain pinching at our nostrils.

"Why am I here?" she asked.

"I'm asking myself the same question." I stared at my callused fingers strumming Tania before looking up. "You're hanging onto this job for dear life. You in some sort of trouble?"

"No," she said, not taken aback by my candor. "I have a nephew. His parents can't find steady jobs, and he deserves more. More than we're giving him. More than constant ear infections. More than drinking milk that expired two days ago because it's cheaper. Just…more."

I poked my lip out, considering her answer. I didn't care too much for my family. In fact, the part I dreaded the most about the tour—along with trying to come up with new songs—was seeing my mum, dad, and older sister, Carly. If I was going to see them at all.

"What's his name?" I asked, not entirely sure why. I never felt compelled to be polite, least of all to people who were on my payroll.

"Ziggy." She smiled. Her smile wasn't as annoying. Dimpled and genuine and Botox-less. Big lips. Small teeth. I liked it. Flaws were intimate. Telling. Pure. Indigo was pretty. Like a wasted sunset, beautiful in a taken-for-granted sort of way.

"Like the David Bowie album?" My eyebrows fell into a frown. I banged up a few notes on Tania, and they actually made sense. Maybe I was remembering "Starman" or "Rock 'n' Roll Suicide." Though it sounded different, fresh.

"My brother is a fan." She stared up and started absentmindedly chewing on her bottom lip. "Ziggy is two years old. Smart, funny, and kind. I always tell him he is Ziggy, and I am…"

"Stardust," I finished, bunching up a few notes into a melody in my head. Of course I was still dressed in the same clothes I'd worn to the gig. And of course I smelled like stale piss in a dark London alleyway. "Silence, now."

She didn't scold me. Instead, she started braiding small pieces of that blue hair as I came up with something…new. I closed my eyes, my fingers trembling a little. Finding a good tune felt very close to finding a flower in the sand. Improbable, rare, thrilling. I played for a few minutes before pulling Tania's strap off of my shoulder and propping it against my door. I took out the little notepad and Sharpie from my back pocket and started writing the notes. When I looked up, New

Girl was still braiding. The troubled look on her face told me she felt sorry for me. The thought was unsettling.

"Tell me about yourself." I ignored her quizzing eyes.

"You'll need to be more specific than that."

"What makes you, you? Your personality. Your secrets. Your quirks."

Another girl would giggle, avert the topic, or play dumb. She didn't.

"I'm left-handed. Hate clowns. Love making dresses. It makes me feel…" She looked up, searching for the word. "Focused."

I strapped Tania back on, my pick moving over the strings without direction.

"What else?"

"I don't have any social media accounts. If I could study anything, it'd be fashion. I used to work at a thrift shop called Thrifty in Beverly Hills run by a seventy-year-old woman named Clara before she closed it down to spend more time with her family. Working there was—still is—my dream job."

She looked at me like I would deem her dreams too small or too insignificant. I bet anything she didn't know I hadn't planned on becoming a hotshot TMZ regular. The initial goal was far more romantic. I got sucked into this world by my childhood mate, Will. We used to have a band together—The Kryptonites—before we'd decided to go solo and live together in London, all five of us—me, Will, Alfie, Blake, and Lucas. I'd wanted to stay indie when Will got that fat, mass-production deal. He was the one who'd hooked me up with Grapevine Records. Who'd made me me, in more than one sense.

My fingers were moving faster, chasing a rhythm, a forgotten song that was always there in my head. This was why I wanted her in the hallway. Somewhere neutral. Not in one of our rooms, where all I'd think about was how to shag her, because she was there, with a pulse, and in all probability willing. I needed her words and her thoughts and her disposition. I wanted to suck her soul dry and pour it onto the pages, *my pages*, getting my money's worth out of my babysitter.

Because she was innocent. And strong. And so infuriating, picking at her brain felt like a necessity.

"Go on, Stardust," I taunted her. She knew it. It wasn't a moniker. It was a dig.

"I have one brother." She omitted her parents' death this time when speaking to me. She'd offered the information to my bandmate freely enough. Maybe she saw me as the enemy and Lucas as an ally—stupid, stupid girl. "I ride my bike everywhere." She paused, her front teeth sinking into her lip again. "And I have something to tell you, but I'm not sure it's my place to say it."

My head snapped up at her last confession.

"What could you possibly know that I don't?"

"Oh, wow." She blew air, shaking her head. "Look, I just want to help you."

"And you are. You're helping me by doing everything short of changing a fucking diaper to make sure I don't dip my nose in the white stuff. That's your job done. Nothing more. Nothing less."

She stared at me, insolent, her gaze telling me she knew what I was doing. I was pushing her away in a last bid to make her leave, but my heart wasn't in it anymore. Not all the way, anyway. She was going to stay, whether I liked it or not, and the least I could do for myself was use her until there was nothing left to take. The way Fallon had used me.

"You annoy me so much, sometimes I want to cry" she gritted through clenched teeth.

I smiled, knowing for a fact I had another set of notes to write down. It was time to finish our session. She'd turned out to be more productive than anticipated. This was all I needed. I'd spend my night writing.

I climbed to my feet, my fingers wrapped around Tania's neck, and knelt forward, getting into Indie's face.

"When I finally lay my hands on you—and make no mistakes, Stardust, I will—you will be crying, all right. My name. Over. And. Over. Again."

Chapter Six

Indie

Melbourne, Australia

Two days had passed since the hallway.

Two days in which my relationship with Alex somewhat improved, despite his killing every bit of goodwill I had in my body to tell him the truth about the leaked sex photos and Fallon's engagement. He was no longer actively bullying me. Instead, he chose to ignore me altogether. I shadowed him like a lovelorn puppy, the equivalent of punching my self-respect to death. We spent the next couple days driving from Sydney to Melbourne, with a stop in some desert town that served mean BBQ ribs and iced tea. Alex spent the majority of the drive at the back of the SUV, trying to write and groaning in frustration. Sometimes he was hyper, animated, and conversational. Most times, he was a step away from a sulk. Blake was always on his phone, arguing with Jenna and Hudson, all while throwing me warning glances every now and again. Alfie was in charge of making sure Alex didn't have Internet access on his phone, a task he took surprisingly seriously. Alex seemed perfectly content being disconnected from the virtual world. Throughout our time together, I noticed he hadn't made any personal calls, which I thought was peculiar, but also none of my business.

Lucas and I got closer.

Partly because he was the nicest of the bunch, but mostly because my loneliness was starting to feel like a heavy coat I was desperate to peel off my body. Luc was twenty-seven years old. Just like Alex, he was from Watford. His father worked at a local council; his mother was a teacher. He and his two siblings had had a dog named Harvey. He'd known Alex ever since they were kids, and moved to Los Angeles from London only three years ago, after he broke his engagement to Laura, a girl back home. Apparently, Alex had had a thing with Laura when they were teenagers. And apparently, Lucas was still somewhat bitter about it. The SUV was driven by the same silent dude who'd picked us up from the airport.

"Alex loves to tell the story of how he took Laura's virginity, and I took her baggage," Lucas said as we zipped through the desert.

I put my hand on his arm and squeezed.

"I'm sorry." I meant it, but Lucas looked far from devastated. He occasionally threw glances at Alex, as if trying to gauge his reaction.

"Don't be," Alfie chimed in from behind us, where he sat with Alex. "Winslow said it once—*once*—and he was just taking the piss. Besides, I reckon Waitrose was over her before she pulled her knickers up after their last shag. You were never into her, mate. We all know that."

Something passed between the three men—Blake, Alfie, Lucas—a secret, by the way their gazes swept through one another.

Blake chuckled. "Laura's the least of Lucas' problems."

Alex's curtain of nonchalance was drawn tight today, and he didn't offer any commentary on the subject.

Rain began to beat on the rooftops and the sky cracked with thunder when we rolled into Melbourne. It looked different from Sydney. Older, maybe. We went through the motions. Circling around the hotel for a good twenty minutes before the road was clear. Again, Alex stopped to sign fans' shirts and mementos, squinting against the rain with a smile. Blake distributed our electronic cards. A floor had been closed and reserved for Alex Winslow and his staff. It occurred to me that this was the norm for these guys. To them, this was what a typical day looked like. Was it any wonder they were all cynical and jaded? There was nothing to chain them to the ground, to one place. They floated through life. Gravity meant nothing to them.

"Hey, Indie," Lucas said when everyone walked into the elevator. Blake was typing a long text message, Alex was moving his guitar strap from shoulder to shoulder and rubbing off the raindrops from his hair, and Alfie was pretending to scratch his nose, even though he was very clearly picking at it.

"Yeah?"

"You up for a stroll? Show's not until tomorrow, and the rain's about to stop any minute now."

I whipped my head in Blake's direction. I couldn't take time off and wander around. I had to babysit Alex. Unless Blake was with him, which he was, most of the time. Blake scratched his temple with his most important organ—his phone.

"It's Saturday, mate. Does she not get any time off at all?" Lucas probed, elbowing him lightly.

Alex dragged his fingers over his jaw, his eyes set on Blake, who flicked his gaze toward the singer.

"Let's talk about it privately." Blake remained cryptic, tucking his cell phone into his front pocket and evading Alex's gaze. It made me feel so uncomfortable my skin crawled.

"Right." I cleared my throat, every feminist bone in my body demanding I do something about it, no matter how small. "Feel free to discuss your plans about me behind closed doors, where I can't hear you."

"That's the plan," Alex deadpanned.

"Alex," Blake warned.

"Don't 'Alex' me. He's been trying to get into her over-the-top dresses since day one. I've had it with this wanker."

The elevator pinged and we all poured out, walking to our designated rooms. Lucas tagged along with Blake and Alex, with the latter refusing to acknowledge the former's existence. Alex was pointing at things and naming songs about them. "Elevators" by U2 when we got out; "Stairway to Heaven" when we passed by the emergency staircase; and "God Only Knows" when we passed by a huge painting called

Portrait of God.

"Don't tell our old mates Paul and John I was singing the Beach Boys," he said, cheerful all of a sudden. "Though I guess they wouldn't give a toss. It was Brian Wilson who was all pissy with the Beatles' success, not the other way around."

"Stop being extra." Blake snorted a laugh.

"I'm not being extra. I despise everyone equally. You think I don't have any complaints about the Beatles? They inspired the Bee Gees and Oasis. That ought to be illegal in some countries."

"Of course, you'll be the only person on earth who has a problem with the Beatles." Alfie gathered phlegm in his throat. "Tosser."

When I was in front of my door, and they were in front of theirs, my instinct told me to turn around and look at them. I did, for no other reason than to see if my intuition was right. Alex peeked over his shoulder, staring me down like I was the enemy. That also meant he wasn't wearing his usual cool façade, and what I saw on his face was raw.

And disarming.

And unbearably pure.

I blinked, swiping my electronic key and watching the small dot flash green.

For the first time since we'd met, I was the one to close a door on him.

Funny how I thought it would feel good, borderline triumphant, when the only thing I'd tasted on my tongue when the door closed behind me was defeat.

Alex

"No." I fell into another foreign bed that smelled of a different detergent, downing an entire bottle of water. "And that's my final answer, so you can drag your sorry arse to the other side of the floor and lick your wounds in private where I can't see you."

Blake and Lucas were standing over me, their faces suggesting I was being unreasonable when, in fact, reason was definitely on my side. I didn't fault Lucas for wanting to shag Stardust. She was, as it turned out, quite shag-able. But if I could ruin something for him, I'd gladly do so. Two years ago, when I'd gone on tour and Fallon had stayed in L.A., Lucas—whom I employed and supported, whom I'd grown up with, whom I shared a flat, and a car, and sometimes a toothbrush with—was there to make sure she'd be as close as she possibly could to Will Bushell. I didn't know why, but my guess was it had something to do with Laura. I'd slept with Laura long before she was on Lucas' radar. Long before he'd even properly met her. I guess he'd gotten to L.A. fresh out of the ruins of his engagement, felt vindictive and bitter, and decided to take it out on yours truly.

And so, in a straight-to-cable movie villain move, Lucas had befriended Fallon, become one of her closest people, and pushed her deeper into Will Bushell's arms every day I was away.

Lucas didn't rest until Bushell's claws had wrapped around her completely.

When I think about it, Waitrose had no place on my tour at all. He was a deceiving, two-faced cunt. But when Will started dating Fallon, the whole group had fallen apart and I'd needed to assimilate all our mutual friends and make sure they were on my side.

So, really, having Lucas around wasn't about Lucas. It was about Will not having any relationship with Lucas, or anyone else we grew up with. If I could shag Will's mum to get her to disown him, I would. But it was too much of an effort, and besides, I liked Will's dad—save for his strange love for Manchester United. Fuck them.

Anyway, the point was, Lucas wasn't going to screw my hanny—hot nanny.

"Why not?" Blake asked.

I looked up. Since when did Blake care about anything that wasn't managing my career and trying to ram his knob into my agent?

"Lucas knows why," I ground out.

Blake did, too. He constantly talked me off the ledge when the urge to fire Waitrose spontaneously struck me.

"Actually, I don't," Lucas said, folding his arms over his chest while resting his shoulder against the door. "Please elaborate."

"It's about you throwing Fallon at Will to get back at me for Laura."

"You need to stop this bullshit. Fallon was a grown-up. She *chose* Will."

"Fallon was an addict. She chose whoever was more beneficial to her at that point in time," I retorted.

"That why you want her back? What a bloody catch. A woman who goes off with whoever would be a better opportunity to her," Lucas growled. He looked just about as furious as I was, maybe even more so.

"You gave her his phone number, drove her to him when her car broke down, then told Will where to find her. Hell, when she OD'd in *my* flat, you told Will what hospital she was at while I was on tour. Who does that? Who?"

"A decent human being?" Lucas blinked, feigning innocence. "Will wanted to support a friend in need. You were on a bus heading south, states away. Look, this has nothing to do with Indie."

I jumped from the bed, the energy coursing through me too much to maintain stillness. My body was tight from the long car ride and stretching it by beating Lucas sounded just about the most appealing thing I could do. "Save it, Saint Lucas. I don't believe you. No, you can't take Indie out. No, you can't flirt with her, pursue her, or have sex with her. She's mine."

"You don't even like her!" Lucas pushed me, and I pushed back. What the fuck did liking her have to do with anything?

"I'm still going to have her." My taunting smile made an appearance. "But don't worry, I'll let you know how she tastes. After all, we're mates, aren't we?"

Blake jumped between us, as if on cue.

"All right, lads. That's enough pissing testosterone at each other's leg for one day."

"I'm going to fuck her." I stared at Lucas, who was grabbing at his hair, pulling it in frustration. Welcome to Random Acts of Meanness. It's just like kindness, but for cunts. Every muscle in my body flexed as I braced myself for a brawl. Lucas' pain was real, and it surprised me. Why did he care about New Girl so much? He barely knew her. "I'm going to fuck her and make sure she's completely ruined for you. Now, how about that, Waitrose?"

He sucked in a breath and stormed out.

I laughed all the way to the bath and didn't even want to drown myself when I stepped into it. Not today.

Today, I lit up a fag, stared at the ceiling, and thought about another fitting song, exhaling from my nostrils.

"Smoke on the Water."

Indie

Jenna: Indigo. It's Jenna.
Indie: Hi, Jenna. Please call me Indie!
Jenna: Hudson is in this chat, too. Is this okay, Indigo?
Indie: ...
Indie: Yeah, absolutely.
Jenna: How's Alex doing?
Indie: Reluctantly sober.
Hudson: Hi, Indie! I heard Alex's been writing with you.
Jenna: ???
Hudson: He stayed up all night writing. Said he had a breakthrough. He voice-messaged me about it at four in

the morning Australia time.

Jenna: He is a rock star. He doesn't need sleep. That's good. Indigo, tell us about it.

Indie: Nothing much to tell. He's just asking me stuff about my life, mostly. I can't see what he's writing, and asking him is futile.

Hudson: Duh. Alex hates questions. Mostly rhetorical, though he is not a huge fan with straightforward ones, either. Which doesn't bode well for me as his PA.

Jenna: Hudson—you're blabbing. Indigo—report back. And soon.

Indie: It's INDIE.

Hudson: Bye, Indiana. 😉

The knock on the door startled me.

A safety pin pricked my fingertip, and I sucked the blood between my lips, rising up from my sewing corner by the window. Yeah, I was the girl who packed a mini sewing machine to a trip around the world. I always made myself dresses, because buying the kind I loved would cost a small fortune. Clara, my ex-employer, was kind enough to give me leftover fabric every time she worked on a piece. And she always had leftovers, which meant I always walked around looking like I was ready for a Victorian ball.

I opened the door expecting to see Blake. Whenever Blake had to leave the hotel room he shared with Alex, he would either call me or show up at my room while Alfie or Luc babysat the rock star, silently watching me put on my Oxfords as I grunted to myself with displeasure. This time, it wasn't Blake. It was Lucas.

"Hey." His hands were tucked in his front pockets and his smile was apologetic, like he knew he shouldn't be here.

"They let you come here. That's a huge step. Maybe I'll be allowed to vote next."

Lucas rubbed the back of his head, then moved his palm to his face and scrubbed his mouth.

"Blake was never the problem. He doesn't care about much other than his phone, and maybe Jenna. Alex, on the other hand...he's got a bit of an anger issue."

"You don't say." I sighed, poking my head out the doorway to make sure Winslow wasn't there, ready for an ambush.

"He has his reasons, Indie. Give him a chance."

A chance at what? I decided not to ask.

"I don't appreciate being treated like trash."

"No one thinks of you as trash, trust me. This has more to do with me than with you."

I left Luc at the door, falling onto the queen-sized bed and slipping my shoes on. Five minutes later, we were outside, hailing a taxi and heading downtown. Lucas was not someone you'd recognize. He was the drummer for a solo artist, not a part of a well-known band. But he still looked every bit the rock star, with his deep blue eyes, sculpted face, distressed denim, and pea-soup green blazer. His red-brown hair was messy to a fault—not as tousled as Alex's, but still rocking the I-just-finished-a-threesome vibe—and I wanted to ask him how they did that. How they always looked like a walking, talking PocketRocket commercial.

Despite the foul weather, downtown Melbourne was bustling with tourists and cyclists. Carriages with couples and packs of teenagers roamed the streets, flaunting their youth. We grabbed Spanish donuts from a food truck and people-watched, sitting on a bench. Lucas *inhaled* the food like it was the first time he'd been introduced to the concept of eating. I took my time, mulling over the last few days in my head and mostly feeling guilty about being there. Knowing that thousands of miles away, my brother and sister-in-law were still struggling to make ends meet and counting their discounted pasta packs. But all that would change in just a week and a half, when I was due to get my first paycheck.

"How are you liking your new job so far?" Lucas asked, tossing our paper plates into a nearby trashcan.

I shrugged, following the movement of a teenage couple in beanies kissing under a lamppost in the drizzle. I longed to be in their story, not mine. Mine sucked. Plus, I wanted to sleep with my villain while my prince—Lucas—looked at me so platonically, he made me feel as sexy as a tablecloth.

"I don't really do all that much. Just pester Alex, basically." I was about to bite my lower lip but managed to stop myself from doing so.

Lucas shook his head, staring at me, not the crowd, like he was trying to assess something.

"Trust me, you're not. I mean, maybe you are, but he needs this. I've known Alex ever since he was a little lad living in a council house in Watford with his parents and sister. He's always had a flare for addiction. Don't mistake the lack of drug and alcohol in his system for sobriety. He's still very much an addict, consumed by resentment and driven by fury. Just look at the way he talks and reacts to Fallon's name."

Every time I heard her name, my heart slowed a little.

"Bad breakup?" I asked. I was sniffing around. Why was I sniffing around? The less I knew about him the better.

Luc shifted on the bench, his velvet tongue peeking out to wet his lips. "You're not interested in him, are you, Indie?"

I rolled my eyes.

"Answer me with words," he said.

I stood up, wanting to do something with my legs. With my *body*. At this point, Googling the hell out of Fallon's name and finding out what had happened between them was a violent impulse, but my phone screen was cracked, and the new one Jenna gave me was blocked. Besides, how was it smart to nurture whatever fixation I had with the biggest train wreck to walk on earth? One I had to save from himself, by the freaking way.

"Absolutely not," I snorted out.

"Then why are you asking?" Lucas' voice was so calm, it was easy to let my wall of defense roll back down.

"Because," I said, the drummer falling in step with me. We started walking toward the hotel, which turned out to be very close to where we were. "I can't believe you're keeping him in the dark about her engagement."

"It's for the best, trust me." He shoved his hands into his pockets again, his signature good-boy posture.

"I don't think he'd agree." I shivered slightly. I'd bought a jacket in Sydney, but Melbourne was even colder.

"It's complicated."

"What's complicated?"

"The subject of Fallon. And I do mean the Middle East type of complicated. I shouldn't even be talking to you about it, because, frankly, I don't think there's one person in the world Alex doesn't blame for their breakup. Other than himself, of course."

I swiveled to Lucas, still light-jogging to raise my body temperature. "He blames you for their breakup?"

"And he's partly right."

"Why?"

"Why do people do stupid things?" Lucas sighed, shaking his head. "Never mind."

The rest of the walk back to the hotel was silent. My heart was in knots. Rusty wires coiled into themselves around it, making it hard to breathe. Alex had a hidden vulnerability. He was like Halloween. Scary on the outside, but when you looked within, there were good intentions there.

Lucas and I parted ways in the hotel hallway. When I pushed the door to my room open, the first thing I did was collect my hair into a high bun and walk to the kitchenette to get myself a glass of water. When I turned around, I dropped the glass to the floor before the water touched my lips.

Alex.

In my room.

In my kitchenette.

Naked from the waist up, with only a black pair of jeans and dirty boots. Oh, and his guitar. If he could staple it to his back, he would. I was sure of it.

Worse than anything else—he was unsupervised, hence he might've relapsed. I took a deep breath, closing my eyes.

"Where were you?" His voice boomed, even though he was not shouting, somehow taking up space like it had a body of its own.

I stole a quick glance at the mini sewing machine, thread and fabrics by the window, and cleared my throat.

"Went to get some Band-Aids. Sewing accident." I didn't know what prompted me to lie. Maybe the fact I was partly afraid he'd kick me off the tour. If he did, all the plans I'd made would be flushed down the toilet.

I knew he wouldn't ask to see the Band-Aids. He was too self-absorbed to even register what I was saying. He was just being a possessive prick. I diverted the subject quickly. "First things first, please tell me you're sober," I uttered as calmly as one could, considering my heart beat so fast it nearly blew up on the carpeted floor. At least it was the same red as the lush rug, hence no extra dry-cleaning bill.

"As sober as a Mormon baby." He made a Scout's honor signal with his fingers, before flipping me the bird with a grin.

"So now to the burning question—what in the hell are you doing here, Alex?" I dropped to my knees, collecting the sharp pieces of glass.

He was still standing there, stoic as a statue, glaring down at me like I was his subject.

"I mean, Jesus Christ, you can't just come in here without warning..." I mumbled to myself, feeling my ears pinking.

Don't look up. You'll only end up ogling his crotch again.

"The hotel doesn't offer laundry services today for some bizarre reason, and Blake is busy taking care of the fact my dick is getting more exposure than The Kardashians, also known as *'Cockgate.'* I don't have any clean shirts for the show tomorrow." He waved a ball of black fabric in his fist. Hah. Blake was cleaning up the mess he'd created. The irony wasn't lost on me. I turned my back to Alex, mainly so my eyes wouldn't assault his chest. He had the most vivid tattoo I'd ever seen. A black raven, its broken wings shattering into miniscule feathers that peppered his entire back and ribs. Symbolizing the dark, broken angel that he was. I disposed the broken glass in the trash.

"Don't you have people on call for that? You seemed to be surrounded by them at the Sydney show." My teeth sank into my lip again. My phone was dancing on the kitchen counter where I'd left it. I knew it was Nat, who'd probably woken up and wanted to check on me. I hated not answering her, but couldn't risk her listening to our exchange. There was no knowing what'd leave this man's mouth.

"I do. I don't like talking to any of them," Alex confided.

"Pretty sure I'm not your number one conversation partner, either."

"The devil you know." He tapped his nose, eyebrows raised, as though he was sharing some great, inspirational advice. "And so, it looks like you're about to do Alex Winslow's laundry. Congratulations, and you're welcome."

"You can tell Alex Winslow—whom you refer to in the third person for a reason beyond my grasp—that doing his laundry is not in my job description." I strode over to the vast Roman-styled bathroom, reappearing with a towel to dry off the kitchen floor.

He stood in the same spot like he'd grown roots I would've been happy to pluck with my own hands. If he moved slightly, I wouldn't have to brush my shoulder against his arm to squeeze past him. But, of course, he remained motionless. Our skin touched. I dropped the towel to the floor, ignoring the sizzling nerves where we made contact, and moved the towel back and forth with the tip of my shoe.

"Actually, it is," he said, his voice saturated with something I didn't recognize. He was larger than life. A one-man show, even when he was off the stage.

I turned around, my face blank. "Huh?"

"Took the time to read your contract today. Jenna gave Blake an extra copy, and I was bored—you know, no Internet, no drugs, no

Hudson to yell at. It's in your contract to help me with any additional personal assistance services I may require." He smirked, cocking his head to the side. "Looks like you're in quite a pickle, Miss Bellamy."

My eyes widened, and flames of hatred licked at my stomach. Or was it adrenaline? I wasn't entirely sure. I stomped toward him, grabbing the balled shirt in my hand and waving it at him.

"If you want me to do your laundry, you're coming with me to watch, because next time, you'll be doing it yourself. There won't be a second time, Alex. I'm not your maid."

"You want me to go to the launderette?" The look he gave me was priceless. Like I'd asked him if he wanted to spontaneously join me in a trip to outer space.

I nodded, throwing his dirty shirt into a paper bag I'd gotten when I'd purchased a jacket. "Now let's go to your room and pick up the rest of your clothes. We better get going before the clock hits five and all the mortals get off work to do their laundry. It can get pretty chaotic out there."

I should know. We don't have a washing machine at home.

"I can't leave the hotel, you little nutter." He chuckled—*chuckled!*—blocking my way to the door. His shoulders were wide and lithe. Still, I was small enough to slip through the gap between his narrow hip and the doorframe, heading for his door.

"You can, and you will."

"Shit, you're mental. Did Jenna do the whole check on you? Psychiatric, personality assessment, etcetera?"

Lord, give me strength.

"Save the jokes for someone who finds them funny, Winslow. You're coming with me."

"I could get sexually harassed," he called after me, laughing.

The worst part was, he was vain enough to actually believe it. I threw the door to his room open and started collecting his scattered clothes from the billiard table, kitchen counter, and the TV stand. There were boxers hanging from a lamp. I wished I could charge him extra for picking them up.

"I have a pepper spray in my bag, and I took some Krav Maga classes last year. Between you and me, we should be good fighting off the thirteen-year-old girls with dubious musical taste who buy your music," I quipped. It wasn't fair, nor true. Not only was Alex Winslow one of the best songwriters to grace the earth since Dylan, Springsteen, and Jagger—but he was actually one of the few artists to try to bring something different to the table with every single he released.

"Wait." Alex braced his arms over the doorpost, frowning. "You think my music sucks?"

I shot him a look. He was different today…lighter. At the very least, he acted like he was making an effort to not be a wanker, as his friends often referred to him. It occurred to me that maybe *this* was his true self, the one he'd been hiding from me in an attempt to make me leave. And his true self was cute. And funny. Whatever his motives were, I didn't care. I craved a truce, knowing it would make my job so much more pleasant *and* eliminate some of the sexual tension that made the little hairs on my arms stand on end every time his brown-green eyes zoned in on me.

"I think your music is great," I admitted quietly.

He smiled a real smile for the very first time, and Jesus, I wasn't prepared. His mouth curled upward like Marlon Brando in *A Streetcar Named Desire*. Tough as nails but stunningly beautiful in the most delicate way. How in the world was I going to survive the rest of this tour? I swallowed, scooped the rest of his clothes into two more bags I'd found, and rushed past him through the door. I thought I heard him snickering behind me but didn't turn around to check.

"Oh my, your fall will be spectacular," this time he *definitely* said that.

Considering he'd told me he was going to have sex with me two days ago, I knew exactly what he meant. I needed to throw him off somehow. His hitting on me was nothing short of disastrous, because he was right. If he kept it up, he might succeed, and he was obsessively in love with another girl.

Plus, he was a rock star.

Plus, he was my boss.

Plus, he was a mess.

Plus, we were going to part ways in three months.

I had every reason in the world to stay as far away as my job would allow me.

The elevator ride was silent.

The walk out of the hotel felt like torturous foreplay.

Then the fresh air hit my lungs, and I made up my mind on how to deal with his advances.

"I like Lucas," I said, pushing the door to the laundromat open.

His mask fell for the second time that day. I knew it without even looking back at him.

The door shut behind us, and I shuddered, keeping my eyes on the washing machines.

"Shouldn't have said that, darlin'. Challenge accepted, and now you're in trouble. The kind your innocent arse can't talk its way out of."

Chapter Seven

Alex

"Wow. You're so full of yourself." Her short, tan feet dangled in the air. She was sitting on top of a washing machine with a "broken" sign plastered on it, staring directly at the one she'd just shoved my clothes into. Hands tucked under her thighs, her indigo eyes fixed on the black mass of fabric spinning lazily through the round glass. I pondered that tan. Her features were quiet and pleasant, like Emma Watson's. Her tan, I decided, was the product of her L.A. lifestyle. I imagined her cycling around town in a short dress, her hair dancing in the wind. Ignoring my half-mast, I humored her.

"Yeah, well, that's because people want to be full of *me*." I plucked a cigarette from behind my ear and rolled it between my fingers. I needed a fag. But I also needed to get over my sudden infatuation with Miss Bellamy. I was only going to fuck her to get back at Lucas. I was fifty percent certain my interest in her stemmed from the fact she was the only female I had with me on the road. The other fifty was her telling me she wanted to shag Waitrose. Perhaps 'shag' wasn't the right word. Stardust was more of the movies-and-ice-cream type of bird.

Stardust? Stardust. What the fuck!

I was wearing a Burberry cap that Chris, my chavvy mate from home, gave me after I won my first four Grammys—same night. No one recognized me, but that didn't make me feel less exposed.

"Do you actually believe those things you say?" she asked, pulling at the band that held her blue hair in a bun. Her looks were growing on me every day. Her over-the-top Old Hollywood dresses were intriguing. Her big lips/small teeth situation was undeniably sexy. And I fucking loved that she sassed around like I wasn't the one calling all the shots here.

"Wholeheartedly." I parked my hip on the washing machine she was sitting on, scanning her face. "Are you going to ogle my cock tomorrow before the show?"

"If you need to pee, maybe."

"Then I'll need to *pee*," I said, mentally correcting myself to *piss*.

She rolled her eyes but smiled. I shifted a little closer to her. The place was growing busier, which wasn't good news for me.

"Speaking of my cock, what do they say about it in the news? Should I get it an agent? I feel like Jenna is busy with her hotshot clients. I might shop around for someone hungrier who can really make it big." Every word held some sexual innuendo.

"My phone screen is cracked and I don't have a laptop. Even if I did have Internet access, your penis would be one of the last things I'd Google. Literally, even after 'what would a chair look like if your knees bent the other way.'"

Penis. She said "penis" again. How old is this girl?

I gave her an odd look, because she was an odd thing.

She clarified, "It's suggested in the search bar on Google, believe it or not."

Shaking my head, I moved on to a saner topic.

"Anything out there I need to know about?" I didn't do social media. I had millions of followers on Instagram and Twitter, and Blake sometimes posted pictures of me from gigs or at the studio to keep my brand's flame alive. Other than that, people knew I wasn't about the celebrity lifestyle. Social media was my idea of licking my own balls.

Look at me.

Check me out.

Pay me attention.

Hear what I have to say about politics/global warming/insert other topic I have absolutely no knowledge about.

Nope. Not my jam. So, when Blake told me to stay off the Internet, I had no objection at all. Indie—guess she was no longer New Girl—rubbed her palms over her face before her teeth reunited with her lower lip, and that's how I knew she was nervous.

"I don't have access to the Internet, remember?" She jumped from the laundry machine just when the washer buzzed. She dragged my wet clothes to the dryer and pointed at buttons, explaining things I wasn't even listening to, let alone trying to remember. My eyes were focused on her bum beneath the flowery swing dress that rode up her thighs when she bent over. Disappointingly enough, her knickers didn't make a cameo.

"...make sure the whites are separated from the rest of your clothes. I also do the towels separately because they're heavier, though I guess the hotel provides the towels, so..."

She was moving. A lot. And talking. Even more. It was evident she wasn't flirting with me, and that alone made me want to fuck Lucas' crush even more. After she shoved my clothes into the dryer and started the machine, she turned back to me and sighed.

"Guess we have an hour to burn."

An hour. I could do a lot with an hour. For starters, I could sleep, which I hadn't done a few nights in a row, composing songs instead. Or watch some mindless TV. Listen to music. Write some. Play some. Fuck some. Or I could do the honorable thing and take my new hanny for coffee to get to know her better. Nah. Taking her places was a last resort. I was going to try to get into her knickers effortlessly first.

We spent the hour staring at the dryer. It was boring, but probably not as boring as spending one more minute with Blake yelling at my lawyers on the phone to send various tabloid sites cease and desist letters. It was only when we got back from the launderette that she actually spoke to me again.

"So, you didn't learn anything from our time in the laundromat, huh?" she asked when we were in front of our doors.

I raised my eyebrows, my veiny biceps popping out as I held on to the enormous clean pile of clothes stuffed into three bags. I saw her looking. And swallowing. And gaze-averting, as all good girls did before I fucked them so hard I left them in pieces.

"I did, actually. Your arse is not bad at all when you bend down to pick up my stuff, meaning my wanting to fuck you is still very much on."

"You're gross," she mumbled, unlocking her door.

"And you're curious. Good night, Stardust."

Chapter Eight

Indie

Jenna: INDIGO.

Indie: He's sober. I swear. I can tell by how grouchy he's been all day. He nearly toppled a technician over last time he had a sound check.

Jenna: Alex told me he's written a ten-minute song and he insists on putting it in his next album.

Indie: So?

Hudson: So it's 2017, not '69 (despite his undying love for the number) and he is not Deep Purple. A ten-minute song is about as marketable as a flat-assed starlet. Talk him off the ledge.

Indie: What if it's really good?

Jenna: Irrelevant. Tell him it sucks when he plays it to you.

Indie: This feels wrong.

Jenna: Trust me, Indigo, it will feel a lot more wrong when his next album bombs and he officially has to pack a bag and go where all rock stars go to die—guest-judging a reality TV show.

Another day, another box crossed out in bright red ink on my ninety-day calendar.

Since sound check wasn't until six o'clock, Lucas, Alfie, and Blake decided to go on a cruise before the show. Blake didn't feel too hot about leaving Alex alone with me for hours. In fact, he'd packed two chargers and his backup BlackBerry just in case, promising the rock star he would be available for him throughout the day. It was only after Lucas and Alfie talked to him privately in the corner of the presidential suite, exchanging hushed profanities, that he'd caved. Eventually, he unglued himself from his client and left, but not before giving me a babysitting list a two-day-old celiac baby wouldn't even need.

Alex had said he wanted to stay at the hotel and write. But really, all he did was lie in bed and chain-smoke to the sound of Cage the Elephant and The Strokes while staring at the ceiling. He didn't talk to me, and I made no effort to strike up a conversation, either. It was hard to tell whether he was depressed or simply being an artist. One moment he'd be charming and engaging—like in the laundromat—the other he would be brooding about nothing and everything, keeping the world at arm's length.

Today was especially hard for me, and all I wanted to do was lock myself in my room and cry myself to sleep.

Which was exactly what I did the minute Blake came back in the early afternoon and discharged me from my duties.

I treated myself to two hours of crying, then consumed everything made of chocolate I could find in the minibar to calm my nerves. After I was done with my mini-meltdown, I picked up the hotel phone and dialed Luc's extension. I wasn't the type to ask for favors, but some situations called for exceptions, and this was one of them.

Lucas showed up at my door an hour later, freshly shaven, smelling like the inside of a fashion magazine and armed with his laptop and a sultry grin. He was easy on the eyes. And the heart. Not to mention the mind. I'd meant it when I'd told Alex I liked Lucas. But it was unfortunate I didn't like him in a way that made my whole body buzz and come alive with need and heat. In a way that made me groan every time his face popped into my mind. *In the way I hate-liked Alex.*

"You're a lifesaver, Luc." I snatched the laptop from him and plopped down on my bed. My room was already in shambles, not looking much better than Alex's, and at least he had an excuse—he was rooming with someone else and had a rock star reputation to uphold.

Luc gave himself a tour of the room, while I logged into the Skype account I'd opened the day before we flew to Australia, and called Nat and Craig. They answered immediately, Ziggy sitting between them with a big smile on his chubby face, his wispy blond hair falling down in waves on his forehead.

"Auntie Stahduh!" he cooed, flinging his Pillsbury arms.

I felt my heart swelling in my chest, a grin spreading all over my face.

"How's my favorite boy?"

"Gooood," he drawled.

"I'll let you guys talk." Nat picked Ziggy up and ushered him to take a bath.

I wanted to protest and ask for more Ziggy time, but knew I need-ed to talk to my brother. Craig remained seated, pulling at his light brown hair. He looked so tired I wanted to wrap my arms around him in a suffocating hug. I was a notorious hugger, but he was…well, *not*.

Lucas was standing in the corner of the room, running his palm through the different fabrics of my next dress. It was a dark green number with black lace cleavage. I was just about to finish it and start on The Paris Dress, the project for the Halloween event at the chateau. I wasn't even supposed to know about it, but now that I did, it was the only thing I looked forward to on the tour.

Part of me wanted to ask Lucas for privacy, but that seemed rude when he was lending me his laptop—and had only ever treated me with kindness. "How're you holding up today?" I asked Craig.

"Our day just started. Ask me again in twelve hours. How about you?"

"Good," I lied.

Today marked the anniversary of our parents' death. Four years ago, we got the call and rushed to the hospital. We'd really thought Mom was going to make it, but the internal bleeding had won the battle. Dad, on the other hand, had stood no chance. He'd died on impact, and his body had been sent straight to the morgue. Craig had refused to let me see him. I was mad at him for years, but now I got it. Apparently, the car nailed him to a tree before fleeing the scene.

"I hope you're not going to act all crazy and angry today. Nat and Zig don't deserve it."

Craig sighed, running his hands through his hair some more. The accident had changed him more than it had changed me, because he was the one who'd had to drop out of college, find a job, and pay the bills. I was the same person with a broken heart. He was a broken person who'd begun to act like he had none. He didn't mean to resent me for it, but it didn't take a genius to know he did.

"I'll try to make an effort." He placed his elbows on his desk, knotting his fingers behind his head. The accident was a hit-and-run. If tragedy had a face, at least we could hate it. I wasn't the feel-sorry-for-myself type. Even when it was evident that with less than stellar grades and non-existent funds, the closest I'd ever get to college was if I cleaned one. I didn't care that my destiny had been written for me. I edited the bastard. And, frankly, up until Clara had retired and sold Thrifty, I'd been content with my small life. Craig, on the other hand, didn't like staying small. Especially since he'd been on the verge of making it to the NFL before tragedy struck our family.

And that was why I hated alcohol. There was no chance the person behind the wheel had been sober. There just wasn't. Which made Craig's affair with alcohol drive me even more insane.

"Thanks," I whispered. "Be strong for them, okay? Nat's given up on a lot to be with you."

"So you keep reminding me. Constantly."

Lucas was coughing from the corner of the room, and that was my cue to end the conversation.

"Is that Mr. Coked Up?" Craig's eyes lit for the first time since we'd started the conversation, but he was more excited by the idea of insulting a celebrity than being starstruck. "Did I just hear Alex Winslow cough?"

"Nope." I flushed red from the mere idea of Alex walking around in my suite. "It's Lucas, his drummer. He loaned me his laptop."

"Right." Craig's voice dropped down to its usual arctic chill. "Anyway, hope you're done with your annual crying fest."

"I am," I confirmed. I wanted to say something more, to end the conversation on a positive note, but the connection was cut from his side and I ended up staring back at a blue screen.

Lucas appeared next to me, squeezing my shoulder. No words needed to be spoken, and I found myself pressing my cheek to his hand, closing my eyes.

He was there.

He was nice to me.

He understood.

And for the first time since I'd left US soil, I was still alone, but somehow, together.

The whole world felt different that night. Like a wonky picture on an otherwise naked wall. Life was illuminated in a way that only tragedy brings out. Being an orphan wasn't just a state, it was a feeling, a type of baggage, and maybe even a personality trait.

I shadowed Alex silently. He let me have my space, but then again he never really tried to talk to me anyway, other than that time in the hallway. When he stepped onto the stage and started the show, I let out a sigh of relief. I needed my alone time. As soon as Alex left my vicinity, I plopped on the couch in his dressing room—brown leather this time—and used Luc's laptop to scroll over pictures of Flora and Bruce Bellamy. Craig had made his profile public on that day because he knew I'd want to see them.

My mother's smile had been infectious, and Dad used to laugh with his entire body. I ran my fingers over Luc's laptop screen, sighing. "Don't hate me for leaving them. I'll come back with enough money to get us out of trouble," I told them, but I knew it wasn't as simple as that.

When the show was over, Alex walked in, dripping sweat. Drops trickled from his chin onto his bare chest, and my stomach clenched and knotted in an unfamiliar way when his tight abs constricted with every step he took. I bit my lower lip, setting the laptop aside.

"Good show?"

"No," he grunted, scooping a bottle of water and unscrewing the cap. Instead of drinking, he splashed the water onto his face from above, then crushed the empty bottle on the table with his palm. "Bloody amazing show."

I didn't even have a smile to spare him, so I got back to staring at the wall. Alex nudged my foot with his boot, plopping beside me and nearly breaking the laptop in two.

"Midnight in the hallway, Stardust. I reckon tonight's gonna last a bit longer. I'm behind schedule with the songs."

"What are you talking about?" I mumbled, rescuing the laptop and placing it on a stand by the couch.

"Gig night is Muse Night. That's what we do after a show." He stared at me like I'd grown a second, green head from my shoulder.

"We're doing that again?" I blinked, trying to kill the butterflies dancing in my stomach.

He rolled onto his side, giving me a spectacular view of his inked chest and abs, his head propped on his bulging arm, his stare as intense as his husky, drugging voice.

It felt different. So different.

Different from the way he usually looked at me.

Different from the way *anyone* had ever looked at me.

Something happened to my body that prompted me to cross my legs and clamp my inner thighs. His lips were close to mine, ruddy and plump from screaming into the mic. I needed to get up. Why wasn't I getting up? Jesus, it was like my ass was glued to the sofa.

"What the fuck is wrong with you, Stardust? You're weirder than usual, and that says a lot."

"I don't wanna talk about it." My eyes dragged up to the window. There was always a window. In each and every one of his dressing rooms. I wondered if he specifically asked for it, and if it made him feel less trapped. Trapped in a situation. Trapped inside himself.

"Well"—he slapped my thigh lightly, and fireworks, in different colors and sizes and shapes burst inside my chest—"I'm not asking you courteously. You're on my payroll, under my wing. You'll be singing like a canary."

I sniffed, ignoring the dull headache that came hand in hand with crying for hours on end. "Technically, you're under my wing."

"Impossible," he said, lifting my limp arm. His touch was like a blanket. Warm and oddly protective. My body felt like a phoenix rising up from the ashes of dormancy and rediscovering it had muscles, and nerve-endings, and flesh that craved to be touched and bitten and nipped at. I swallowed hard.

"You can't fit me under this thing. My knob is probably the length of your leg. You're under me. All puns intended. Now tell me what's wrong. Trouble in Lucas and Stardust paradise? Finally figured out he's a knobhead?" One of his devilish eyebrows arched sarcastically. He made it sound like Lucas and I were a couple, which wasn't the case, and I wanted to believe there was an edge in his voice, but why? He wasn't interested in me, and even if he was, Jenna had warned me about him. *The world* warned me about him.

"Seriously, Winslow, you don't want to know." I gave him one last fair warning, waving him off tiredly with my hand. It wasn't my job to protect him from the truth. The truth was ugly, and real, and open like a wound full of puss. The way I figured it, Alex was used to the photoshopped version of women. Not the likes of me, who came with two tons of baggage and actual flaws.

"Spit it out, *Bellamy*," he enunciated.

"It's my parents' deathaversary."

"Come again?" He leaned forward, his muscles taut with…what?

What exactly was he feeling?

"Four years ago today, my brother and I got the phone call that they were involved in a hit-and-run near a restaurant in Koreatown. My parents worked three jobs between them and never went out. But every wedding anniversary, Dad took Mom to an all-you-can-eat buffet to celebrate. Some psycho ran them over when they crossed the road into the reservoir to take a walk, and took off, leaving them to die. They lost their lives on their anniversary. Hence the title, deathaversary."

We just stared at each other. I couldn't read him, but for the first time, I didn't care. This was my heartbreak. My pain. My *life*. I didn't need to try to make it fit his. And so what if he looked tortured by my confession before darting up to his feet, walking over to the virgin mini bar across the room.

"You were…what? Seventeen?" He schooled his voice, steeled his expression, put his usual poker face back on.

"Junior in high school." I nodded. Up until then, I'd been a straight-A student. I'd soared. I was going to ride my grades all the way to a full scholarship, but after the accident, they started slipping, fast. Partly because I needed to get a part-time job that ate into my studying hours, but mostly because I lost the drive without Mom's support. By senior year, things got so bad, I barely graduated. I flunked Spanish and am pretty sure my English teacher took pity on me. Alex scratched his chin, downing tonic water with lime and staring out the window.

"You probably hate me a little extra for getting arrested for DUI." He sounded like nice, normal Alex tonight.

I collected my bag and Lucas' laptop and started for the door. If I stayed, I would tell him the truth—yes, I hated alcoholics, and I loathed people who thought it was okay to get behind the wheel when drunk and put not only themselves in danger, but innocent people walking home from their anniversary dinner. As I was heading out, Lucas was coming in. We bumped into each other, and he chuckled, running his fingers through his brown hair.

"Been looking for you." He offered a sweet smile, his gaze jumping to Alex momentarily before landing back on me.

I handed him his laptop. "Thanks for that. You're a lifesaver, Luc."

"No worries. Are you feeling any better? You seemed on edge earlier in your room." There it was again. The look he gave Alex. He was looking for…something. A reaction, maybe.

I opened my mouth, about to answer, when Alex appeared behind my shoulder. I looked up, getting a view of his chin. He was much taller than me, and although lean, packed with tons of charisma, we didn't even look like we belonged in the same species. His fingers strangled the doorframe and his nostrils flared.

"Her *room*?" He rolled the last word on his tongue like it was a curse. "What business did you have being in her room?"

Lucas cocked his head, confusion marring his features.

"She asked me to lend her my laptop."

"Could've stayed in the hallway. No, wait. That's a foreign concept, right, Waitrose? Talking to a girl without monopolizing her life, time, and space," Alex retorted.

I was sandwiched between them, my back to Alex, my face to Lucas, feeling hot, and not just from blushing. Both men released enough heat from their bodies to fry a steak, and it was wrong, especially considering the poor timing, but my pulse throbbed in my neck with arousal.

"Oh, that's rich, Winslow. If your cock had an autobiography, it'd be thicker than Bill Gates." Luc kept his voice light but his intent heavy, offering me his open palm.

My eyes widened in disbelief. This was a blunt provocation, and they both knew that. I sidestepped, my back to the wall. They stared me down, waiting for me to say something. Lucas' hand was still open, but not at all inviting. Alex pushed it away, making Luc's arm dangle beside his body. He got into his drummer's face, and before I knew what was happening, Lucas was glued against the wall beside me, the fabric of his damp shirt gathered in Alex's fist. They were nose-to-nose now. There was no mistaking the bad blood that ran between them, because it was thick and angry like a river.

"Let's get one thing straight—this girl was *not* hired as a parking space for your dick. She is *my* assistant. She takes care of *me*, caters to *me*, answers *me*, and only *me*. This means if I ever catch you in her room again—and I'm planning to keep a closer look now, Waitrose—I will throw you off the tour without even batting an eyelash. Don't forget you're just a fucking drummer. Any roadie with two sticks can replace you."

My heart was in my throat. For all the evil Alex Winslow exhibited whenever I was involved, he'd never spoken to any of his friends like this in front of me. Lucas pushed Alex away, causing the rock star to slam against the opposite wall.

"Oh, piss off. You've been acting like a miserable cunt since the second you left rehab. If your mission in life is to make everyone hate you, you're excelling big time, Winslow."

Alex immediately swung his arm back, preparing to pummel his fist into Lucas' face, but luckily, Blake appeared down the hall, sprinting toward us.

"Oi! You two, stay away from each other," he yelled, waving his fisted cell phone in warning. Words couldn't express how awkward I felt standing there like an idiot and watching the exchange wordlessly. There were many things I wanted to do, including but not limited to screaming at Alex that I wasn't his possession, then telling Lucas to stop acting like an insecure five-year-old who wanted to get a rise from the hotheaded boy down the street. However, I decided to lecture them both separately when they'd cooled down for better impact.

Blake shoved his body between them and stretched his arms, forcing each guy to a different wall.

"Second time in twenty-four hours. What the hell is happening?" he demanded.

"Same thing that happened yesterday. Waitrose is hitting on my babysitter." Alex huffed a piece of hair from his sweaty forehead, and damn, he was still shirtless, and I was still trying hard not to ovulate as a result.

Lucas sneered. "Let's try again, muppet. Officer Cokehead won't allow Indie to breathe without him around. Apparently, we're no longer allowed to hang out because of his small dick syndrome."

"Small dick!" Alex exclaimed, as if Lucas just told him the earth was flat. "My cock already made more money than you this year and will soon need a full staff to manage his career. Don't you fucking disrespect him."

Was I really standing there listening to three grown-up British men discussing Alex's penis?

"Okay, okay, okay." Blake pushed both of them harder toward the opposite walls as they tried getting in each other's faces again.

I'd never seen Lucas anything less than calm and poised, and Alex's feathers had never been this ruffled before, either.

"Listen to me carefully, you two—Alex, Lucas is allowed to hang out with your babysitter, who is not, in fact, in your possession just because she works for you. Lucas, you can try to chase Indie's tail—no offense, Indie, but that's quite what he's doing—without doing it so blatantly in Alex's face. Am I understood?"

Alex stared at Blake like he didn't understand nor agree to anything that had left his mouth. His pupils spat fire and his mouth was pursed into a thin line. After a few seconds of silence, he shook his arm out of Blake's grasp, his eyes never leaving his manager's. "We'll discuss this in the suite. I'm going for a drive. Indie. You're leaving with me."

"Am not," I corrected, on the verge of strangling him while simultaneously screaming. "I'm leaving in our SUV with the rest of the guys."

"Well, then," he said, smiling, "I guess I'll have to get going. Scoring coke in a foreign city is always a hassle."

I was about to stomp in his direction when Blake stopped me, putting a hand on my shoulder.

"I'll deal with this," he said.

A dressing room door opened down the hallway and Alfie appeared, pink-cheeked. There was a gorgeous brunette in a red minidress next to him, and they held hands. I didn't fail to notice that her scarlet lipstick was smeared all over both their faces.

"Can you shut your gobs for one bloody minute? Kinda busy spreading the love here."

"The love or the STDs?" Alex muttered, lighting a cigarette, his go-fuck-yourself expression on full display.

Lucas folded his arms, yawning. "Sorry, mate, you'll have to take a rain check. Your boss is threatening to relapse because he can't take seeing his drummer and babysitter hanging out."

"Hanging out, huh?" Alfie chuckled.

Stay strong. Don't hit anyone. You don't need the criminal record.

"You guys are all idiots," I concluded, storming down the hallway toward the back door where the SUV was waiting for us. "All of you. No exceptions. Big-ass babies with fat wallets and too much time." I turned around and stomped away, throwing two middle fingers in the air for emphasis. "I'm going to sit in the SUV and try not to choke from anger. Hope by the time you guys get there, you grow up a little."

"All grown here." Alfie grabbed his crotch, and this time it was Lucas who slapped the back of his head.

"See you at midnight, Stardust!" Alex yelled to my retreating back.

The brunette squeaked, "Ohmigosh! Alex Winslow! Can I have an autograph?"

I picked up the pace and recited the mantra I'd told myself earlier—that it was just about the money. Temporary and completely meaningless.

But the truth was, Alex wanted into my pants.

Lucas wanted into my life.

And I wanted to get out of this tour alive and whole.

Heart, body, and soul.

Chapter Nine

Alex

George Carlin once said, "What does cocaine make you feel like? It makes you feel like doing more cocaine." George Carlin, ladies and gents, was, in fact, right. With cocaine, I felt more alert, less anxious, and a lot more confident. Coke made me all wired-up and worthy of my ridiculous net worth. Coke also made me more sufferable—I'd been less of a dick because I wasn't so worried my shit was shite all the time—and more *in*sufferable—because it made me think I was The Shit.

Now I was sober and acutely aware of the fact I needed to justify the money sitting in my bank by coming up with a spectacular album. The word 'overrated' flies around way too much once your art translates into sports cars, high-profiled relationships, and Malibu mansions. Money is also the beginning of the end to art, the kiss of death to creativity, and the cancer to integrity. More on that later. Point is, insecurity is like a snake. It can either suffocate or eat you alive. Your choice, really.

The new album made me uneasy, and being uneasy made me a dick. The first people in my line of fire were my staff, so it was no wonder I'd decided to take it out on Waitrose and his easy smile and unscrupulous intentions. Though really, was he expecting me to just sit there and let him fuck my very fuckable hanny? Fuck no.

"What's up with the sitter?" Blake echoed my thoughts, tucking his phone into the front pocket of his trousers.

I stopped strumming Tania and looked up. We were sitting in the back of a taxi, driving through Melbourne's interesting bits. The Eureka Tower, MCG, the Botanical Gardens, and the Shrine of Remembrance. I knew that since Blake had actually put away his phone to ask me that question, it meant it was serious.

"Specify." I flicked dirt from under my chewed-up nails.

"You never cared when we hit on your nannies before. And we always have. Christ, Alfie shagged two, and none of them lasted over a week."

My eyes moved to the window, and I tapped my knee to a tuneless rhythm. Oh, my life, two lines would fix everything. Unclog the lyrics and make me do what I'd been wanting to—drag Stardust by the hair to the balcony overlooking Melbourne's skyline and fuck her senseless until she moaned out of key.

"Allow me to refresh your memory, Blake—none of my sobriety companions made it past the three-day mark. That's the first fact standing in your way. The second one? This nanny is on the road with us, probably for the remainder of the tour, and I don't need the drama. Third and last—unfortunately, she's no longer disposable. I sort of found a good use for her."

Silence sat thick between us. Then, "Now it's your turn to specify. What is this something?"

Blake wanted Jenna. That much I was certain of. The first time they'd met, he'd asked her about the massive ring on her finger before he asked for her name. She answered she was wearing it specifically for idiots like him, who she wanted to avoid. His sniffing around Indigo made zero sense. I plucked a fag from my pack with my teeth and lit it, ignoring the driver who shot me a silent frown from the rearview window.

Puffing, I unrolled the window. "Indigo turned out to be a bit of a muse to my next album. She's down-to-earth; I'm sky-high. She makes me want to write about the L.A. of the old films. Just look at her. She dresses like one of those Marilyn Monroe impersonators on the Walk of Fame. I'm starting to come up with the narrative of the album, and she's part of it. The blue-haired girl in the vintage dress, cycling around on her bike, going around trying to piece her heart back together."

I was talking out of my arse at this point. My explanation sounded artsy-fartsy at best and delusional mumbo jumbo at worst, but that was the beauty of being a musician. No one could dispute your process, even if it essentially involved sitting on a Chinese takeout joint's rooftop, stark naked, balancing a fruit bowl on your head while singing "We Are the World"—undoubtedly the worst song to ever be written in the history of, well, the written word.

"Huh." Blake stroked his chin, carefully considering the load of crap I'd fed him with a spoon. I knew he'd do whatever it took to help me write a good album, including skinning Waitrose and using his flesh as a new case for Tania. The next bit was a tad trickier. See, being an arsehole is an art. I probably needed to do this without blatantly pissing all over the meaning of "friendship," but when it came to Lucas, I genuinely didn't care. If anything, I'd be delighted if he'd found out I was fisting his little girlfriend to the sound of The Pussycat Dolls.

"I'm also going to fuck her."

Blake's jaw slacked, then eased back as he let loose a smile he was trying to bite. Why did he look so satisfied? Did he know something I didn't?

"I didn't say it'd be a threesome," I clarified.

He schooled his face back to a scowl. "Shut up, Alex."

The cab stopped in front of our hotel, and it was dark and cold, and for the first time in weeks, I wasn't feeling like my soul had been run over by every vehicle in a two-hundred-mile radius. The crisp air pinched my nose as I slid out of the back seat. Two doormen approached us while Blake paid the driver, tipping him extra for the cigarette stench I'd left in his car. One of the doormen held an umbrella above my head. The other offered to take my guitar. I *tsked*. No one touched Tania except me. Blake matched my steps into the building, and for a second, we weren't Alex Winslow and his dapper manager. We were normal twenty-seven-year-old blokes, and I was getting shit from my mate for being so insufferably self-centered. There were no barricades, no barriers, and no bodyguards to shield me from the world.

"Waitrose wants Indie. He made it clear," Blake said matter-of-factly when we stepped into the elevator. "You've already dipped into the Lucas pool, mate. Remember Laura?"

Vaguely, and only because I didn't have the pleasure of being high at age fourteen.

"We didn't even have hair on our balls back then. Besides, I shagged her long before he started dating her." I waved him off dismissively. "Laura left him because he was a miserable sod who gave her very little attention. He'd been itching to go on this tour and join us in L.A. When they broke up, I took him in, bought him a plane ticket, brought him to California, same as I did with you. The way he repaid me was throwing Fallon and Will together. Guess what? I still hired his arse as my drummer. Well, now he owes a debt, and I finally chose a way to collect it. He's going to see what it feels like when the girl slips from between your fingers. Spoiler alert—it's not pretty. Not by a long shot."

The lift door slid open. The walk to our suite was so quiet our footfalls on the carpeted floor echoed on the walls in dull thuds. It was eleven fifty-four. Part of me wanted to see if Indie would come out to the hallway at midnight willingly, but the greater part didn't give two shits. There were songs to be written. She was going to help me whether she liked it or not.

"You staying outside?" Blake rubbed his forehead tiredly, his other hand already on the doorknob.

I nodded toward my babysitter's room. "I'm finishing this tour with an album." It was a declaration, not a wish.

"With the amount of mess you're creating in the process, you goddamn better." He pinched the bridge of his nose, slamming the door in my face.

Eleven fifty-five.

I stood and stared at her door, wondering if Lucas was there. Surely, he wasn't so daft as to try to mess with what was mine. And that was the naked, raw truth. Indigo Bellamy was mine. I paid her to be here.

She was at my disposal, for better or worse.

I was going to use her.

And fuck her.

And taunt Lucas with her, because he had nowhere to go—he'd literally have to see it. Day after day. Night after night. Like I saw Fallon and Will on every website, in every magazine, and every media outlet in the world. Kissing, hugging, smiling for the camera. *"Bushell Finds Love!" "State of the Art: Will Finds His Muse!" "Love on Lankford Lane."*

Eleven fifty-six.

I swore her door was taunting me.

I was sober enough to recognize this wasn't logically plausible, yet somehow, it was. I needed to knock and get it over with, but something stopped me.

Eleven fifty-seven.

A sound came from behind the door. A cross between a groan and a moan. Was Waitrose touching her? Was she touching herself? My blood heated in my veins, my dick hardening in my briefs. I imagined her mounting a white hotel pillow, clutching it between her sun-kissed thighs and riding it with her fingers deep inside her pussy. She was so small, I wondered what she'd look like from the inside. Pink and tight and easily bruised. I wanted to stick my tongue in and check. To rip her panties and see if her bum was the same color as her bronzed face and shoulders. The need to know was carnal. Like this was the greatest mystery one could possibly unearth.

Oomph, my cock strained against my zipper, swelling to a point where I felt my pulse thudding through its veins.

Eleven fifty-eight.

Footfalls fell along her room. Back, forth. Back, forth. She was probably packing, *not* masturbating. I cupped my dick through my jeans, rearranging my junk and cracking my neck. Right. I needed a fuck. Stardust was still a no-go. She was the get-to-know-you-first type of bird. I made a mental note to jog from the plane the minute we landed in Japan and stick my cock into the first set of open legs I could find. Maybe even at the airport. No matter if I got caught. It wasn't like there was one person in the western world who hadn't seen my cock yet. Including Indie herself. And the way her eyes had brightened when she'd looked at it...

Eleven fifty-nine.

Restless. Why the fuck was I restless? She was nothing to me. And yet, she was obviously something. It was the album, I decided. It was doing my bloody head in.

Midnight.

The door was still closed. I didn't hear her little feet or feel her approaching, and I should have. Body heat had the ability to move through wood and steel and space. My jaw clenched and my fist curled around her doorknob. It was pointless. The door was automatically locked, and even I was perceptive enough to acknowledge I had no right to barge into her space.

Twelve oh-one.

The girl wasn't going to comply. What a little spitfire, she was. I raised my fist to knock on the door. The second my knuckles were about to connect with the wood, it swung open. Indie stood there, her eyes swollen and red. Somewhere in my throat, there were words I couldn't say. Mostly profanity, so it was probably good I kept silent.

"I need someone to hold me tonight," she croaked, hugging her midsection. Her eyes fluttered in defeat at her own sincerity, like she was giving me something precious. Her weakness. And of course—I took it. I stepped into her room. If there was anyone doing any holding of Indigo Bellamy on this tour, it was going to be me. She pushed me away, her palm connecting with my chest, and stepped outside into the hallway with me.

This evening, when she'd told me about her parents, I'd felt sorry for her. It looked like her parents had actually been decent human beings.

"Let's keep it impersonal, shall we? Weren't you the one who made the rule about staying out of each other's rooms when we write? The hallway is neutral."

"We're way past neutral, and fuck if you aren't being difficult again," I grunted.

"I'm allowed to be whatever I want tonight." She sniffed.

She was probably right. I wasn't an orphan, but I might as well be, with parents like mine.

Not giving her the chance to resist, I immediately wrapped my arms around her body, holding her like breakable china. She wasn't as boney as I'd thought she'd be. In my mind, she felt like hugging a sack of marbles, when in reality, she was soft everywhere. It made me tighten my arms around her, like she could slip through my fingers, like mist.

My chin rested on the top of her head; her nose was buried in my armpit. She was warm and silky. Delicious, really. I wanted to take her like a drug. All at once, in one gulp. I wanted to overdose on her like cocaine, and heroin, and crack, knowing the destruction I was willingly inhaling into my body. Because Indie, like drugs, was a temporary fix. Once our three months were up, she'd leave my surly arse and run back to what was left of her dysfunctional-yet-loving family.

I wouldn't blame her.

Hell, I wouldn't even stop her.

Because deep down, I knew a bastard like me couldn't keep her.

Indie

The rudest bastard in the world, as it turned out, was also a welcome distraction.

Because here I was again, sitting in the hallway, face-to-face, soul-to-soul with the most troubled of them all.

Initially, I was going to stay put in my room, even if the entire world collapsed and Alex tried to break down my door. But then Natasha had called me shortly after the show, and I'd realized the last thing I needed was to stay in my room and stew. She'd sounded panicked on the phone. Apparently, Craig's version of being a good husband and father today had been to go MIA the minute he'd stepped out of bed. Nat had gotten a call from her friend, Trish, saying Craig dropped Ziggy at her place wordlessly, already stinking like an Irish brothel. Nat had had to leave work and rush to pick up Ziggy, then aimlessly look for Craig on the streets while clutching her toddler to her chest.

My brother was going to show up back home. We both knew that.

He was also going to apologize profusely, promising it'd never happen again.

'Just a blip.'

'Not after all we've been through.'

'Come on, Nat, you know my family is my *everything*.'

Oh, yes, my brother was charming. He'd never raise his voice to his wife, or push her, or blame her for his troubles. Nat would stay, and the crack in their foundation would widen further, with Ziggy's happiness slipping through it.

"If you wanna talk about it—do." Alex's glacial voice pierced through my dark thoughts, his boot between my stretched legs. It only touched my ankles, but still somehow felt deeply inappropriate. Then again, we were in the hallway, in plain sight, like all delicious secrets that were meant to stay that way.

I considered the unlikely idea. "Would it be helpful to your songwriting?"

He did a one-shoulder shrug. "If I knew the answer to that question, I'd have thirty albums under my belt, not four, and probably enough money to buy the entire city of Los Angeles and consequently burn it down."

"You're charming." I rolled my eyes.

"Doubtful. I'm not prolific, either."

"There are solutions for that. Time management classes are kind of big these days," I babbled.

He shot me one of his dry looks. "What a great time to be alive. So. Your hissy fit today," he detoured back to the subject.

I tilted my head, studying him. His frown. His natural, bee-stung pout. Clean-shaven face, softened by youth but hardened by life. If it wasn't for his tousled hair and life's-a-bitch-and-then-you-die scowl, he could actually pass for someone else. Less intimidating. Less soul-sucking. *Less dangerous for my heart.* He was so beautiful, and talented, and adored, and *miserable.* How could you have so much and feel so little?

I opened my mouth, knowing the truth would come out, but afraid of hearing it.

"I always knew my life would have this big, colossal catastrophe. Even before it actually happened. It was like I was waiting for it, in a way. For something to define me. I spent my youth sitting in my room sewing clothes, content with being a weirdo, as you so diplomatically put it. My brother, Craig, was just the opposite. Hotshot football player with the cheerleader on his arm."

"And did it?" Alex asked, his army boot caressing the inside of my ankle, riding up my calf. The worst part was that I let him do it. Yesterday, I wouldn't have. And tomorrow, I would swat him away. But today, I was fragile enough for him to make me feel good, even if it was a bad decision. "Define you, I mean."

"No. It didn't. I have this chip on my shoulder I carry with me everywhere I go. Of the girl who's been robbed of her parents. But I still smile, and laugh, and spend time with my nephew and friends. My tragedy is like an ugly scar that's hidden from the world. Only I can see it."

"Mine's the opposite." He smirked, fingering the strings of his guitar absentmindedly. "My tragedy is an open wound every fucker in the universe can poke and look into. My fiancée left me for my ex-best friend publicly, after it was revealed in the tabloids that she'd been fucking him while we were still together while I was on tour. I'm an addict, a knobhead, and a bitter arsehole who can't even sit still when his enemy receives a Grammy. Everyone can—and does—see my scars. No exceptions. My soul is empty, because I whored it out. I signed fat contracts with huge labels to get big money. For the last six years, they've dictated my every move. And whatever they didn't suck out of me, the crowd did. Because every night you go on that stage, Indie, you give your fans your everything. Every. Fucking. Thing. Then you wake up the next day and do it all over again."

I was so surprised at his admission, the fact I uttered anything at all was nothing short of a miracle. "Is that why you act this way?" Not that it gave him an excuse, but the need to understand him better burned me from the inside.

Alex rolled his head against the wall. "Enough with the philosophical bullshit. So. This is not inspiring at all. Tell me about your sex life."

I gave him a look, my walls stacking up again, brick by brick. "No."

"That 'cause you don't have any? Because that could be rectified."

"It's because it's none of your business, and while we're on the subject, I'd appreciate it if you stopped hitting on me."

He put his guitar down, snatched a cigarette from his open pack by his feet, a notepad, and a blue Sharpie and started writing. *Blue Sharpie.* Just like in the article. Alex was a creature of habit. I wondered what it was about the color.

There was something incredibly sexy about seeing him, an unlit cigarette hanging between his straight teeth, making art in front of me. I had no idea what he was writing, and I doubted he'd let me know if I asked. But the idea that I might hear it on the radio someday made me shiver.

"If you want me to believe you about not wanting me to fuck you raw, you should probably stop looking at me like that. Like you're already mine," he said, his eyes still focused on his notepad. I looked away, my face growing ruddy and hot.

"You're crass."

"And you're full of bullshit." He looked up, catching my gaze. "You really like Waitrose? Really, *really* like him? I don't believe that. Not for one second. Know what the difference is between you and me, Stardust? You watch me, but I see you. And what I see is your truth. You wear your heart on your sleeve, and it bleeds into the real world, which means you're a remarkably terrible liar. You look at Waitrose fondly. Like you would at a stranger's baby down the street. You look at me with dynamite in your eyes, waiting for me to light up the match and finally set you on fire."

Everything stopped.

The air.

The world.

My heart.

He said all that with his lips still pursed around the cigarette. With dead eyes and a sultry, rough voice he'd tone down and sweeten when he recorded his music. A door opened and closed in the distance, and we both snapped our heads in its direction. It was Alfie, ushering two giggling girls in miniskirts toward the elevator. He smacked their butts as he rushed them between the doors, not even sparing us a glance. They skipped, their voices pitching high, while he barked like a mad dog, pretending to bite and nibble at their necks. He hadn't noticed us.

"We're heading to the airport in less than two hours." I cleared my throat after the laughter died down. Alfie and the girls rounded the hallway. "Did you get everything you needed?"

"Not by a long shot." He leaned forward, his hand clasping my wrist. His gaze held mine hostage. "And neither did you."

I rolled to my knees quickly and stood up. Alex did the same, his guitar and notepad still on the floor. We stood in front of each other, not like strangers anymore, and that scared me.

"One for the road," he said, hooking his finger into the neckline of my hoodie and jerking me close. His arms enveloped me, the tip of the cigarette in his mouth tickling my neck. I felt his hug in my stomach, in my groin, and in my toes. His arms felt coarse, but the moment felt eerily soft. I squeezed selfishly, burrowing into his white V-neck tee while closing my eyes, inhaling, inhaling, inhaling.

I miss you, Mom.

I miss you, Dad.

It's when you memorize the small things in a person that you realize you're screwed. I liked the stale scent of cigarette smoke between his fingers, and the sour, masculine smell of his neck. The way his wavy hair curled at the sideburns, silky and boyish, and the way his strong jaw looked almost comical in contrast with his stupidly cute ears. When he finally loosened his hold on me, I looked up, and he looked down, and every sense was floodlit. A ping rang between us. The elevator, probably. But he couldn't have noticed. Not with the way his browns held my blues. This was his chance to make a move. He'd said he was going to have me, and tonight, I wanted to be taken. After all, if you make one horrifyingly bad choice in your life, better do it on a day that represents your parents' deathaversary, right?

His lips were close.

His pulse quickened under his shirt.

Warm, warm, *so* warm.

I took a deep breath.

Closed my eyes.

Opened my mouth.

Stood on my tiptoes.

And…stumbled forward into nothingness.

As my eyes cracked open, the emergency door at the end of the hall slid shut automatically, still pushing the last hints of his intoxicating scent. I looked down. His notepad and Sharpie were still there.

Cold, cold, *so* cold.

He'd gone to smoke that cigarette.

And left me all alone.

Chapter Ten

Indie

Indie: I think the ten-minute song is going to be really good.
Jenna: I hope you didn't tell him that.
Indie: No. I told him it's unmarketable.
Hudson: And what did he say?
Indie: He said I sounded like a Suit, specifically like Jenna Holden, and that Jenna Holden was hired to get him Balmain deals and negotiate fat deals with record labels, not produce his next album. He also said he'd once caught you nodding your head at a Maroon 5 song, and the fact that you're not dead to him after that is a miracle in itself, so you should not push your luck. Again, his words, not mine.
Hudson: Classic Alex.
Jenna: We'll have to work on that. Indigo, how's his mood? Does he look okay to you?

I didn't know how to answer that. Alex constantly looked like his soul was shattered, but his bravado was steel and metal. I didn't know him well enough to know if his current state was good, bad, or indifferent. He didn't look like he was having suicidal tendencies, but I wasn't exactly a qualified shrink.

Indie: He's crabby, but fine.
Hudson: That's his default setting.
Indie: He and Lucas aren't getting along.

Hudson: When did they ever?
Jenna: Keep us posted, Indigo.
Jenna: Indigo?
Indie: I said I only answer to Indie.
Hudson: BURN.
Hudson: Also, I think Alex is rubbing off on you a bit.

Oh, he had no idea.

Alex

Tokyo, Japan.

Not so fun fact: when you're an alcoholic, holding a bottle of champagne in your hand is the equivalent of clutching a semi-automatic weapon. Destructive, but somehow still fucking legal in all fifty states.

I don't know who the fucker was who kept on sending them to every room I'd stayed at during this tour, but whoever they were, they had inside information, malicious intent, and a lot of free time on their hands. Every time we rolled into a new city, Blake, Jenna, and Hudson all made sure to call the hotel and warn the local staff to empty the minibar of alcohol. I was kept away from everything I could get high on, including mouthwash, dust remover, and hand sanitizers. I swear, the fact I still smelled remotely pleasant was a fucking miracle. And though I was too busy hating the world to actively look to score or get pissed, my sobriety was mainly a product of circumstances and laziness. And now I had a bottle of champagne and a minute by myself.

Fancy that.

Knowing Blake would come upstairs to our hotel room any second and that Indie had a key card to my presidential suite, I quickly wrapped the bottle in a hoodie and shoved it into one of my suitcases.

They'd both lose their shit had they known I'd found the bottle on the threshold. The first time Blake had opened the door to find a bottle of Jameson, he'd tossed it out of the window and cursed, watching it swan-dive into the ocean. The second time, he'd hired a PI and treated himself to a twenty-minute meltdown in the bathroom. And Indie... she would go on a hunt all over the world to track down the twat who'd tried to throw me off the wagon, turning every stone over until they were found. Never mind the fact I thought I knew exactly who the bastard was—and where he was. In bed, with my ex-girlfriend.

Which reminded me, I needed to throw the plan of fucking Stardust into high gear *before* I got back with Fallon. She may have been a cheater, but I wasn't.

The decision wasn't calculated or even particularly smart. Sure, I saw Indie balling into herself like a kitten on the couch of the private jet with her head on Lucas' thighs—his *crotch*—but it wasn't like I was jealous. My heart rolled in my chest helplessly like a wounded soldier, because Waitrose didn't deserve anything, much less the only girl on the tour.

The. Only. Girl. On. The. Tour.

If anyone was going to fuck this girl, it'd be me, not my backstabbing drummer and frenemy.

Rising up from my open suitcase, where the champagne had been placed carefully on the side, covered by clothes, I walked across the darkened room—the wrought iron chandelier looming from the ceiling like a devious monster. The wallpaper was black, with Japanese letters smeared in red. I stopped by the kitchen island, flipping over my notebook with the notes from last night.

Progress.

My soul didn't feel quite as empty when I strode over to the floor-to-ceiling window overlooking Tokyo.

Clean. Busy. Sophisticated. Tokyo was built high, wide, and in long strokes, like she'd been painted by a confident artist. I'd been here once before and had made some pretty sweet memories in the form of a foursome and a dirty underwear vending machine I'd emptied.

When my phone rang, I didn't immediately move. The only people I spoke with were already on the tour, as pathetically tragic as it may sound, and Jenna and the rest of my management usually liaised directly with Blake, because he was less likely to be a volatile tosser. I withdrew my mobile from my back pocket, frowning.

Mum.

Not today, Mother Dearest.

I let the call die, watching as the screen lit up again with another call as if on cue.

She hadn't called when I broke up with Fallon.

Or when I'd been thrown into rehab the first time.

The second time, she hadn't even answered said phone when I'd been desperate enough to want to talk to anyone, her useless arse included.

In fact, the only time she *had* picked up the phone to talk to me was after the Grammys' incident, to tell me I had circles around my eyes and that blue is not my color.

This meant she either needed to break some bad news or ask for more money to nourish her plastic surgery/gambling habits. Unfortunately for her, I was working on not letting people screw me over. Since Mum was about as constructive in my life as fucking leukemia, I chose to cut her out.

Blake walked through the door, talking to Jenna on the phone. "Jenna. Jenna. *Jenn-a,*" the last one was peppered with exhaustion. "I've got it all under control, trust me. And if, by any chance, I need to leave him for a few hours, Indie will take over. Girl watches him like a hawk."

I flicked my cigarette into the trash, the amber tip still burning. The scent of something unnatural melting—plastic or polyester— spread around the room and I plopped down on the low, black couch and stared at the ceiling.

"What's up?" Blake asked, boomeranging his mobile across the black marble island.

I stole a bottle of champagne, and I'm probably going to drink it in one gulp next time you take a shit.

"I wrote a song." *Much better.*

"Is it any good?"

Blinking slowly, I tried ungluing my teeth from my tongue. "Think I would've told you if it was shite? Of course it's good." Though, really, who the hell knew? Art is like love. It's too subjective for you to see it clearly.

"Wanna play it for me?" Blake collapsed on the loveseat across from me.

As if on cue, Alfie and Lucas walked in the main door, waltzing toward the sofa I occupied and taking their seats. The new track was ten minutes long. Way longer than the average song, but for the first time in ages, I believed in something I'd done. It felt good.

"Yeah, play it for us, Winslow. Serenade us like you mean it." Alfie batted his eyelashes, clutching the fabric of his shirt over his heart.

Lucas looked tense and didn't say a thing, which was probably good, considering how our last conversation had ended. I smirked.

"I still need to polish a few things, but I'll give you the notes soon."

"Notes for what?" Alfie shoved his bacteria-infested hand into a bowl of chocolate-coated strawberries in the middle of the coffee table. No way was I touching those strawberries, or that table, or anything else in the fucking suite now. I wasn't much of a germophobe, but the bloke was made of fifty percent flesh and blood and fifty percent jizz.

"My new song."

"You wrote a song?"

"I wrote a song."

"Let me guess," Lucas said. "Indie helped?"

I paused for one second before deciding I was above acknowledging his existence.

"I told Lucas I saw you guys hugging down the hall yesterday," Alfie volunteered, his mouth full, red juice dripping all over his chin. "Just, you know, to spice things up."

"Wanker," Blake muttered, shaking his head.

Lucas continued to stare at me like I'd killed his fucking kitten. The fact he had feelings for Stardust was bizarre to me. They'd known each other for less than a week. Where had he acquired all those feelings? His newly found vagina?

"She was there when I wrote the song," I said noncommittally, refusing to make her a bigger deal than she was.

Lucas' jaw was tight and square. "The moment we saw her at the Chateau, you knew I had my eye on her."

"Yeah, well, maybe that inspired me to have my eyes on her, too." I shrugged, turning on the TV and flipping channels.

Waitrose closed his eyes and fell back on the sofa, releasing a sigh.

"It's not a good idea, Alex. Even if it wasn't for me, you are not in the right headspace to start a relationship. You need to battle your demons first."

"Relationship?" I laughed. "Who the fuck wants a relationship?"

The end game—Will Bushell—was waiting for me around the corner, in Paris, in just a few weeks' time. Lucas' presence reminded me that Fallon was going to be with him, and it was time to reclaim her. Lucas reminded me of a lot of things, but most of all, he reminded me I was a competitive bastard, and every single thing I did, I did to prove one thing—I was still number one.

Best artist.

Best musician.

Best lover.

I got up from my seat, peeling off my wrinkly tank top.

I *was* a semi-automatic weapon, fully loaded and ready to fire. I was my own downfall, and deep down, I knew it.

Yesterday I lay with you in a bed of glass
We broke together trying to survive your past
Still, in your pain I found magic

The beauty in something so raw and tragic
When life feels banal and ordinary and beat
Run to me, my blue-eyed girl, to the place where pleasure and pain
meet

The. Crowd. Went. Nuts.

A veteran artist knows how to recognize a real buzz from miles away.

There's the usual buzz. The we-like-everything-you-do type of excitement. Then there's the promotional buzz. The one that smells of glossy brochures and PR women in pencil skirts and brunches at The Ivy to close a nice, fat deal with a top-notch radio station. Then there's the real buzz. *This* buzz. It hums in your veins—not unlike morphine—floods your entire body until every hit of oxygen feels like downing a shot. I watched my fans beneath my boots, clawing out of their own skin with elation. They skulked over security, desperate to get to me. Yelling, screaming, begging.

More. More. More.

The flashes blinded me as I finished playing "Secondhand Love," the song I wrote after I left Stardust standing in the hall. Nine minutes and twenty-three seconds of anger, frustration, and passion.

I could have kissed her.

And another bloke probably *would* have kissed her.

But where was the fun in that? I liked playing with my food, and that included driving her crazy until she could take no more of it. I wanted to make her cunt ache and drip for it. Because when I finally touched her, the star *would* turn into dust.

Pacing the stage, I threw them a crooked smile over my shoulder. I was shirtless, first sign that I was in a good mood. Usually I didn't like the whole Justin Bieber see-my-abs shite. This wasn't Hooters, and once you let your record label fuck you in the arse, the least you can do for yourself is keep your bloody shirt on. But I felt like I was standing in the middle of a bonfire singing that song to a crowd for the first time. Sweat trickled down my torso, and I could see on the huge screen behind me that the cameraman zoomed in on the drops running down my V-tap. I wondered how long it'd be before the video hit YouTube, and which would be more successful—my new song, or a picture of me fisting that starlet while coming all over her tits. Probably the latter. I decided to Google it sometime. It wasn't like I fucking cared what people said about me, anyway.

"There's more where that came from." I adjusted the mic on its stand and walked across the stage.

The screams became louder, more frantic. Yeah, this wasn't polite encouragement. This was hunger, immediate and greedy. I was vindictive and complicated and back. Fuck, I was *back*. I had lyrics in me and they were gushing out. It was futile to pretend Stardust didn't have a hand in this. She did, and I was going to keep her until the last drop of greatness poured out of me. Or her. Whoever it came from.

I looked down at my fans. Then up at the inky sky. Then in-between, to the space where a golden cloud of body heat and bright lights powdered above their heads, and smiled.

I put my lips to the mic.

My fingers strumming my guitar, I started to play "Man Meets Moon," one of my earliest tunes. When I didn't need a blue-haired girl to save me. When I was a teenager with an agenda and a lot of fucking mind to speak. A kid who didn't know where the Chateau Marmont was and only knew about caviar from the movies. The video of "Man Meets Moon" had been filmed in Lucas' basement by Blake. I'd had a zit the size of Beirut on my chin that day, but it still gave me the big break I'd needed.

Alfie, Lucas, and the back guitarist followed suit. I gave the back guitarist a slight head nod, and his eyes widened in disbelief. Everyone on my tour knew what it meant. I hadn't done that in two years, but it was time. He needed to cover for me while I crowd surfed.

And I was going to crowd surf.

Because tonight, it felt so real and right.

Good and bright.

Just. Like. Coke.

Chapter Eleven

Indie

"**O**h, my life, that was bloody epic!" Blake jumped on Alex before the rock star could stumble all the way backstage.

His bare chest glistened with sweat, and the red marks painting his abs and back made a blush creep up my neck. I knew they were put there by his fans, and I also knew what these fans thought about when they raked their fingernails over his skin. It was the same thing I thought about when I watched him move so confidently across the stage. Like an angry god. Mars. Out for blood.

Blue-eyed girl.

Just hearing his husky, hoarse baritone say those words made me rub my thighs together, trying to relieve the tension between them. He'd written about me. He'd sung about me. And, true, he'd referred to me as a mental rebound, but who the hell cared? He'd given me a song. I hadn't even given him a kiss.

I inhaled sharply, drinking him in. For the first time since I'd boarded the plane in Los Angeles, I was anxious and curious about my time with Alex tonight. About the hallway. Something had changed yesterday when we'd hugged. Better and worse.

It was like we'd become closer and drifted apart at the same time.

Standing in the shadows backstage, I let Alex have his moment with his friends. Alfie clasped his shoulders and shook him with an evil laugh. Fans took pictures of him. Lucas was smiling so hard I thought his face would split in two. Then Luc turned to me, almost in slow-motion, walking over and snaking his arm around my waist, yanking me into a hug, and burying his face inside my hair. I gasped. Sure, we were close. Kind of. We hung out, mainly on the plane and in hotel lobbies, but nothing more than that. There wasn't some brave, soul-linking friendship between us. There wasn't a bond. So, this came out of left field. Always one to please, I plastered on a reassuring grin and joined the claps in the circle of human appreciation that had formed around Alex, politely ignoring Lucas' advances.

"Brilliant, wasn't it?" Luc squeezed me into his shoulder again.

I hmm-hmmed in response, my smile faltering. Alex's laughter continued as he took in the people around him, the boyish glint in his brown-green eyes making my stomach do cartwheels, and his head swiveled in slow-motion until his eyes landed on Lucas' arm flung across my shoulder.

The smile dropped.

So did my heart. Straight to my underwear.

Wicked heart.

Traitorous heart.

Unreliable heart.

"Stardust," he barked, and I didn't know why his referring to me by my moniker made me blush, but it did.

I swallowed hard and pretended to comb my hair away from my face, when really, I was hiding from the world. "What's up?"

"Need you for a sec. C'mere."

I disconnected from Lucas, walking over to Alex without glancing at any of the people around us. Most of their faces didn't even register to begin with, which was becoming more and more of a problem when Alex was around. He surprised me by taking my hand in his and ushering me through the narrow, black maze backstage. I didn't ask him where we were going. If he was feeding off of my fear and hesitation, I didn't want to give him anything I wasn't willing to part ways with. Like my dignity. Alex Winslow was a two-faced man. One was the cold, asshole devil he gave me now. The one who wanted me to kneel. The other was his playful, relaxed self. The one I'd hung out with at the laundromat. Needless to say, both versions were unpredictable, and I did the right thing by being cautious.

We stopped at the end of the hallway on the opposite side from the dressing rooms. A small balcony overlooked the crowd of yelling fans, most of them still hopefully milling around, their eyes pinned to the stage. Pleading, wanting, wishing for their star to come out and maybe give them an encore. Another sliver of greatness. Alex led me to the black, metal bannisters, until we were in complete darkness, cloaked behind the huge projectors pointing at the stage.

We were alone.

In the dark.

The chill of the Tokyo air whispered against our skin.

Alex flattened a hand over my lower back, gluing me to the bannisters until the cold metal dug into my stomach. He crept behind me, his breath shallow and warm against the shell of my ear. His torso was still naked and he was hot, smooth, and hard everywhere. I longed to feel him, *really* feel him.

"I told you to stay away from Waitrose."

"And I told you I'll do whatever the hell I want in my personal life," I whispered back, both our eyes still staring down at the screaming fans.

"Are you gonna give me trouble?"

"Me?" I gasped. Kinetic energy flowed between us. My skin felt prickly and agitated, like I needed to step out of my clothes and feel his skin or I'd die. "Why? I thought I was just a sport." I threw the words he'd told Jenna when we first met. No, I hadn't forgotten. Yes, they still stung. Just not as much as being so goddamn poor.

He chuckled, his breath tickling my skin, his nose nuzzling into my neck. "You're an enjoyable sport. Like footy."

"See how much you like me when I knee you in the balls," I muttered.

"Hmm," he said.

"Hmm?"

"I was just thinking about you massaging them while you suck my cock."

"Never gonna happen." I shifted, my center physically aching with want.

"Oh, yeah?"

"Yeah."

"Help me choose her, then," he rasped, dragging his lips up from my shoulder to my jawline.

I let him. Let him touch me despite knowing everything. That he was an addict, a rock star, and an asshole. That he was in love with a girl named Fallon who'd broken his heart, and he'd never quite managed to glue it back together again. That his broken heart meant he could never love again, not in the way I deserved to be loved, and so he was nothing more than a painting. A beautiful thing that could never be of use.

"Her?" I asked gravelly.

"The girl I'm going to be inside of while I imagine fucking you tonight." The taunt in his voice had a lilt.

My eyes broadened as I stared down at them. My competition. All young and pretty and keen. I wanted to turn around and slap him across the face, but that would only serve as a reminder that I cared, and I didn't want him to know that.

Slowly, I brushed my palm against the railing, smiling at nothing. He viewed me as a sport, which meant there would be a winner and a loser in our little game.

"Isn't gig night also hallway night? Are you bailing out on me for a playdate, Winslow?"

He kept silent for a few beats, and my heart picked up speed, before he swiveled me, his hand on my waist. We stared into each other's eyes. The fans beneath us shuffled and shouted and hooted, yet it felt like we were all alone.

"Are you fucking him?" His thumb pressed against my stomach.

"If I am, you'd be the last person I'd confide in." I took a step sideways. "I'm leaving now."

He caught me by the elbow, turning me around. My chest crashed into his, his now-cold sweat mixing with the fabric of my dress.

"Lucas is a nice lad. But he's not what you're after."

"Oh, and you are? You're in love with someone else." I laughed bitterly.

"I never said anything about loving you, Stardust. Now, fucking you is something else entirely."

"Well, when you put it that way." I rolled my eyes before walking back to the busy hallway.

He followed behind me, not catching my steps, purposely staying behind me. Preying.

"Her," I heard him say, and I snapped my head in his direction, my eyebrows pinched together. I couldn't keep up with his stupid games.

"Her, who? Stop speaking in codes, Alex."

"There's no code. Look at where I'm pointing. Her. I'm going to fuck her tonight." His finger was pointed at a pretty brunette who stood by a vending machine backstage, clasping a clipboard to her chest and talking on the phone. She was wearing tight jeans, a cropped Alex Winslow shirt, and looked deliciously sordid, every movement and curve in her body designed to seduce.

I took a deep breath, trying not to lose it. It was hard, with Alex attempting to provoke me every step of the way.

Think about Ziggy.

Think about Craig.

Think about the big picture.

"Mazel Tov. Do you want me to hold your hand while you're with her?"

"That would be logistically challenging, but cheers for offering. Just have her sign an NDA before I take her back. I don't fuck without a non-disclosure since Cockgate." He lit a cigarette, strolling toward the guys, his back to his next conquest and me. My whole face flamed with anger.

I took a few deep breaths to calm myself before following him. "You want me to go to her and ask her to sign a non-disclosure agreement before you have sex with her? And you haven't even approached her yet?" I matched his step. Jesus H. If this was how Alex behaved completely sober, I dreaded to think what Blake and Co. had gone through when he'd been high as a kite.

"Correct."

"What makes you think she'll say yes?"

He tapped my nose with the hand that held the cigarette, smirking down at me like I was the simplest creature in the world.

"So fucking precious, Stardust. Just do it. We're heading back to the hotel in ten."

And off he walked.

I wasn't his assistant. I was his sobriety companion. It occurred to me I wasn't obligated to help him score. Furthermore, for the most part, it was probably for the best if I didn't do that. I mean, there was no mistaking the current moving through my body. I was jealous beyond words, belief, and logic. But maybe that was exactly why I needed to let it go and comply.

I needed to show him I didn't care.

I needed to show *myself* I didn't care.

We were one week into a three-month tour, and already he'd declared his intention to get me into his bed and turn my life upside down. I couldn't give him this power over me. I had my family and future to think about. And they were more important than any British hunk with eyes like molten gold and a devastating smirk.

I cleared my throat, squared my shoulders, and walked over to the girl. With every step I took, I inwardly prayed she was like me. Guarded and rational. That she would laugh in my face and tell me to take a hike. That she would turn red, personally walk over to Alex Winslow, and slap him in the name of feminism and self-respect. I stopped about a foot from her, tapping her shoulder to grab her attention. She turned around, a mixture of surprise and annoyance between the creases of her frowny face.

"Hi." I smiled, swallowing down my nervousness. Every muscle in my face betrayed me, and I was sure I looked at least a little psychotic. "I work for Alex Winslow. He sent me here because he's interested in"—*driving me nuts*—"spending the night with you. So I'm wondering if you'd like that, and, if so, would you be willing to sign a non-disclosure agreement?"

I wasn't even sure where the hell I was going to find one, but my instincts told me Blake must have them handy. He was legally-savvy. Come to think about it, he was everything-savvy.

The girl's frown disappeared, replaced with a nose-wrinkled expression of disbelief.

I know, right? What a bastard. So just say no and we can all go back to pretending this never happened.

"Alex Winslow wants to spend the night with me?"

"Seems that way." I hated her for not slamming the idea right away, hated him for sending me over to her, but most of all, I hated myself for being stupid enough to go ahead with it to prove something to the world.

"I don't believe you."

I turned around, did a little hand-wave toward the guys, and caught their attention. All of them swiveled to stare at me. Lucas looked pained. Blake looked tired. Alex smiled his arrogant wolf's grin, raising an eyebrow and his hand, tipping it slightly forward in a 'hi' motion.

I hope she has an STD. I hope she has all the STDs known to man, and a few new ones she'd created all on her own.

"See?" I turned back to the lady in question. "He's in."

"Oh, my God. Then so am I! I mean, I'd like to look at this contract, but…" She had an Aussie accent. Suddenly, I took all of her in, gulping every detail. Her luscious black hair. Her dark, feline eyes. Her pierced navel and Snow White skin. My wide-eyed, freckled, average self hated every inch of her. And that made me feel guilty.

I mustered a smile. "Fantastic. Be right back. Don't go anywhere."

I soldiered on to the boys, adding a fake bounce to my step. Two could play this game. I may not have a lot of experience, or millions of fans, or billions of dollars, but I was good. I was strong, and I was worthy. And, yes, I sure as hell was equal to him.

"She's in," I said, yanking a bottle of water from the long table of refreshments behind them and unscrewing the top. Turning toward Blake, I took a slow sip. "Can you provide her with an NDA? She said she'd like to look at it, but judging by the time it took her to say yes, I'm pretty sure she's a skimmer."

"Well, damn, Blue." Blake's eyebrows were kissing his hairline. "No wonder Jenna likes you. You have a good set of hairy balls on you."

"Not sure about hers, but mine are waxed." I winked.

All the guys laughed as Blake sauntered over to the girl with an agreement in his hand. It was the first time he'd called me Blue, and even though the moment felt like the end of the world, it also felt like a beginning of something. Of acceptance.

All the guys laughed but Alex, who stared holes into my forehead, his look alone threatening to kill someone, preferably me.

"You're one cool bird, know that?" Lucas moved beside me, brushing his shoulder against mine.

Alex grabbed the bottle of water I'd opened and put back on the table and downed the entire drink. "Pushover."

"Come again?" I asked, willing myself to stay calm.

Alex angled his body toward mine, a dark smirk on his lips. "I said you're a pushover. You did what I told you to do, never fighting back, never saving face."

"Saving face?" I blinked rapidly, trying hard not to scream in his face. *This. Man.* "I don't need to save any face. You wanted me to hook you up. I did. You're just disappointed I didn't fight over you. But guess what? I'm not them. The fangirls. The women with stars in the eyes. When I look at you?" I took a step toward him, and he took a step forward, too, and it was all too wrong and too close and too intimate all at once. "When I look at you, I see something broken that isn't worth fixing. And you look at me like I'm a cheap thing to replace the expensive one that's been stolen from you. See, we're all vases. And you're the one scattered on the floor, shattered beyond repair. So I'll let someone else pick you up. It's really that simple. Have fun with your temporary glue." My gaze swept across the room to find the mystery girl already giggling and signing the contract she pressed against Blake's back while the latter was texting on his phone in boredom.

Alex unleashed a toxic smile, his gaze narrowing on mine as he broke our physical stare-off and began walking to her.

"Congratulations, Sport. You just became a war."

That night, I heard them through the wall.

Their hands. Shuffling. Feeling. Searching. *Finding.*

Walking down the hall. *Our* hall. Right outside my door.

Stumbling. Giggling. Breathlessly whispering.

Stop it, heart.

Stay still, heart.

Fight it, heart.

Her name was Gina.

I knew, because he leaned down and let her sniff his neck when she said he smelled like the malest thing she'd ever met. 'Malest' wasn't even a word. And I immediately hated all the Ginas in the world.

"*Gina,*" he rasped her name like a dirty secret.

I peeked at them through the peephole, every bone in my body shaking with rage.

"Darlin', if you only had a clue."

Darlin'. He dropped the G. For Gina.

I was so consumed by their moment, I found it hard to breathe.

"Oh, I saw." She laughed, her sultry voice perfect against his skin, nothing like my high-pitched one. "Your cock's all over the Internet, Alex."

To that, he said nothing.

He stopped by my door, took out his chewed gum from his mouth, plastered a small note into it, and slammed it against the peephole.

Then I heard his door open.

Then I heard his door close.

I opened mine quickly, slipping my arm to take the note he'd left for me.

YOU ARE THE GLUE.

I turned around, squeezing my eyelids and banging my head against the door.

Three.

Two.

One.

Alex

Three.

Two.

One.

The sound was faint, but it was there. The exasperation in her movement lit something in me. I felt her pain. Tasted it on my lips and savored it like hot honey on my tongue.

I smiled into my kiss with what's-her-face. My tool, my container, my bait. My prop for this lesson.

Finally, Stardust was beginning to get it.

It.

Us.

We were going to fuck. Her head banging against the door assured me of that. Lucas was going to pay.

He was going to pay for giving Will the keys to my apartment when I was on tour and Fallon OD'd. He'd found her.

Lucas was going to pay for giving Fallon Will's phone number when she'd asked for it to thank him after he'd rushed to save the day. Pay for helping them slip under the radar at the Grammys three years ago, when she was on my arm but ended up fucking Will in the bathroom.

Pay for all of those things with the most precious thing money couldn't buy.

Lucas was going to pay for them with his heart.

Chapter Twelve

Indie

Indie: Anyone up?

Jenna: I am. It's the middle of the night there. What's wrong?

Indie: Nothing's wrong. Sorry. A question for future reference—is Alex allowed to bring girls to his room? I mean, they might have alcohol or drugs...

Jenna: They might, but they probably won't. Yes. It's fine.

Jenna: Or maybe it's not completely fine for YOU...

Indie: All is good. I just wanted to make sure.

Jenna: Did you tell him about the ten-minute song?

Indie: Yes. He's keeping it. The crowd went nuts for it today. He also wrote a political song.

Jenna: Of course he did.

Indie: It's great, actually.

Jenna: Great will get you nowhere in the music industry. He needs catchy. And fast. People DNF three-minute songs these days.

Indie: DNF?

Jenna: Do. Not. Finish. How are you two getting along?

How much time do you have, lady?

Indie: Well, he's no longer actively trying to get rid of me.

Jenna: And Blake? You and him are on the same wavelength?

Indie: We are. Are you?
Jenna: Did you actually just ask me that question?
Indie: Yup. I had nothing to lose. Jenna needed me there. Plus, they weren't exactly secretive about hating each other.
Jenna: Blake and I are complicated. I have contracts to sort through. Keep me updated.
Hudson: :-O

Singapore.

I spent the plane ride Skyping with Nat and Ziggy, curled on the sofa by the window.

Alex was wearing Wayfarers and a black hoodie, his arms folded over his chest, draped on a couch, asleep. He had earbuds in his ears and looked like the closest thing to women's porn while being fully clothed. I tried to tell myself it was a good thing that he'd done what he did with Gina. It clarified what we were, and more importantly—what we weren't.

"He came back in the middle of the night." Nat rubbed her red eyes, bouncing Ziggy on her thigh. Her hair was a knotted mess. "Drunk as hell and reeking of puke. Said he'd been looking for the killer all day. Knocked on people's doors. Yelled at them. Do you realize how crazy this sounds? He needs help, Indie. Fast."

She was right, of course. I was starting to believe my brother needed much more than a job. He needed rehab. With the money I was making, we could afford to send him to a decent one. Even more incentive to stay on tour and tolerate Alex. I cleared my throat, glancing sideways to make sure no one was listening.

"Eleven weeks and I'll be home," I soothed. "Just hang in there, Nat. I promise, I'll set him straight when I'm back."

"It's like he's not even the same person anymore. I mean, I get it. He's still hurting. But...I married a stranger. I had a baby with a stranger. I look at him and don't see the boy who serenaded me outside my window. I see a slacker who doesn't want to get better. A slacker that boy would have hated."

I opened my mouth, about to answer, when the flight attendant breezed in, wearing a satin, baby blue uniform and the best customer service smile I'd seen in years.

"Gentlemen, Miss Bellamy, we're getting prepared for landing. Please buckle up."

"I need to go." I wrinkled my nose, hating to cut off the conversation prematurely.

Nat looked older, like her last few nights had been as long as years.

"At least tell me you're having fun over there? It would make me feel a lot better."

"Sure." I smiled. "Great time."

"Manage to catch a glimpse of any English rock star sausages?" She replaced her exasperated frown with a heartened sniff.

Oh, God.

Alex's pouty lips twitched, even through his pretense of sleep. My face burned all the way up to my roots, then down to my toes. She couldn't have known he was right there. The plane was quiet, with everyone either napping or watching a movie.

"No," I said.

"Yes," he announced at the same time from his place on the sofa, flicking his sunglasses to a nearby table and standing up. He swaggered toward me, his devil-may-care smirk on display. My heart did that thing again, where it disobeyed my mind and wanted to jump into Alex's hands.

What the hell was Winslow doing?

"Oh, she saw my cock, all right." He dropped on the loveseat next to me, breaking the news like it was an international matter. His arm snaked behind me, his chin almost resting on my shoulder. "And she stared. Real long. Which prompted me to ask her how many cocks she'd seen in real life, a question I still have no answer to. Maybe you could enlighten me. Cute kid, by the way."

Natasha's jaw dropped, and if it weren't for the fact Ziggy had managed to slip out of her embrace and skip away toward the kitchen, she'd be sitting there and ogling Alex until we were back on US soil.

"You look great in real life," she breathed out, eyes as wide as saucers.

"Not technically real life, but I'll take it." Alex's broad, tight shoulder brushed into mine, and I winced, inching away from him. "I'm trying to convince Indie to warm up to me. How do you think I should do that?"

You're trying to get me into your bed, I wanted to correct. *And here's the first thing on your to-do list: don't ask me to hook you up with random chicks named Gina.*

"She likes cycling." Nat's smile was sinister and sweet at the same time, and I wanted to be that way. Dangerous and unassuming at the same time. "She would cycle all day if she could. So, I'd start with that."

He nodded. "Good idea, Natasha."

"Oh, wow. You know my name."

"I pay attention when she speaks." He was putting his charmer face on. Great. No one could say no to that, Nat included.

"He's a keeper," my sister-in-law said before turning off the camera.

I shook my head. He was the opposite of a keeper. He was the guy I knew for sure was going to walk away. I shut the laptop screen, my heart drumming against my throat. Alex tilted his body forward, his lips close to my shoulder blade.

"I'm going to have you," he whispered, *"glue."*

My eyes burned, and I stared ahead at Alfie's blond curls as he looked down, playing a Nintendo game.

For the first time in a long time, I knew I was in deep trouble.

Something I couldn't control.

Because Alex Winslow was a broken vase.

But I wasn't the glue. I was the stupid cleaner who was about to try to pick up the pieces and, inevitably, get cut.

The minute I stepped into my hotel room, I started pacing.

Fingers laced behind my neck, I walked in circles. My limbs felt different. Shorter, heavier, more tense. It was the lack of physical exercise and all the crappy food, I concluded. I hadn't cycled at all since we'd started the tour, plus, Alex had a thing for gas station sandwiches and street food, which left us without decent catering, and therefore, eating junk or too-rich room service most of the time.

I dropped my head, worrying my lip. Being away from home felt like a betrayal. Guilt ate at my insides for not being able to help Nat with Ziggy when she needed me the most. But what truly horrified me was that I still found myself being occupied with Alex Winslow's privates when so much was at stake.

A knock on the door made my head shoot up. All the hotel rooms I'd been in so far were different—some bright and some dark, some classically furnished and some contemporarily decorated—yet held the same melancholy of a place that never offered true intimacy. This room had peachy walls, high ceilings, and linen the color of gold. It looked luxurious beyond words, like something you would copy and paste from a bridal catalog. And I couldn't enjoy it when my loved ones were suffering two continents away.

Another knock, this time harder.

"Geez, I'm coming." I made my way to the door, still dressed in my black and white plaid dress, one of the first I'd made for myself. My hair was a mess, and my eyes were red-rimmed. I swung the door open. Alex stood on the other side of the threshold.

He'd changed from his usual plane attire. Now he was wearing skinny jeans and a Smiths T-shirt.

He looked delicious.

He also looks like a man who slept with someone else last night, Little Miss Dementia.

"What do you want, Winslow?" I cut straight to the chase. I had neither desire nor the need to be polite to him. He shouldn't even be walking around by himself. Where was Blake?

"Stardust." He rolled the nickname on his tongue, his British accent slicing through the letters prominently.

"To what do I owe this dubious pleasure? Also, am I talking to the charming, playful Alex today, or to the jerk who made me help him score last night?" I quirked an eyebrow, collecting my hair into a high and messy bun.

"Glad we finally established I'm charming."

"Sometimes, when you're trying to be. Big difference."

"But it's working?"

"Not really," I lied.

"All walled up and waiting to be defrosted. That's how I like you." He grabbed my hand and jerked me out of my room in one swift movement. "You're like a piece of delicious toffee in a thin wrapper. It's tedious work to peel your layers off, but whatever's waiting for me inside is too sweet to pass. I'm about to smash those walls of yours to dust. It will take you years building them back, but I won't be there when it happens, so no big deal."

I glued my feet to the carpeted floor, looking around us. He had a show in six hours. He was probably going to try for some hanky-panky in the hallway. He ushered me down the hall, and I dragged my feet like he was leading me straight to the gates of hell. Still, I couldn't turn around and leave him in the hallway, alone and dangerously free to do whatever he wanted. Besides, there was a surprise at the end of this journey, and I wanted to see what it was. Alex slapped his open palm against the elevator button and turned around. He crowded me with his body. I stepped back. He stepped forward. A tango I was getting used to by now.

"Where's Blake? Why are you here?" My eyes narrowed.

"Chained him to my bed and nailed him to the headboard."

"Does he know you're with me?" I ignored his stupid joke.

He bowed a playful brow. This particular expression drove me mad. It implied I was his cute baby sister who'd just made macaroni art and showed it to him.

"Let's get one thing straight. Blake? He's on my payroll. Waitrose? On my payroll. Alfie? Gross human being *and* on my payroll. So are you. You're answering to me, and right now I wanna be with you. So I will. It's really that simple, you see."

I opened my mouth to say something that would make me feel crappy and push him away, but the elevator pinged and he pulled me in by the little belt of my dress, my back slamming against the wall. He leaned against the opposite wall, and that's how we stared at each other, like two opponents in a very screwed-up game.

For the first time, he seemed to notice how red my eyes were. He squinted down at me. "What's on your mind?"

"My brother is acting up back home. It worries me. Natasha is pretty much taking care of Ziggy by herself, and working full time, and…"

And I was blabbing. I looked away, at the mahogany wood and mirrors around us.

He didn't say anything, and for that I was grateful. I didn't need empty words of encouragement. I knew my situation, owned up to it, and was working toward fixing it. The elevator slid open and we both stepped out. Alex directed me to the hallway behind the main reception, not the front entrance of the hotel, where we walked through a darkened passage leading to the underground parking lot. I said nothing and felt everything. When he finally stopped, I looked up from my feet and saw two blue city bikes. My eyebrows shot up.

"Bikes," I breathed.

"Perceptive," he sassed.

I swear British people were born with more sarcasm running in their veins than blood.

I laughed, swatting him lightly across the shoulder, too relieved to get mad at him. I ran to one of the bikes and swung one leg over it, squeezing the handles in my palms. They felt different from my bike at home. The seat was higher than I was used to and the fabric was tougher—not as worn-out as mine. I kicked the brake, allowing the bicycle to slide a few feet forward inside the hot and humid underground parking lot. It was mostly empty.

"I could cycle around here and blow off some steam," I voiced my thought aloud. He was still standing next to the other bike, staring at me.

"Or"—his voice was particularly un-icy—"you can get your little bum outside." Just as he said that, he slammed a button on the concrete wall behind him and the metal garage gate slid up, light pouring in inch by inch. My eyes widened at the skyscrapers and huge, dazzling harbor spread before me. My breath caught in my throat. I gulped in the Merlion spitting water, the integrated resort of Marina Bay, and the unbelievably systematized cityscape. Before I knew it, his elbow touched mine and he was on his bike next to me.

"No helmets?" I grinned despite my best intentions. Manwhore or not, I missed biking around the city. And it was just a little trip. Not a love declaration.

"I like to live on the edge." He licked his lower lip.

"I like to live safely within the lines," I retorted.

"It's a comfortable place to be, but nothing ever grows there."

We rode through the Merlion Park. He had his shades on and the same Burberry cap he'd worn at the laundromat, so no one could have guessed he was Alex Winslow, the man who kept the paparazzi awake at night. The sky was gray; the air was dense and moist. The weather reminded me of the apocalypse, and maybe it was fitting, because he'd destroyed so many of my walls that day.

Everything was clean and foreign. I might've been a more experienced cyclist, but he had longer legs and the stamina to keep up with me. We cycled silently for forty minutes before he jerked his head toward a little coffee shop by the promenade.

"Thirsty." A statement, not a question.

I nodded, and we both took a curve and rested our bikes outside the small café. We were about to head inside, but then he hesitated, took one look at the busy tables outside the shop, and groaned.

"Go order. I'll wait out here," he said, swinging his long leg back on the bike and staring ahead at the sapphire ocean.

I made my way to the counter, relishing the idea that, unlike him, I *could*. I wouldn't know how I'd feel if I couldn't even order coffee or a sandwich without the fear of being ambushed or photographed.

I placed an order for two coffees, two waters, and a pastry we could split. When I turned around, I saw him throwing little rocks he held in his fist into the peaceful water, still on his bike. He looked... happy. Like he wasn't used to doing something so mundane and casual. Alex smiled when I got back and hoisted myself back up on my bike, and my heart almost threw itself at him like a stupid groupie throwing panties. That heart of mine was starting to feel a lot like a liability. I wished I could surgically remove it and stay alive. I handed him his coffee and water, putting my cup of joe to my lips.

"What are you thinking about *now*?" he asked, his eyes still hypnotized by the water.

I wondered why he wanted to know that all the time. Did he really find inspiration in whatever'd gone through my head? Then something even more depressing occurred to me—no one else had asked me that in years. Not since my parents died. Craig and Natasha, they loved me, but they were too busy surviving to care. Feeling wanted and desired was addictive, and he doped me. If you want to put a spell on someone, make them feel special. That would do the trick.

"I'm just wondering"—I let the hot liquid burn my tongue, but continued without even flinching—"why are you after me? You seemed to want me gone, and now you want to sleep with me."

"I figured if I couldn't get rid of you, at least I can have fun with you."

"I'll never sleep with you." I poked at the pastry without even considering eating it. Alex took a big gulp of coffee, still looking at the ocean.

"Why?"

"Because I'm not as stupid as to willingly put myself in a position where I get hurt."

He swiveled his head to face me, and suddenly, I couldn't breathe. Like all artistic geniuses, he had an expressive face. Kind of funny-looking. Sort of imperfect. The type you couldn't look away from. Mick Jagger, Steven Tyler, Jimi Hendrix, Keith Richards. They all looked a little funny. A little too mischievous. With mouths too wide and eyes too droopy and smiles too open. Alex's face was like a great book. Every time you looked at it, you found a different something.

"I'd never hurt you. I will leave you kindly. And you will leave me happily. That, I can promise."

"How can you promise me that? How can you promise me I wouldn't fall in love?"

He looked up from his coffee, a sad smile on his face. "I'm sort of unlovable once you get to know me."

Silence.

"My appeal is in my mystery, you see."

Rain started pouring down on us, seemingly out of nowhere. Tropical weather. Short sleeves and a downpour. He tilted his head to the other side of the promenade.

"Come, Stardust. The night is young and full of promise."

We rolled to the parking lot, dripping and laughing.

And I decided not to ask Alex Winslow any personal questions, just to keep my sanity at bay.

Chapter Thirteen

Alex

A nother show.

Another hit.

Blake speculated that the YouTube video's views of "Secondhand Love" that had been leaked from Japan were so high, whoever had posted it was making twenty grand a day from ads alone. Not gonna lie, writing a great song numbed the notion of being categorically defective as a human being, and for a day there, I'd even forgotten about Fallon and Will and revenge and *the champagne*—side note: the latter sat in the back of my mind the whole time. I didn't even like champagne. Getting pissed, though, was another story.

When I got off the stage, I rushed to the dressing room, disregarding the shambolic queue of staff and local celebrities milling around trying to get a moment with me. I threw the door open and collapsed right on top of Indie, who was sitting on a silver sofa, sewing.

"Alex, gross! Get off my fabric." She pushed my chest, but there was laughter in her voice.

I climbed atop of her like a monkey and tickled her armpits— and what do you know? Indie Bellamy was ticklish. She squirmed and made the most fuckable sounds, making me want to stuff my fingers into her mouth and take out those little sounds and put them in my pocket.

"Off, off, you caveman, off!" That hint of a giggle bloomed into a full-blown laugh.

Something had changed. *We'd* changed. She'd melted a little, and I wanted to shove off the ice and see what was underneath. Alfie, Blake, and Lucas walked through the door, watching us from the threshold, mesmerized. It thrilled me, the look on Lucas' face. I didn't even need to lift my head to see it to know it was there. He was hurting. Not in the way I was hurting when he'd booked the hotel for Will and Fallon under his name so they could fuck when I was still with her, but still.

"Make me," I growled into her face, so close I could see every individual, orange freckle peppered across her nose.

"This is sexual harassment." She laughed breathlessly.

"Don't embarrass yourself." I pinned her to the sofa, my crotch on hers, my lips on her cheek so only she could hear me. "I bet if I slide my fingers up that fancy dress of yours and push your knickers aside, I'm going to find you so soaked and ready for me, it would take me an hour to lick you dry."

Her body stiffened beneath me, and I elevated my upper body, glancing down at her. Her blue eyes were so wide and curious. I wondered if she was a virgin. Indie with another guy. I couldn't picture it, and not because I was attached or some sentimental crap along those lines. She just seemed too reserved. Too proper.

"Alex," she warned, too afraid to move underneath me, knowing my erection was dangerously close to her cunt.

It was crazy, but this was perfect. *This.* Me on top of her. The only things between us were fabric and the idiots watching us from across the room. Her body was humming, and I could feel it beneath me, struggling between lust and logic. I lowered my face to hers when some cocksucker grabbed me by the belt loop and yanked me away from her.

"Get off her, you wanker," Lucas barked. When I turned around, he looked pink and pissed, not unlike Babe the pig. "You're out of control!"

"So is she." I fished for my cigarette pack in my back pocket and lit one up, blowing smoke into his face. "It's called passion. You wouldn't recognize it if it pissed directly into your mouth."

"You're such a twat, you know that?"

"Know it, live it. Sorry, Saint Lucas. Not all of us can maintain such high moral standards."

"*Alex!*" Indie scolded.

Fine. I shut up.

The ride to the hotel was wordless. Indie looked out the window, Lucas looked at me, Blake looked at his phone, and Alfie looked at his watch.

"I'm expecting three fans in half an hour. Think we'll make it in time?" The latter poked his lower lip out.

Everyone groaned, and I threw the blue pick he'd thrown at me in L.A. right at his face.

He laughed. "Oh, we've come full circle now."

In the hallway, I flat out collapsed by my door, watching Indie do the same. It was past midnight, and everyone went to their rooms. Lucas knew better than to push me by loitering around her. Indie had her cloth duffel bag, with a patched dress stuffed into it, the one she'd been working on backstage.

I plucked the notepad and Sharpie out of Tania's case and stared up at my muse, waiting for her to feed me spoonfuls of her soul.

Knowing I didn't deserve her.

Knowing *she* didn't deserve *this*.

Knowing how fucked everything was, but not being able to stop, because I wanted revenge, and an album, and solace. And Indie? She would get her money—hell, I might even throw in a couple more hundred grand to sweeten the deal for her—and I'd be to her what I was to so many others. A good story to tell her mates when she was piss-drunk at a hen party. *I fucked a rock star once, and it was great.*

"What're you working on?" I jutted my chin to her bag.

She grinned.

"What?"

"Nothing. It's just that you're the only person who asks me stuff. Most people just *tell* me things, you know?"

"Well, you're not utterly boring, and you're here, so you might as well spit it out."

"A dress. For Paris. My favorite city in the entire world."

"I thought you'd never been on a plane before?"

"I hadn't!" She batted her eyelashes and did some little girly-claps, looking so utterly ridiculous, it was almost endearing.

"Looks patchy," I observed. There were white and pink and cream patches sewn together deliberately out of order. Like a patchwork blanket.

She fingered the fabric with her thin fingers. "It's a little ugly. Isn't it beautiful?"

It was my turn to smirk. I strummed my fingers on Tania.

"You find ugly things pretty? Tell me more."

What she said came out in one breath. Like she'd been waiting to tell me this. Waiting for our midnight date.

"Anything essential is invisible to the eye."

My eyes shot up. I'd recognize those words anywhere. "*The Little Prince.*"

"Have you read it?" Indie asked.

I snorted. "You can say that again."

She squeezed the tip of my boot, her eyes probing. Was I really going to share this with her? Whatever. Why the fuck not.

"My family was the furthest thing from bookworms. I don't think we had one book in our house, save for the Bible. We were skint as hell. But my dad had a brother, George, who lived in Notting Hill. Made his money composing songs for kids' shows. It was my dream to go live with him, but George was a womanizer, and a terrible drunk, and even though he loved me, he certainly didn't love me enough to give up on his precious vices. When I was eight or nine, George gave me a rare birthday gift. A hard copy of *The Little Prince.* He said to look for the meaning of the book, and once I found it, he'd buy me my first guitar. He said that no musician deserves as much as a pinch of success before they truly understand the meaning of life, and that he'd know if I cheated and asked, and anyway, I didn't want to. I wanted to *earn* that fucking guitar. Wanted her to come to me justly and deservingly. For the next couple years, I was consumed by this book. Every year I saw him at Christmas, I tried my luck, decoding the meaning of this goddamn book. All I got was nonsense about some little twat asking people to paint him a sheep. Until, two years after he gave me the book—now worn and old and stained with mustard and milk—it dawned on me. All true meanings are hidden. Life is full of secrets, and narrow-minded people, and sugar-coated, empty conversations that hold no weight. What's real is what's inside us. What's important is what *we* feel. That day I rang him, and he picked me up from Watford, even though I could've taken the train. That day, I got Tania. That day changed my life."

I squeezed the length of my acoustic guitar. I'd stopped playing Tania at unplugged gigs years ago, but I still carried her everywhere—you don't throw away your gran because she gets too old to bake your favorite pie. Tania was, after all, my first and only genuine friend. Indie caressed the fabric of her work in progress in circles, nodding.

"I always loved *The Little Prince* because it always felt like I, too, belong on another planet. Like I can barely even survive the world I live in and don't necessarily understand why things are the way they are," Indie licked her lips.

She tucked her chin to her chest, her eyelashes floating on her cheeks. I stared. Gulped. Averted my gaze. Fuck. She was beautiful. It was hard to believe she was the same girl from the Chateau Marmont. The one I'd looked at and seen a strange lass with a funny dress, weird hair, and a too-freckled face.

I looked down at my notepad and started writing.

Can you keep a secret?
Sometimes I look at you and all I see is regret
My little passion pit is out of this world
Dictates my every lyric and note and word
I do all the things I want to do to you in the dark
But time knows and sees and notices every mark
And sometimes I want you

But most times I don't
I should leave you alone, but we both know I won't.

I realized I was running out of paper, but the words kept on gushing out. They rushed in a stream, and I needed to capture them as they were. Desolate. Feral. Un-fucking-hinged. I grabbed Indie's hand and pulled her into my body. She stumbled across the tight space between us right onto my lap, her mouth falling open. I didn't care. It wasn't about sex. It was art, and art was divine—it overruled everything. And this wasn't even my bullshitter speaking. I actually believed that.

"I need you to take your dress off." I tugged at the thick fabric of her frilly number.

Her eyes widened, and she jerked away. Oh, how I wished she were one of my groupies in that moment. But if she were, we wouldn't be here. I wouldn't be feeding off of her memories, and stories, and reveries. That was the thing about Stardust. She stood toe-to-toe with me, even though I was taller, stronger, richer. She made me feel…*real.*

"Here? Jesus H, please don't tell me you're drunk." She looked around the hallway, checking that it was empty.

I gripped the hem of her dress and dragged her toward me, my eyes roaming, looking for the buttons or zipper or whatever to get her out of her dress.

"I need to write on something and my notepad is full. No one will see you. The lads are fast asleep, and Alfie's girls only just arrived. Even that dickhead can keep them busy for at least twenty minutes. The whole floor is reserved for us. It's just you and me, Stardust. I need your back."

And your words.

And that song that kept playing in my head.

I'm the king with no subjects
The vain man with no crowd
The drunk twat who's always so fucking loud
And you're the rivers and mountains

Maybe even the oxygen itself
You're the wind that carries me from place to place
The only high I always chase

"No."

Inside, I screamed my frustration, but on the outside, I just looked at her with mild disinterest.

"No?"

"Just write on my arms. Better yet—on yours. They're thicker."

"Not enough space, and I need to break it into paragraphs."

"No."

"Why?" My eyelids were twitching. I was pretty sure that wasn't a good sign.

"Because you slept with someone else yesterday." She looked surprised at my even asking.

I licked my lips slowly before opening them, enjoying the way her gaze clung to them. "I didn't sleep with Gina."

"Huh?"

"Never intended to, either. I kissed her, right. But only to piss you off, and honestly, I don't remember what she tasted like, just your reaction to it, which made my cock really fucking happy. The only person I want to fuck right now is you. The second I heard you across the hall banging your head against the door, I threw her in Alfie's room and went into the bathroom for a quick wank. But don't feel sorry for our little friend Gina. Alfie gave her what she needed and then some. I meant what I said, Stardust. I want to screw the words out of you. Just you. Until the end of this tour, it's only you and me."

The silence between us reminded me that seduction was like a game of Monopoly. It required patience, and planning, and reading your opponent. Just because I'd hit the jackpot and had a pocket stuffed with fake money didn't mean shite.

She could still say no.

She could still win the game.

Not giving her the chance to deny me, I brought my callused palm to her back and rolled the zipper down. She let me, if for no other rea-son than the relief she felt knowing I hadn't slept with that Aussie bird. Or maybe she finally understood what we were. Floating in the world, with no roots or ground or gravity. Mistakes, and sins, and errors were the bones of my kingdom. Everything felt different away from home, and so she allowed herself *not* to be herself, just for tonight. When the top portion of her dress slid down, Stardust turned around quickly, covering the small, perky tits I didn't get the chance to see.

I uncapped the Sharpie with my teeth and started writing on her smooth back, taking great pleasure in knowing it was going to stay there for days. The Sharpie danced along her spine, and I gulped each time her body shivered against the bright red tip of the marker. My cock sprang to life, but now wasn't the time.

And I would travel from asteroid to asteroid
Trying to find the one that would be ours
Building palace after palace until it feels like home
From London to Paris, from New York to Rome

The Little Prince, Alex Winslow

I paused, staring at my own terrible handwriting.
Her skin blossomed again.
"It's cold." She cleared her throat, grasping for her dress, her tits still covered by her arm. Bullshit. She was hornier than a unicorn. "Let's go inside. You can copy it onto a notepad."

I leaned forward and kissed the valley between her shoulder and neck, her skin coming alive and heating under my lips. The next words I whispered as seductively as I possibly could. I didn't normally need to put in an effort, but with this one, I had to.

"If I don't fuck you soon, I will die, and it will be on your conscience."

"Jesus Christ."

"You can call me that in bed, if you're inclined to," I retorted, my lips skimming her drug-like skin. What was it about her that felt like home? It was senseless. I didn't even fucking *like* home. I didn't fucking *have* a home. Home was where my useless parents sat on their arses all day spending my money. "Isn't that what *The Little Prince* is about? Being tamed and taming others? We don't have to do that, here, Stardust. It's just us. No grown-ups."

"*We* are supposed to be the grown-ups."

"No one is a grown-up when given a choice. It's something you're forced into."

Pause.

"I've already told you, Alex. I'm not a fling type of girl."

"You're young, and available, and fit. You shouldn't be so closed off. Get drunk. Fuck famous blokes. Post pictures of yourself all over the world on Instagram. You should live and make mistakes, and I'm offering to be one of those mistakes, because you have nothing to lose. We have an expiration date. We have a deadline. We have endless five-star hotel rooms and an album to write and your family to save and just fucking admit it—all arrows point in the same direction. *Us.* Together. For now."

"And after now?" She turned around to stare at me. "What happens after now, Alex?"

"What do you mean?"

"When the tour is over. What do we do then?"

"We go our separate ways." Wasn't it obvious? Did she want a fucking boyfriend? Because I didn't do that shit. And even if I did... Fallon was the first and last girl I tried monogamy with. She held my heart between her manicured fingers and squeezed hard every time I considered moving on. Even if I wanted to give Indie something—which I didn't—I wasn't sure if I even could.

"You will likely run into Fallon in Paris." Indie was candid. And honest. And raw. She didn't beat around the bush, asking the tough questions, giving zero fucks if it made her sound clingy or committed. She didn't pretend to be someone she wasn't.

"Then we end in Paris." I brushed a lock of her hair behind her ear. "We end whenever Fallon and I begin again."

Where in the fuck had that come from? I mean, it was the truth, but the truth could always be softened while being shoved into someone's face. "Prior commitments" were my version of "I don't fucking want to do it," and "busy schedule" was "I'd rather choke on someone else's cock than meet you for coffee." But I wanted to get a rise from her. In fairness, I realized I was being a massive hypocrite. Here I was, just about ready to sack Lucas and throw him off the tour if he so much as looked at my sobriety companion, but I had no issue telling her—while trying to fuck her—that I was going to try to win my ex-girlfriend back. Where was my tact? Wherever it was, my charm and logic were hidden in the same dumpster.

"Wow." Her eyebrows shot up. She pulled the straps of her dress back on her shoulders and pushed up to her feet, not even bothering to zip up. The step she took to her door was shaky and clumsy and told me everything I needed to know.

I'd fucked up royally.

"You're such a bastard, calling you one is an insult to every bastard inhabiting this world. We need to invent a new word for what you are."

"I think the word you are looking for is 'cunt,'" I offered, dropping the open Sharpie onto the carpet and rising, about to follow her into her room. Pissed off or not—she still had my lyrics on her back. "It is what it is. We're infatuated with each other, but not enough to lose our bloody minds. Eyes on the prize, Stardust. You need the money. I need the muse and the warm body at night."

"In what universe does making me sound like a whore equate to a good flirting tactic?"

"I'm not paying you for the sex. I'm paying you to keep me from falling off the wagon. Side bonus: you're officially not allowed to hang out with Waitrose, so it's not like you have any other options to choose from."

She turned around, giving me the same sugary smile she used when she wanted to knee my bollocks and stitch my lips together with her sewing machine.

"Just out of curiosity, Alex, are you asking me to stay away from Lucas as my friend or my future fling?"

"I'm *demanding* this as your fucking boss. Never forget that, Indie."

Another thing I knew would piss her off. Her door slammed in my face so hard the frame almost collapsed inward. I stared at it blankly, debating whether I should punch and kick it until she opened up or just take the spare card Blake kept, swipe it, and storm in. I wanted to threaten her, tear her apart, then pick her up and throw her onto the bed and make her see all that we were. But all my sorry arse ended up doing was plastering my forehead to her door, closing my eyes, and taking a deep breath.

Three.

Two.

One.

Chapter Fourteen

Indie

I glued my back to the door, the room coming into my vision in fragments behind the wall of unshed tears.

Three.

Two.

One.

I wanted to open the door and hurt him. To tell him he was a world-class asshole for doing this to me, for making me feel all these things. Even though he'd made it perfectly clear I didn't stand a snowball's chance in hell at ever being with him the way I deserved. Because Alex Winslow didn't do love. He only did hate. I wondered if he knew that. That he wasn't capable of giving his precious Fallon half the things a person you love should be given. Security, unconditional support, and kindness.

I knew what I needed to do. I needed to march over to his room, knock on the door, and tell him to stop. Stop hitting on me, stop trying to make us happen, stop seducing me with his goddamn lips and lyrics and buckets of rugged charm. My lips throbbed from another kiss that had never happened, and I was irrationally angry at the world. Steam. I needed to get rid of it. *Now.*

With those things in mind, I turned around, about to swing my door open and give him a piece of my mind. That's when I heard someone hammering on it from the other side.

Blinking, I pulled it open and peeked through the slit.

Alex stood there with red eyes and a mist of sweat covering his forehead, like *not* kicking down the door left him labored and sticky. He pushed the door the rest of the way open, silently walked in, cupped the side of my face, his thumbs on my cheeks, and kissed me.

Hard.

I stumbled back, off-guard and unprepared, but that only made him more aggressive in his kiss. I sucked in a desperate breath just as he darted his tongue out, stroking mine. Our tongues rolled together, hungry and vicious, in a wild dance without rhythm or pace. I moaned, and he groaned, sucking on my lower lip and digging his teeth into it on a warning bite. *Do not disobey*, the bite said in his English accent. *Or you'll be sorry.*

Admittedly, I didn't think. Not about how he'd managed to corner me deeper into my room in a lust-filled haze, and certainly not about the consequences. That's why when he cupped both my ass cheeks and pushed me, my back slamming against the antique dresser, I let him. He bit my lip again, this time harder, and I winced. I wanted him to know I wasn't surrendering to him—I was surrendering to my own needs. It was different. And selfish. And *mine*.

"I always wondered, you know." His lips ghosted mine, wet and drenched with dirty intentions. "What it feels like when you do that, gnawing on that sexy, fat lip of yours."

All I could do in response was sigh into his mouth. He tasted of the virgin lemonade he had after the show and the bitter bite of his last cigarette. Delicious in a hardened, unapologetic way. My fingers found the silk of his wavy, brown hair and I twisted it, my hips grinding against his abs. He grabbed the back of my thighs and brought them up to circle his waist, crashing his groin into mine. I clenched around nothing, desperate to feel him inside me, but knowing better than to unzip him.

He took my hair in his fist and pulled hard, forcing me to stare at his face. My scalp tingled, but he didn't hurt me. Not too much.

It felt like I was dipped in cold fire and caressed by a thousand feathers. My whole body tingled, and I'd never felt so awake in my entire life. He laid me on the queen bed and hovered on top of me, much like he had earlier on the sofa, and it reminded me I'd already lost the battle. The one where I drew lines and lived comfortably within them. Because—and this was the really sad part—I'd already crossed so many limits when it came to Alex Winslow, and not one of those decisions was conscious.

He rolled his hips between my thighs, his erection sliding along my thin leggings and his jeans.

"Look at me," he said. I didn't. Couldn't. This moment was mine. The fact he was in it was completely irrelevant, or so I tried to tell myself. I kept my eyes closed, kissing him fiercely.

"Look. At. Me." He took my hair in his fist and pulled hard, forcing me to stare at his face. Whatever he saw in my expression made him loosen his grip on me, but the intention was there. Alex Winslow played rough, in and out of bed.

"I apologize in advance." He cocked his head to the side.

"For?"

"Ruining you for any other man on this planet. I'm going to fuck you, Indie. So hard you'll think about me years from now, when you lie under your boring, missionary-loving husband. I will own every orgasm, every shiver, every wave of pleasure inside you. From here on out, it will be me. Just me. And for that, I truly am sorry."

"You're so cocky." I ran my lips down his neck, and he did this thing, where he ground his jeans against my sex through our clothes fast and rough, creating so much friction my clit swelled and screamed for release.

"That doesn't make me any less right."

"Are you going to make me sign an NDA before we go to bed together?" I grinned, and for that, I got my chin bitten.

"When I fuck you, Stardust, you'll scream so hard, the whole city will know I'm finally inside you."

I raked my fingers along his broad back, and it felt good, marking him back. After all the times he'd taunted, teased, and messed with me, finally, it was my turn. He scarred me. I decorated him. But at the end of the day, we were both tainted by each other. "We're not going to have sex. I'm not…super experienced."

He pushed up from me, running his hand through his lightly stubbled jaw. "Are you a virgin?"

I shook my head. "Nope. Just…I haven't been around much."

"How many?"

That again? Ugh.

"One."

"When?"

"High school. Junior year."

"Give me his address when we get back to L.A. Promise, I just wanna talk." He cocked one eyebrow up.

I laughed and swatted his chest, and he locked my wrist in his palm and brought it to his lips, breathing hard against it. I shivered again.

"Okay." His tone was low. "No fucking tonight. We'll take it slow."

A kiss on the lips. The nose. The forehead.

Jesus Christ, heart.

I'm trying my best here, heart.

Enough, heart.

"I'm tired," I said, even though it was a lie. I was buzzing and high and in need of a release. I wanted him to get the hell out so I could run to the bathtub and release the ache between my legs with my fingers.

He pushed off me without an argument. It shouldn't have surprised me, but it did. Alex Winslow was an accidental rock star. I knew it when I watched his bigger-than-life figure moving in the luxurious hotel room, and knew he didn't belong there. He belonged in some dingy underground pub in the bowels of London, screaming to the microphone about anti-fascism and anarchy. He'd lost his soul somewhere along the way, and I was just another piggybank he shook, trying to see if what was inside resembled what he was looking for. And at that moment, I knew I'd take it.

He was going to break the pig, and I was going to let him.

"I found my well in the middle of the desert," he said from the threshold of my open door. "Now it's time to drink from it. Every. Single. Drop."

Chapter Fifteen

Alex

Moscow, Russia

The plane ride was the closest thing to hell ever recorded on planet earth.

Partly because Blake and Jenna were yelling at each other in decibels that threatened to bring the aircraft down—she was on speaker, since Blake had to answer emails simultaneously—but mostly because Lucas insisted on not getting the memo that Stardust was not for the taking and lay beside her on the L-shaped sofa, gazing at the ceiling like a fucking John Green character and talking to her about life. Which was ironic, really, considering the fact I was about to end his if he kept throwing himself at her. Alfie was curled up beside me, playing a video game and making sure I didn't use any of the laptops or mobile phones around us to go on the Internet. I was bored, and agitated, and fuck, hadn't I told her she couldn't hang out with Waitrose? Obviously, I had to put my point across more blatantly.

Because subtlety is clearly my forte.

"Ever seen a cockpit from the inside, Stardust?" I asked Indie from across the room, sprawled on a recliner high and plush as a cathedral.

She looked away from Lucas and at me lazily, putting her patched dress down. She was sewing every spare moment she had. Compulsively. Wasn't that the only way to make art?

"So many sexual innuendos from this one." Alfie smirked to

himself, eyes still hard on his Nintendo screen.

"You know the answer to that question." Her scowl warned me not to screw with her unnecessarily.

Fair enough. I *did* know the answer. The only times she'd ever been on planes had been with me, and I'd never offered to show her anything other than my boot inside her arse as I sent her away. I shot to my feet and sauntered over to them, stretching my open palm in her direction.

"You'll like it. Lots of buttons to push," I enunciated the last sentence, in case Lucas didn't quite understand what kind of fire he was playing with. I wasn't a match. I was the kind of flame that burned down an entire forest.

"I can show you, if you prefer." Waitrose looked over at her, still holding the next patch she was meaning to sew. Surely, he couldn't have been that daft. But of course he knew exactly what he was doing. He wasn't only pushing my buttons. He was prodding them so hard, they cut deep.

Ignoring him, I turned my head back to her.

"Time is money, Blue," I used the nickname Blake gave her, for no other reason than to remind everyone they didn't have exclusivity on anything Indigo Bellamy.

She scooted her perky bum from the sofa and followed me, silently refusing my hand. Which was fantastic, because it only served to turn me on even more. Her defiance was refreshing. She should patent, juice, and give it to the next girl I dragged into my miserable life.

"Thanks for doing that," she muttered behind me.

"Sure." I had no idea what she was referring to. My mind was set on one thing, and that was finding out what color her knickers were today.

"Can you take a picture?" We were out of the main space, advancing inside the narrow corridor.

"Of what?"

She hesitated. "Umm, me in the cockpit?"

I'll show her a cockpit…

She was still mid-step when I pushed her hard against the bathroom door and locked us both inside. I had no illusions about making her a member of the mile high club. She needed more prepping. Still, messing around was part of the process, so I needed to make sure she wasn't skipping any classes.

Her back dug against the sink as I lifted her thigh up and curled it against my waist, dipping my groin against her clothed cunt without warning. This couldn't have been a comfortable angle for her, but I had a point to make.

"Feel that?" I was fully hard and strained against my jeans, my balls already swollen and heavy with need. "Feel what it does to me when you go and shit all over our arrangement?"

"There's no arrangement. Lucas and I are friends." Strong words, spoken by a woman who sounded almost believable, if it wasn't for the fact she was grinding her sweet groin against my crotch.

"Lucas wants you."

"Debatable. And even if he does, he can't have me."

"But I can."

"For a while." Pause. "Maybe."

Fuck. Your. Maybe. Lady.

I crushed my mouth to hers so fast and so hard, she stumbled backward, even though there was no space to fall into. Grabbing the back of her neck, I bit her lower lip until I produced the sound I was after—the moan I knew had sat somewhere at the back of her throat since the day she fucking saw me—as I slowly but surely thrust between our clothes, dry-fucking her. My firm torso against her soft everything made both our bodies tremble. She whimpered every time my cock hit her groin, and I inwardly cursed the pretty baby blue dress that separated our skin and matched her hair so nicely.

She pulled her lower lip away and flicked her tongue into the roof of my mouth, dragging it leisurely, making my skull break into goose bumps. The surprise alone made my cock jump in appreciation, and it was already straining inside my tight jeans. Why couldn't I be a rapper? They had such great attire for erections. I could hide two Indies inside Lil' Wayne's trousers and no one would know.

"Fuuuuck." I bit her shoulder to suppress a frustrated scream. The need to be inside her matched the need for a drink and two lines before stepping onto stage at Madison Square Garden. It justified making out with a girl six years my junior like some sort of a desperate teenager. Only I was a grown-up. No. No, I wasn't. I was a fucked-up kid with a babysitter. A babysitter I was going to eat alive. She trailed her tongue up my neck, to my chin, all the way to my mouth. I laughed, because it was so unsexy, yet so her.

Real.

Sweet.

Indie.

"You taste so salty," she breathed into my mouth.

"You taste so innocent," I countered.

She didn't smoke or drink or cuss. She didn't fuck around or try to get back at the world. She was pure and untroubled. Her problems were external—fucked-up brother, lack of money, dead parents. Inside, she was unsoiled. It helped. The idea I was wrecking her.

The act of corruption fed my power hunger.

"Alex." She rolled her head to the side, giving me access to her neck as one of my hands ran down her ass and squeezed, the other snaking between us and skimming over her pussy. She wore thick leggings. Guess I couldn't fault her for that. It was close to freezing on the airplane, plus Moscow was going to be a shitshow weather-wise, and she knew better than not to check the weather, thanks to my cunty remark when we'd first arrived in Australia. I hated myself for riding her ass about her clothes. I also hated her leggings and all leggings in general and declared war on them. I rubbed her slit, salivating at how wet she must be under the layers of fabric between us.

"For fuck's sake," I groaned, throwing my head between her shoulder and neck. I needed so much more, but she was tiny. There was literally not enough to satisfy my hunger for her. My fingers were pushing so aggressively through the material of her leggings, I was sure I was about to tear them apart or set them on fire from the friction. Neither was an option that would score me brownie points on my way to her bed. "Strip for me."

To my surprise, she pushed me away, wiggling out of her knitted stockings while standing up, her cheeks so red I *did* want to take a picture this time. Because she looked like foreplay, and foreplay and music were the reasons I'd been put on this earth.

"God, you're beautiful." And oh, was she ever. Like a painfully short, brilliant song that keeps you thirsty for more.

She dumped her leggings on the floor and launched at me. My back hit the glassed shower from the other end—viva la private jets— and we stumbled in together, so turned on we were fighting for each breath.

"Oh...oh...oh!" she screamed in pleasure as our tongues met and danced together, my fingers nudging her panties aside and fluttering over her slit. Shit. She *was* soaked, and I didn't even dip one in. I rubbed my thumb up and down along her cunt, feeling my cock growing so impossibly hard and erect, it was reaching the point of painful. But I couldn't rush her, and I didn't want to, anyway. This was fun. Fun in the pre-adulthood kind of way, when you actually had to work hard and didn't wash your hands for two days straight after fingering a girl.

"Oh, indeed." I found her shy little clit and flicked it up and down, falling to the floor, the showerhead above our heads, while she straddled me, still in her dress.

"I'm going to hate myself in an hour." She bit her lip, but a loud groan escaped, anyway. She was a moaner. A real one. Not a fake one. Not an I-want-you-to-like-me one, and there were too many of those, especially when your net worth matched Adam Levine's. Hell, Fallon had put on a West End-worthy show for the first six months of our relationship. It was only after eight months or so that I realized she didn't even like it up the arse and had just been humoring me so I wouldn't leave—cheers, Fallon, for the vote of confidence.

But I didn't want to think about Fallon. Not when I had a perfectly fuckable girl in my arms.

"Shit." I laughed, our teeth clashing together in another messy kiss. "Moan louder and you'll take over pirate radio stations in Mongolia." I only guessed we were flying above it, though geography was not high on my list of interests at that point.

She pulled away, her eyes colored with confusion and embarrassment. "Really? Should I be quiet?"

Why had I said that? Did I have a built-in cock-blocking device along with my huge red button of self-destruction? There was absolutely no way in hell we were going to stop messing around because of those fuckers outside. Even if I had to throw them out—and yes, I was aware we were 35,000 feet in the air. I extended my arm above my head and turned the faucet on. A stream of spluttery, cold water rained down on us with a hiss. I rolled the handle all the way to the left, and steam bellowed over the glass around us as the water heated. It felt good. Forbidden. Crazy, just as we were.

"That's better. Hit those high notes for me, Stardust, and go to town on my fingers. I wanna watch your face as you come, and you better come, because we're not leaving this airplane until you do."

I slipped two fingers into her pussy, studying her closely. She flinched at my rough touch, but there was no mistaking how hot and wet she was for me.

There was a bucket of ice with glass bottles of Coke beside my shoulder—Alfie enjoyed long baths and cool soda when we were flying—and for the first time in a long time I wasn't an angry piece of shit because of that.

"Your cunt is so warm." I sucked in a breath, still watching her. Our clothes were heavy and drenched. Indie moved her hips to create more friction between my hand and her pussy, and I tried hard not to grin like the perv I was.

"Oh, God," she croaked when I pushed my fingers in and out of her. "I don't even want you."

To this, I curled my fingers, burrowing in her wetness, and pulled them out slowly, sucking her warm juices into my mouth. She tasted like a thousand orgasms, and like a fucking liar.

"No?" I asked, holding her gaze.

"No." At least she had the decency to try to look away.

I jerked her by the back of her neck in one movement and shoved my tongue into her mouth, forcing her to taste herself. Our tongues collided and danced, and she drank herself up on a loud moan. I pulled away and held her face.

"Your cunt begs to differ."

I grabbed an ice cube. She protested, grinding her pussy into my cock and making me want to grab her by the hair and fuck her on the floor.

Not yet. Soon, but not yet.

"More." The pain in her voice made pre-cum gather at my tip.

I shoved the ice cube into her pussy and she shrieked, her entire body coming even more alive on top of mine as I sat on the floor, my back pressed to the Jacuzzi. I clasped her chin between my fingers, guided her back to my mouth, and silenced her with a kiss as I fucked her with the ice cube, feeling how it melted inside her sweet, warm folds. Pushing in and out, I made sure I stretched her good. She was too innocent to just drive into, and I was an arsehole, but not a sadist.

"Such a decent girl." My breath was hot against her skin.

She relentlessly chased my fingers and ice cube, looking drunk, on the border of shit-faced. All I needed to do was touch her clit once and she'd explode like I'd pushed a red button. Which was exactly why I didn't do it.

"But you'll be dirty for me," I added.

To that, she didn't reply. I slipped my hand into the bucket again and shoved another ice cube in, and she winced, arching her back before rubbing her pussy and clit all over my abs, wanting a lot more than ice and fingers inside her.

"Answer me," I growled.

"I'll be dirty for you," she rasped, riding my hand like she did it for a living.

"Take my cock out," I ordered, my voice dripping chill almost as much as her pussy. She stopped grinding against me for a second, staring at me through dreamy eyes, the droplets coming down from the tips of her eyelashes and plastering her hair onto her forehead.

"There's an orgasm at the end of this journey." I smirked.

She reached between us and unbuckled me, taking my cock out with shaky fingers. She spent a few moments gaping at it, just as she had when I took a piss in front of her the first day we were on tour.

"You're uncut."

I wanted to laugh, but was too aroused to function. Her eyes were big and wide. Did it really matter? It never did to any of the women I'd been with before. Then again I *was* Alex Winslow. I was told by Blake and Alfie, though, that sometimes American women were a bit iffy about the blanket on the piggy. I took her palm and wrapped it around my shaft, squeezing my hand around hers and feeling the pearl of pre-cum between us dropping onto my clothed thigh. "Problem?"

She shook her head. "It's just…different."

"You've only been with one guy." *The fucker.*

"I know, but still."

We weren't going to talk about the benefits of circumcision today. I moved her hand back and forth, showing her how to rub me off rough, the way I liked it. "Make me come, and I'll do the same to you."

"I don't come on demand." Her eyes met mine.

I slid three fingers into her needy pussy and curled them, hitting her G-spot at the same time I pushed my callused thumb just above her clit. "New game, new rules: you come when I tell you to."

"Ohhh…"

Yeah. Ohhh was right, with extra fucking foreskin.

She gave me a wank while I fingered her delicious cunt. The water pounding between us was a constant reminder that people were probably asking questions, and even more importantly—that we were going to walk out of here soaking wet or worse, wrapped in towels, giving them the answer they didn't want to hear. Not that I gave a toss. Actually, it was better if everyone knew once and for all who she belonged to. Because it definitely wasn't Waitrose.

Stardust gave a terrible handjob. She didn't use enough pressure and treated my cock like it was about to fall off my body. But I was so high on what we were doing—and *where* we were doing it—I got off anyway. And when I felt the climax pressuring the base of my spine, climbing up like a ladder, I finally put her out of her misery and gave her clit some TLC, rubbing the swollen thing in circles while shoving my tongue into her mouth like I wanted her to choke on it.

"Jesus! Shit, oh, wow!" she exclaimed. She sounded surprised, and that made everything so much hotter, even though Jesus got the credit for all my hard work.

"Say *my* fucking name when you come," I hissed.

I didn't know what to expect. Maybe she would call me Winslow, as she often did, like I wasn't a person but a brand.

But when the name "Alex" rolled out of her lips, I shot my load onto her baby blue dress, groaning and pushing her to the floor, on her back, to finish the job. I didn't let her come on my fingers. No. I pressed my knee between her thighs and let her come on nothing, empty and deprived, with just a little taste for more.

I bent down, kissed her lips—thumbs on cheeks—and watched her squinting under the drops. Her face was rosy, her lips puffy from my abuse on her mouth.

I stood up and left her on the floor, thinking, for the first time in years—*this is better than alcohol. Better than the champagne I smuggled.*

"Don't give yourself a hard time, darlin'. Especially as next time I touch you, you will be on your knees for me."

Indie

The minute I came down from the high, I realized how low I'd gone.

And once I did, everything became clearer, just like the steam that had dried off of the glassed shower. My feet felt like a thousand hornets had stung them, cold and hot all at once, and I shivered quietly.

It wasn't so much the shame of letting Alex finger me—*finger me!*—in the shower, although that was grossly out of character for me. We were both single and weren't hurting anyone. It was the fact I'd allowed him to do that on a plane, with people right outside, and now they were all going to know what had happened.

I'd never be able to live it down. Even if his friends didn't care— which I'm sure they didn't, I wasn't the first girl to fall into Alex Winslow's trap. He was made for legends, almighty like an angry god. Too bad he knew it.

Alex yanked his jeans down, kicking them through his army boots and wrapping his waist in a clean, dry towel.

"All right?" He threw me a glance down his nose, his thick eyebrows drawn together.

I was still sitting on the edge of the Jacuzzi, combing my hair through wobbly fingers. Maybe I was stuck up, and a goody two-shoes, and a prude. But life had taught me a valuable lesson, and that lesson was that sometimes, the people you were attached to don't come back. With my parents, I hadn't had much choice. But with Alex—I did, and I'd knowingly let him in. Into my thoughts, and now my panties.

"Sure." I rose to my feet with the intention of squeezing my clothes dry. He turned toward the door, forever blasé.

"There's a blow dryer in the left cabinet. Step out of your clothes before you dry them, unless you want third-degree burns. I'll go bullshit your way out of this one."

"Do you think they'll buy it?" I munched on my lower lip again.

"I'm a recovering drug addict. At this point, it's easier for me to lie than say the truth."

"Oh," I blurted. Apparently, I was not the most eloquent human being after getting fingered by a rock star. You live, you learn.

He left the room, and I immediately glued my ear to the door in an attempt to hear everything outside. It was pitiful, but no more pathetic than everything else I'd done so far on this tour.

"You're in a towel," Blake observed matter-of-factly when Alex re-emerged from the bathroom. "Why on earth are you in a towel?"

"Stardust dumped her coffee all over my crotch."

"For fuck's sake. Why?" It was Alfie's turn to speak.

I grinned to myself, my heart thrumming in my chest wildly.

"I don't know. Who knows why women do anything? She's probably on her period."

"Your shirt is gone, too."

"She dumped *my* cup over my head."

"Damn, mate, she really hates you."

"Clearly," Alex's voice dripped sarcasm.

I covered my mouth, suppressing a laugh. That was my problem with Alex. He was too charming for his own good. Beneath the cliché of a tortured rock star who escaped to the arms of drugs and booze and had enough ink on his skin to print an entire edition of *War and Peace*, he was a lost boy. A fantastically witty lost boy. A lost boy who was incredibly lovable, even though he may not have thought so.

"Where's Indie, anyway?" Lucas' voice was different from the rest. He sounded annoyed rather than amused.

"Bathroom, last I checked."

"How come?" Blake grumbled.

"She's suffering from massive diarrhea. This may or may not have to do with that beef fried rice we had before takeoff."

"I knew it! My stomach's been feeling funny, too." Alfie slapped his thigh by the sound of it.

I. Was. Going. To. Kill. Alex.

My hands balled into fists, and I used every ounce of my self-control not to waltz out and tear my vocal cords yelling at him.

Then he *continued.* "I think it's gonna get loud in there, so I suggested she use the blow dryer."

I tried to tell myself he was protecting my dignity.

In his own twisted, backward, exceptionally uncultured way.

"Brutal," Blake mumbled.

"Bullshit," Lucas spat out.

I pressed my forehead to the door and squeezed my eyes shut. My cheeks hurt from the huge smile on my face. My heart squeezed for an entirely different reason. I turned the blow dryer on and heard them laughing.

Damn you, Winslow.

Chapter Sixteen

Alex

I was lying facedown on my bed in Moscow, listening to my heartbeat through the silence of the pillow, when Blake walked into the room. It was the first time in weeks he left me unattended for more than two minutes. I'd fault him for being so distrusting, but I did think about that champagne in my bag more than I wanted to admit. My own, bloody security blanket at this point.

"There's something you should know."

I stayed silent, allowing him to finish his grand announcement. If Fallon were here, she'd call his behavior "extra." Which, in itself, was extra. Hollywood just made people really insufferable.

"Lucas was saying he felt bad about Blue catching a stomach bug earlier. He's going to the drug store to get her some crackers and Advil."

I elevated my head, ignoring the dull pain it sent to my neck. "Is he fucking deaf?"

Blake kicked his smart shoes against a dresser, unbuttoning his smart shirt.

"I'm serious," I grunted. "Is Stardust's pussy worth his job?"

"Is Fallon's worth *yours*?" Blake retorted. Spastic. I was engaged to Fallon. Lucas barely knew Indigo.

"At any rate, he might already be on his way to her room," Blake said, now standing by the bathroom door. "Look, I'm not sure what's going on between you and her, but I know you were in the bathroom together, and not for a short time, either."

I rolled to my back and stared at the ceiling, marveling at his words.

Hanging out with Indie was the opposite of what I was trying to do. Singapore had been a one-off. I'd wanted to show her we were compatible, and I had. Now it was time to take our relationship to the strictly sexual zone. On the other hand, the idea of Lucas spending time with her was even less appealing than doing it myself. And she was going to say yes to Lucas, not giving much damn about the restrictions I put her under.

She wanted to see the world.

She was going to see the world.

Whether I liked it or not.

I had two choices—be the one who'd show it to her, or watch my backstabbing frenemy do it.

"Cheers for the heads-up." I jumped up, padding to the walk-in closet. Whoever Blake had hired had already hung up all my crap and ironed my stupid jeggings—forever a great liar, I moved the champagne from my suitcase to my duffel bag before they got their hands on it. The concept of having it, in itself, kept me saner. Or at least less crazy. Like a suicide pill.

I slipped into a dark gray coat. Blake watched me silently from the threshold of the bathroom as I walked into my shoes on my way to the door, stuffing my wallet into my back pocket.

"Let me accompany you," he said politely.

"Fuck off," I answered, also politely.

I slammed the door just to be a dick and sauntered down the hallway. My first stop was not, in fact, Stardust's room. It was Lucas' door. I took a step back toward the opposite wall and crashed my foot into it, leaving a foot-sized dent. I'd told him, time and time again, not to mess with my babysitter. This was a warning to let him know that next time, he was going to hitchhike back to England, because I was going to fire his arse and empty his bank account. Also, Britain was an island, so I hoped to fuck he was a good swimmer, because the odds of him completing the tour weren't in his favor. I made my way back to Indie's room—it was in front of mine, as per usual—and drummed on the door with open palms dramatically. She opened after a minute, looking fresh, her hair dried, a silky beige dress hugging her tiny figure. She had a matching wool scarf a shade darker wrapped around her delicate neck.

"Stardust." I placed my elbow on her doorframe, staring down at her.

She looked a little confused by my being there. Like she still couldn't believe I actively sought her out.

That makes both of us.

"You look pissed," I observed.

"You told your friends I'm having a poop crisis." She blinked slowly.

"Telling them the truth would've given you a heart attack. Besides, Alfie and Lucas started looking at you like you were their next meal, and I didn't like that. Two birds. One stone."

"Why are you here?"

Because I can't bear the thought of Lucas standing in my spot.

"Wanted to check if your head is still intact and not blown up from embarrassment for doing something dirty with a boy. That's the chivalrous thing to do, correct?"

She hugged the door and nibbled on that poor lower lip of hers, all cracked and bruised. "First of all, you're giving yourself way too much credit, and second of all, you're as chivalrous as a Tasmanian devil. Your business is hanging all over the tabloids, literally and figuratively. Your penis is the new kittens on YouTube, for Chrissake."

"I see you finally decided to Google me."

She shrugged. "Lucas gave me his laptop until the end of the tour."

Red cloth.

Angry bull.

Clenched fists.

Don't kill Lucas. He's not worth the jail time.

I grabbed her hand and yanked her out of her room. You just

earned yourself a new laptop. My treat."

Indie

I bet if I'd told Alex that Lucas let me crash at his place, he'd buy me a whole house just to spite him. It was obvious that whatever was happening between him and me was also a direct result of trying to keep me away from his drummer. A different girl may have taken a step back, but my life was such a hot mess, on and off the tour, Alex was the least of my problems.

After he bought me a laptop—which I insisted on not taking, but he maintained I'd make use of after the tour ended—we took a ride. Moscow was cold, gray, and old, like a stern grandmother. When I got back to the hotel, I immediately installed Skype and tried to call Natasha, but she didn't answer. Then I stared at my crack-screened phone and willed it to ring, feeling hope slither out of me like blood from an open wound. Finally, I threw in the towel and started working on my Paris dress. It was well after eleven p.m. local time, and I was just starting to relax, the hum of the mini sewing machine lulling me out of my anxiety about Craig. Only two more months until I'd get back and take care of them. Already, the bi-monthly payments helped pay for so many necessities back at home.

This particular dress I was working on was a difficult one to make, because I had to write on the patches with a fine pen. It took twice the amount of time to produce, but I knew too well that things we earn through hard work are always more precious.

My window overlooked the Red Square, which I'd been to earlier that day with Alex. We had a driver, and that made me feel like some kind of a princess, and not in a good way. When we were walking toward the Kremlin, Alex gave me the brief history of the place. He said it costs two hundred thousand dollars a year for the museum to maintain Lenin's corpse in perfect condition, and that it was already one hundred forty-seven years old.

"I'm telling you, Stardust, I've seen pictures. He doesn't look a day over fifty-six. A little waxy, sure. But no more than the average Hollywood starlet."

Alex told me he'd been to Moscow three times before, and if the tour wasn't so condensed, he would've loved to have shown me around. I didn't believe him at all, knowing he was a liar, but it was still nice to hear. When darkness blanketed the Russian capital, Alex asked the driver to take us to see "the ugliest, most awesome thing in the world." I laughed as I tucked myself in the back seat of the Renault Duster and tried to swallow down my excitement when butterflies cartwheeled in my belly. He scooted so close I could feel his breath on my skin again, and my thighs clenched when I thought about the last thing he'd said to me about being on my knees for him.

"It's pretty dark out." I tried to sound indifferent to spending time with him. Alex wasn't wrong, I decided, when I drank in Moscow like bitter coffee with a bite. It looked new, with skyscrapers and mani-cured parks and smoggy air, virtues of a fast-paced city. At the same time, it looked old, with trains of mass-built buildings from its Soviet past stretched out for miles.

I found out what Alex was talking about when the car rolled to-ward an embankment. The driver cut the engine and sat back. The monument was unmistakable, because it hovered over the Moskva River like a monster. Winslow, once again, had been correct. It was huge, elaborate and…scary. Yes. Plain creepy. Like something out of *Game of Thrones*. Of a man on a ship. The statue was holding some-thing in his hand, staring in the distance.

"That is…" I started.

"The tenth ugliest building in the world according to the Virtual Tourist," Alex finished for me, sticking his head near my shoulder and grinning to catch a glimpse of the statue, too. "Peter the Great. The irony is, not only is it quite ugly, but Peter the Great didn't even like

Moscow. He changed Russia's Capital to St. Petersburg before they switched it back. Welcome to human logic."

Our driver started texting, making himself invisible, and it was easy to forget we weren't alone.

"How do you know all these things?" I asked.

"I like history."

"Why?"

"Because it gives me better tools to understand the future."

I nodded. Alex wasn't being patronizing or blabby. In another rare time since the first time I'd met him, he showed genuine interest in something, and was sharing it with me. It frightened me. The idea that he could be open and real. Because the very thing that held me together was the idea that Alex Winslow was, in fact, a pile of stereotypes sewn together into a persona even he couldn't distinguish anymore. He ticked every single box: rock star, troubled, drug addict, tattooed. It was embarrassingly familiar.

I swiveled my head to the window again.

"Can we go back to the hotel?"

"Why?"

Because I want to survive you.

"I would like to call my family."

Alex shrugged in a women-huh-what-can-you-do, catching the driver's gaze in the rearview mirror, who returned the same international 'man, woman' signal.

We rolled forward.

A soft knock on the door made me snap out of my reverie. I frowned, turning off the sewing machine positioned by the drawn curtains. I stood up, knowing it couldn't be Alex. He was never lenient, always rough and dirty, and maybe that was why my heart throbbed fiercely every time I did as much as hear something drop in the other room. I opened the door, staring back at Lucas.

"Hey, sleepyhead. Where have you been?" Lucas flashed me a tentative smile.

I took a step sideways, leaving it for him to decide whether he wanted to come in. I didn't give a damn about Alex warning us both off, but I wasn't sure where Lucas stood on our boss' threat. He'd probably come here to grab his laptop, anyway. I turned around to seize it from the desk, but Lucas snagged my wrist.

"Can you tell me one thing?"

I looked up at him. His face was angelic, even while tense. Open, fresh. He was Alex's age, but he didn't share the same internal hardship, and that somehow made him look so much younger. Alex was wrong. There was no way Lucas could be bad or vindictive. I read faces the way bookworms reread their favorite paragraphs. Religiously. And I knew that whatever Lucas was doing, he had his reasons.

"Maybe," I answered. "I need to know what it is first."

He licked his lips. "If—and I'm not asking you to tell me what's going on between you and Alex because that's none of my business— at some point he's too much for you, would you let me know? It probably looks like we hate each other, he and I, but trust me, we go way back."

I stared at him blankly.

"I'm just worried."

"For who? Me or him?" I asked.

"Both of you. In different ways. You're a strong girl. He's like a black feather. Less resilient than he appears."

Pause. I stared at my feet. It looked like Lucas didn't want us together, and I was starting to feel like maybe Alex had a good reason to think his frenemy wanted me.

"Never mind." Lucas shook his head. "Just let me know if you need me. He thinks I want in your knickers—hell, you probably feel the same way, too—but trust me, I just want to be here for you," he said.

My eyebrows nearly touched at this. Maybe the tour was forcing me to embrace my inner cynic.

Luc rushed to add, "You're on the road with a bunch of blokes you've never met before, and your boss is giving you crap. Whatever's going on with your family back in L.A., I'm sure it's not easy on you."

"It's not," I admitted.

"I'm here to help." He offered me his hand.

This time I took it, unaware of the chain reaction it would prompt.

Unaware of all the secrets we held between our palms.

Chapter Seventeen

Alex

I n my defense, Ozzy Osborne snorted ants and Keith Richards snorted his *dad*, so, in comparison, I wasn't being that crazy.

Having said that, I had, indeed, been pretty fucking out of my mind when I'd decided to turn around in the middle of a gig, walk over to Lucas's drum kit, and smash my silver boot right into the bass. It had collapsed right into Lucas' spread thighs, and he widened his eyes, his arms still mid-air holding the sticks, watching me like this came as a great surprise. It shouldn't have. Fucker could have seen it from three countries over, and he'd kept pushing and pushing until I had no choice but to shove him out of my life.

But I digress.

It had started half an hour before the show. I'd already been on edge because Blake had locked us both in my dressing room and launched into one of his self-righteous monologues that served to stroke his own ego. It had taken me a few minutes to understand what, exactly, he was yelling and sweating about.

The champagne.

He'd sifted through my shit and found it. Which was quite ironic, because the past few days were the first in a very long time where I hadn't wanted to drown my sorrow in alcohol.

"When I find the cunt who keeps sending them to you, I'll kill them. But in the meantime—why play into their hands? Why, Alex? You have so much going for you. You have *everything* going for you.

You're rich and young and talented and adored. You're a religion, for fuck's sake. You're writing what might be your best album yet. All you have to do is not fuck it up. Is it really that hard?"

Was he kidding? Of course it was that hard. Did he think the entire zip code of Hollywood wanted to be addicted to painkillers, alcohol, cocaine, and plastic surgery? Did he reckon I was just so bored with my perfect, wholesome life? Finding happiness as an intelligent person was like finding a real-life unicorn. Blake was pacing the room and throwing his arms in the air, exasperated.

"I'm trying. I really am. Trying to make you and Jenna happy, even though you both give me very different instructions on how to make it happen. I'm trying to respect your wishes not wanting to take Hudson along because you hate big entourages and still make sure that you're sober. But it's so difficult. *You're* so difficult, Alex. Most of the time, I think the only reason you're sober is because we're watching over you all day."

"It is," I said from my place on the couch, lighting up a fag. Now that Blake was riding my arse about it, of course I needed a fucking drink. Oh, Irony, you and your twisted sense of humor.

Blake stopped in front of me, hands on his waist, eyes to the ceiling. "It's not good enough. You need to make more of an effort to change. That means taking better care of yourself. Eating better. Actively trying to get over your addiction. And, yes, talking to your parents. You'll have to see them soon, so I'm not sure why you keep postponing that conversation."

He was right. My entire staff—all fifty roadies or so plus my band and my manager/babysitter—were sober because of me, and I hadn't even made the smallest effort by throwing the champagne in the trash. I'd kept it because I was *still* an addict. I still thought about alcohol and cocaine every single fucking day. I missed it. I didn't resent it. I was like a rich, spoiled sonovobitch who got caught doing something bad and had his parents buy his way out. Just because I was physically clean didn't mean I'd learned my lesson. My only drawback from drinking the champagne was: A) I was never alone, and B) I was momentarily occupied with getting into my hanny's knickers and was so close to my goal, cocking it up was out of the question.

I needed to grow up, but growing up meant letting go of who I'd been for the past seven years. The last time I was sober was when I was twenty. I didn't know myself anymore. Not without the drugs. There was a stranger in my house, and that stranger was *me*.

The only thing I didn't agree with him about was my parents. I didn't need to talk to my family. My family did enough talking about me. To the press. Often. *Twats.*

If Blake thought it was some kind of a pivotal moment where I snapped out of it and finally understood how low I'd stooped, he obviously gave me too much credit. I knew I was in deep trouble, and that I was a piece of shit, but I still had a few more inches of abyss before I really hit rock bottom. Blake dragged the coffee table between us aside and squatted down between my legs. It felt intimate and weird, and I groaned with annoyance. He plastered his hands on my knees.

"My PI can't track the person who sends you alcohol. Can you? Think hard."

"It's Bushell," I said without as much as a blink. "Who else could it be?"

Blake shook his head, sighing. "Stop it, mate. He's not after you."

Bollocks, but whatever.

"Maybe it's Lucas," I sneered.

"You're insane," Blake muttered.

I decided to bend my mate a little harder, see if he could break. There was something beautiful in fucking up my own life and alienating people by choice. It gave me the illusion that I was in control. That the choice was mine.

"I don't know, Blake. Maybe it's Alfie. Maybe it's Jenna. Hell, maybe it's even you. Maybe you want me to cut this tour short so you can go back and fuck her like you've been planning for the past few years. Who knows? Every single person I work with wants to either fuck me or fuck me over. Some—both. Nothing surprises me anymore, other than the sheer astonishment at finding someone who doesn't want or need anything from me. You wanted me to go to rehab? I did. You wanted me to write an album? I am. Now you want my trust? That can't happen, Blake. Not anymore. You've done so much shit in the name of saving my brand, you don't get to keep the fucking friend title." I stood up, adrenaline running in my veins as I shoved his hands aside. These words had sat dormant inside me for far too long, I realized. Blake always wanted what was best for *us*. His career was intertwined in mine, and he had good intentions—Billboard hits, sobriety, and stability in mind—but he didn't think twice or ever stop to wonder before he ran people over on his way there. Including yours truly. He'd covered so many of my scandals by dumping the blame on other people, and putting the blame on *me* when he fucked up things, I knew better than to think he was the same guy I'd shared a two-bedroom flat with in Clapham. We were both different. Blinded by money and destroyed by fame. Want to ruin a relationship in less than five steps? Put a few million quid between the two people and see what happens.

Blake shot up, so now we were in front of each other, panting hard, ready to yield our verbal swords. It was liberating to finally let all the shit that bubbled beneath the surface rise.

"Everything I've done was to help you. I saved you." He bared his teeth.

"And I *made* you," I said, dumping my lit cigarette on the floor and stomping on it. I balled his shirt and crushed our noses together. "Never forget that, Blake. Before you were Alex Winslow's manager, you were just a loser from Watford who had to split rent three ways to live in South London. I made you, and I will undo you if need be. So I suggest you find the bastard who sends me alcohol—because by now I think we both know it's not the hotel staff that brings it to my door. It's who has access to a lot of people or can bribe his way with the hotel staff. And that's the last time I hear you talk about my family. If I want to see them, I will. Right now, I'd be more worried about our relationship, *mate*."

It was the last word that made his face crumple.

I slammed the door so hard in Blake's face, I wouldn't be surprised if his ears rang deep into 2034. Stalking down the corridor, I took deep, desperate breaths, trying to get to the break room without killing anyone on my way. I needed something strong. Or a good lay. Where the fuck was Indie, anyway?

Blake was right. At the heart of it all, I was still an addict. If there had been alcohol or coke anywhere near me, I would've consumed the hell out of it without even taking a moment to think it through.

Maybe it was time to call in some groupie favors.

Maybe it was time to live up to my reputation and snort my frustration away.

The only reason I stopped by Lucas' slightly ajar door was because I heard weeping. It was soft and polite, like the person who was crying didn't have the guts to do it all the way. I halted, my back to the wall next to Lucas' door.

"I'm so sorry," I heard Waitrose say, and to that, Indie cried even harder. What had he done to her? Nothing, most likely. She was crying about something else, which threw my mind in overdrive.

It was probably family-related. She'd been dealt shitty cards in life, but unlike me, she was still deep into the poker game, trying to fool people into thinking she could win. And Waitrose was the person she'd run to when sorrow found her.

The thing about flashbacks is that they really do your head in. His relationship with Fallon was the first to spring into mind. I'd been on tour, and he'd stayed in Los Angeles to help Blake and Jenna with the demos I'd left behind. He'd been there for Fallon when she'd overdosed, and when she needed to pour her little, black heart out. He'd been there for her the first time she sought out Will Bushell, and he'd been there for *them* when they snuck around behind my back and started fucking at the very same Chateau Marmont I stayed at these days, because I'd had to sell my L.A. apartment and couldn't even stomach the idea of calling myself a permanent resident of that god-awful city.

"Let it all out," Lucas said.

I leaned forward and watched them through the crack between the door and the frame. They were sitting on the same loveseat, her head pressed against his chest.

He kissed her forehead.

He kissed her forehead.

He kissed her forehead.

He kissed her goddamn fucking forehead.

"I love my brother, Luc. But I don't like him. At all."

"We'll sort it out, Indie. We will."

We? Since when were they a 'we'? He was barely a fucking 'he,' acting like a pussy every turn of the way.

Stardust sniffed and pulled away, wiping the tears on her face with the back of her hand. "It's like ever since we lost our parents he's just this crazy, volatile person. Who does that, Luc? Who does what he did tonight?"

"Your brother is hurting," Lucas said, and something inside me twisted like barbwire. Her brother sounded a lot like me. Maybe it was premature to think she'd get attached to me. Why would she want another knobhead to stress about?

"Sometimes I think I should just hand in my resignation and go back. Now's not the time to be away from home."

"Stay." He squeezed her palm. "The money you make will be able to help your family more than any pep talk you could give Craig, and we both know that."

I wanted so badly to push the door open on them, waltz in, yank her up, and escort her outside before I beat him senseless. In fact, the only reason why I hadn't done that was because Stardust seemed genuinely distressed, and for the first time in forever I allowed someone else to steal a small slice of the limelight and have it their way.

She didn't need me; she needed him.

Did it make me want to kill him? Yes.

Did it make it any less true? No.

Anyway, that's the short story of how I ended up ruining Lucas' drum set.

I was six songs into the gig when I turned to take a breather from looking at all the faceless faces below me. I caught Waitrose glancing sideways and smiling at someone. At the someone I'd fingered twenty-four hours ago. That had done it. I'd walked over and broken his drums, admiring the fact I'd held back from yanking out the stand and smacking him with it. Baby steps, right?

"What the fuck!" He'd jumped up.

"The fuck is you're fired," I'd said, already storming backstage. "And what a fucking fuck that is indeed, my friend."

I was now chasing Indie. *Chasing* her. As in, spotting her and going after her. Perhaps it was not my finest hour, but it made sense to do it at the time. She turned around and power walked toward the main dressing room, probably to Blake, most likely to make sure I didn't kill her or anything. I grabbed the tip of her flared black dress and yanked her into my chest. She gasped, falling into my body, and to her horror—my erection.

"I get that you're going through shit, Stardust. We all are. That's the nature of being born into this chaos called life. But this is getting a little old, and not so fun anymore. So I've decided to fire Lucas, just to make sure you don't run off to him next time your brother pisses you off. Where's my thank you for that, huh? We both know it should've been you I gave the boot to."

She turned around, and my heart had a hard-on at the prospect of how she was going to react. Not one to disappoint, Indie's cheeks blazed red as she raised her hand and, instead of slapping me, pushed me with every ounce of power in her, slamming my back against the wall.

"You don't have to fire me, because I quit," she announced, her voice pitching high. Just then, Blake appeared from my dressing room, looking ready to admit himself to the ER with a severe heart attack.

"You stormed off the stage?" He looked so wired I thought he was going to explode. A drop of saliva decorated his chin. He looked rabid. I kept stalking behind Stardust, who was still running away from the scene, even though there was nowhere for her to go. She couldn't leave the stadium without us. Blake followed both of us. *Cirque de stupid.* And, of course, I was the leading clown.

"I fired Waitrose, too."

At least he had the courtesy not to ask me why. The answer was obvious, and he knew it, because he was there to talk me off the ledge every time I thought of throwing Lucas out of my life. I followed Indie until she was faced with the end of the hallway and had nowhere else to go. She turned around, narrowing her eyes at me and plastering her back to the door, clinging into her personal space.

"What do you want from me, Alex?"

Everything. I want everything, and then all the things you've already given away to other people. I want them back, too.

"Don't play coy." I grabbed her wrists when she tried pushing me off again, but she didn't really mean it—I know it sounds creepy, but it was true—her hips bucked forward, and her breath was fast and husky. "It's gig night, and I just fucked up royally. We have work to do tonight, Stardust."

She threw her head back and laughed, the voice she was producing so sardonic I barely recognized it as hers. "Work? Your whole tour is crumbling. You fired your drummer, your babysitter quit, and you walked off the stage."

And hid a bottle of champagne.

And began messing with you only because Waitrose showed the slightest interest.

The list was longer and acutely embarrassing. "You can't quit."

"Why?"

"Because you need the money too much, and I need you too much." What was I saying? What was I doing? I thought I heard Blake gasp, and I couldn't even blame him. I hadn't subconsciously drunk that bottle of champagne and then blacked it out, had I?

Stardust took a step toward me and cracked a smile, with teeth and all, and I finally saw her for who she really was. A cunning pixie, a thief of hearts. She was shy and reserved, but she had power now, and she knew it. It made our game so much more interesting.

"I'll stay for the money, but I won't help you anymore. What are you going to do to me? You can't force me to talk to you. All I signed up for is watching you."

"Oh, Stardust." I thrust my face into hers, laughing. This was where I thrived. In our cruel banter. "You have no idea what I can do to you, but you're sure as hell about to find out."

Chapter Eighteen

Indie

Jenna: Has Blake been fooling around on the tour?

Indie: Does Alex usually fool around on tours?

Hudson: Ladies. I'M HERE FOR THIS.

Jenna: Don't mind Hudson. He can solely communicate with you using offensive GIFs.

Hudson: Not true.

Hudson: Okay, a little true.

Jenna: Alex is…complicated. He's mostly ambivalent toward women. He'd engage in one-night stands occasionally, but not as often as one might think. The only woman he ever talks about is Fallon, and even that is drenched in negativity. Your turn.

Indie: Blake has not been seeing anyone or fooling around. He works and argues with Alex, then works some more. He hasn't even looked at a woman since we boarded the plane to Australia.

Hudson: Jenna. Talk to us. Are you and Blake finally going to bump uglies?

Jenna: Hudson, leave the chat.

Hudson: Like hell I will.

Jenna: You tell Alex everything. Go away.

Hudson: No!

<Jenna Holden removed Hudson Diaz from the chat>

Indie: …
Indie: Are you dating Blake?
Jenna: No.
Jenna: But we slept together.
Jenna: And I'm pregnant.
Jenna: I sound like one of the idiots I used to laugh at when I'd read teenage magazines when I was fifteen.
Indie: 1) cruel, and 2) you need to tell him.
Jenna: I don't know. I don't even know if I'll keep the baby. Don't tell him.
Indie: I won't. But you should.

It took Blake, Alfie, and Lucas to throw Alex into the van. He put up a good fight, but what struck me even harder than the fact it had taken three grown men to shove him into the vehicle, was that no one cared he'd fired Lucas. They'd all acted like everything was normal, dismissing Alex's authority.

I'd needed to talk to someone when I'd found out my brother had been arrested and was spending the night in jail for assault. And I'd wanted to talk to Lucas specifically because he was more logical and emotionally balanced than Alex.

When we got to the hotel, I unlocked my door quickly to avoid the Alex-storm that had been brewing in the hallway behind me. The minute his arm reached behind my shoulder to stop me from entering, I turned around to face him. He looked serious, determined, and…what was the third thing? Exhausted. It couldn't be easy to live life the way he had, but I was worn-out, too.

Flashes of his breath skating down the nape of my back when he retrieved the lyrics he wrote on me made my skin blossom into goosebumps. God, I was in trouble.

"I don't want to write tonight." My eyes followed the trail from his square chin to the collar of his gray Henley. His neck was slender and masculine at the same time. I wanted to lick it.

"Me neither. I just want to talk." He lowered his forehead and pressed it against mine, his breathing labored. "And maybe give you oral sex. But that's it."

I laughed through the ball of tears that had formed in my throat. What were we doing? Weren't we fighting five minutes ago?

The door clicked behind me and we both fell in. The room was eerily quiet under the weight of the night and both our shitty days. I careened to the virgin minibar, eager to do something with my hands, and plucked two bottles of water.

"Sorry about your brother." He braced himself over the TV stand, his face lined with worry.

I felt the burden of his whiskey eyes on my shoulders as I passed him a bottle and watched him set it aside. I didn't know why it was so easy to talk to Lucas and so difficult to talk to Alex. Maybe because Lucas always felt platonic. Maybe because Lucas didn't have any ulterior motives. And maybe it was because it felt like the air in my lungs was on fire and all my nerves concentrated in one spot between my naval and groin, the minute Alex was in the same room with me. I cleared my throat.

"Yeah, uhm, Craig got arrested tonight. It's his first offense. The guy was coming out of the strip club under our apartment block. He was very drunk and tried getting into his car with the intention of driving home. Craig was equally drunk and tried to pull him by the shirt through his window. Natasha said everything is fine, but I know she doesn't want me to worry."

Alex paced in my direction, his predator stride sleek and calm. He stopped, pressing his palms into the wall behind me and his lips to the crown of my head, inhaling—not kissing—my hair.

"I'll send someone to bail him out tomorrow and lawyer him up good."

"You don't need to do that," I said quietly, my face warming up. I felt more ashamed than I'd ever been before, because I knew it was one favor I was going to accept.

His eyes darkened, and his jaw tensed. The change was subtle, but it was there. From afar, Alex Winslow looked like nothing could penetrate his armor. But he was an artist—and an artist's armor is full of bullets and cracks. That's how the lyrics and notes seep through. My breath hitched at his stare, at the nakedness of it, so much so that I felt a damp spot forming in my underwear. He didn't say a thing, but by not saying much, I knew—I *read* through the lines of his forehead and mouth and eyes—he hadn't done that because he liked me. He did that because that's what he did. He took care of the people around him, because he didn't know he had the option not to.

Alex dropped his face to my neck and kissed the hollow part where the shoulder and the sensitive vein met. I closed my eyes, my hand flying to the desk behind me for support. I clutched The Paris Dress in my fist.

"Do you ever feel so lonely you're not sure people are real anymore?" he asked.

"All the time." I swallowed, adding, "The Little Prince was lonely, too."

"He was. And he died. All broken princes die at the end."

I shut him up with a kiss. Alex thought about dying, and I thought about how I'd do anything to keep him alive, even if it killed me. The notion only intensified the magnitude of the kiss when our mouths closed on one another. He dragged his lower lip along mine and brushed his nose on my cheek, slipping his tongue into my mouth and claiming it as his own. His tongue thrust between my lips again and again. I lifted my hands to cup his cheeks, deepening our kiss even more, and somewhere along the way I lost my balance, because before I knew it, my back was plastered across the desk with my legs wide-open and him between them. We were all over The Paris Dress and dozens of needles and threads.

"Bed," he barked into our kiss. "Right now."

He yanked me up and threw me onto the bed like a ragdoll. I laughed like a drunk, and he jumped right after me, making a huge splash in the covers like he was cannonballing into a pool. I scooted up until my back hit the headboard and we were face-to-face. He grinned, advancing toward me on his hands and knees like an animal. We were still fully clothed—hell, my shoes were still on—and I pressed my heeled boot to his chest in one last bid to stop him. I didn't even know why I bothered at this point. It was obvious I was going to give him whatever he wanted, consequences be damned. He grabbed my ankle and brought my leg to his mouth, sliding my glittery blue pump off and pressing his lips to the base of my foot.

"How many leggings have you packed for this trip?"

"Four."

"So you won't be needing these anymore." He grabbed the fabric of my leggings between my legs roughly and tore them from my body.

I yelped and tried pushing him away, before my bare legs were exposed in front of him. I slid down the bed, trying to fight him, and he took both my arms and pinned them above my head, sliding over me so his groin was on mine and his unmistakably hard shaft was digging deep between my thighs. His eyes blazed with so many emotions, I felt nauseated on his behalf. It made my stupid heart forgive him for acting so cruel and aloof all the time.

"Do you trust me?" he asked.

I nearly choked on a laugh. "Of course not."

"Fair enough, I'll rephrase. Do you think I'm a rapist?"

"Doubt it. It's too available for you to take by force."

"Serial killer?"

"You don't give enough of a shit about anyone to kill them."

He paused, his mouth curving into a smirk. "Close your eyes."

"Let go of my wrists first."

"No chance. It's a part of the process."

"And what process would that be?"

"The one where I make you come so hard you'll need a spine transplant because I'll turn you into goo."

I grinned despite my best intentions. I didn't think I'd ever smiled so much in my entire life as while on tour with Alex Winslow. Which was insane, considering he also made me so mad and frustrated in the same breath. Alex kissed a path down my collarbone—dirty, wet kisses full of hunger and promise—dragging his teeth down the valley between my still-clothed breasts. He rubbed his thumb along the black silk of my dress, his other hand still pinning my arms above my head.

"How long does it usually take you to make a dress?"

He wouldn't dare.

"No." My breath was shaky, my voice thick. I was delirious with need. "Don't you dare, Alex Winslow."

Phhhsshhhhttt!

He tore my precious silk dress, disposing it on the floor like I hadn't ridden my bike eight miles each way every day to save money to buy the fabric, like I hadn't sewn it deep into the night. "You assho—"

But I never got to finish the word, because my panties found the same fate as my dress, and before I knew it, his head was between my legs and oh. My. God.

Confession time: no one had ever gone down on me before. I'd only had one sexual partner in high school, and, like a lot of high school kids—he was pretty selfish in bed. I'd never given, nor received, oral sex, so I didn't know what the fuss was all about. That's why my eyes almost rolled out of their sockets straight to the floor along with my tattered clothes the minute his hot, wet tongue pressed into my center and gave my slit a thorough, long lick.

My pussy contracted so hard, I nearly came on the spot. I closed my eyes, too embarrassed to look at what he was doing to me, and dragged the pillow from beside me, pressing it over my head to stifle the moans that followed every time he put his tongue at the base of my pussy and dragged it all the way up to my clit, flicking it gently with an arrogant asshole smile I could *feel*.

I thrust my hips up, wanting more, and he pinned me down in response, growling.

"Open wider."

I did.

"One leg over my shoulder."

I clumsily raised my right leg and propped it against his broad shoulder, painfully aware of the fact he was still fully dressed and I was so physically and mentally naked.

"Look at me."

I froze, exhaling all my anxiety into the fabric of the pillow. Shit. Did I have to?

"Look. At. Me." Apparently, I did have to. "Or I'll stop, but before I do, I'll make sure you get to the edge before I yank you right back. Don't make me be cruel, Stardust."

Slowly, I slid the pillow down and peeked at him through the valley of my breasts. His eyes looked drunk and mean, a combination I never thought I'd find appealing. He stared at me as his tongue penetrated me hard, and I choked on a shaky breath.

"Alex..."

He reached over and kneaded my right breast, his fingers rubbing my pebbled nipple and making me yelp. My legs started to tremble around his head, and that's when his tongue began mercilessly fucking me like it was much more than a tongue. I clutched his gorgeous hair between my fingers, his tongue buried so deep inside me I could feel it filling me in ways I'd never been filled before. He looked so rough and male, his tattoos crawling from the edge of his Henley, his locks mussed and wild, and his stubble making the insides of my thighs burn deliciously. I whimpered, clamping around his tongue, my butt cheeks so tense I couldn't breathe.

"Fuck, yeah." His voice was gruff and low as he grabbed my butt and hoisted me up, pushing me into his face, eating me like a starved man while deepening his tongue inside of me.

I clinched around him again, and he let out a laugh—*a laugh*—like my body was an instrument for him, a tool, a toy. Like I was Tania, and he knew all the notes by heart, and strummed on my cords, producing the angriest, craziest song in the world.

"I'm coming," I panted, feeling a ball of fire rushing down from my spine and to my groin. I'd never felt this way. Lit up like a Christmas tree. Like my body was a bundle of sizzling nerves. Everywhere he touched—and he was roaming now—tingled and danced with electricity.

But Alex only played by his own rules, and he was good at bending them, depending on his mood. Mid-orgasm he decided to grab my hips, flip me over roughly, and press my cheek to the pillow. Snaking his arm under my stomach, he propped me up and kicked my legs open when I was on my knees. I was wide-open and exposed now, and my instincts told me to close my legs and run for my life. Coincidentally, my instincts were dead the minute he put his hot, wet mouth to my clit from behind and started sucking on it ravenously.

"Holy…" I began, when he thrust two fingers into me. The pressure of an orgasm was back in full swing, even though I'd just come. I swiveled my head around to watch him, getting a rush from the mere idea of him working me up like I was his only passion in life, but he grabbed me by the hair and turned my head back.

"Not so shy anymore, are we?" His voice was muffled, and I felt the words inside my core. It made my want for him trickle right onto his tongue.

I felt him moving behind me. My body began to spasm as he fingered and sucked me with his mouth, the new position allowing him to be deeper and rougher than before. And there was another thing that made it hotter than anything I'd ever done. The slight humiliation of having my butt wide-open for him to see. I just found the whole thing out-of-this-world hot, but that's what you get for messing with a rock star, right?

Alex moved more quickly, more urgently, and I chanced another glance at him when he was busy biting my clit and inserting a third finger into me, my loud moans making him far too high to notice what I was doing. I found him thrusting into my bed, still in his jeans, dry humping it to oblivion and back. I was so consumed by getting off, it hadn't once occurred to me he was in need of a release, too.

"Alex," I whimpered when my legs finally gave in, and I collapsed on the bed. He withdrew his fingers, pressing his mouth to my slit and sucking all my juices like it was water in the desert. I came hard on his face. It took me a few seconds to realize what country I was in—Russia—and what time it was—one in the morning—before I turned around to stare at him like he'd broken me. He was still in his jeans and shirt, his back to me, sitting at the edge of the bed and lacing the boots he must've kicked off when we started fooling around. I jumped and crawled on my knees all the way to him, placing a hand over each of his shoulders from behind.

"That was…"

"I know," he finished for me, and I nuzzled his neck, smelling myself on his hot breath. Why was it such a turn-on? Because I was everywhere on him. He smelled of my sex and my lavender and rosemary shampoo. I put my lips to his jaw and sucked. "You need to stop completing my sentences for me."

"Why? I always get it right," he said dryly.

I stood up and walked over to grab my bottle of water, taking a slow sip. I stared at him from the other side of the room. I was still naked. The bob of his throat told me he noticed. I didn't want him to leave. Not before I got him off, too. His eyes raked over my body, sizing me up. When he opened his mouth again, the world faded, and he was the only thing clear enough to see.

"Don't start what you're too scared to finish," he said.

A dare.

"I will finish, Alex. And so will you."

A promise.

I took a step toward him, feeling brave. He liked what he saw, and he had a hard-on the size of a salami to prove it. His glazed-over eyes warned me he needed nothing more than a few strokes to explode in delirious pleasure. I wanted to take him to the same place he'd taken me. I wanted to take him to heaven.

"Do you make a habit of eating girls out for forty minutes and leaving without any reciprocation?"

His Adam's apple moved again, but his eyes remained cool and dark, scanning me coldly.

"I haven't eaten a girl out in a year," he admitted, his eyes traveling down to my core before he licked his already slick lips. "And I never give without taking."

I sat beside him, not feeling half as weird as I should have, considering I was oh, so very naked.

"I'm more than willing to give."

He grabbed the back of my neck and jerked me toward his face. I thought he was going to kiss me, but his mouth traveled past mine to my temple. He put his lips to my ear and hissed, "Kiss my cock through my jeans, Stardust. Show me how hungry you are for it."

I erected my spine, waiting for him to fall down to the bed so I could straddle him. He didn't move from his spot. Reluctantly, I got down on my knees in front of him and prodded his legs to make myself some room.

"Told you I'll get you on your knees willingly, *Bellamy*."

I blushed. He used my last name as a weapon, and it worked. I didn't like to be called that. It was at that moment I decided to stop calling him Winslow.

When my head was leveled with his groin, I put my lips to his zipper. I pressed close-mouthed kisses all over his groin, my pulse quickening in my neck. He didn't touch me. He didn't even look at me. In fact, if I didn't know any better, I'd think he'd turned on the TV behind me and was watching something mindless. The only proof he was with me in that moment was the way his chest moved above me with uneven breaths.

I opened my mouth and licked his jeans, kissing his clothed groin eagerly, finding myself rocking back and forth. What was wrong with me? I'd never been that forward with a guy before. I wrapped my lips around his shaft and moved them up and down, tracing the size, width, and the curve of his penis. I could smell him, his penis, and that made me elated with need. The feeling confused me. I'd never wanted to go down on a guy before. I thought it was gross. Maybe even dirty. And Alex wasn't even my boyfriend. He wasn't my anything.

"All right, that's enough of your cock tease. Take it out."

I undid his jeans, maybe a little too quickly, because I heard him chuckling above my head.

"Put it in your mouth."

"I've never done it before," I muttered, more to justify it to myself the moment I screwed it up.

"It's not rocket science."

"Don't be crude."

"Don't stall. You said you want to suck my cock. Now's as good a time as any."

I covered some of his shaft and sucked. Maybe half of it. There was still more skin I couldn't reach, so he took my hand and curled it around the base of his dick.

"Squeeze."

I clutched it, and he closed his eyes, looking tortured. A beautiful prince giving in to the moment. It inspired me to squeeze even harder, sucking on his hot, silky flesh and moving my mouth up and down. He pushed inside me, slow at first, but steady enough so that his tip touched the back of my throat. I gagged, my eyes burning with tears. He grabbed my shoulder and yanked me on top of him, so that he was lying on the bed and I was still sucking him off, naked, but on top of him. His fingers grazed my damp slit again, and I purred into his cock, which made it jerk in my mouth. *Rapture. Euphoria. Stars in my eyes.* No one had ever told me sucking someone off could make you feel powerful, rather than degraded. I felt like I owned Alex in that moment, and the feeling was...priceless.

I pumped my hips into his hand, wanting more, sucking him off eagerly. He grabbed the back of my head and changed the pace, going faster, and deeper, and so much rougher than I'd ever imagined it could be. He was propped up on one elbow, watching me, and the position made his abs tense with every thrust he made into my mouth. He retrieved two fingers coated in my warm juices from my pussy and pinched my clit with them, playing with my arousal and rubbing it along my slit now.

"Ohhh," I cried, which made Alex shut me up by driving even harder between my lips.

"Remember it's my turn to take? The only thing you should be given right now is my spunk down your throat. Everything else is a bonus, and you're definitely not allowed to make demands."

Bossy jerk. Yet there was absolutely no way I could stop what I was doing. I felt him jerking inside my mouth, and he scooted up quickly to lean against the headboard, keeping my head on his crotch by fisting my hair.

"Fuck, yeah. Suck me good, Stardust. You're a natural."

Thanks...I guess. I did like the idea of taking control and being able to give him what he needed.

"I'm coming."

It was a warning, which I appreciated, but I kept my lips firmly on his cock as he came in spurts. His cum was warm and salty—sticky—coating my tongue and teeth. I groaned, sucking every drop, until Alex let out a deep sigh and dragged me by the hair to look up and sit on my knees. He looked nonchalant and unflustered as ever. Other than his cheeks—stained in pink—he looked completely normal.

"You swallowed yet?" he asked, patting his back pocket and producing a cigarette pack.

I couldn't believe what I was seeing, only I could. It was classic Alex. I still had some of his cum in my mouth. It was too thick to swallow in one go. I shook my head.

"Open your mouth," he ordered.

I did. He lit up a cigarette—no doubt taking a small pleasure in making me wait—then pushed my bottom lip with his thumb, cigarette in mouth, and watched his cum drip from my lower lip to my chin. It was filthy and mortifying, and...hot. He swiped his index finger over my tongue and rubbed some of his cum on one of my nipples, and we both watched my body reacting to his touch, blooming into goose bumps, my nipples pebbling like little rocks.

"Pity I can't keep you," he said around his cancer stick.

"Who said I want to be kept?"

He put his palm on my cheek and squeezed, a sad look in his eyes. "Who said you had a choice?"

Chapter Nineteen

Alex

"**C**ongratulations, eejit. Jenna is officially going to kill you." Blake slammed me to the door the minute I stepped into our room. Even before I got in, I had a feeling I should've stayed at Indie's and burrowed into her scent and heat and sweet, innocent existence. The shit with Blake and Jenna was getting old. Like it wasn't enough my soul had been gangbanged by a bunch of Suits on a daily basis, I also had to answer to them every time I fucked up on stage.

I would say that Blake and Jenna acted like my mum and dad, but truth was, my parents didn't give a shit, and my manager and agent mostly gave a shit about their paychecks.

"Waitrose had it coming." I pushed Blake away. His back bumped into the opposite wall, his eyes narrowing, honing in on me like I was a moving target.

"Just tell him you like her, Alex. Is that really so hard? Instead of making grand announcements about how she's yours and you're the king of the world. You're starting to sound like Mussolini on steroids."

"Why is it so important that I tell *anyone* I like her?" I fumed, galloping toward the minibar and yanking out a bag of crisps. Holy crap, I was hungry. I'd come so hard I'm pretty sure Indie had swallowed enough little Alexes to form an army. "Plus, I don't like her," I maintained. Actually, that was a lie, but as I'd said before, lying was second nature. Or a first one. Whatever.

"It's important for us to know that your sobriety companion meets your expectations." Blake cleared his throat and added quickly, "To Jenna and me, that is."

I stared at him like he'd just informed me he was going through a pickle transplant to replace his cock, my crisp mid-air on its way to my mouth. I threw the crisp into my gob and chewed loudly, trying to figure out his game. It was unlike him to focus on Indie instead of the fact I'd walked off stage mid-gig after slamming my foot in the drum kit.

"Are you high?"

"Are you sleeping with her?" he asked simultaneously.

"That's none of your business. Even if I were, she signed an NDA."

"That's not why I'm asking."

I blinked. He'd never given a damn about any of my babysitters. Then again, I'd never gotten close to a girl after what had happened with Fucking Fallon. Blake leaned over the kitchen nook, running his fingers along his hair, looking skyward. Then he did that big, dramatic sigh. The one I got every time he threw himself a pity party.

"The Halloween event in Paris...we need to be there. Fallon and Will are attending," he said, his words slow and careful, like he was dripping gasoline into an invisible fuse in my head while I was smoking.

I gave him a flat look. I felt like Rob from High Fidelity, sans the love for pop music. Basically, I was a loser and everyone pitied me, even though I pitied them, too. "And?"

"And I don't want you to do anything stupid. Like trying to win her back."

"I won't." I scratched the back of my neck. Was it a lie? Maybe. When you lie so much, it's difficult to distinguish the truth. In retrospect, Paris would be the night when my life changed forever. Indie's, too. And Fallon's, the most. But of course, I didn't know that when I stared deep into Blake's eyes.

Beat. Beat. Beat. Beat.

"Okay," Blake said, withdrawing from the nook and walking to

the bathroom. It was then I noticed he still hadn't changed from tonight's show. "All right."

I watched his back, trying to figure out what had just happened.
What. Just. Fucking. Happened?

In the end, it was more of the same.

Blake gave me shit about the incident at the gig for days afterward.
Jenna highlighted that sentiment by sending me a basket of baklavas
when we landed in Istanbul with a note:

I dare you to pull something like this again, Alex. No, really. Try me.

I played nice with Lucas, but found other ways to taunt him.
Mainly by devouring Indigo every spare moment I had in public. We
wrote every night in the hallway so we could concentrate on work, then
I'd sneak into her bedroom and eat her out on the balcony overlooking
Athens, or finger her in a cab on our way back from a gig in Berlin, dry
hump her against the wall behind a coffee shop in Milan, and eat ex-
otic fruit off of her naked body in Barcelona. She always had that look
on her face when I made her come. Like the intensity of what we were
doing stunned her. It was like deflowering her every single day, even
though we hadn't actually had sex. Yet. *Yet.* But we were getting closer
every day. Plus, she'd finally taken a step back from Lucas, and he, in
return, remained polite and pleasant to her, not overstepping the red,
imaginary line I'd drawn between them.

Luckily, she didn't bore me despite Waitrose's lack of interest in
her.

It was probably the fact I hadn't shagged her yet.

Though, let's be honest—it's not exactly like I was charming her
into a fucking Shakespearean love story. I was certain a big part of
the reason why Stardust could stand the sight of me was because, the

morning after the Moscow gig, Howard Lipkin, one of the biggest at-torneys in Los Angeles, had bailed her brother out and dragged him back home to his wife and kid. Craig was on house arrest, and that made Indie feel pathetically content. Like he couldn't possibly fuck up from the comfort of his home. Which, from experience, was bollocks, because both my parents were unemployed and had managed to dam-age Carly and me just fine, even though their arses were forever glued to the sofa, watching *EastEnders* and Jeremy Kyle into the afternoon— is there ever anything more depressing than watching daytime TV? I thought not, and I still do.

Barcelona was our last stop before we took a week off in London. Technically, I had a gig at the Cambridge Castle on Friday, but that was the extent of it, and the Cambridge Castle was my home field.

Barcelona was a turning point. It was a turning point because it was the place where I stupidly thought it'd be a good idea to walk into a British hipster coffee shop and grab some black coffee and English breakfast for my entourage. Should've known nothing good ever comes out of trying to be considerate.

Indie was up in her room, probably sewing The Paris Dress. Blake was loitering outside the shop on his goddamn mobile. With my bean-ie, Wayfarers, and head down, I knew I wouldn't be recognized. It was the kind of place that would play Nazi propaganda before playing someone who managed to break onto the Billboard list, so I doubted they'd even recognize me. I was Satan to them. Suits' Satan.

I took in the deep blue and pale pink tiles of the shop, the people in flashy blazers and thick-framed glasses and women in trendy pet-ticoats. The breeziness of their lives. They looked so grounded. Like they had the virtue of gravity working in their favor. Me, I felt loose. Tied to nothing. Not to people and not to objects, other than Tania. I just floated through life, and the worst part was, drugs and alcohol had actually been one of the only constant things in my life. I stood in the queue. No one recognized me. It was a relief caked with worry. There was always a gnawing anxiety that nibbled at my ego whenever people overlooked me.

Was I still big?
Was I still famous?
Was I still worth it?
Was my career going downhill?

Cue to wanting to throw up my own soul for giving a fuck.

The queue was dragging. That was fine. I didn't have anywhere to go. I thought about Indie. How we only hooked up at night. During the day, I acted like I couldn't be bothered with her, and she acted like I exasperated her. It was only at night when we peeled our masks and our clothes off that life became bearable.

There was a row of flat-screened TVs plastered above the counter. One had the menu, the other played the show *GossipCave*. Menu, *GossipCave*. Menu, *GossipCave*. Bright colors and bold fonts. Showbiz programs are like junk food, so beautifully wrapped. The volume was quite high, and my eyes drifted up despite my best efforts. A bunch of millennials and a gay bloke in his mid-forties were swiveling on neon chairs in their cubicle-style, ultra-futuristic office, the floor-to-ceiling window behind them exhibiting L.A. in all its Botoxed glory. They were talking so animatedly, you'd think they were discussing the Middle East conflict.

"Do you think there's going to be a showdown?" The older man in the Polo shirt and impeccably styled hair rested his elbows on top of some guy's chair. All the reporters and editors nodded enthusiastically.

"Oh, absolutely," a blond, malnourished girl exclaimed. "There's no way around that. Alex Winslow is unhinged. I mean, he's definitely cooking something delicious, what with the snippets from his 'Letters from the Dead' tour." She clapped her hands together excitedly, brushing her tongue over her glossed lips in a way that was calculated and overtly trying and not at all like Stardust's nervous gnawing. "But Winslow is still every inch of the reckless rock star we know. Like two weeks ago, when he attacked his drummer. He's definitely going to let Will Bushell and Fallon Lankford know how he feels about them."

"Apparently, he didn't attack the drummer. There were severe sound issues and he was just frustrated. He was later photographed hugging Lucas Rafferty outside the hotel," a guy chipped in.

Right. About that.

That had been Blake putting out one of the many fires I'd created. There were no sound issues—though I'm sure someone got fired for the non-existing one Blake reported—and the embrace I'd given Lucas outside our Berlin hotel had almost snapped his neck.

"Either way, will they even meet? I mean, chances are they won't." A brunette girl with bold red lipstick picked dirt from under her acrylic nails.

"They're all going to be at Chateau De Malmaison's Halloween event in Paris." The older man snapped his fingers.

Someone tapped my shoulder, and I realized the queue had progressed, but I'd stayed rooted to the floor. I took a few steps forward, my eyes still glued to the screen. There was something cathartic about the pain coursing through me. It made me feel so human. So vulnerable.

"There'll be no media at the event. And they'll all wear masks." The blond girl sounded disappointed. At least someone still got a mental hard-on for my personal life. Shame it wasn't me.

"Mask or not, Will and Fallon owe Alex an explanation, don't you think? Their engagement came as a surprise to everyone."

For a second, I was in purgatory between my life the second before I'd heard it and my life after.

Engagement?

En-fucking-gagement?

I sucked in a slow breath. Fucking Fallon was the hottest mess Hollywood had had the displeasure of producing in this decade and Will was happily married to his work. What business did they have getting married?

"The preparations for the wedding have been going on for weeks now. Do you think they'll invite him?"

Weeks? They'd been engaged for weeks and no one had told me? Then it dawned on me like hail. Trickling down at first, then all at once, pouring down on my fucking parade.

No Internet.

No social media.

Stay away from the laptop.

Channels in my hotel rooms hooked on news and porn and nothing else because of...

Cockgate.

Blake had created Cockgate. My jaw locked so hard my teeth meshed into dust. He'd do whatever he needed to divert the scandal from "British rock star loses his shit and goes on a three-week bender consuming every single gram of cocaine in Europe" to "British rock star fucks a random starlet and leaves her a souvenir."

My blood boiled, and I made a U-turn, pushing the door open and storming out. Blake was still on his mobile. He had one eye on me, like I was going to drink myself to death in a coffee shop in the middle of Barcelona. I motioned for him to follow me up to our hotel with my hand, and he did, the device still cemented to his ear.

"All right. Gotta go. Talk later. Bye."

We got in. Into the lobby. Into the lift. I was sick and tired of Blake and Jenna pulling shit like this. I had a babysitter, I was not allowed on the Internet, and every time I acted in a way that didn't suit them, they'd dump the blame on other people and bark at me, like in Moscow.

Not to mention I suspected he put my fucking dick on the Internet.

Yeah, enough was e-fucking-nough.

"What crawled up your arse?" Blake's defiant eyes dragged to meet mine when we were in the lift, and I had to tell myself, *not now. When we get to the room. When we get to the fucking room,* which only served to make every second tick like a year.

The minute the door behind us clicked shut, I grabbed a vase and threw it across the wall. I wanted to scream, but this time we didn't have the entire floor for my entourage.

"How long have you known? About Will and Fallon. Don't lie." I wasn't a bad man. I knew that. I paid my taxes. I always made sure my sexual partner orgasmed before I kicked her out. I took care of my family and mates, even when they let me down. So this didn't make any sense.

"How did you…" He gulped, widening the loop of his tie like it tightened around his neck. "What…"

"They have fucking TVs in Spain, that's how!" My voice hitched up, the control I'd clung to seeping slowly out of me. I looked aside. I needed air. I didn't have air. Not in the physical, but fucking spiritual sense. I always had someone babying me. I could drag Indie from her room and have her accompany me, but I didn't want to do it. As it was, she was overworked and dealing with personal bullshit. Plus, I needed to be alone. Bollocks.

Bollocks!

"Look, I can explain." Blake held his palms in the air in surrender.

How many times had I seen him in this position? One too many. That was the exact number. And I was sick and tired of it. I pushed him, bloodthirsty for a fight.

The more I had money, and power, and fame, the less I had freedom, and happiness, and the ability to be me. And the person I'd become was imperfect. He occasionally fucked things up, including his drummer's kit. The person I was wanted the truth. The person I was—*I am, I always will be*—couldn't settle for the life he had. A life where I worked for so many people—Jenna, Blake, my former publicist—and the only thing that kept the illusion of control was the fact I'd taken the biggest slice of the pie. A pie I was no longer hungry for.

I didn't need guardians.

And babysitters.

And people who leaked pictures of my dick on the Internet.

I needed to get out of there. *Now.*

I made my way to the door before my fist could make its way to Blake's face. My manager panicked and grabbed my wrist to turn me around. What the hell did he think he was doing? The minute I swiveled and he saw the look on my face, his eyebrows popped.

"I did it for your own good, Alex."

"Fuck you," I spat, shaking his touch off me. "You don't get to pretend it's even half-true after everything you've done."

"Where are you going?"

"Doesn't matter. Wherever it is, no one's coming with me. Not Indie, and definitely not you." The minute I said these words, I realized it was a demand I'd been afraid to make months ago. Sure, I'd bullied my past babysitters and taunted Indie, but I'd never put my foot down. I'd never said no. Until now.

"Alex." He jumped in front of me, blocking my way to the door. "I'm afraid if you leave now, you'll make a huge mistake. If a punch in the face is what I need to tolerate to keep you sober, I'll take one for the team."

I threw my head back, shaking it on a bitter chuckle. "Aren't you a goddamn saint." I shot him a serious look. "Out of my way."

"Alex…"

"Now!" I grabbed the first thing I could get my hands on and swung it in his face with force.

He tripped sideways to prevent the hit. Tania crashed with force against the door, chipped wood flying everywhere from the thump. She broke into two pieces, leaving me standing there, choking the neck of my guitar while the rest of her was lying on the floor. She lay under my feet like a dead lover. Beautiful and broken and no longer mine. She was all the diaries crammed into one object. The empty box that was full of tunes and lyrics. She was the most special, important gift I'd ever received, and the only possession I actually cared about.

And she was gone.

Tears pooled in my eyes, and I squinted to prevent them from falling. When was the last time I'd cried? Never. I mean, I'm sure I did—who hadn't?—but it was so long ago I couldn't imagine it was after I hit thirteen. So. There was that. I was crying. I was fucking crying.

Blake was standing behind me, his pulse so fast I could hear it thrumming in my ears. He wanted to offer an apology but knew better than to speak. I'd kill him. Shit. Tania. Shit.

I don't think my world had ever been so silent as it was in the moment I stepped out of the room. Indigo stepped out of hers at the same time, like she could sense me. When I looked at her face, all I saw was another mouth I needed to feed. I bypassed her. She stood there barefoot, with that Paris dress she always worked on clutched in her hand.

"Alex? What happened?"

"Whoever is stupid enough to follow me will get fired on the spot," I said coolly, then left.

I wandered around the streets. Alone. It was reckless, and stupid, and kind of cool. I bought a pack of cigs and finished them as I walked. I thought about everything. About Will and Fallon, who were on the same continent, probably not many miles away. About their wedding. I thought about my life and what it had become. About my mates, or the people I referred to as such. Of Blake, who pulled no punches to further his career and mine. Of Alfie, who was oblivious to anything other than his dick's desires, and about Lucas, who'd tried to seduce Indigo. Then I thought about Stardust, about the way she'd made me feel. Like I was living in a semi-normal universe, where I didn't have to worry the girl I was shagging would sell our sex tape to *The Sun* or lure me into buying her something expensive. She was, perhaps, the only real thing I had in my life, and that was utterly pathetic, seeing as she was my employee, and only on tour because I paid her to save me.

But I'd saved her, too, hadn't I?

In the only way I truly mattered.

With my money.

It was only when I strolled back to the hotel that it occurred to me what my heartbreak was really about.

Tania.

Blake.

Alfie.

Lucas.

The list wasn't short, but it was telling. There was one thing omitted from it—two, actually—and those were the things I should have considered the most.

Will and Fallon. They made me feel nothing.

And that, somehow, made me feel everything.

Chapter Twenty

Indie

<Jenna Holden added Hudson Diaz to the conversation>
Hudson: No longer on your period, Jenna?
Jenna: You can say that again. Indie, how are things?
Indie: I hate your client, Jenna, and your boss, Hudson.
Jenna: What has he done?
Indie: Is Fallon really all that amazing?
Hudson: She's pretty the way the Eurovision is. Fascinating, but ultimately makes you want to puke. Why?
Indie: Alex found out she's engaged to Will. He was not happy. We can't find him.
Jenna: ???
Jenna: ELABORATE.
Indie: Blake is roaming the streets, along with Alfie and Lucas. They asked me to stay in the hotel in case he shows up.
Jenna: Keep us posted. I don't need this right now with everything that's going on.
Hudson: What IS going on?
Jenna: Doesn't matter.
Hudson: Tell me, Indie, is Alex still mad at Luc?
Indie: Very much so. Why?
Hudson: Oh, no reason. If you ever get to it, tell Lucas he's a jerk. He'll know why.

Unattainable. Cold. Disturbed.

I knew that. I wasn't, after all, stupid. But maybe that was what drew me to Alex. He was categorically unreachable—he would never give me his heart or future or even the greater chunk of his presence—but he still gave me something. Some fuel to run on as I knitted together patches full of stupid dreams and idealistic ideas about us. And I did. I absolutely did. Despite my best efforts, and what I so often told myself, I wanted Alex in more ways than he wanted me. It was very easy to figure out, actually. Every time we touched, it was always in my room, always in the dark, always on his terms. I was his little doll. The one he'd bend over and finger under the dinner table, his fingers ascending up my underskirt, meeting my wet flesh and playing with me while he was engrossed in a conversation about record labels with Alfie at the hotel ballroom. I was the just-for-funsies girl he'd pin to the bed—arms above my head, always, legs spread wide—and kiss until I begged and panted and made a fool of myself. I was now the girl I'd always detested. The one who took something, even though she wanted everything, because in the end, she settled for less.

I tried to convince myself I was after the desire, and not the desired. That he was just a tool, and that with time, and space, and distance, I'd forget about him.

I'd realized how wrong I was when I stood in the hallway, The Paris Dress clutched to my chest. I'd been about to walk over to Alex's room and ask if they had an extra pair of scissors, since I couldn't find mine.

He stormed down the hallway, taking the stairs, not the elevator, despite the fact we were on the twentieth floor. His door was still open, and his scent was everywhere in the hallway, so different and masculine and uniquely his. Blake looked back at me from the threshold. I quirked one eyebrow, silently asking him to explain. Alex's eyes shone, and the pain etched on his face couldn't be mistaken. It was there, and it was raw.

"He found out about Fallon and Will's engagement."

I pulled my lower lip into my mouth with my teeth, my eyes widening. The dull pain in my chest intensified. For him. For me. Maybe even for Blake. The notion that this was over—that we were over—took over me.

Maybe we'd reached a boiling point.

Maybe we were done.

I spent the remainder of the day in my hotel room, watching TV. I'd Skyped with Natasha, Craig, and Ziggy. Craig couldn't leave the house, and Natasha wouldn't bring him any booze, which prompted him to stay reluctantly sober. It wasn't fun to watch him moping around, but I hadn't seen him look so healthy in years. His cheeks had a natural pink hue again and his skin looked smoother. The bags under his eyes were less prominent. And he was functioning. Ish.

Yet, I didn't find myself happy about it.

"Craig, go fix Ziggy his dinner. There's mashed potatoes and chicken in the fridge," Nat said that day.

I smiled tiredly at that. They could afford chicken. I was glad, despite everything, that I was still touring with Alex. Whoever had said money can't buy happiness was never truly poor. Money could buy happiness, but that doesn't mean you need too much of it.

When Craig and Ziggy were out of earshot, Nat took the extra step and grabbed the laptop, jogging to her bedroom and shutting the door behind her. She jumped on the bed and fixed the monitor so she could see me better.

"What's going on?" she whispered. "Tell me everything. And there are things to tell, I bet. There was a paparazzi picture of you guys in Greece. It looked like Alex was half-hugging you, half-grabbing your ass."

Oh, shit.

I mentally browsed through everything that had gone down in Athens. The guys had wanted to go sightseeing, and I'd had to watch

Alex extra carefully, because apparently, he used to party in London with some drug dealer who'd moved to Greece, and Blake was on edge about it. I'd worn a polka-dot blue dress and a scarlet smile that day. The weather had been glorious. We'd admired the ancient ruins with a bunch of starstruck tourists from Japan and Germany, taking pictures of the Parthenon, when Alex had slid his hand over my butt when everyone else was walking ahead of us, listening to the tour guide, and pressed his mouth to my ear.

The Parthenon was the temple they'd built for their goddess, Athena, the tour guide explained. Athena was the symbol of arts and freedom.

"Two things you remind me of." Alex's lips had dragged to my neck, his voice gruff with cigarette and lust. "But tonight, darlin', you'll be the one to call me god."

He'd dropped the "G" in 'darling.' For me.

"That's corny as hell."

"I like corn. Corn is good. And we're so hot we could make popcorn."

"Jesus, Alex!" I'd laughed.

"See? I haven't even touched you properly, and you're already half-religious."

I'd been so happy at that moment, which only reminded me how unhappy I was now when my face heated and Nat's smile widened.

"Holy hell, Indie! You're sleeping with a rock star. My inner slut is cheering for you. Or should I say my former slut? I think I'm still her. I'm just reining in on that shit since I'm married and have a kid and all."

Another arrow of sorrow shot to my heart. Nat deserved so much more than Craig was giving her. Had she brought the subject up a few hours ago, I might have felt braver. Safer. Like it didn't matter at all that Alex was looking forward to Paris so he could pursue his former flame.

"It's not like that." I pulled a lock of my blue hair and fingered the ends, my eyes concentrating hard on them instead of on my sister-in-law.

"What's it like then?" I heard her grin.

"It's really casual. He's still in love with his ex."

"And that bothers you?"

"Of course not."

"So, why the long face?"

Because I'm a liar, just like him.

"I should probably end it," I said aloud, making the idea real and scary. Not that I was in love with him, or even needed him. But he was the one thing in my life that made me feel good, and the list of things that made me feel that way wasn't very long.

"Maybe you should, but you definitely won't," Nat said, and I looked up to see her expression, which turned from amused to worried. "Remember, Indie. Three months. Enjoy what's there, and leave it at that."

Easier said than done. I changed the subject, and we ended up talking about other things. About Clara from Thrifty, who had been calling Nat and asking about me. Then about Ziggy's new obsession with pulling his pants down, which Natasha was very happy about, because she thought it'd meant he was ready to be potty trained.

After that, I ordered room service. Philly cheesesteak and fries. Not exactly authentic Spanish cuisine, but I was desperate to feel like I was back on US soil, even for a little while. I was drawing figures on the plate with a French fry and ketchup when he pounded on my door. I didn't need to open it to know who it was. Alex was always minutes away from crashing the door down with his force. I ignored the knocks for the first ten minutes, but after that knew I was entering a dangerous territory. If he was drunk or drugged up—two ideas that weren't farfetched, seeing as he'd disappeared for hours on his own—I needed to deal with that. No matter how hurt I'd felt, this was still a job, and one that paid well. Well enough, in fact, to get Ziggy the tubes he needed in his ears. He had a consultation appointment next week. Plus, I wanted to put Craig in rehab and get Nat's car running so she didn't have to take three buses on her way to her temporary job. That meant that no matter how foolishly angry I'd felt about Alex being devastated about Fallon's engagement, I had to swallow my pride. But that didn't mean I'd humor him anymore when it came to us.

I walked to the door and swung it open. He stood in front of me, his white V-neck crumpled and wrinkled, his black skinny jeans and impossible height both familiar and imposing. He smelled of cigarettes and the fresh bite of the cool evening air. He looked sober, and miserable, and extremely huggable. I folded my arms over my chest to keep myself from reaching toward him, staring up into his amber eyes with the green and gold flakes that swam in circles, like a gold pond.

I'm so happy I didn't sleep with you. If I had, I wouldn't be able to stop myself from giving you everything you came here for tonight.

"Can I come in?" His eyes looked wrecked. Bloodshot.

I should say no. I knew he'd pour his heart out, and once he did, I wouldn't deny him of anything in this world. He made me weak and exposed, and that alone should make me run for the hills. I stood there wordlessly, not quite ready to say no, but not stupid enough to say yes.

"Please." He saw the hesitation on my face, but his voice was hard and coarse. Leave it to Alex Winslow to ask for something nicely one time in his life and still make it sound like a demand. "I need to talk."

"Talk to someone else. You have plenty of friends."

He snorted, rolling his eyes to the ceiling. From that angle, I could see the dark circles under his eyes. "Some friends they are."

"Not my problem," I said quietly, hating myself for every word. He'd been cruel to me, but that didn't mean I had to be cruel back. There's strength in choosing kindness even when you're being dragged into the well of malice. I'd never been this way, and yet, I couldn't stop myself. I was angry. Angrier than sympathetic. He knitted his brows and stared me down. I watched as his eyes turned in slow-motion from exasperated and sad to dark and interested.

"The fuck happened to you?"

"You happened to me. Unfortunately." I was about to shut the door—he was sober, my job was done—but he slipped his arm through the crack and stopped me.

I was about to slam it anyway when he said, "I'd reconsider if I were you. This arm is insured for twenty million dollars. If I can't play my guitar, a lot of people will be upset. All of those people you don't want to piss off."

Feeling lava bubbling in my chest, I kept the crack open, painfully aware of how his finger brushed the strap of my dress up my shoulder.

"Why are you mad?" His thumb rode up to my neck, to my pulse that quickened by the nanosecond. The change in mood confused me, and that's exactly how he liked me.

"I'm not mad." A chuckle died in my throat.

He pushed the door open all the way and sauntered in like he owned the place, doing his usual inspection. Alex liked to look and examine everything, like I was hiding dozens of dead bodies in my room.

"You are. You're looking at me like I ran over your pet cockatoo."

"I don't have a pet cockatoo."

"Yeah. Don't. They're a lot of work. Fallon had one."

Fallon. Her name on his lips sounded like a profanity.

"I just don't see why you'd even come here. You're upset about Will and Fallon's engagement. You should be dealing with it either by talking to them or with someone who can help you. I definitely can't."

He walked toward me, making me walk backward to avoid his touch. He wasn't slow or particularly predatory. Just...nonchalant. When my back hit the dresser behind me, I finally exhaled some of my rage. He just stood there and didn't say anything. Needless to say, that annoyed me.

"Say something," I growled. His eyes tapered into slits.

"You knew." He meant the engagement.

"I did," I admitted, without missing a heartbeat. "Blake said you'd go on a bender if you found out. My job is to keep you sober. You are a job, Alex," I reminded myself more than to him.

He pondered my words, rolling a lock of icy-blue hair between his fingers. Any trace of his sadness was gone from his face now, replaced with quiet, burning desire. One that runs deep and doesn't end in your lower stomach, but buzzes all the way down your toes, kissing every nerve in the process.

"That is cold," he said, his fingers sliding down my shoulder again—warm and rough and so callused—slipping the strap of my swing dress back down. "Especially for someone so warm. You really hate me, don't you?"

"I don't hate you." I swallowed. A truth for a truth. Would he give me one, too? "Do you care about me at all?"

"Yes," he admitted evenly without blinking, no trace of emotion on his voice. "I care about you."

"Then let me go. Let me work here and stop this...this..." What were we? What the hell were we? It felt like more than a fling but less than dating. "This thing between us. You're in love with someone else."

"No," he said, in the exact level tone, his body crowding mine further and further until the handles of the dresser dug into my lower back. Our limbs were entwined, but other than that, I had no excuse to the way my body reacted. Like it wanted to dance and fling itself off a cliff.

"Why?" I breathed.

"You need this. *We* need this. Today wasn't about Fallon. The engagement came as a surprise, sure, but it wasn't what made me lose my shit. My mates taking every ounce of power and freedom from me did." Pause. Beat. Swallow. "I accidentally broke Tania."

My stomach flipped, a shiver running down my spine. He killed Tania. His turtle's back. Tania inspired him, protected him, was there for him. My mouth fell open.

"How..."

"I went mental on Blake for leaking those dick photos. For hiding so much from me. I didn't even realize what I'd done. I just grabbed the first thing in reach and swung it his way. It hit the door. Remember this next sentence, Stardust, for it's important, and a rare fucking truth: I'm not upset about Fallon. Granted, I'm not happy about it either, but today wasn't about her. It was about my fucked-up life and my fucked-up mates and the fucked-up way I mixed business and pleasure like a rookie. I no longer know who's there for the money and who's there because they care. And it gets worse—if I could know, I'd still choose not to. Because it'd hurt like a bitch. The stupid, over-rated truth."

Something moved between us. Some kind of silent understanding. Alex was a liar because he hated his truth. But he was there, in front of me, his face so naked and raw, and at that moment, I didn't care that he'd break me just the way he had Tania.

We needed each other. Now. On this tour. Like air, and oxygen, and the pulse beneath our flesh. For once, I understood what he'd meant about being above gravity. There was a world outside, I knew it. But there was a smaller asteroid on which we lived, and that was the only place I wanted to be in that moment.

Silence.

Silence.

Silence.

Music.

It came from somewhere downstairs. A street party, I think. As soon as it started, our lips crashed together, and we wrestled each other out of our clothes. The soft thuds of fabric hitting the hard carpeted floors filled my ears even with the festive music on, and Alex hoisted me up to curl my legs around his waist, his signature move, and walked me around the room. He always opted for the Jacuzzi, the balcony, or while I was bent over the kitchen alcove. He liked it awkward and savage. The un-photoshopped version, as he'd called it.

Alex dumped me onto the cold sheets of the bed, and I arched my back, the sheer surprise of him wanting to do it in bed startling me. He dragged his teeth along my skin, and I wrapped his hair around my fingers, giving him better access to everything. When he kissed his path down my stomach, I started feeling the butterflies swirling around my belly, my sex tightening around nothing in anticipation. He was always so smug, like he had the world at his feet—and he really did. That was, perhaps, the entire irony of it all—but never when we were in bed together. When it was just us, his lips hovering over mine, his thick cock grinding into my body, he looked humble, and grateful, and pained.

His mouth found my sensitive bud, and he started playing with it as I let go, forgetting about my family and my heartbreak and the discarded plate of French fries that made the room smell funny. It was just me and him. Me, him, and the pleasure.

"I need to fuck you," he murmured, his voice vibrating and tickling my inside. "I need to be inside you the way you're inside me. So deep I want to peel my skin off just to get rid of you. I need to get rid of you," he repeated, and my heart dropped, my breath catching in my throat, as my clit began to throb, my lower lip shaking with an impending orgasm that had threatened to ripple through me like a storm. He loved to suck on my clit so hard my vision dotted with thick, white clouds.

"No." My voice quivered, my pelvis rocking into his mouth as he began to thrust his tongue into me over and over. He was relentless. Dirty and shameless. Like the way he spread his fingers under the back of my thighs and pushed me back and forth to make his tongue go deeper and deeper into me. Or the way he pressed his cock to my thigh until his zipper tore at my leggings from grinding me so roughly.

"I told you, I'm never going to sleep with you," I said under my breath.

But it was a lie, and we both knew that. There was no difference between sleeping with him and letting him eat me out every night. Finger me at public dinners and play with my nipples while he was talking on the phone with Jenna, yelling at her about some appearance he'd never agreed to do.

He chuckled into my warm flesh. "But I'll break you."

You already did. Today. I said nothing to that. My thighs began to shake uncontrollably and my mouth dropped into an O as I clutched tighter into his hair. I was sure it was painful for him, but he didn't complain. He never complained. For all the jackass things he did outside of the bedroom, once the clothes were off, he made me feel comfortable. Comfortable to scream, to moan, and to demand. Comfortable to hungrily suck on his shaft and wipe the drool with the back of my hand at how incredibly aroused he'd made me by simply looking at me the way he had. Like touching each other would take all our troubles away.

I came hard on his tongue. He flipped me over, and before I had the chance to protest, mounted me, burying his cock between my ass cheeks—completely bare—and sliding up and down.

"Oh, fuck," he said.

He loved doing things to me from behind. I think it was because he knew I could see everything on his face when we were together. The worry, and sadness, and fear. We weren't having sex, not technically, but boy, was it getting harder and harder to tell myself I had red lines with this guy. I needed to just give in to him already. Give in to *myself*. Ask him to put a condom on and have sex with me. But not putting out made me feel like I was in control, and I craved that no less than I craved his body.

His cock pulsated between my cheeks, and I felt the warm precum gathering at my tailbone. I didn't know why I found it so stupid hot to have him masturbate on me this way, but I quickly pushed against him, taunting him, prompting him to smash into me from behind. I didn't know what I was doing. Not fully. I was too delirious with lust and relieved at his reason for heartbreak. I shouldn't have taken pleasure in knowing he was devastated about Tania breaking, but at least it wasn't about Fallon.

"Why do you taunt me?" He fisted my hair and pulled me up, making me arch my back. Once my stomach rose from the mattress, he used his other hand to play with one of my tits, pinching my nipple on a hiss. "Why do you take so much pleasure in driving me mad?"

My skin prickled with goose bumps at his menacing tone.

"To get even." My voice was hoarse, suffocated by the position we were in, my neck fully extended as he rubbed himself harder and harder into my ass, his thrusts almost punishing—both to him and to me—for not being able to penetrate me. "Just returning the favor, Mr.

Rock Star."

"I think we're on a first-name basis now, *Stardust*." His dick started twitching along my skin, and I knew he was about to burst. His teeth dragged over my neck. "Seeing as next time we do this, I'm going to be so balls deep inside you, I'll be able to tickle your fucking lungs."

With that, he came on my back. I felt the ribbons of hot cum on my skin. He then collapsed on the bed, disconnecting from me like I was nothing but a container to put his sperm in. My face was still buried inside the pillow, which was for the best, with the way I blushed.

I lay there, in the same position, waiting for him to say something. To clean me up, seeing as I couldn't do it myself. Not unless I got into the shower.

I waited for many things, but a few minutes later, I heard the door open and shut, and knew he'd left me there, like the disposable fuck doll he'd wanted me to feel like.

Because when Alex was hurting, he wanted the entire world to hurt with him.

And in that moment in time, I was his world.

I should have felt disgusted by what he'd done. I should have wrapped myself up in a towel, stormed after him, and given him a piece of my mind.

But all I did was smile into the pillow like the stupid, lust-struck girl I was.

My Alex.

My little prince.

My fallen star in the dark, dark skies.

Chapter Twenty-One

Alex

E xcitement is like a contagious disease. It catches like fire, spreads, and there's nothing you can do about it. You can't tame excitement, or piss on someone else's parade when they're truly enthusiastic about something. Which was why I was extra bitter when the cab picked us up from Heathrow Airport and drove us through London, up to Watford.

Everybody was just so jolly about seeing their families.

Blake was staying with his parents down the road from me. Alfie was crashing at a mate's house in Kentish Town, and Lucas was going back to his perfect family in their perfect converted barn. Kent, not Watford. They'd moved somewhere with sheep and fresher air and inbred, posh neighbors when the eldest Rafferty graduated from university. All of Lucas' siblings were already married to horsey-looking partners with great jobs. I'd once told him his family put the "promise" in "compromise."

Maybe that's why he dedicates his life to ruining yours, arsehole.

I had two rooms booked at a London hotel, close to my family, but not too close that I actually had to see them. The rooms were for Indie and me, though I'd asked Hudson to cancel the extra room so she and I would finally sleep in the same bed. I wasn't even entirely sure what my feelings toward her were. I just knew she made some of the bullshit go away, and that was enough to pacify me.

I missed Tania.

I felt naked, moving around the world without her on my back. I'd purchased another acoustic guitar, but she didn't feel the same. She was rough—not soft-wooded like Tania—the strings too tight. She felt weird on my lap, like an average-looking fangirl begging to be fucked. Every time I tried playing it on the plane, Stardust shot me a look of pity, which made everything so much worse somehow.

If there was, indeed, one good thing about the entire Fallon and Will engagement ordeal, it was that now I had fewer restrictions. I wasn't talking to any of the lads—just to Indie, and not too much— but I could go on the Internet and watch whatever the hell I wanted. I knew Stardust had been privy to the engagement and the dick pics ordeal, but her betrayal wasn't as soul-crushing. She wasn't my childhood friend. She owed me nothing. In fact, she hadn't even asked to be employed by me, which made everything about the revelation that she knew less stinging.

"Ready to go home?" Blake sniffed, staring out the window at the gray London landscape.

I didn't answer. The constant drizzle reminded me why I loved my city. It was so unapologetically shitty. *Rainy with a chance of a very public meltdown.* People came here to survive, not to live. But surviving made you feel so much more alive.

"Would I be able to get a day off? I want to check the London Eye and the Dungeon. The House of Parliament, too," Indie muttered, her eyes glued to the window. I didn't know why it'd surprised me so much. Like I didn't expect her to make any plans other than riding my cock and my face. She always seemed like an open book, eager to be stained by ink in different colors. Everywhere we went, she always wanted to bike around the main streets and eat the local food. Other men might find it cute, her lust for life, but I just found it depressing. She was so much happier than I was, and I had so much more than her.

"I'm sure we can sort something out. Right, mate?" Blake elbowed me, his whole body angled toward me. He'd been working hard on being less of a micromanaging cunt since the loss of Tania.

I chose not to answer Blake—again—and flung my arm over Stardust's shoulder, eyeing Lucas, who was looking at me like I'd stabbed him in the soul.

"Sounds good. Let's go there together and make some memories," I gritted out.

Her head popped up, her skeptical gaze sliding along my face, my jaw, my eyes, my lips. An inventory she knew all too well, which was why pink spread over her cheeks and neck, cluing me in that she absolutely thought about all the things we could do while sightseeing. Grinding into her from behind in the London Eye in front of horrified Japanese tourists or cornering her in a dark spot at the London Dungeon sounded like paradise. Half the fun was watching her get flustered and annoyed with the way her body reacted to me in public.

"Whatever happened to you being sexually harassed by people? I thought you didn't do public appearances," she teased.

I shrugged. "I might have to punch a teenager or two. It'll be on your conscience."

Indie couldn't help herself. She shook her head and laughed. "You're so weird."

"Normal is grossly overrated," I muttered, hating that I cared if she thought it was good-weird or bad-weird.

And I didn't want to break her. Not at that moment.

It should have been an alarm bell, but I chose to ignore it.

By the time I figured out how to call it, it was too late.

If you ever wondered how Indie would look if she found out I killed every puppy on her street, let me tell you: I now knew.

All it took for her to make this expression was telling her she was going to share a room with me. She didn't like the idea. Not. One. Bit. Indie had only found out about our shared accommodation when we were actually in front of our presidential suite's door. She turned around, asking for her digital key.

"What key?" I asked with a straight face, prolonging our inevitable showdown.

She rubbed her open palm over her nose, which I thought was adorable—another clear warning sign I chose to ignore—and cocked her head sideways.

"The door to my room. What's up, Alex? You're not even jet-lagged."

I placed the card of our shared room in her hand and curled her fingers around it.

She said, "No."

To which I replied, "Did you know the world is suffering from overpopulation and vast waste of natural resources? We're going to save a lot of water and electricity sharing a room for a week."

"We'll be saving a lot of oxygen, too, because one of us ought to strangle the other." She walked over to the opposite door. She thought I was joking. Clearly, we needed to be doing more talking and a lot less fingering, because this woman didn't understand me. At all. I watched as Indie's smile evaporated gradually from her face each time she slid her key card into the slot and the red dot blinked back at her, spitting out the card. By the fourth attempt, she turned around, stomped her foot, and released a feral growl. "Alex."

For the record, I spared her my shit-eating grin when I leaned against our already-open door, arms crossed over my chest.

"Alex," she said again, her tone warning this time, indigo eyes begging me to put her out of her misery.

I didn't get it. The only difference between the entire tour and London was that she'd be spending the night next to me. Even that wasn't much of a big deal. I wasn't a spooner.

I crooked my finger and motioned for her to come in. She stayed rooted to the floor.

"Why?" she asked.

"Because we're going to write music together. And get drunk on words. And bone against the glass door. Because we make sense.

Because I'm tired of your fears. This is our tour. Our album. Our soul."

The thing about being a compulsive liar is at some point, you don't stop and think whether what you said is true or not. But at this point, I knew, we shared a soul. It was inside her, and I borrowed it. And I *needed* it. Losing Tania was a game-changer. I needed Stardust much more—maybe even after Paris—and I was beginning to accept that the way one accepted a deadly disease. With a healthy dose of disinclination.

She peeked behind my shoulder to the empty room, then back at me, her fingers clutching her duffel bag, knuckles bone-white.

"On one condition."

God, if you exist, please make her not ask for Louboutins or a Porsche.

"I'm listening."

"If we do this, I want you to see your family."

Now, here's the thing. Stardust and I had talked. A lot. About *The Little Prince* and about music and, yes, about our families. We talked like our life depended on it when we were writing every midnight. So she knew everything about my gambling mother and drunk father and slag of a sister. She knew I'd never been hugged as a wee boy and that I wrote about love in the same way people write about sci-fi: solely from my overworked imagination. Which prompted me to believe she thought my relationship with my family was salvageable. Look, I got it. She didn't have any parents. But living vicariously through me was not the way around it.

"No." I glued my forehead to the still-open door, acutely aware of the fact she was still in the hallway. What was it about us and hallways? Why were we always so reluctant to let the other person in? Note to self: write a song about it. Foyers. Relationships. Metaphors. Blue-haired girls.

"Well, then, you better get me a room." She spun on her heels, advancing toward the lifts.

I needed to let her go, and deep down, I knew it. But my soul couldn't, so I ended up grabbing her wrist and jerking her back to me.

"First of all, you don't know my family."

A hint of a triumphant smile decorated her lips when she looked up at me. "I know enough. I know you have one. You, Alex, have a family. Everyone needs a family."

"That's bullshit. Do you honestly *need* Craig? Need this wanker's drinking problem, hot and cold behavior, and stupid violent spurts?" I couldn't believe we were spending our time fighting instead of fucking. I also couldn't believe how similar Craig and I were. How could she be attracted to a guy who represented every vice that had made her life a quiet hell for the last few years?

She thought about it—actually thought about my question, not just spat out an answer—before answering.

"Yes, I need Craig. A big part of loving people and feeling loved is taking care of them, even when they infuriate you. You build confidence and security not only in being taken care of, but also by taking care of your loved ones. I want to help Craig. Hell, I want to *change* Craig. But that doesn't mean I don't need him. He's my brother."

It was my turn to think. Did I need Carly? No. Or, at least, I didn't think I needed her. She was never much good at anything, other than popping babies, and I wouldn't touch that department with a twenty-foot pole. I didn't need my parents, either. They clung onto my fortune like a skunk's scent, and I only ever spoke to them when I needed to, or the customary Christmas and birthday phone call. But I needed Indie, at least for this tour. I didn't have any illusions about her. She was a girl with small dreams and big problems and we had nothing in common. Nevertheless, she did make "Letters from the Dead" bearable, and I needed to keep her close until we finished the tour and I could give her what she wanted, even if what she wanted was to stab my soul until it bled the rest of its vitality. Because that's what me sitting in the same room with my parents and my sister, watching them drink canned lager and eating unrecognizable fried food from a newspaper funnel would do to me.

"Jesus Christ." I waved a dismissive hand her way. "I'll meet them, okay? Just get the fuck in here and stop loitering in the foyer. For all I know, they're going to sell the security footage to TMZ, and then I'll be the cock-exposing, washed-up druggie rock star who also has to beg his babysitter not to leave him home alone."

She took a step in my direction, her grin infuriating and cock-hardening in equal measures. "You're cute when you beg."

I hooked my finger into her barely existent cleavage and pulled her into me, planting a wet kiss on her smart mouth. "We'll see who's going to be doing all the begging tonight."

Chapter Twenty-Two

Indie

Jenna: I'm not keeping it.

Indie: Talk to Blake first.

Hudson: :-O :-O :-O

Jenna: Clearly, the hormones are taking over my brain. I forgot Hudson was here.

Hudson: My baby is having a baby!

Jenna: You're not my mother, Hudson.

Hudson: I was actually talking about Blake. His Hugh Grant charm makes my panties wet.

Hudson: Actually, it doesn't make any sense. But still.

Jenna: I swear, I'll kill you if you tell anyone. This is TOP SECRET. Indie, how's Alex?

Indie: Good.

Jenna: Elaborate.

Indie: He's been writing steadily, and he seems to be really excited about his next album.

Jenna: And the ten-minute song?

Hudson: He decided to split it into two songs.

Jenna: I didn't know he consults you artistically.

Hudson: He does. Sometimes. When he sits on the toilet and gets bored.

Hudson: Where do you think I got the nickname Little Shite? LOL.

Jenna: What made him change his mind?
Hudson: A girl.
Jenna: Elaborate.
Hudson: The right girl. ;)

I'm the first one to admit that, sometimes, you push things to the back of your head to protect yourself from heartbreak. Like the memory of losing your dog. Or like the time your first crush turned you down. Or that your brother is not completely sane and normal and *okay*.

Before I'd gone on tour with Alex Winslow, I'd thought talking to Nat and Craig would be the highlight of my day. Turned out it was the last thing I'd looked forward to. Every time my cracked phone rang, I half-wished it was my credit card company telling me to chill.

But it was always Nat, and she was always crying. This time, she'd caught me in a relatively good time. Alex was taking a shower, and I was sitting on the king-sized bed in front of the pale green wall, wondering if he knew how close we were getting to the deep end of feels. I should've told him no. Already, I was in over my head, and it wasn't just my body that wanted to be claimed. The minute I answered the phone, I realized Alex was the least of my worries. Craig was. Craig was always a worry.

"Hey, Nat."

"Why didn't you tell me about the shoebox above the cupboard before you left?" She sniffed tiredly. Her voice was different. Wary. Sad. She used to sound like sugar pops exploding in your mouth. Sweet and enthusiastic and open—so open—to hug the world and whatever it threw her way. It enraged me that my brother was the one to turn off the light inside her.

My eyebrows crinkled. I tried to remember what I'd put in that shoebox. I didn't have too many things of interest or value. Some stupid diary I'd written when I was a kid. Love letters from boys in elementary school, not that there were many. Some pictures...I squinted toward the curtained, wide window overlooking SoHo. Then it hit me. All at once.

The pictures.

Oh, God.

Of Mom holding our neighbor's baby, sweet and blond-curled like Ziggy.

Of Dad bouncing Craig on his lap, pointing to the camera, smiling.

Of both of them helping us build a faux snowman outside our house one Christmas, when it was so hot out the ice cream my mom brought us melted in our hands, and another photo from the same day where we all licked our sticky fingers and laughed.

Memories. Sweet, precious memories.

Memories I was so afraid I was going to forget, I'd had to put them somewhere safe. Somewhere that was only mine.

Memories I was so afraid to remember, I'd hidden them in a shoebox. On a cupboard. Somewhere I couldn't reach easily, because going there was toxic. I'd never have them back. They were gone.

"Tell me he didn't do anything stupid..." I said slowly, hysteria gripping my throat. Craig was not allowed to leave the house. I didn't even want to know what the consequences would be if he had.

"He did." She burst into tears, just as Alex walked out of the shower, wearing nothing but a towel and a smirk. His dark hair was dripping, just like it did in his gigs, and my lower belly tightened, despite the fact that my heart and mind were an ocean away, in America. He shot me a questioning glare, to which I replied by turning my back to him so he couldn't see me at my weakest. With my lip trembling and my nose aching like I'd been punched.

"Where?" I cleared my throat, shooting my gaze to the ceiling, steadying my voice. "Where did he go?" I repeated. "Do you know? And when did he leave?"

Nat was about to answer me when Alex snatched the cell phone from my hand and put it to his ear. He walked toward the master bathroom of the suite, and I jumped up immediately, stalking after him. The jerk was fast. It was those damn long legs. He could outrun me while crawling.

"Natasha, I want you to call my PA in Los Angeles. He'll help track him down." Alex jumped into the conversation like he'd been a part of it all along, which made my simmering blood chill a little in my veins. "Yeah, I'm sure. I've got private investigators to last for a decade in Hollywood and enough connections with the LAPD to take a shit directly on the booker's desk and still get out of there unharmed." He stopped by the bathroom door, his eyes unblinking. When I half-heartedly went for the phone, throwing my arms in the air to try to grab it, he plastered his palm over my forehead and pushed me away, making us look like a cartoon where the giant is blocking the little mouse, who is running aimlessly in the same spot. Even though we were physically comical, there was nothing funny about the way he made me feel. He wanted to help, and right now, I knew better than to refuse him. He owed me absolutely nothing. I'd betrayed him by not telling him about Fallon and Will and about the guys' plan with his leaked photos, and all he'd done so far was bail out, and now search, for my brother.

"Write it down," Alex ordered, giving her a cell phone number, then a code you needed to dial to put you through the line. Alex never gave his number out, and, normally, he didn't need to. Blake and the others were always around. It was weird to think it was just Alex and me now, and even weirder to imagine he'd be actively working for something. Something to do with me.

"Text me when he finds him," Alex added, pressing my phone between his shoulder and ear and lighting up a cigarette. He was commanding and forbidding, his expression so distant, you wouldn't think he was dealing with feelings. And this, perhaps, was the part of him that would be my ruin. He was kind without being kind to me. I parked my waist against the nearby closet facing the bathroom and watched him as he killed the line and tossed my phone across the room and onto the mattress. He swiveled, pointing his cancer stick at me.

"Get dressed."

I shook my head, watching him from under my lashes. "You can't go out. You're a superstar, remember?"

"I'm also a goddamn person. Two bodyguards are on their way here."

"Bodyguards?" My spine straightened on cue. "You hate bodyguards." I didn't even have to ask him to know that it was true. I saw the way he'd reacted every time one or two had had to tag along throughout the tour. Apparently, Alex Winslow was one of the rare celebrities who didn't have full-time bodyguards on their payroll. He just hated being babied. *And I was his babysitter.* The fact he was nice to me at all was a blessing. He sauntered past me, grabbed his skinny jeans, and black muscle T-shirt, throwing his leather jacket on top, already lacing his army boots.

"Hey, ho. Let's go."

"I didn't peg you for a Ramones fan," I said.

Alex was the greatest music snob of all time. Especially considering he'd sinned by making sweet, Ed-Sheeran, let-me-hold-you-in-my-arms music at some point in his career. The glint in his eyes told me I was right.

"I'm not. I'm a let's-go-fucking-eat fan."

One could argue Alex Winslow was one annoying, eccentric, arrogant man. But there was no disputing this weird mixture was enchanting.

Slowly—so very slowly—I made my way to the shower, the hot steam still clinging to the glass. He was really going to do it—get out of the hotel, knowing he was going to get noticed. Alex hated crowds. And people. And the paparazzi. The only humans he was okay with tolerating were his fans. I was worried this might prompt a breakdown, which would later lead to drug use.

I hesitated over the threshold, throwing him another look. "The paparazzi will probably see us."

"I know."

"And you don't care?"

"Giving fucks is not exactly my forte." He quirked a thick eyebrow, turning on the TV and making himself comfortable on the bed. "Chop, chop, now, Stardust. I turn into a pumpkin at midnight."

"It's noon, and you turn into an artist at midnight," I corrected, stepping out of my dress in front of him. Bare for him, I watched him as he watched me. Like he understood me. Like our intimacy was a living entity, sitting between us, its warm, ultraviolet rays caressing me softly.

"I'm always an artist. Sometimes, I'm an artist who gets screwed over by Suits," he amended, blowing smoke through his nostrils like a vicious dragon and smirking to the ceiling. "Now, go."

I had a quick shower, then proceeded to try on a dozen dresses. I knew we were not a couple. Of course I knew that. But I also knew the tabloids would be speculating, and I didn't want to be the mediocre-looking girl with the funky hair and cheap dress. I tied my locks into a loose chignon, tresses of arctic-blue waves slipping down my nape, and wore my classic, maroon velvet dress. Lipstick. Mascara. Mental pep talk. I was ready as one could be.

I stepped out of the bathroom.

Alex didn't react to me. Not at first. He was engrossed with something on his phone, and when he looked up, something on TV caught his attention. I stood there for a few long seconds, my heart vaulting behind my ribcage. For once, I wasn't the one talking to my heart, but it was the one talking to Alex.

See us.

Feel us.

Love us.

I was no longer able to quiet it down. My heart wanted Alex to love it. The rest of me did, too. And when his head whirled, almost in slow-motion, his mouth fell open, just an inch, his golden eyes twinkling with something I'd never seen there before. Or maybe I just wanted to see it, and it wasn't there after all.

"Midnight Blue," he whispered. "Illicit and elegant at the very same time."

I tucked a curl that had escaped from my chignon behind my ear and cleared my throat. "Let's go eat."

When we were walking down the hallway and toward the elevators, a thought occurred to me. It was so obvious, it made me want to laugh and cry all at once. Alex didn't want to go out. He didn't want to move around with bodyguards on his tail. And he definitely didn't want to board the rumor train and have people talking about us, especially after *that* picture in Greece, which Blake, of course, maintained was photoshopped every time he'd been asked about it.

"Thank you," I said while we were waiting for one of the elevators to ping.

He grunted, knowing exactly what I was talking about.

He was distracting me from thinking about Craig.

He was saving me from drowning in dark thoughts about my family.

He was no knight in shining armor, a far cry from a savior. He was just a broken, sad boy who was given a great gift that put him on display for the world to see and to judge.

And that boy saved me that day.

Again.

The good thing about walking with a Londoner in London was that you saw it through their eyes. Alex knew London like an old lover. Every curve and line and beauty spot. He was originally from a town on the outskirts of the English capital, but this was where he hung out. This was his domain. And he ruled it the way he did all things: mercilessly and methodically, like every inch of it was his.

First, we hopped into the underground train, to which he referred to as "the tube." The bodyguards, Harry and Hamish, were sitting a few seats away, pretending to read a local newspaper. Alex and I sat together, and maybe it was his beanie and shades, or maybe it was just how casually he'd acted, but no one took notice of us. Once we poured out of the train at Camden Town station and took the escalators up, we visited a little market where we inhaled two portions of vegan tacos, each. They were delicious and spicy, and we washed them down with chocolate milk we'd bought at a nearby convenient store. Then Alex showed me around. He said the market was going to turn into a massive mall soon, and that he was happy he wouldn't be there to see it happening, because it was the equivalent of tearing a piece of his heart and using it as an ass transplant for a Hollywood starlet. I laughed and asked him how his soul was these days.

"Good. And it will get even better once I break it to Jenna that I want to produce my own album. No more Suits." Our pinkies collided and curled around each other.

"No more Suits," I repeated.

We walked through the gray streets of Camden Town, past pubs that reeked of stale, warm beer and cigarettes. The scent of fried food constantly floated in waves, and it could have been a lot less pleasant if the air was not so fresh from the rain. We walked uphill until we reached the Cambridge Castle, a small pub with a two-floored apartment building above it.

"This is where I said I'd live if I ever made it big." He pointed at the apartments above the red banner of the pub.

"So how come you're not living there?"

He shot me a look I couldn't decode. A mixture of disappointment and annoyance. "I'm an idiot who lost sight of what's important. I really should be living there, shouldn't I?"

It looked kind of small, kind of old, and kind of stuffy. But it was a part of his dream, and when life gives you the tools to fulfill your dream, it's your duty to do so.

"Definitely." I nodded.

Alex took my hand in his and jerked his chin to the chipped, wooden door. "Drink?"

"Virgin," I warned.

"I'll rectify it later."

We had cranberry juice and chips—see: "crisps"—at a secluded table. It was just us and the bartender, who was new, and even though he couldn't remember Alex's golden years at the venue, he still asked for an autograph and five selfies.

Afterward, we took the tube to London Bridge and visited the London Dungeon. It was really scary, and I found myself jumping several times and clutching Alex's leather-clad arm. We were walking around with a group of tourists from Eastern Europe who didn't speak a word of English, which worked in our favor.

Though they asked for autographs and selfies, too.

We decided to head back to the hotel at six o'clock. We took a black cab, watching the streets of the capital flashing by. London was gorgeous and cruel, just like Alex. Too busy. Too hectic. Too brooding. Too dark. Yet I couldn't help but drink her in like I did Alex. Like I'd finally found the one thing I hadn't known I was missing.

Alex took off his beanie for the first time since we'd left the hotel room, and his wavy, shaggy hair was sticking out to one side, which was so adorable I needed to look away to protect my heart.

"I love your London," I blurted out to the window. "I love that people shoulder past me and avoid eye contact and have a no-bullshit attitude. I love that no one looks the same. I love that it's rich, but grim. Poor, but classically beautiful. It inspires me."

"I hate your Los Angeles," he replied. "I hate how it doesn't suit you. I hate how it's flat and sparse and shallow. The agreeable weather and the big-teethed people. You deserve better, Stardust. You deserve to be inspired. All the time."

"Maybe," I said. I wasn't unhappy. But I wasn't happy, either. I just didn't know if Los Angeles was to blame, or the general chaos that was my life. "Maybe when it's all over I'll travel from planet to planet, city to city, to find what I'm looking for."

"You should know, though"—Alex's voice sounded sad and far, like he was already drifting away from me—"Craig is your rose. He will root you in place and never let you go. I've had these kinds of roses back at home. You don't have to put up with Craig's shit in order to still be there for Ziggy and Natasha. You need to tell him to get better, or he never will."

Turning around to look at him, I put a hand on his cheek. "Are you happy, Alex?"

"I'm an artist. My job is not to be happy. My job is to feel, to suffer, and to conjure the same feelings in others."

I wanted to tell him he was wrong. That he could create greatness whilst holding onto his bliss. But I didn't know if it was true, and I knew better than to hand out empty promises, like the ones my brother gave me.

I said nothing, even when Alex slipped his hand into mine and laced our fingers together.

My heart was loud enough to hear, even in the midst of London traffic.

And it spoke all the words I couldn't give him.

Chapter Twenty-Three

Indie

The most important dance you'll have in your life is one that does not require music.
Alex Winslow, Broken Hearts Blvd

That night, he practiced what he preached. Each movement was an impulse, an instinct, a compulsion. We didn't need to practice that dance. It was a necessity, like breathing. As real as something could feel.

We got into our suite silently. I walked backward as he cornered me toward the bed. Pressure was building inside me, and I knew he was the only one who'd be able to unknot it into an orgasm. His hard breaths came down on me as he peeled his jacket off and rolled the zipper of my dress down all the way to my tailbone, where he stopped, pressing a teasing finger to the slit between my ass cheeks until he pushed me toward him, my stomach meeting his throbbing erection. His skin burned with an animalistic need, and I touched him everywhere to make sure he was real. He felt so alive under my fingertips. So terribly human, despite his god-like status. The pressure between my legs became agonizing before my panties dropped to the floor. I don't remember how we got naked. I just remember how it felt a second before he laid me on the bed.

Final.

It felt so final.

Like there was no going back from this. Without words, without a warning, and without a condom, he hovered over me, his dick poking at my belly. He put his hot lips on my neck and sucked on it with a private smile I could feel, and I stared at the ceiling, my pulse rioting all over my body. It was like my heart was working on overdrive, desperately pumping blood into the rest of me, trying to match how alive Alex was in that moment. He positioned himself between my thighs, his tongue swirling over my throat, driving me mad. I clawed at his back like he was already inside me. In a way, he was.

"Condom." My voice was barely audible; I had to repeat the word to make sure he heard me. "We need a condom."

He leaned back and stared at me, flushed. His chest was moving up and down, and I wanted to believe it wasn't like this for him with all one-night stands. There was no way Alex Winslow responded like this to every girl he rolled between his sheets. Like I was the very asteroid where he wanted to live on. Forever.

"I'll finish out."

"Alex, what the hell?"

"I just really need to feel you."

"You will. Through a condom."

"No. All of you."

"You can't have all of me." But even I knew that was a lie.

I wondered if he really expected me to agree to go bareback our first time while he picked up his jeans from the floor and sorted through the pockets until he found his wallet. There was one condom there—just the one—and the wrapper looked crumpled and old. My heart cartwheeled happily at that. I watched as he sheathed himself, his eyes focused on the condom he rolled over his shaft—upper teeth biting his lower lip—before he returned his gaze to me. His cock pressed onto my lower belly.

"Stardust," he breathed, shaking his head slightly. "Stardust, Stardust, Stardust."

Then he thrust into me all at once. I whimpered, threading my fingers in his hair and bringing him down, his forehead pressing into mine. I chattered, "Alex."

He thrust. Again. Then again. His movements were rough and callused. Every time he drove into me, his hips ground on mine painfully, like he wanted me to feel how he felt, trapped inside his body, inside his thoughts. I had no illusions about Alex's nature. He was an addict and a tortured soul, and he wasn't going to stick around. But this felt like everything I didn't know I could wish for. This made me settle for 'For Now' instead of 'Forever.'

"Christ," he muttered, his lips on mine, then on my chin, my ear, back up on my cheek. We were a heap of flesh and limbs. I felt him rattling something inside me, and my womb clenched every time he pushed into me. He grabbed one of my legs and hoisted it over his shoulder, sliding even deeper than before, and I cried out so loud, I was sure every resident in the hotel could hear me.

"It's so intense." I sucked in a breath, but that only made him go even harder. He knew what I needed—we always knew what the other needed. That was the tragic thing about us. We were compatible in so many ways—and used ourselves as weapons against each other.

"I'm going to come." My body was quivering from the inside. Goose bumps crawled over my skin as tiny, steady hot waves of pleasure began to wash through me, head to toe. "I'm coming…"

I threw my head back and shuddered in his arms, feeling like a lit match.

"Fuck, if we don't change position, I'll come, too," he growled, flipping me over on my knees and driving into me again.

"Ohhhh…" My mouth dropped open in pleasure.

Alex snaked his arm around my waist and started playing with my clit, nibbling on my earlobe. I knew he was going to say something. He took special pleasure in talking into my ear like that when I couldn't see him. *When I was at his mercy.*

"Come for me again, Stardust," he said, fucking me mercilessly, and tears pooled in my eyes. It felt so intimate and promising. And he knew how I'd felt about empty promises. "Come all over my cock like the good, bad girl that you are."

I came again, falling to the mattress with a thud as he continued driving into me and playing with me at the same time, the overstimulation making me twitch now.

"Fuck, fuck, fuck." He drove into me once more, jerking inside me and slapping my ass at the same time as he collapsed over me, his entire weight on my back.

He stayed inside me, little grunts of pleasure escaping his lips, his chest plastered over my back. I wanted to turn around and look at him, but I couldn't move.

"I should start asking you for rent money if you decide to stay on top of me any longer. You're not light, Alex," I grunted softly.

He laughed and slapped my ass playfully again, rolling on the bed, pulling out of me gently.

"You should. I'd pay good money to stay in this position." He went for the pack of cigarettes on the nightstand, but I put my hand on his arm, stopping him. Our eyes locked.

"We're sharing a room now. I wanted to tell you earlier, when you lit one up, but I was too busy with the Craig thing. You can smoke on the patio. Not here."

"Is this a joke?" he said, looking incredulous. It didn't matter that he paid for the room. I was the one who was going to need to pay for the medical bills when I got cancer from all the secondhand smoke.

"I'd like to believe my sense of humor is better than that," I replied.

He stood up, still butt naked, and walked to the balcony with his pack of cigarettes. His dong was swinging from side to side, and it would look ridiculous and embarrassing on anyone else, but not on a rock star. No. Alex looked perfectly confident and horrendously cool.

"Wear something!" I called out from the bed, wrapping my chest in a white sheet.

He whirled and walked backward, smoothly opening the giant glass door as he flashed me a wolfish grin, canine teeth galore.

"Why, I'm wearing the most beautiful thing one could wear, darlin'. My smile."

Alex

The problem with the world is when you're having fun, days seem to stick together into lumps, but when you're miserable and alone, every day is a year, an island, a padded room you cannot get away from.

Three days had passed since I'd gotten into Indigo Bellamy's panties. Three days in which I'd made it a point to drive into her in every position, angle, and location in Greater London.

We shagged in the Jacuzzi—twice—taking a shower—three times—in bed—four times—and in a black cab—one time—and I'd had to stuff her face with a Mind The Gap shirt while she was sitting on top of me wearing a long dress. We went sightseeing. We visited my old Clapham neighborhood, and other times we just stayed in our room, fucking or watching reruns of *The Mighty Bush* and *Never Mind the Buzzcocks*—both of which she thoroughly enjoyed. Fallon always thought my favorite shows were stupid.

Though, to be completely honest, Fallon was the least of my worries in London. For the first time in years, I actually enjoyed myself. I even answered Blake's calls, though I did keep it professional and curt. Alfie dropped by our hotel room one day and brought Afghan food, which we all ate on the floor, watching *Shaun of the Dead*. I couldn't be mad at the tosser. He literally had the social awareness of a chapstick.

Then, on the fourth day, Indie nudged me. "Your parents. We need to go visit them."

Right.

I didn't know what bothered me more. The way she'd included herself in the plan to go and see them—*why wouldn't she, you wanker? She's your babysitter. It's strictly business*—or the fact she would actually meet my train wreck of a family. I rang my mum up while Indie was in the shower that morning, and, of course, she was delighted with the news.

"I saw you were in the UK in them tabloids, luv. Was wondering whether you were going to ring us or not. I'm glad you did." She snapped her gum in my ear.

I didn't dwell on the fact *she* hadn't bothered to call *me*, even though she'd known I was there. As long as I threw money my family's way every now and again and stayed out of their way, they were all right with my existence. I exhaled loudly and tossed myself on the bed, staring at the chandelier.

"I'm not coming there alone," I warned. My way of telling her she needed to behave for a change. My parents cheated on each other all the time. It was such an ordinary thing, cheating might not be the word I was looking for. I could count at least six times in which Mum and Dad aired their dirty laundry—literally—in front of the entire neighborhood, on the street. They lived in a semi-detached on a busy Watford road where everybody knew everybody. They loved yelling at each other at the top of their lungs with people gathering at their windowsills and doors, peeking through curtains. If you ever wondered who those people who go on Ricki Lake, Jerry Springer, and Jeremy Kyle are—they were my parents. That's who. The worst part was they'd cheated on each other with local folks, too, so it was all a big, hot mess of middle-aged people who looked like they'd missed every single dentist appointment ever booked for them.

"Is that the lady friend we've been seeing in the papers?" Mum asked, half-laughing like a hyena. What was so funny? Maybe the fact Indie was the exact opposite of Fallon. Tall, curvy, blond Fallon, who looked like a carbon copy of every Victoria's Secret model from the last five years. Indie had blue hair and funny dresses and enough personality in her scrawny figure to stuff a hundred Fallons.

"Yeah," I ground out, narrowing my eyes, "that's the one."

"A bit of a funny thing, ain't she?" I could practically *hear* my mum filing her pink acrylic nails while she popped her gum, once again.

And this, ladies and gents, was why I chose narcotics over people.

"I expect you to behave when she's there," I warned, my voice dripping ice.

"Stop talking like you're the parent here," she cried, adding as an afterthought, "I should ask Carly and the wee ones to come on over."

I loved my sister's kids. They reminded me of myself with George. They were incredibly smart and perceptive. Dwayne was a little terror, but he had good rhythm and could probably be a great guitarist if he ever got a guitar—he would, I promised myself. And I wouldn't let him read a book five hundred times before I gave it to him. Chayse was sweet and sensitive, kind of like how I would have been had my parents not dented me so thoroughly. Bentley was a proper comedian, even at the tender age of eight. The only part I didn't like about this idea was seeing their mother and my sister, Carly.

"Yeah," I said, anyway, watching Indie walk out of the shower wrapped in a towel only, my lazy gaze following her every movement. "Sure, it'd be great to see her. I'm calling a cab now, so…" *Clean up the piglet.* "Get ready, aight?"

"Aight." Mum laughed, then hung up.

"You ready?" Indie smiled at me.

"Never."

I didn't know why she'd laughed. It wasn't supposed to be funny.

Chapter Twenty-Four

Indie

Jenna: Indie. What do you want to be when you grow up?
Indie: Thrift-shop owner.
Indie: Why?
Jenna: No reason.
Hudson: Aww, Indie. That's...random. LOL. Jenna, how's the baby?
Jenna: Shut up, Hudson.
Indie: Have you talked to Blake yet?
Jenna: No. But he suspects something is up.
Hudson: Why?
Jenna: Because I can't help but be nice to him. Because I cried the other day when we talked on the phone and he was online shopping for his niece's birthday.
Indie: So what's the problem? He's obviously into you.
Jenna: He's also obviously eleven years younger than me.
Indie: Tell him. I feel bad not telling Alex.
Hudson: As you should. He's crazy about you.
Jenna: ???
Indie: ???????
Hudson: Yes. Every time he talks about you, he doesn't even sneer. It's weird. Last time he spoke that way about something, it was about Jack White's Acoustic Recordings album.

Indie: Does he talk about me a lot?
Hudson: A gentleman never tells.
Jenna: What about you, Hudson? Are you dating someone?
Hudson: Only my left hand and a Neil Patrick Harris poster.
Jenna: Sad.
Hudson: Less complicated than your situation, girl.
Indie: What did you want to be when you grew up when you were a kid, Jenna?
Jenna: An astronaut.

The black cab stopped in front of the red door.

Hamish and Harry nodded us a somber goodbye from the front seats. Alex figured he didn't need an entourage, seeing as he was just visiting his family. On our way to Watford, in the cab, we'd negotiated the time and length of the visit.

"Three hours, Stardust. A minute more and I'm dragging you by the hair." He looked out of the window, tapping his foot on the floor, his black Wayfarers giving him an extra layer of asshole.

"I think you'd very much like dragging me by the hair," I remarked, flipping a fashion magazine. It was amazing how small things brought so much color into my life. I would've never bought a *Vogue* magazine in Los Angeles. But now I had some pocket money. Also, Blake was very good at shoving his business credit card at the cashier every time I tried to pay for my stuff at airport kiosks.

"Of course, but I wasn't planning on doing it until after dinner," he said. I laughed. He was so wrong in thinking he wasn't lovable. Alex was lovable to a fault.

The Winslows' front yard was neglected, with bald patches and beer cans peppered throughout the thin grass. We sat in the cab for a few seconds before Alex pushed the door open. I followed him out, and we both made our way, burrowing into our coats. The house looked depressing. Everything was either peeling or torn. I spared him from that observation. I didn't live in a mansion, either.

"I love the little church across the road." I jerked my thumb behind my shoulder. Anything to make him feel slightly more at ease. He squinted at it, his gorgeous face twitching. *This man was inside me,* the thought, creepy as it sounded, made my heart warm, *and I think a part of me is inside him, too.*

"That's where Father John touched me." His lips flattened into a scowl. My eyes widened at his admission, before he rolled his eyes and pinched my ass.

"You should've seen your face."

"I want to *punch* your face."

"Let's settle for you sitting on my face. Tonight. Now come on, let's get it over with."

Alex's parents, Louisa and Jim, both looked like older, bloated versions of him. His father was pasty white with a pink nose of someone who always had a bottle of something strong in his hand, but also had the same sharp, cut lines. Strong jaw and square chin. His mother's body was wrinkly, tan, and plump, but her tawny eyes were bright, mischievous, and compelling.

The house was clattered with stuff—useless stuff, stuff you order from the shopping channel. Carly, his sister, had highlights in her chestnut hair and wore bubblegum lipstick and matching sweatpants, and her kids, all between the ages of four and nine, looked so different from each other, I found it easy to remember their names.

We sat at the dining room table and ate industrial mashed potatoes and a roast. Louisa had microwaved the entire meal, coughing into it in the process of serving it to us. They cracked open a few cans of beers, which made me want to cry for Alex. Every time someone took a sip I balled my fists and tried breathing through the pain.

"So...*Indigo.*" His dad rolled my name like it was a bad joke.

I locked my spine, raising my chin high. I would not be ridiculed about my name. I didn't choose it, and, frankly, would never change it. It was one of the most important pieces of memory I had from my parents. Bonus points: blue really was a fantastic color. Especially when it was dark and bottomless. Like my name. Like their son.

"Mixing business and pleasure, aye? Our lad here sure knows how to lure a girl into his clutches." His dad chuckled, spraying bits of mashed potatoes from his mouth as he elbowed Alex, who sat next to him, right across from me. Alex's eyes narrowed, his angry tick, and he pushed his dad away with his own elbow.

"Let it go," he hissed, his tone so low and cold, chills rolled down my back.

"Oh, come on, he's just having a laugh," Louisa chimed in, piling another bulk of mashed potatoes onto Alex's plate. "So, how are things going? How are the lads? Alfie's doing well for himself. Funny, innit? He was the one who could never get shagged to save his life."

"That's a great observation to be making in front of the kids," Alex said flatly.

"Sex is natural," his mom retorted.

"Talking about it over family dinner—not so much." Alex looked kind of pale.

Silence. I coughed, wishing someone would say something, anything.

"At least Alfie posts pictures on Instagram so we can keep up with him," Carly huffed, breaking up a food fight between Bentley and Chayse as she spoke. Bentley sprung from his seat and ran for the living room, shouting obscenities. Alex's dad burped loudly, and if I wasn't mistaken, also deliberately. I was beginning to feel guilty for asking Alex to come here. It was pretty presumptuous of me to assume I knew something he didn't. He didn't feel comfortable here. And I could see why. I stretched my leg under the table, lacing it with his. It soothed him a little, I think, because his broad shoulders eased, but he still looked like he could spit fire at any moment and burn down the entire house.

"The lads are fine," Alex bit out, dragging his fork along the plate and producing an unnerving sound, his eyes dead on the stale mashed potatoes.

"And Fallon? She called to wish me a happy birthday two weeks ago. *And* she talked to me for more than the obligatory five minutes." His mother gave him a pointed look of her own, and that was my cue to dissolve into a cloud of humiliation and sail away from the table.

I shifted in my seat, my shoulder accidentally brushing hers.

"You talk to her more than I do. Ask her yourself," Alex mumbled, running a finger smack in the middle of his plate, separating the mashed potatoes and gravy from the roast. "Scratch that—I don't talk to Fallon anymore. At all."

"You don't?" Carly chipped in.

I was being ghosted, live from his kitchen. This plan had really backfired in my face.

"Yeah, we stopped communicating sometime after she fucked one of my best friends and sold the engagement ring I bought for her to fund a new pair of tits."

"Alex, the kids!" Carly moaned.

"What?" He smirked, cocking his head sideways. "Thought you said sex is natural. And enough about Fallon."

"But surely you'll bump into her in Paris. I'd love to see you together again. You made a gorgeous couple," his mother persisted, a sinister smirk decorating her face. It reminded me of Alex's smile when he bullied people, only her jab was directed at...me. By the look on Alex's face, he did not appreciate being on the receiving end of mistreatment.

"Hey, Mum, don't you have a juicy piece of gossip to share with us that doesn't have to do with my life? My life is, after all, boring. So boring, in fact, that save for the time you needed money two months ago, you haven't rung me once since I got out of rehab. Now, come on. I'm sure you can do really well. Tell us something good. Have you been messing around with a new lowlife from Ladbrokes? Found Dad with a new bird in bed? The possibilities are endless. Oh, I know! Maybe Carly is pregnant again. That'd be fun, right?"

The whole table quieted down, all eyes on Alex. He stood up coolly, collected his plate, and dumped it into the kitchen sink on his way upstairs. I stood up and excused myself, ready to follow him up, when my phone buzzed in my purse. I took it out. If it was about Craig, I didn't want to miss it. I didn't want Alex to think I wasn't there for him, but Craig's situation was urgent.

"I'll take this outside." I waved the hand that held the phone and jogged to the front door. When I pressed the phone to my ear, my lungs released a strangled breath of worry.

"He's here, and he's okay." Nat sniffed, sounding all teary.

I rubbed my face, walking back and forth in the narrow trail leading to the Winslows' front door. "Who found him?"

"Hudson. He just brought him back. Your brother's been drinking again, but, thankfully, he wasn't harmful or violent in any way. His probation officer is on his way, but I'm sure we'll be able to smooth things over. Hudson called the nice lawyer who helped us the other time, so I think—"

"Put Craig on the phone," I cut her off. Maybe it was being bullied by Alex's family, but I was in the mood for confrontation. For years, I'd felt sorry and apologetic for Craig. For his lost opportunities and shattered dreams. Well, I no longer did. I felt sorry for his doting wife, for his beautiful, healthy kid, and for his sister. *Me.*

"Indie…"

"Put. Him. On. The. Phone," I enunciated every word, like Alex did when he wanted people to feel like idiots. Which he did. Often.

A few seconds later, the labored breaths of someone who had a lot of adrenaline—and alcohol—in his veins sounded from the other line, and I took a shaky breath to slow down my pulse.

"Craig Bellamy, you're an asshole," I said. When he didn't answer, I continued. "You've been given so many opportunities throughout my short yet stressful trip across the world, and you blew every single one of them. It's fine. You don't owe me anything. You really don't. But that wife of yours? You owe her the world. She didn't sign up for this when she married you. Your son? He deserves so much more. He is worthy of a loving dad who is there for him, who takes care of him, who teaches him stuff, and takes him places and reads him books. He deserves what you had. And you're not giving it to him. I'm so mad at you." I realized two things as the last words fell out of my mouth. The first one was that I was full-blown crying, and that was new. I didn't usually cry. I was more of a holding-it-in-until-I-burst type of girl. The second thing I noticed was that I wasn't alone. There was a man, wearing a black coat and a ball cap, standing on the corner of the street, lurking. He was talking on his phone and holding something in his hand. I glared, making sure he knew that I knew *I* was being watched.

"Since when are you in charge, Indie? Hanging out with your famous friends has gone to your head. Don't think I haven't seen how he's parading you around like some kind of consolation prize from his *real* fiancée. You're delusional if you think that…"

I didn't bother to listen to the rest of Craig's rant. I dumped my phone into my purse and took a few steps forward, leaning against the broken gate of the Winslow household, watching as three more men dressed in the same attire snuck into the neighborhood. They were multiplying by the minute, more and more of them flocking near the park and the church across the street.

The paparazzi.

My stomach coiled into knots and the need to storm down the street and give them a piece of my mind slammed into me so hard, I nearly toppled over. And I would. I so freaking would. Because Alex didn't need this right now. At the same time, I knew that confronting them was a PR nightmare waiting to explode. If I confronted them, they'd just record the whole thing and upload it to every media outlet out there. And that would result in more of a mess in the already chaotic world of Alex Winslow. I curled my fists beside my body, took a deep breath, turned around, and walked through the door. Alex's family was still in the kitchen. His parents were fighting loudly while Carly barked at the kids. I climbed upstairs, into the narrow hallway with the stained carpet and yellow wallpaper, drawn to Alex's room like a magnet. The door was ajar. I leaned against its frame, watching him sitting on the edge of his childhood bed.

His room was small, square, and clean. A single bed—too short and too narrow for his out-of-this-world frame, was pushed against one of the walls. There was a Morrissey poster above his pillow, a Cure poster right next to his old-school computer monitor and cheap desk, and the guitar stand I assumed belonged to his late Tania, naked and empty of his favorite thing in the world. He rubbed the back of his neck, looking up at me.

"Happy now?"

My heart shriveled in pain, especially as the next words left my mouth. "Don't look out the window."

He walked over to the small window, ignoring my plea and scanning the neighborhood through dead eyes. "Oh, fuck."

I couldn't summarize the situation better. "I don't know how they found out."

He turned to me. "I do. My parents are going to get a nice check from this little stunt."

Everything that happened from that point forward was so quick, so fast, I could hardly catch my breath. Alex stormed down the stairs two at a time, while I followed, calling after him to *stop* and *think* and *don't react*. Which was very rich, considering I'd never been so deeply betrayed by my own family members, even when Craig was being unbearable.

"You cunt," Alex growled, invading the small, crowded kitchen and pinning his father to one of the walls, his hand grabbing his dad's neck firmly. The kids shrieked and, without thinking about it clearly, I gathered their hands and ushered them out of the kitchen.

"Here. Play with this." I dumped the entire contents of my purse on the coffee table. My money, cell phone, snacks, everything, splayed before them, and I watched them tearing out the five and ten quid notes from my wallet, shouting through the roof. I hurried back to the kitchen, where Alex stood over his dad, hissing at him like he was about to kill him.

"You piece of shit! You sold me out! Again!"

"That was all on your mother, son. She wants new tits for

Christmas. Kind of like Fallon. Mummy issues, much?" His father cackled, as if the entire thing was a joke Alex should be taking more lightly.

Louisa tried to break them apart without really putting much effort into it, careful not to get her pink nails broken in the process. "Calm down now. Just give them what they want and they'll go away, Alex. A few kisses to the camera with the missus. Just like in *Notting Hill*."

"Where did you get the idea that my life is a fucking rom-com? Who the fuck let you take me home when you gave birth to my sorry arse? Bloody hell." Alex released his dad from his grip, running his big palms through his hair.

"Don't talk to your mother like that," Jim said.

"You talk to her a lot worse," Alex deadpanned.

"Well, I'm her husband. I'm allowed to."

Alex paused, stared at him like he was the very cause for the Ebola phenomenon, and sneered. "You're a pig."

"And you're no different. Only thing is, you're a pig with money, so you get better pussy, really."

Alex's fist connected with Jim's nose immediately, and I jumped in to pull him away. I grabbed onto his arm just as he was swinging for a second punch, and he must've had a hell of a lot of momentum, because his elbow collided with my eye. The sharp pain made me stumble back, and I fell flat on my butt once my back hit the wall. My hands immediately went to my left eye, and I winced. Damn, that hurt. I could feel my tears running freely now—not from emotion, but from the sting. Everything around me blurred, but I still caught Alex squatting by my side, his hand on my shoulder.

"Shit. Fuck. Are you all right?"

"Hmm." I nodded, even though I really didn't know that for sure. "I'm good."

"Let me have a look."

"Oh, it's okay."

"It's not, Indie." He peeled my fingers off my eye, his own eyes flaring when he caught a glimpse of me. Not magazine material, I gathered from the look on his face.

"Black eye," he muttered.

"Really? Already?" I asked, feeling more deflated than angry. My eye felt numb now. But it still stung. Like my eyelashes had curled backward into my eyeball.

"I'll get her some ice," Louisa said.

"Sorry, luv," Jim offered.

"I fucking hate both of you," Alex seethed, grabbing a bag of frozen French fries his mother handed him and pressing it against my eye. "It's gonna hurt like a bitch, but you need this right now."

Same could be said about you.

I nodded, feeling the bite against my skin intensify with every second the cold bag was on my heated flesh. Alex took out his phone and demanded Siri *call Blake*.

"I need a cab back to the hotel from my parents' house. Now."

There was a pause before he said, "A hundred? You're fucking joking."

By the look Alex shot behind his shoulder to his shrugging parents, I knew Blake wasn't joking. A hundred photographers waited outside. His parents must've told the entire world and its nephew that Alex was coming over. Carly was sitting down at the table, staring at her hands. I wondered what part she'd taken in all this. Not once had she tried to interfere with the confrontation between Alex and his parents. My gaze wandered back to Alex, who frowned and stared at me with a mixture of exasperation and wonder.

"Well, the only way I'm spending the night in Jim and Louisa's place is in a fucking body bag. So sort something out."

Jim and Louisa. He didn't even call them Mom and Dad anymore. Man, I felt shitty for pushing him into this whole thing. I shook my head, placing my hand on his arm. He immediately relaxed under my touch. Like he'd been waiting for some confirmation that he wasn't a complete monster for giving me a black eye. Which he wasn't. He had no idea I was behind him.

"If we need to stay, we'll stay." I gave him a weak smile. Ouch. That hurt the entire area under my eye.

"We never thought it'd be that big of a deal," Carly finally murmured from her place at the table, still staring hard at her hands. "You always deal with them. We thought it would be just another day at the office for you."

Blake was saying something on the other line, and Alex sighed and hung up, dropping his forehead in defeat.

"Is that okay?" His hand cupped my knee, his thumb brushing over it in lazy circles. I didn't know if he meant his touching me or staying the night at his parents' house to make sure the coast was clear and prevent them from seeing my black eye. "Sure."

"Harry and Hamish should be at the front door at six a.m. to pick us up. The paparazzi will clear up by then."

That made sense.

Louisa opened her mouth again, about to say something, but Alex shut her up, jerking me upward to stand in front of him.

"Spare me the excuses, Louisa. This is the last time you fuck me over."

Chapter Twenty-Five

Alex

Uncomfortably close, intolerably far away.

That's how I felt about staying at my parents' house. Stardust and I would sleep in my old room. I didn't believe in sentimental shit. Not usually. I was too hardened by life, circumstances, and the very people I shared a roof with. But there was no point pretending it wasn't a little monumental. To have a girl in my room. A girl whom I'd given a black eye to—by accident, sure, but fuck it, it looked so bad, more so since it was tainting her beautiful, olive skin—a girl who was willing to sleep at a strangers' house for me, without batting an eyelash.

When Indie went to take a shower, I was still watching the paparazzi swarming under my window. One raised his head and spotted me, and I flipped him the finger. He immediately raised his camera and took a slew of pictures of me, his mates following suit. I shut the holey, twenty-year-old curtain before they got any good shots. Stardust walked in with a towel wrapped around her body. Her hair was wet, clustered into little snakes, dripping water onto the beige carpet. She wiped her chin with the hem of the towel and stared at me, her bottomless blues not dimmed, even by the black eye I'd given her.

"Hey, you." She attempted a smile.

I hated that she was the perfect combination between sweet and tough, because it made letting her go less easy. And letting her go was not fucking optional. I had Fallon to recollect—to punish her for what she'd done—plus, even if Fallon hadn't been in the picture, Stardust was simply too good. Once we went back to the real world—where days and the weather and family mattered, the world outside this tour—it'd be very easy for her to walk away. And walk away she would, because I was a fuck-up, an addict, and I'd screwed up everything with her before it even started.

I'd given her a black eye, for fuck's sake.

Instead of answering her with words, I walked over to her—towering over her tininess and liking *us* even more for it—and shut the door behind her back. She looked up; I looked down. I laced our fingers together; she didn't resist. I'd fucked Stardust many times, in many places. I'd fucked her hard, and then rough, and then lazily, all while shoving my fingers in places that made her eyes widen. But when the towel fell off and pooled at her feet, her freckled, tan skin and toned body bared in front of me, I didn't want to destroy her like I had all those times in London.

My hands on her neck. *Gentle.*

She flinched at the memory of how I'd held my dad, but melted when I put my lips to her forehead and backed her to the single bed.

"We'll need to spoon, you know." She grinned, catching my lower lip between her fat, juicy ones and sucking. "Bed's too small."

"I don't do spooning. We'll be forking instead."

"What's forking?" Her hoarse giggle poured into my mouth, skating right into my dick, making it salute between her thighs.

"It's porking, but with an F that stands for fuc—"

"Crude alert!" She shut me up with a kiss that was far dirtier than my words.

We tumbled into the bed, and I let her strip me, slowly, the way she'd always wanted to strip me a minute before I kicked my shoes and tore my clothes so I could drive into her like a sledgehammer. She lay down on my childhood bed, and I hovered over her. A demon, destructive and undeserving. Yet still there, despite everything.

"We need to keep it quiet. Your parents might hear us," she whispered.

I pinned her arms above her head and buried my face in her luscious hair. "I don't give a fuck about my parents."

"Well, I do."

She did. She gave a fuck about everyone. Every Tom, Harry, and Louisa. And I needed to start respecting that, even if I didn't respect *them*.

I grinded myself on her, bare, feeling her damp, clean flesh against mine. Her skin was gold, her hair silver-blue. Her eyes—her fucking eyes—a dark spell enveloped in a sweet girl who brought so much light into my miserable life. I pushed between her thighs, fumbling for the condom and unwrapping it with my teeth. The scent of latex attacked my nostrils, but not even that took away from the moment. The sheer moment of elation. Of having her, submissive and mine—so utterly and entirely at my mercy—despite her promise to me, and to herself, that we would never sleep together.

I felt like a flower that had just endured weeks of hail and rain, finally feeling the soft kiss of the sun, and knowing that somehow, someway, things would be all right. Maybe not tomorrow, and certainly not today, but they would.

I drove into her and closed my eyes, plastering my forehead to hers. She felt so good, so tight, so fucking wet. I moved slowly, allowing her a second or two to adjust. Our eyes were eloquent, our expressions self-explanatory. Hers were the ocean. Mine were the earth. She moaned when I thrust into her, slowly and deeply, biting that lower lip.

"I don't want to fall in love with you," she croaked. It wasn't a statement as much as it was a plea.

I thrust deeper, my forehead wrinkling in concentration as my balls tightened.

"You don't seem to have much choice," I answered.

She moaned louder, looking away from me, at the wall, at The Cure, at Robert Smith, hung above us on a wrinkled poster, eyeliner, lipstick, and ridiculous hair galore.

After a few minutes, she began to rock into me while I poured into her.

This wasn't fucking. This was something else entirely, and if I were a good man—if I were halfway decent, even—I'd stop, flip her over, drive into her from behind, and make sure to bang her head on the headboard for good measure. But I wasn't a good man, so I let her fall in love with me in that moment, because she was the only person who took my loneliness away.

"I'm coming," she said, sinking her short, square nails into my back. I liked her nails. They were the epitome of her. Chipped and clean, always coated with a funky color. "I'm coming so…so…hard."

I felt it, too. In my body. In my balls. In my veins. The release wasn't immediate. Like our sex, it trickled down gradually, from my neck, down my spine, feeling my muscles spasm and slack as she quivered and tightened around me. Robert Smith and Morrissey watched silently as I did to Stardust what they had taught me.

I put her under my spell, to make sure she was mine.

Scribbling onto her the notes only I could play.

Now that Tania was gone, Stardust was my main instrument.

And it saddened me, because I knew I had to break her, too.

Chapter Twenty-Six

Indie

You.
I was already a goner.
By the time you found the rest of me.
You sought me out.
And left me to deal with the girl I never thought I could be.

You.
You carved your name into my heart.
Gutted it out like I was a dead fish.
Held it in your fist.
And left me to drown.

You.
You took my heart and held it in your teeth.
Then we kissed.
Then we fought.
Then we made out.

You.
You said you loved to see how we burn together.
So you took a match.
Lit us up.
And now we burn forever.

I tucked my stupid poem into one of the many compartments of my suitcase, my heart heavy with emotions. Alex was still in bed behind me, sleeping on his stomach, his wild hair blanketing his perfect face.

The twilight was glorious that morning. The sun nearly kissing the stars. I wanted him to watch it, but I didn't want to wake him up. I settled for taking a picture with his phone. He'd see it when he woke up.

Later that morning, we snuck into the Mercedes. Harry and Hamish met us in the living room. Alex's family stood in line like soldiers by the door—Jim, Louisa, Carly, and the three boys, from tallest to shortest—staring at us through the lens of regret and tragedy.

Alex patted the boys' heads and ignored the adults altogether. He bent forward to speak to them, his voice hushed. "Be good. I'll come back soon and give you stuff. Meaningful stuff, I swear."

Sadness pierced my soul as Alex's house became smaller and smaller in the rearview mirror of the SUV. The silence, choking and suffocating, was loaded with so many words I didn't want to say in front of these strangers. I took his hand in mine and squeezed.

"I'm sorry I made you do this."

"I'm sorry for thinking with my dick and doing this," he shot back, his words not malicious or angry, but simply frank. "And also for the black eye."

Jenna: I heard Alex had a little accident with your eye. A dozen Ray-Bans will be waiting at the hotel. Make sure you wear them until the black fades. Oh, and don't worry about the paparazzo who photographed you. We paid him well to destroy the photos.

To live in Alex Winslow's world.
We stopped at a little café and had a full English breakfast, then

zipped straight into London. It was close to eight o'clock in the morning—still far too early for the local shops to open—when we stopped in front of a fancy-looking building on Piccadilly Circus. Alex jumped out of the SUV and helped me out, and we both walked under an arched entrance leading to the back of a block. Someone buzzed us inside, and a second later, we stood in a red-carpeted foyer.

"Close your eyes," he croaked.

"Why?"

"Because everything is so much more beautiful when you can't see it."

I bit my lower lip, allowing my eyelids to flutter shut. Alex took my hand, not gently—the way he did everything, with the kind of coarseness I'd grown to love—and ushered me a few feet until I heard a door opening and closing.

"Open."

I was spellbound before my eyes were fully wide. *Fabrics.* Hundreds and hundreds of fabrics. Lace. Satin. Velvet. Chiffon. Organza. *Colors.* So many gorgeous colors, swirling together like a carnival of beauty. Merlot red. Electric pink. Paradise blue. Metallic silver. Rich and soft and inviting, I wanted to roll inside them like a caterpillar. Swim in them. Live in them. Love in them. I ran to a corner where the velvet sat in long rolls, stocked on neat shelves in the vast, old-school room.

"This is perfect," I exclaimed. "This is everything."

"*You're* everything," I heard him say, still standing at the door.

I turned around. His hands were stuffed inside his pockets. His gaze was a little warmer than his usual indifferent face. To some, it may look like he had melted and yielded to what we were. But I knew better than that. There was fire in him, and it was going to consume him one day. One day soon. That was why I'd written him the poem that morning.

The poem I knew I would give him someday.

Someday soon, when we said goodbye.

Someday soon, when I'd need to forget.

Alex

The lads didn't join us until Paris.

Which was a good fucking thing, because every minute alone with Indigo "Indie" "Stardust" Bellamy, I felt like I could breathe deeper. It wasn't that I didn't like my mates. I did, in my own screwed-up way. Despite everything they'd done—and maybe even *because* of it—I knew they always had my back. But I also acknowledged that I wasn't in the best state of mind.

I needed to be tamed.

So they'd tried to tame me.

And that's when the monster inside of me came out.

Spending time with Indie, the monster was tucked in. Sure, Stardust watched over me, but she wasn't *them*. She was fresh, pure. We weren't stuck between the walls of the past, a foundation that had been steadily crumbling with every hushed phone call and white lie meant to *save* me.

By the time we boarded the plane to Paris, after my Cambridge Castle gig, I wasn't even pissed off at Blake and Lucas anymore. That elusive feeling of contempt, one that cannot be bought, purchased, abused, and monitored with measurements of lethal powder or amber liquid, was strange to me. I was happy, but I couldn't control it.

It came to me in small, steady doses, not all at once, with a rolled note and a few sniffs. It came to me as all good things should be experienced—in time, and in effort, and with caution.

By the time we got to Paris and Stardust's face glowed like a thousand fireflies, I'd forgotten who I was.

I'd forgotten my name was Alex Winslow.

I'd forgotten how it was going to explode in my fucking face.

And I'd forgotten all the mistakes I'd collected over the years since hitting it big.

Well, I was about to remember.

Chapter Twenty-Seven

Indie

Paris, France.

How do you know you're in love?

For me, it was in the kiss. I knew I was in love when I found myself opening my eyes when Alex and I were kissing. I no longer needed to close them to concentrate, to withdraw the curtain so I could feel the magic, so to speak. Alex *was* the magic. And every time we kissed with our eyes closed, I missed him. It was corny. Gag-worthy even, but nonetheless true.

It was under the Eiffel Tower that he'd told me his existence had felt different the past couple of weeks. Like his living and breathing were more significant, somehow. "Remember in Berlin, when I asked you to sit by the stage, where I could see you?" he'd asked. I'd nodded, taking a sip of my foam cup. The coffee was better in Paris. Come to think of it, everything was better in Paris. Alex had jerked me to his body with the collar of my coat, our lips touching as he'd spoken. "The way you look at me when I sing and play reminds me why I started doing it in the first place. It reminds me there's nothing else I want to do—*can* do—and even though there's something tragic in that, a man with one destiny, you take the edge off."

"How does your soul feel these days?" I'd smiled.

"Pure," he'd answered.

Had I known this was the last time Alex and I would be this way, peaceful and whole and unassuming, I would've spent a few more minutes sipping that coffee. A few more moments kissing him under the perfect blue sky. But I hadn't known, and we'd had to go back to the hotel and get ready for the charity gala. I don't know if he'd realized it, but Alex had had a smile on his face the entire time. Even when Blake had forced a disgusting herbal tea down his throat to help his vocal cords. Or when Lucas had sat between us and stared at him with the same kind of pained, pissed-off expression Lucas only produced when he looked at Alex. Hell, he'd even laughed at Alfie's completely inappropriate jokes.

The last thing I remember from that afternoon was when we were in the snack room before the limousine came to pick us up for the gala. Alfie had been loitering by the entrance with a few fans, Blake had been on his phone to Jenna, and Alex, Lucas, and I had been sitting in the hotel lobby, sipping orange juice from champagne glasses. I remember the way Lucas had looked at me when Alex pulled me into his lap after I'd paid a quick visit to the bathroom. Alex had circled my waist with his arms and spread his lean thighs apart to accommodate me, his fingers playing with the hem of my dress as he'd talked shop with someone he openly referred to as French Suit Number Three.

I remember thinking I'd gotten it all wrong.

I even remember the sound the penny made when it dropped.

And most of all, I remember asking—why? How? And—for how long?

I didn't know I'd be getting the answers to all of those questions the same night.

And that as soon as I'd make sense of them, I'd want to forget them. Forever.

"Do Re Mi" by Blackbear played as we sauntered through the huge double doors of the chateau. Ironic, considering the song was tailor-made for Fallon and Alex's story. Fallon, the girl whom I hated without even knowing. We hadn't seen her yet, but she was everywhere. The room was heavy with her presence, and I knew it wasn't a matter of *if*, but *when*. The whole evening felt like a huge middle finger to me, and I didn't even know why.

I wanted Paris.

I craved this ball.

I was dying to show off my dress. The Paris Dress, as all the guys referred to it.

Everyone was wearing masquerade-style masks. Silver, gold, black, and blue camouflaged the beautiful faces of the rich attendees. Mine was one of the rare white ones, lace curving over my eyes and forehead. Alex had a simple black Zorro mask that showcased his strong jawline even more. Alfie, of course, had opted for a flamboyant mask with feathers and glitter. His playfulness was growing on me.

"I'm going to head to the ladies' room. Let me find Blake." I put my hand on Alex's arm, and he squeezed it, prompting me to look up and meet his gaze. We hadn't spoken about Fallon, or about our very near future, but I didn't want to let him out of my sight. Which was exactly the reason I should.

"Perfectly capable of not fucking up for five minutes. Go." He jutted his face toward the restroom. "Anything to drink?"

I hesitated for one second. I shouldn't be leaving him unattended in a place that openly served alcohol, and I was perfectly aware of that. At the same time, I couldn't treat him the same as before. We were no longer an employer and an employee, and treating him like he was strictly business was borderline inhumane. Especially since he was so much more now.

Alex saw the doubt etched on my face, locked my chin between his fingers, and slammed his mouth down on mine. His other hand caressed the side of my tit, darkening my thoughts with lust. "Go take a piss," he hissed, his hand sliding backward and cupping my butt. "I promise not a drop of alcohol will meet my mouth tonight. All I intend to get high on is *you*."

"And Fallon?" I hated that I asked him that.

"Fuck Fallon," he said, unblinking.

The joy that filled my body in that moment was so pure and real, I felt like I could fly.

I wobbled to the restroom and stood in line for ten minutes. It sucked, because most women were there to powder their noses, and that was precisely the thing I was afraid Alex was going to do when no one was looking. Every minute made hysteria bubble and simmer inside me, hotter and deeper. I had the fastest pee in the history of urine, washed my hands sans soap, and rushed back out to the main drawing room where people danced on white and black marble floors, chandeliers twinkling above my head. My eyes darted to the spot where I'd left Alex.

He wasn't there.

Of course he wasn't. He was an addict, and all three things he was addicted to—alcohol, cocaine, and Fallon—were there tonight.

My eyes roamed. I spotted Alfie flirting with someone at the bar, Lucas dancing with a girl in a Victorian dress, and Blake talking on his phone on one of the balconies overlooking the Paris skyline. If Blake knew I'd lost Alex, he would maim me. And rightly so. I started walking around in circles, searching for him. Black tux. Black mask. That was pretty much half the attendees of this Halloween charity ball, but the knowledge that so much was on the line for me—my job, my salary, my *heart*—made my heeled feet run from spot to spot, searching for the troubled rock star.

I peeked into every face and studied every curve of jaw before deciding he wasn't in the ballroom. Then, I began to look through the balconies. All eight of them. The first one was filled with couples making out. The second had a yelling Blake, and thankfully, he hadn't noticed me. The third one was occupied with smokers, the fourth was empty, the fifth had a couple fighting in French...when I reached the sixth balcony, I stopped. It was empty, but I heard voices. One of them was familiar. Ragged breath on tough-as-nails accent. The familiar hoarseness that came with smoking like a chimney. I erased the space to the white marble railings with three steps.

And there, standing on the terrace below me, I had the perfect view to my very own version of a horror flick.

Alex and Fallon on the balcony of the first floor, face-to-face.

Without masks. Without pretense. Without *me*.

The lower terrace was deeper, almost twice the size of the one I stood on, so I had a crystal clear view of them.

She was prettier in person than I'd expected. Her hair was blond, long, and shiny. Her hourglass figure was hugged in a red silky dress. A seductive Juliet. The beautiful Disney Princess in the perfect dress. The way they looked at each other alone paralyzed me. Good. I'd had it coming from day one. Wasn't I the genius who'd gotten into bed with the baddest rock star in the universe, who—by the way—had warned me he was after his ex?

She took a step toward him. He didn't take a step back. No words were spoken, and that somehow made everything worse. She cupped his cheek, looking up. He bowed his head, looking down.

Then she got on her tiptoes and kissed him. Softly. Heartbreakingly slowly. I watched them, surprised the moon didn't drop into the earth and the stars didn't rain down on me. It felt final, bitter, unexpected. Suddenly, I found it hard to breathe.

Three.

Two.

One.

Three seconds. That's the time it took him to tear his lips from her. Three seconds that felt like a lifetime as I stood there, in my stupid dress, with my stupid hair, being my stupid self. His lips disconnected from Fallon's, but his eyes were still heavy and his expression was tortured. Anger washed over me. How could he do this to me in my favorite city in the whole world? How could he do this to *us* after London? After Watford? After the whole, entire freaking world?

He took a step back, and she threw herself at his chest, wrapping her arms around his neck. He grabbed her wrists and untangled himself from her, schooling his features to their usual icy look. "No."

"Why not?"

"How much time have you got?" He chuckled bitterly.

"Alex…"

Timing can make or break you. I learned that the night my parents died when they'd decided to cross the road at the exact same moment that psycho had driven past—and then over—them. And it was in perfect timing that a patch of fabric detached from my elaborate dress just then on the balcony, sailing down like a feather, old ink on antique pink. I didn't need to read the words I'd scribbled on it to remember them by heart. I knew every patch on The Paris Dress. This one was, coincidentally or not, my favorite. It had the lyrics of one of the best love songs ever to be written, and it was written by the guy who'd just broken my heart in the most romantic city in the world.

I don't want your yesterday.
And would never expect your tomorrow.
But if we can have today, I will show you what love tastes like.
And maybe, just maybe, we'll forget about all our sorrows.

The patch fell between them, a symbol of their infidelity, and the air burned like there was a fire nearby. Only Alex hadn't cheated on me. He'd said so himself—he wanted me for fun. Not for today, tomorrow, next week, or even the second after we said goodbye a couple of weeks from now, in L.A.

They both looked up, and I wanted to leave, but my legs were rooted to the floor. A statue made of broken hopes and dreams. So out of place, the party behind me still fizzing with laughter, music, and alcohol.

His eyes widened. Even in the dark, I could see how unnaturally big they were. Alex wasn't the kind of guy to panic, and this look on him—the surprise, the regret, the dread—was new. He took off before I could blink, chasing me. Fallon stayed put, her blank gaze scanning me like you would dirt.

A slight smirk spread on her lips, and my brain tried to will the

rest of my body to cooperate and move. I knew my heart was disobe-
dient, but didn't think it'd make the rest of my organs rebel, too.

"He won't give you a head start." Her grin widened, as she swiveled her head to the view and parked her forearms against the railings, giving me her back. Paris was lit up in black and gold before us,
the Eiffel Tower like a needle that could pierce your heart. "When he
wants something, he always gets it."

"He didn't get you," I whispered.

"He always had me. I just waited for him to come and get me. I
did absolutely everything in my power to get his attention, but I never
had it. Not all the way. You're not listening, Indigo Bellamy. Take off
before he gets to you. You two don't belong together. We do."

"We don't belong together," I repeated. It was true. He'd bullied
me, told me he wanted someone else, and then went and kissed her
the minute I'd turned my back.

"You better start running."

I snapped like someone punched me from the inside.

I took my heels off without even being present in the moment,
collected them in one hand, and took flight. I ran and ran, and then
ran some more. The chateau was an elaborate labyrinth. Every floor
had a long hallway full of big rooms. I took the stairway to the floor
down, knowing Alex would go up to get me, and started opening
doors, looking for the busiest room I could hide in. The faint echo of
the bass thudding against the ceiling was the only evidence there was
a party upstairs. My heart raced faster than my mind. I didn't have a
plan. The only thing I knew was that if I saw him now, I would accept
his explanation, and maybe even apology. I would forgive him, and I
would take him back.

Until the next time Fallon came around.

Until the next time temptation knocked on his door.

Alex Winslow was both an addict and an addiction. Pure and wild. The notion that I couldn't refuse him was bone-deep, so I did the only thing I could tonight. *I copped out.*

Jogging into another empty room, I glanced around to see if I had somewhere to hide in it. I couldn't hear any footsteps, and for all I knew, he could've given up and gone back to kissing Fallon until their lips fell off.

It was a fairly small maintenance room. The door was unlocked, and I still had cell phone reception, so I decided to stay there until the party died down and I could call Lucas and ask when we were heading back to the hotel. I dragged the heavy door behind me shut and flicked on the flashlight on my phone. The screen was broken, but it still shone just as bright, much like Alex.

I dragged my back against the wall and squatted, gathering my knees in my arms and resting my chin on top.

You were right, heart.

I'm sorry, heart.

Never again. Never again. Never, ever, ever again. Ad infinitum.

Ten minutes passed. Maybe more. Somehow, it didn't surprise me when the door flung open and light poured through the crack. Then he came to me, like in a dream. Tall, commanding frame, confident footsteps. Fierce brutality stemming from his mere existence on this planet. Everything I'd studied and admired for the last couple months assaulted me when he entered the tight, dark space. I didn't know what to expect. Maybe for him to apologize, or to be mean and his usual terminally indifferent self. For him to tell me I always knew it was going to be this way. That we were temporary. That Fallon had his heart. That I had his body, and a few rebound songs that always left me balancing on a thin thread of flattered and furious.

"Get up." His voice was like a whip. He grabbed my hand and pulled me to his chest in one, effortless movement.

I groaned and glued my back to the wall, pushing him away. "Go away."

He tried to yank me closer, his movements becoming desperate and impatient, when I pushed him off again, this time harder.

"The dress!" I tried to control my labored breaths. "It was for you. The patches were you. That's why I made it. Out of your songs, Alex. If you looked closely." I tore a patch of the dress, waving it in his face.

Go tell your friends that I'm the one,
Other guys have had their run,
Your soul is mine, and that's the end,
I don't even care, that you fucked my whole band.

"I did it for you. Because you're layered and multicolored and different and...and..." And torn. My dress had fallen apart. Nothing I ever made fell apart. Other than The Paris Dress. Other than *his* dress. I inhaled, squeezing my eyes shut. "Just...leave."

"Why?"

"Why?" I laughed, struggling to keep my tears at bay. I wasn't going to cry. Especially over him. "You kissed your ex-girlfriend in front of me while I was in a dress I made for you. Because I feel like the stupidest girl in the world right now, and I think I'm allowed this one moment of quiet meltdown without an audience. You can sympathize, right? Understand the need to be broken without the limelight shining all over your ugly-cry face?"

Why was I being so brutally honest? I'd only stroke his inflated ego. Though I wasn't sure his ego was so huge anymore. I actually suspected it was as fragile as my current state of sanity.

"First of all, I didn't kiss her. She kissed me. And second of all," he exhaled, punching the wall behind me with both fists and boxing me between his arms. I didn't fight him. For the first time since we'd met, I didn't need to. I knew I wouldn't let him have me. Not when his lips were ghosting someone else's tonight. Feeling in control over my body again was, sadly, anticlimactic.

"I felt nothing," he said.

"You love her," I insisted, praying to hear him dispute those words. "You said so yourself."

"I love her?" He snorted, shaking his head. "What part gave me away, Indie? Huh? The part where, in every single conversation I've ever had about Fallon, I wanted her down and compliant and submissive, begging for my forgiveness and love again, or the part where I chased your sorry arse across the world? Tell me, *Stardust*, is that what love feels like? Feeling the need to steal, and destroy, and ruin your love interest just so you could breathe for one fucking second without feeling like a cockless loser? I don't love Fallon, I don't even like Fallon, and I sure as hell don't fucking *want* Fallon. It was you I wrote songs about. It is you I see first thing in the morning before I open my eyes, like you're carved into my fucking eyelids from the inside. It's you I see at night, a second before I fall asleep, like you're printed on every goddamn ceiling in Europe. I don't want this to end, and my reasons are purely selfish. You made me forget about the drugs and remember about the art. But I've a feeling I'm not the only one who's enjoying this arrangement. Why fuck it up? Because of a brief, one-sided kiss? Fallon is not a threat. Fallon is not even a hiccup. The only girl I'd like to be with until I'm back in L.A. is you, Stardust."

Until I'm back in L.A.

Just an arrangement.

My reasons are selfish.

It killed me from the inside to know the man who came up with some of the most inspiring words about love was also capable of offering something so half-assed, partly-baked, and indecisive. And what slayed me even more was that I was fully ready to take it. Maybe not tonight, but tomorrow, or the next day, once my heart slowed down and logic kicked in. He hadn't cheated on me. If anything, he'd peeled her off and told her no.

I felt Alex on my skin, even though he was smart enough not to touch me. He was waiting for me to speak when the door opened again.

Fallon appeared behind his back.

She looked horrified.

And broken.

And...dangerous.

Like a fatal disease that crawled to your threshold without

knocking on the door, asking you to open your mouth and let it poison you. Most of all, Fallon looked high. Her pupils were dilated and wide as saucers, her skin clammy and gray. She thrust herself at Alex, trying to peel his palms from the wall above me with quivering fingers. Cold sweat misted her forehead, and her shudders were as violent as her eyes. It scared me so much I momentarily forgot to hate her and was more worried we should be calling for an ambulance.

"You weren't supposed to find her," she growled, tears running down her face. She wasn't crying. She was shedding tears. I didn't even think she was aware she was doing it. Her face was emotionless, ill-looking. "How do you think it feels to read about you in the news, Alex? New love. New album. New songs. I'm hurting, too. Don't play into their hands. It's us, baby. You and me. I don't need rehab, and you don't need her. All we need is each other."

Who the hell were they?

"Fallon," he bit out, more exasperated than emotional, like she was an annoying kid he tried to tame, "busy here. Where's your fuckboy, Bushell?"

"I don't know!" She threw her arms in the air. "Probably doing charity stuff or something boring along those lines. Oh, my God. He's *so* boring. How was he even your friend? You guys have nothing in common. I need to talk to you."

"The only thing you need is rehab. Go back to your boyfriend. Fiancé. Whatever."

"Don't do this, Alex. Don't play into their game and let them win. This is not who we are. We do us. We've always done us."

I had no idea what she was talking about, and one look at Alex's face told me he was just as oblivious to what was going on. He parked his waist next to mine, turning his head and narrowing his eyes at her.

"You're engaged to someone else."

"They *forced* me. Jenna paid me, and I needed the money. Will won't give me access to shit unless I go to rehab."

"What are you bloody talking about?" Alex growled.

"They wanted you to hook up with this girl! That was the plan!

They wanted her to make you forget about me! About the drugs." She stomped her foot, waving around and pointing at me. "Oh my gosh, like, how can you not see that? You don't need a sobriety companion. You have Blake, who's attached to you by the hip, and Lucas, who would goddamn-near kill for you!" she spat out, growing twitchier by the second.

I mulled her words over. She looked crazy, but the things she said added up pretty correctly, and that worried me. Had Jenna hired me to make Alex forget about Fallon? It sounded extremely farfetched, but I'd heard stranger things.

"Bollocks!" he yelled into her face. He was losing his cool, too. "How would you even fucking know that? No one from my team talks to you. No one!" Alex took a step in her direction, so mad I thought he could push her.

I dragged him by the arm back to me, and the mere touch between us made his face soften a little. Still, he looked scarier than I'd ever seen him.

"I know that because Will was in on it," she cried on a full-blown sob. "Will loves me. I know he does. But I don't love him. I love you. They wouldn't let me talk to you." She sniffed. "They said..." Now she was crying for real, and I wanted to cry with her, because things had gotten so much more complicated. "They said I ruined you and that you're better off without me. That she was sweet and proper and will make you feel better."

"Lies." He shook his head. "No, no, no."

"Will only ever wanted the best for you. For me, too. Blake, Lucas, and Alfie were in on it, too. Why did you think Lucas was pushing himself on this girl so hard? Is she really worthy of the attention of two rock stars? I mean, no offense." She raked her eyes along my body, meaning the offense and then some.

I took a step toward her, about to give her a piece of my mind, but now it was Alex's turn to pull me into him. My head was spinning with the revelation, even though I wasn't even sure it was true.

"If you're lying—" Alex started, raising a finger in warning.

"I'm not lying," she cut through his words, stomping her foot again, a reoccurring tick that was more suitable for a toddler. "Why the hell would I lie? You know these people. Will wanted to save me and love me and blah blah blah. Then he felt guilty about us, so he ganged up on you with your friends and agent, who would do just about anything to keep you sober and productive. But you're not happy, Alex, are you? How can you be happy without me? I thought about you every day."

"This is bullshit." Alex shook his head. "Will is not a martyr, and Waitrose is not a saint, and none of them would listen to you, anyway. Let's go, Indie." Alex pulled me by the hand, and the relief I'd felt at leaving the place was instant, but then Fallon grabbed his wrist. Up close, I could see madness dancing in her eyes, and I wondered how could they even call what they'd had love? If they were both high all the time, they never even had the chance to truly get to know each other.

"You never did the math, did you?" She laughed bitterly, losing any trace of self-control. "You never figured it out on your own."

"Figured what out?" Alex asked, squeezing his fingers into his eyelids tiredly. He'd had enough of her. I could see it now. He wasn't in love with his ex. He was merely annoyed that she'd left him for someone else. "What are you talking about, Fallon?"

"The accident," she said. "The day you helped me?" She tilted her head, and there was something in her eyes that made my skin crawl. "It was her parents."

The next few seconds moved in slow-motion.

I looked up at Alex.

He looked down at me.

His face was white. That's the last thing I remember. Ashen, with realization and grief. I didn't feel the fall. Rather, I saw it, as the sound around me muffled and their figures became dotted with inky black spots. My eyes watched Alex's shoes and Fallon's dress a second later. They closed despite my efforts to stay awake. More than anything, I wanted to hear what they were saying. They were yelling through the fog of lightheadedness. I strained my ears to listen.

"Fuck, fuck, no!" Alex yelled. "Fallon, no!"

"I'm so sorry," she cried. "I'm so, so sorry."

I blacked out, never coming up for that air I needed to survive.

Everything around me fell apart. And I fell with it.

Hudson: Sup, girls?

Jenna: Hi.

Hudson: Is it just me or did Alex look uber hot at that London gig? Indie, are you in charge of his wardrobe? He looks so much less hobo.

Hudson: (I'd tap it either way, but don't tell him)

Jenna: Where is she?

Hudson: Ghosting our asses. But why?

Jenna: Indie, answer.

Jenna: Indie.

Jenna: INDIE.

Jenna: INDIGO!

I came to in a bed.

My Parisian bed.

Or, should I say, *our* Parisian bed.

God, I wanted to throw up.

Alex's stuff was still in our room, as if nothing had happened. I looked around, examining the collection of fancy water bottles and organic snacks on the dresser, the guitar picks, the strewn notepads, Polaroid pictures of Alex and me from London, which we took when we found Blake's camera in his suitcase. The room felt saturated with deceit, swollen with lies. My head pounded, and I wanted to stand up, walk over to Blake's room, and hand in my resignation.

I was alone.

Swallowing the sour taste of puke that occupied every inch of my mouth, I wiggled in bed, trying to summon the energy to get back up and start packing. A minute after I woke up, Alex came out of the bathroom. His eyes were red-rimmed and his hair was a mess. He wore gray low-hanging sweatpants and nothing else. He looked like he'd just attended his own funeral. I tried to drag myself up and rest my back against the headboard.

"I'm going to make this right, Stardust. I'm going to—"

"Don't," I growled, my voice so harsh I couldn't believe it came from me. "Don't pretend like we're still okay. We're not. I want you to tell me everything. You're a liar, Alex, but this time I need every truth you have to give me. That's the least you can do after everything we've been through."

He sat on the edge of the bed and stared at his hands on his lap. Yesterday, I hadn't known how I could look at his face without my lungs contracting like he held them in his fist. Today, he was a stranger dressed as the man I loved—yes, loved. I fell in love with him earlier than I'd realized—with one version of him, anyway.

Once upon a time, a mere mortal fell in love with a rock god. You probably know this is not a fairy tale by now. Mortals and gods don't mix.

"Four years ago, Fallon came home looking like hell on heels. We'd just moved in together. I was sober back then. Sort of. I was mostly on painkillers, a functioning alcoholic. I didn't do cocaine and didn't know I had a problem. I thought I just lived hard and played harder. So many people in my industry do. Anyway, she came back, and she was high as a kite, but she was also very upset. Said she ran over a deer on her way back from Calabasas and asked me to go take a look at the car. I did. It looked…" Alex rubbed the back of his neck and stared at the ceiling, sighing. "It was wrecked. I asked Fallon, again and again and a-mother-fucking-gain if it really was a deer. There was so much blood. She maintained it was a deer and asked me to help her get rid of the car. So I did. I...I..."

"You helped her cover it up. Even though you knew, deep down, that she was lying," I finished for him, my eyes hard on his face. "That's what you're telling me."

He shook his head, raking his fingers through his hair. "I was drunk. It wasn't the only thing that didn't make sense. So many things looked wonky. It was just another thing on that list. But I'm going to make sure she turns herself in, Indie. If she won't, you bet your arse I will."

"Spare me the excuses."

"I said I'm going to make it right."

"You're also a self-proclaimed liar," I felt my lower lip trembling like a leaf.

"I'm not lying to you now. I promise."

"You let her get away with murder." My voice pitched high, too high, and I became dizzy again. He scooted toward me, and I slapped his hand away when he tried to take mine. "No."

"I would've never let her get away with it had I really known. I *didn't* know. I just suspected, but half the fucking time I was seeing and feeling things that weren't there. I was paranoid. And shit-faced. No matter how bad it looked, I chose to overlook it and buy what she was telling me."

I squeezed my eyes shut, willing myself to take the next breath. I missed Mom. I missed Dad. I missed normalcy, and Saturday dinners, and Christmases, and even the dreaded Sunday mass. I missed the opportunity and promise of being normal, whole; I missed my big brother and how he took care of me. I even missed the great father Craig could have been to Ziggy, had Alex picked up the phone and called 911 when Fallon came home that night.

Then, maybe, my mother would have survived.

Then, maybe, I wouldn't be on this tour, my heart shattering into a million pieces as I tried to hold it together, feeling like my pain was bursting at the seams, my whole existence gathered together with pins and needles stapled by my old sewing machine.

"Consider this my official resignation," I said, eyes still closed.

"No," he said. "No, no, no, no, no."

"I wouldn't push me, Alex. You've done enough. Respect my wishes and let me go." I opened my eyes now, staring at him, at everything that he was. A traitor I'd opened the door to and willingly let into my life. It had taken him mere weeks to slip from the hallway and into my domain. He'd conquered every single inch of me and used it against me, unbeknownst to him. I didn't see his beauty, his sex appeal, or his dazzling bone structure. I didn't see the funny, complex, tortured guy I wanted so badly to fix. All I saw was a broken prince with pleading eyes who was on the verge of tears. Man tears. Not angry or exasperated or annoyed. But real and sad and deep.

All broken princes die. Hadn't he said that? Maybe he was right. The scariest part was that, at that moment, I wanted him to be right.

I smiled, surprising myself. I didn't know I had a mean streak, but I guess Alex had dug it out from deep within me and dumped it onto the morgue table along with my heart. I knew that once he'd find my poem—the one I'd written after our night in his childhood bedroom—he'd see why this was over. Why we could never be together.

"If you leave me," he said, "you take my soul with you."

"It's always been my soul," I said, my tone quiet and defiant. "You don't have a soul. Not for a very long time. You proved it by turning a blind eye all those years ago when you could have saved my mom. You don't need me. You need *you*. Time for you to pack a bag and travel the different planets. Find your soul, Alex. You'll never truly be happy without it."

Chapter Twenty-Eight

Alex

She left me a note.

    On a sheet of paper.

    From a notepad.

My notepad.

The notepad I'd used to write songs. Songs she'd inspired. Songs that were meant for her, and maybe even *to* her, and held her legacy, each word pregnant with so much more than its meaning. It was a cross between a poem and a letter. About us. About me. About the fucked-up thing that we were. Then, underneath it, underlined and in red, something else. More recent. The ink pressed so hard against the paper, it had torn around the letters.

*You're beautiful, Alex, but you're empty. No one could die for you. And no one **should** have died because of you. –Indie*

She'd quoted *The Little Prince*, and somehow, that hurt even more. *The Little Prince* was ours. I'd written her a song about him—and she'd twisted it against me. It dawned on me, in a Parisian hotel that looked exactly like all the rest, but also very different, that I'd finally found her. The girl who was worth all these songs I'd written. Then I'd lost her. The girl whose life I'd helped ruin.

There was a light at the end of the cold, dark tunnel of my existence: even I knew I couldn't cancel the remainder of "Letters from the Dead" tour. Jenna was going to rip me a new one and stuff it with dynamite if I even mentioned such possibility. The insurance company was on my case, my record company breathed its rancid, corporate breath down my neck, and I was actually making a decent comeback and building a buzz around my next untitled album. Besides, my mates relied on me. Mates who, as much as I wanted to kill, I owed, too. Our relationship was messy and abnormal and completely off the rails. They constantly betrayed me in a bid to bring me back to life. And it had worked.

Until now.

I made a promise to myself that no matter how this shit was going to pan out, I was going to make sure Fallon did the right thing by Stardust and her family.

I stood by the kitchen island of my hotel suite, clutching her note until my fingers almost snapped. The scent of Indie was still in my nostrils and on my pillow and inside my fucking guts, when the door behind me opened. I'd been trying to get high off of bath salts unsuccessfully for twenty minutes when Lucas walked in and shut the door behind him.

Yeah, I was using again. Or at least trying. Shit, I wasn't even good at being a drug addict. How embarrassing was that?

"Don't even think about it." I sniffed, trying to light up the little rocks of salt. How the fuck could you get high on them? I needed new mates. New, young, loser mates who'd teach me how to get high on pathetic things. And it hadn't even been a full four hours since she'd left. I dreaded to think how I'd fare a week from now. Heroine? Crack? *Riverdale*? I'd die if I became the very thing I loathed.

"Don't think about what?" I heard Lucas moving behind me, but didn't turn around.

"Everything. My answer is no, no matter what. Don't talk to me. Don't apologize. Don't offer your condolences. For the last time—I shagged Laura long before you'd met her. There was no need to shit on my only serious relationships, twice in a row." I dumped the salts onto the counter in frustration, essentially walking right into a conversation with him. Idiot. I was an idiot. A part of me—albeit a small and insignificant and muted by the general bullshit swarming in my head part—realized I deserved it. Everything that had happened to me. Indie leaving. Fallon acting like a crazy bitch. My mates and agent babying me, lying to me, micromanaging every single breath I took, from my love interest to my records, deals, interviews, and general wellbeing. Lucas appeared by my side and wiped the marble counter with his arm, throwing the half-baked salts to the floor.

"You think this is about Laura?" he screamed into my face. "Are you mental? What's wrong with you? It's not about Laura, and it's not about Fallon. It's not even about Indie. It's about you, you arsehole. I'm in love with *you*." He shook, spitting the words in my face.

I turned around to fully face him. The words trickled in like rain through a cracked ceiling. Slowly but surely. If only I could wrap my head around them. "Huh?"

He took my arm and pulled it. I let him, too stunned to think of something coherent to say. Our faces were inches from each other, but far enough that I could see his expression. Tortured, almost like me.

"I'm in love with you. Have been for the past—hmm, let's see, I don't know, twelve years? Everyone knows. It's obvious and plain for everyone to see. I started playing the drums because of you, for fuck's sake. You needed a drummer, couldn't find one—no one wants to be the drummer, it's a lonely, reclusive job—so I did it. I wanted to be close to you, and you wanted to start a band, so I learned to play an instrument. Then I *became* your instrument. Then I picked up your leftovers—Laura, your idiotic lady friend, Fallon, and everyone else around you—to have more pieces of you. More precious pieces of Alex-fucking-Winslow, the guy who, unfortunately, possessed *it*. The charisma, the talent, the presence, those eyes. Those damn eyes, Alex." He let go of my arm and cupped his hands over his eyes, shaking his head in exasperation and pacing around the room.

I wanted to light a cigarette to do something with my mouth—I sure as hell felt too inadequate to speak—but was too shocked to move. Everyone knew? Was I even living in the same universe as my mates? They seemed to have been keeping a lot from me.

"I broke you and Fallon up, not because I liked Will, or her, but because I love you. And loving you comes with the price of completely disregarding my own wishes and needs. Fallon made you fall deeper into drugs and depression. She was toxic for you, so I kicked her out of the way. And I'd do it again if I could. In a heartbeat. I would slay for you, Winslow. Now, Indie did the opposite. She rebuilt you. But of course, watching you fooling around made me want to hang myself every day. Knowing I'd pushed you into each other's arms just about killed me. And I still did it. For you."

Lucas threw himself across the black velvet couch, burying his face in one of the pillows. I inwardly wondered what kind of arsehole goes around living his life not knowing one of his best mates is in love with him. Me. I was that arsehole.

"You're gay," I said, rather dumbly, rubbing my sweaty temple. I wasn't sure why I was so sweaty, but it might have had something to do with the fact I was so numb, I couldn't even distinguish how fucking hot the room was. I'd been too busy trying to get high and to not think about Indie. Two things I'd categorically failed at.

"Gay as they come. And please, no Alfie jokes." Lucas started rolling the zipper of his leather jacket. *Up. Down. Up. Down.*

It was weird to talk about him when my own world was in shambles. But I could no longer afford to be a shitty mate, and acknowledging that was a start. Plus, he looked like a sulking child. Sad and annoyed and defeated. I fell down to the settee beside him and nudged his shoulder with mine.

"I'm sorry." I wasn't even sure what I was apologizing for. Not being gay? Parading half the female population of Hollywood at the Chateau in front of him? Making him play fairy godmother to me for over a decade? Inadvertently destining him to become *a fucking drummer*?

"Don't be sorry. I'm nearly thirty and still mostly in the closet. I lied to you for years. Pretty sure we're even." Lucas wiped the snot from his nostrils with the back of his hand, staring down.

I didn't know it was possible for my heart to break even more after Indie, but it did. It broke for Lucas. I jerked him into a hug.

"Oi," I said, honing in on the wall in front of us. Nothing was okay, and yet I had to assure him it was, because Indie was right. I needed to find my soul and show it to people around me. "Look at me."

He sniffed again and looked up.

"When did you figure out you like dick?"

"When we were twelve? Maybe thirteen? I'm not sure. I just remember wanting your heart long before wanting your dick. It was a January evening. I spotted you walking up and down the road with Tania on your back, yelling to the closed windows, 'who knows how to tune a guitar?' and thought...*this sonovobitch is going to have a bathroom full of Grammys someday.* You looked like a loser, but you were so far into what you were doing, I couldn't help but admire that. Your voice had just broken, and so had your chin, with a dozen pimples or so. Do you remember that?" He laughed. "God, you were a joke."

"I'm still a joke." I smirked. I remembered that day. Dad's mate, Duncan, had finally agreed to tune Tania and taught me how to play the first few chords of "Smoke on the Water." "It's just that, I'm not really sure if me being a joke is funny anymore."

"You're definitely still funny," Lucas said, swatting my chest. He'd never done that before. Maybe he'd always wanted to, but didn't know how I'd react. The thought depressed me.

"Please don't relapse, Alex." Lucas was serious again. But it was too late. Even though I hadn't gotten high that evening, I knew with certainty that I would. And that I'd regret it. And that it'd take at least some of the pain of what had happened with Stardust away.

"Question," I averted the topic. I took a fag out of the pack on the coffee table with my teeth and lit it, my arm still wrapped around his shoulder like he was my little brother. "If we were together, would I be top or bottom?"

Lucas laughed harder through his tears. "I'm always on top."

I said, "Bollocks."

He said, "See? Still funny," and pressed his index against my nose, smiling miserably.

I still thought about Indie the entire length of the conversation. Wondering what she'd think about all that.

Chapter Twenty-Nine

Alex

Alex,

Remember when we first moved to L.A. and promised ourselves we'd never change? That we'd still be the same blokes from the same shitty town with the mutual hate for Manchester FC (fuck ManU, man, fuck 'em). Well, I think it's suffice to say we all broke that promise.

I'll give you one thing—even when we stopped being mates and became competitors, you always had the upper hand. You got the better lass, and the better album, and the more prestigious Grammy. You got the Rolling Stone and NME covers, while I got the Billboard crap. You were still cool to the hipsters even when you broke into the mainstream, while I got invited to the Country Music Awards.

And you got our mates. All of them. Yours.

I want you to know how the idea of Indigo Bellamy started, and, more than that, that I am not your enemy. Never was. Never will be.

I think I owe you an explanation. You think I stole Fallon from you, when, in practice, all I wanted was to save you both. Do I love her? Yes. Will I ever have her, all the way, the way you did, the way you own everything? No.

The night Fallon was involved in that accident, she came back from my party in Calabasas. You were sick at home. She was doing drugs and going behind the wheel.

I knew that.

I let it happen.

I take full responsibility.

There were so many people, I didn't really care who came and who went. But the day after the accident, she contacted me. Sought me out.

She panicked, and she knew you would leave her if she didn't go straight to the police.

From that point on, Fallon and I started nurturing a toxic relationship. We became closer, and I fell more and more into her, while she fell more and more into drugs.

We cheated on you, and then the whole thing exploded. I don't blame you for cutting me from your life. If anything, it's probably best we stay far away from each other.

But I always knew about Indigo Bellamy's parents.

And I know it might come and bite me in the arse, but it's true. I did. I'm partly accountable. I'm a shameful, shameful man.

After everything with Fallon went down, Alfie, Lucas, and Blake said they'd never talk to me again. But they did. Sometime after you kicked your eighth babysitter to the curb, I contacted Jenna Holden, who ordered a meeting with Alfie, Blake, and Lucas. We all agreed that you were spiraling again, and I was the stupid idiot who'd followed Indigo and Craig around, feeling guilty and disheartened about what Fallon did and got away with, and their lives were shitty, too.

I said the plan would be perfect, and they agreed.

I wanted you to fall in love and to get better.

I wanted you to rival me in the Grammys, not in my nightmares.

I knew it would better your life, and Indigo's life, and if everything went according to plan, maybe Craig's, too.

Indigo didn't know who circled that Wanted ad she ended up calling. She thought it was her brother or sister-in-law. It was Hudson who slipped that paper into her bike's basket while she was shopping.

Not for one second did I think Fallon was still so into you. So fiercely in love with you. What kind of person confesses a crime like she committed? A desperately drugged one. That's who.

You might look at this and see betrayal, but your mates only wanted the best for you. I did, too. I'm sorry it didn't work out, and I'm somewhat re-lieved—although mostly terrified—for coming clean. Do with it as you wish. I'm done hiding. I'm done playing kismet. I'm done fucking up my life and others'.

But don't take it out on your team. They love you. They chose you.

You win.

P.S.

I still pretend to spit every time someone mentions Alex Winslow's name.

Faithfully,

William George Bushell

Here's the thing about addiction: that arsehole friend who comes sneaking into your life when you're down and low? That's it. My addiction crawled in, because I could no longer purge it out. I had no reason to behave, because she wasn't there, and everything felt hopeless, and wrong, and final.

So. Fucking. Final.

I found out a lot in the three weeks that marked the end of the tour. The first thing was that when you want to get your hands on narcotics, you do, even when the entire world and its sister are watching you. I snuck groupies into my room with coke stashed in their bras. I didn't touch them, but I definitely touched the drugs. I downed a bottle of vodka in the bathroom in Canada and popped some Xanax in New York. When we landed in Tennessee, I dropped in to say hi to a country singer I mentored on a reality TV show and drank a bottle of whiskey in his bedroom. It was pathetically easy, almost to my dismay. I'd had my chances all along. I'd simply chosen not to use them for, I don't know, whatever reason. Actually, the reason was crystal clear to me now. *Her.* Stardust. She kept me high on something much stronger than coke. Even before I'd gotten my hands on her little body, she was there to taunt, and fight back, and keep me entertained.

Once an addict, always an addict.

The worst part is that you don't quite understand the severity of your addiction until it's already five steps ahead of you, running toward the finish line, ready to ruin your life. I had my gaps between lines and bottles of alcohol, so I tried to convince myself I was still relatively sober, and when I was relatively sober, I called her. All the time. She never picked up. I got her email address from Blake and sent her messages. Stupid messages. Creepy messages. Messages that could have landed my arse in a lot of trouble.

To: Indiebell1996@gmail.com
Subject: I need you

I met Jesus at Times Square after a gig and he told me we were all going to die and that I should count my blessings, and I could only count one thing, and it was you.

Are you mad at me, still? Actually, don't answer that. We'll talk about it when I get there. I shouldn't be contacting you. Blake thinks it's an apology email, and I guess it is, but I'm not going to stop at that. He and Jenna are going to kill me if they know, but you and I, we are bigger than them. Bigger than this.

Jenna is pregnant with Blake's baby, btw. She said not to tell anyone, so I'm telling you. Because you're my someone. I think I'm going to circle back and delete this paragraph later. Too cliché. Did you know the album I had produced by that boy-band fuckboy was my best-selling one?

Huh.

Maybe I'll keep this line in after all.

Alfie is on a pussy bender. Says he's worried about me and that it's his outlet. Blake is sleeping with his mobile pressed to his ear. Lucas rarely even talks anymore, and I…I drink.

It started with a vodka bottle the other day. I miss you. I didn't know about what Fallon did that night. I swear. She's in rehab. I gave her an ultimatum about coming clean. Please answer my calls. Or…not.

Don't tell Blake.

A.

To: Indiebell1996@gmail.com
Subject: How?

I can't believe this shit's for real, Stardust. How can you not answer me? How can you not need me the way I need you? How is it fair that I found you, and you found me, and we both know damn well how rare what we have is, and you still let me go?

How do I let you go?

Stupid question, I don't.

Two more weeks. I'll be coming to get you. You know I will.

Yours (even if you think you don't need me),

A.

To: Indiebell1996@gmail.com
Subject: I wrote a song

It goes like this:
Answer me.
Answer me.
Answer me.
Answer me.
Everyone and everything is falling apart. The Chicago gig was a shit show. I forgot most of the lyrics. Don't ask why, Stardust. You know.

Hudson joined the tour to keep me from taking a shit on what's left of my career, because Blake is back in L.A. playing baby daddy. I think Lucas and him are hooking up. Lucas and Hudson, that is. Not Blake. I hope they are. That's good, right? That I'm wishing good things upon good people.

Oh. Side note. Lucas is gay.

I want you to know I thought about it, and even though I'm a sellout, I do love the rough material for the new album. It bleeds your personality. I can't wait to share you with the world. Share your soul. You were right. It is your soul, but I told you I'd borrow it. You don't mind, right?

I'm coming to L.A. in a week.

A.

To: Indiebell1996@gmail.com
Subject: Once upon a time there was a prince…

Remember, in The Little Prince, when the fox wants the boy to tame him so they'd always have each other? I think that's what you did to me. You tamed me. I needed you. And you unleashed me back into the wild, domesticated and YOURS, and now I'm not sure wtf I need to do to survive. Which, I think you'd agree, is ironic. Everything considered and such.

I'm on the road from Chicago to Oklahoma on a tour bus. You would have liked it. We banned Alfie from Mexican food. I think about you a lot. I wank to our Polaroids a lot. I haven't touched anyone since you left. Okay. Full disclosure: I cupped a tit while taking a photo with a fan. But she'd just had a boob job, and it was for her birthday. And I didn't enjoy it. At all.

It's so weird to be here, to do this, to not be chasing you like every bone in my body tells me to. Blake says to give you time, but what does he know about relationships? He and Jenna are a train wreck.

I saw a squirrel today. Its tail was cut. It

was still furry, just…short. Ever seen a squirrel's tail up close? It's quite magnificent. I felt bad for the squirrel, but reminded myself it didn't know that its tail was cut.

Then I realized I'm the fucking squirrel, Indie.

I'm the fucking squirrel who ran around with half a tail, and no one told me, so I lived in blissed ignorance. Then you came in, walked away, and guess what? Now I know. I know I'm incomplete and my soul, which I thought was dying, is actually in Los Angeles, riding a French bike in a ridiculous dress.

I know I'm making this about me, and I know you're going through a load of crap right now, but I guess that's what addicts do.

And I'm an addict. Again.

Four days, Indie. You. Me. Us. Always.

Blake came back from the OB-GYN appointment he had with Jenna the same week. When he found out what I'd been doing, he took away the laptop Indie had left behind and begged me to stop. Which, naturally, prompted me to call her some more and to order Jenna and Hudson—the latter had reluctantly dragged his arse back to L.A.—to check in on her every week. They said she was doing well. This, consequently, made me feel like shite. I wanted her to hurt like me, and I wasn't even ashamed to think that. And that was a problem.

Oklahoma, then Texas, then straight back to L.A. By that time, I knew my cocaine and drinking habit was in full swing, but I had a bigger issue to tackle—win the girl.

Everything else—the drugs, the alcohol, the addiction, would be sorted out afterward. Love conquers all, and all that jazz.

The gigs were fine. The drugs pulled me through. But I no longer wrote songs, and I no longer gave the crowd the electric show they'd heard about when I'd toured Europe. "Letters from the Dead" officially featured a corpse—hah. I should write that down somewhere.

The flight to Los Angeles was wordless, and the first thing I did when I landed at LAX was give the driver Indie's address. I didn't even care that the others wanted to be dropped off at their flats. Fuck them. They'd sure fucked me over by introducing me to the blue-haired soul-thief.

I hadn't come empty-handed. I'd thought about it long and hard, then gotten her the perfect present. I thought it symbolized what I wanted to say perfectly. Unfortunately, my gift had the potential of dying. I had no time to waste.

Indie lived in a shite neighborhood in an even shittier building. There was a strip club under her flat, so you had to go around through an alleyway to reach the rusty metal staircase leading up to her complex. I knocked on her door three times and rang the doorbell for good measure. I knew she was home. It was six o'clock. And she had nowhere to go. She didn't have a job. I'd made Hudson check.

A blond, tall woman opened the door. *Natasha.* I recognized her from Indie's laptop time. She arched one eyebrow and looked at me like I'd taken a shit on her welcome mat.

"Can I help you?" She acted like we hadn't bantered on Skype before, and I wondered how much Stardust had told her.

She told her everything, you little twat. What do you think?

"I'm looking for Indie."

"Indie doesn't want to see you."

"Indie will have to see me at some point, because I'm not going to stop until she does, and she'd probably need a restraining order against me if she really is serious about cutting me from her life. Side bonus"—I waved my full fist with her present, signaling Natasha that I hadn't come empty-handed—"I made her something. She'll understand what it means."

Nat stared at my gift for a moment, looking torn and embarrassed for me. Even I was a little embarrassed for myself. I wasn't entirely above begging at this point, and shit, if I didn't look like an idiot holding my dripping, half-dead gift.

"Indie! It's him," she yelled into the small apartment.

Indie appeared at the door a few moments later. Was that all it took? I was confused. But then I saw the look on her face and the elation of seeing her after three full weeks evaporated completely. Her eyes—her expressive blues that shone when I played the guitar and wrinkled at the sides every time she came on my fingers and tongue and cock, were turned off. This woman in front of me was nowhere near as present and alive as the girl who'd left me in Europe.

I reached out and gave her the present before she could speak.

"*It is the time you have wasted for your rose that makes the rose important,*" I quoted *The Little Prince*, word-for-word, because it seemed important, somehow. She stared at the roses clutched in my palm, not exactly scowling, but far from touched. "Roses don't have a blue gene," I explained. "You can't get them in that color. Fact. I dyed you some blue ones. It took me hours." I followed every twitch in her face with hungry eyes, trying to decode what she was feeling, but I got nothing. I continued at double-speed, stumbling over my words. "See, I spent the time. On the roses. Because I care. About you. And I guess what I'm trying to say is, I deserve a second chance."

I was pretty proud of that little speech. Which, in retrospect, goes to show how bloody out of it I'd been. I couldn't read the situation, let alone read what was clearly written on her face. This wasn't a rom-com, where the problem would solve itself with the help of a few roses and a Godiva box. She watched as my arm remained stretched with my offering, and when I thought she was going to collect the roses, she withdrew her hand and let them fall between us with a thud.

"Huh?" I *huh'ed* her. True story. Because in my stupid, dysfunctional brain, she was still my secret girlfriend. And this was a lovers' quarrel, solvable and pregnant with the potential of leading to now-or-never, I've-seen-the-light-now-let's-get-shagging, intense sex.

"How much did you drink and snort today?" she asked, her voice even. She looked good. Dressed in a kimono-style emerald dress.

"Not much," I hiccupped, not realizing she could smell the alcohol from across the threshold. "I need you."

"Right." She shook her head, releasing a chuckle. "Listen to me, Alex, and listen good, because you can threaten to come here every day for the rest of your life, but it won't change the outcome. I don't want to hear from you. You're the most self-absorbed, selfish man I've ever met. Don't bother dropping by tomorrow, because I won't be here. Wherever I'll be, you will not be welcome there. Thanks for the flowers." She kicked them out of the threshold.

Slammed the door in my face.

And locked the bolt from the inside.

Leaving me alone.

When I was a kid, maybe six or seven, my sister had forced me to watch *Beauty and the Beast* with her. I did it, for no other reason than she was older and knew how to make microwaved popcorn, and popcorn and a movie was some kind of Holy Grail in my books.

There was one part that really got me. The part I asked her about for days after. When Gaston finds the Beast's castle, when shit hits the fan, when they're engaged in a battle, there's a part where the beast just...gives up. He allows Gaston to take him and win the fight.

"Why?" I asked for the four-thousandth time.

"Oh, my God, you little muppet. What's not to understand? He lost the girl! His life is pointless! He's better off dead than living like an old, lonely sod. Without her, he'll stay a monster forever."

No truer words have ever been spoken, even though these particular ones were uttered by someone who'd later on go and claim the questionable nickname TTB—*The Town Bike*, because everyone had a ride. Hardly an authority when it came to romance.

I don't think I ever told Indie that story, and the thought I never would nearly suffocated me.

I was well into my second pack of smokes that day, wondering what was the point of all this. Of staring at nothing and watching time and air move—despite their invisibility—dragging like a dead, heavy body you had to carry with yourself everywhere. I was high on cocaine and drunk on whiskey.

And I had questions. So many. All of them the wrong ones.

Where was Indie?

What was she doing?

How was I going to make it work?

Did I even have a chance anymore?

I had one phone conversation with Fallon, and it was to tell her that if she wasn't going to say anything about what had happened, I sure as fuck would. Consequently, Fallon had come clean and spilled everything to the police. She'd gotten a visit from plain clothed cops in rehab. Will had been there to hold her hand. She'd been given the opportunity to finish the rehabilitation process before being taken into custody. Blake said that legally, I was in the clear. Like I cared. Like I fucking cared.

I texted Indie to let her know about Fallon, even though Blake and Lucas told me not to. She hadn't answered. I didn't know if it made it better or worse for her. On one hand, I reopened her wound. On the other, I offered her some closure.

The doorbell rang three times. Old Alex—AKA Tour Alex—would've furrowed his brows. New Alex was the beast that didn't care if Gaston was barging in. Someone was an enthusiastic bastard today. All the lads had a key to the apartment I'd rented when I got back to L.A. to be close to Indie, so it was probably a UPS bloke who was eager to get on with his route. Had I ordered something? I didn't remember ordering anything.

Two more rings and a knock. Peeling myself off of the couch felt like trying to remove a hundred-ton brick from my shoulders. Since when was my body so heavy? I hadn't eaten all that much since Paris, and had probably lost a few pounds, which prompted me to believe the feeling was exclusively psychological.

"I'm coming," I groaned, shuffling to the door. I glanced through the peephole out of sheer habit. A guy with light brown hair and soft features stood on the other side. He was wearing sweatpants and a jersey and looked like a complete maniac. Beast or not, I wasn't going to roll a red carpet down the hallway and invite him to slice me into pastrami.

"Who is it?" I asked. It was encouraging to know I still had a logical bone or two in my body.

"Craig Bellamy." His head snapped up as he screamed—actually screamed—straight into the peephole, as if it were a mic.

Stardust's older brother. He existed in my mind as a ghost, a pivotal tool that had brought us closer by fucking up so I could clean after his mess repeatedly. I'd hardly considered he was even real. I was just thankful he was the one little shit who'd actually behaved worse than I had. I knew I had to open the door. Even if he wanted to murder me—understandable, and I considered it poetic justice—maybe, just maybe, I could still find out where she was. Hell, I was half-elated with the idea of being punched by a person who shared her DNA.

I opened the door and said the stupidest thing to ever come out of my mouth, "Where is she?"

Craig ignored my question, pushing me deeper into my apartment. I let him, even though we were the same height—I might've been slightly taller, actually—and around the same build. I probably looked like I'd been run over by every lorry in the state, but he looked like he'd been living in a damp cave in the Afghan mountains for the past couple years. Indie deserved so much better than the men in her life.

"You know? My sister doesn't open up to many people. She is guarded by nature. Growing up, every time I threw a party or had friends over, she'd lock herself not only in her room, but in her closet. And she would listen to music and sew. Some of the music she'd listen to was yours," he said as he crowded me, making me walk backward.

I didn't know how to respond to that, but Craig wasn't waiting for an answer. He gave me another shove, and this time I stumbled towards the open-plan kitchen.

"I had parties almost every week to try to numb the pain away, but she never said anything about it. See, Indie is just *that* good. Even when I knocked Nat and dropped out of college three and a half years ago, and screwed up everything, she stood right by my side, squeezed my hand, and looked at me like I was important."

The third push made my back crash against the kitchen sink. I barely winced, too engrossed in his story and where he was going with it. Craig got so close to my face, I could see the little hairs in his nostrils. He smelled of alcohol and sweat and the kind of desperation I recognized, because I'd worn it like a cologne for years.

"I knew she was going to give you her everything the minute she signed the contract. That's my sister. A classic do-gooder. Always gets attached. I thought, fuck it. She ought to learn this lesson on her own, right? I thought you'd play with her, discard her, but we'd be there to pick up the pieces. And, eventually, she would move on and find a decent guy. You'd be a blip in her existence, a good story to tell her friends on a girls' night out. Never in my life did I imagine you'd ruin her so profoundly. Not just her, but us. You and your cokehead girlfriend took a family, ripped it apart, and threw every single plan and dream we collectively had into the trash, then came back to cause more heartbreak. Now, you tell me, Winslow. How would you react if you were me?"

We stared at each other. His eyes were a shade lighter than Indie's. Bluer. Commoner. Softer. They lacked that smart zing artists have. Suddenly, the need for him to hurt me was overwhelming. He felt like an extension of Indie, and I wanted her to purge all the shit I'd put her through.

"I'd kill me," I said, my voice steady and dry. "Maybe not kill-me, kill-me, because jail time would be a drag, but I'd definitely leave a few forever marks. Fuck knows I left a few on your family."

I'm not sure I even finished the sentence before his fist flew to my face. It was exactly how I'd imagined it would be. Shocking at first, then came the burn, then finally, the pain. The warmth of the blood trickling down from my right nostril prompted me to lick my upper lip, and I straightened back into position.

"You know?" He laughed to himself, shaking his head. "My mom could've been saved. She didn't die immediately. If only she'd had the mercy of a selfish prick, she could be alive today."

Another fist, this time to my stomach. I folded in two, coughing whatever oxygen I had in my lungs. Shit. Guy had some strength in him. I jerked back, my eyes blurry. I could still see him. I could still fight back. I could maybe even take him. My sister's words came back to haunt me.

I'd lost the girl.

I *was* a monster.

And that was how Indie was going to see me. For the rest of our lives.

Craig tackled my midsection and threw me sideways to the floor. I made no effort to fight him off, letting him pound his fists into my face repeatedly, until I stopped feeling anything from the neck up. His face—at this point nothing but a pink swollen thing spitting animalistic growls—was contracted in pain. I wondered if he realized how alike we were. How we loved the same girl—granted, in very different ways—and how the same girl loved us, and wanted to save us, mainly from ourselves.

"Where is she?" I repeated, coughing up blood. Their mother could have been saved. I hadn't known that back then. And if I had— would that have changed the way I'd reacted when Fallon came home that day? Yes. It would.

I'd begged her to tell me the truth. *"Come on, darlin'. We can fix whatever shit's happening, but I need to know."* I'd replayed that night countless times in my head since it happened. Even before Indie and Craig walked into my life. The answer had always been the same.

I would have compromised my relationship with my girlfriend

and gone straight to the nearest police station to file a report. I couldn't have done more than that—she'd been adamant that she hadn't hurt any people, and maybe she'd been high enough to believe it at that time. But I wouldn't let her get away with it, because that was where the spiral had begun.

That was the final step into the abyss. From there, everything fell down and crumbled like an elaborate beautiful castle made of fucking cards.

I had started snorting cocaine.

And speed.

And drinking even more than I ever had before.

I'd distanced myself from Fallon, not quite willing to let her go yet, but depressed enough that I didn't want to touch her anymore.

I couldn't write. Not anything decent, anyway.

Cock My Suck, my failure of an album, was supposed to be a huge fuck you to the Suits I worked with, but really, it was a massive, angry dick pissing on my own career. Because it was full of angry, empty, soulless songs.

Maybe I had invited Will Bushell to take Fallon away from me. Could I really blame her for choosing him? I hadn't wanted to touch her. I was always too busy to actually deal with her. And he was responsible, smart, sober, and savvy. But this was ancient history, and now I had my future to worry about.

"I hate you so much," Craig spat the same words his sister told me in my face, yet again not answering my question. It was weird, how I couldn't feel my flesh anymore, but I did feel his warm saliva dripping on the side of my cheek.

"I know," I ground out. Despite everything, it hurt to hear it. Not that I normally cared. I had people telling me I ruined music, people making voodoo dolls of me, and endless stalkers trying to harm me, and their existence was meaningless to me. But this was different. This was the guy whose sister I was in love with.

That was the first time the thought hit me fully, a wrecking ball straight to the brain, denting it well and good in the shape of Indie. I was in love. I'd known it, I'd felt it, but using the exact word at the exact time made everything clearer.

"You need to go to the hospital." Craig sniffed, righting himself with a high stool by the kitchen island and standing up.

I made a *humph* noise, not bothering to move. The floor felt quite comfortable at that moment.

"Where is she?" I asked again.

He shook his head like I was a lost cause. "Seriously, man, what the fuck? Why didn't you fight back?" He started coming back to my vision inch by inch. He looked like hell with stubble and dripped sour sweat right into the open wounds on my face. But he'd asked a question, so it was only fair I give him an answer.

"Because I love her," I said. There was nothing to worry about when you told the truth. The truth was factual, and facts are things you can't change or bend to your will. "Because I love your sister and because I deserved to get my arse kicked," I finished.

Craig squatted down, squinting at me like I was the most ridiculous thing he'd ever seen. Maybe I was.

"You love my sister?"

"Probably more than I love sex and The Smiths and my Les Paul Gibson guitar combined." I tried to nod, but that was a mistake. It hurt like a thousand bitches in heat.

"Then what the hell are you doing here sulking like a pussy? Didn't you Brits write some good-ass, solid love songs back in the day? Get your ass in rehab. Get clean. Find her. Grovel to her. Win her back. And love her."

"Rehab," I repeated. The plan had always been to get her first. Who had time to rehab when you were on the edge of love?

"Rehab"—he gave me a curt nod—"That's my plan anyway. I can't lose what I have. I just needed to beat the shit out of you, making one last huge mistake before I start doing things right."

It filled my stomach with something. Maybe it was an internal organ that had exploded there, but perhaps it was hope. Call me optimistic, but I suspected it was the latter.

Craig stood up again. "I'm calling you an ambulance." His voice was detached.

I shook my head, but even that prompted me to wince. Had he broken my neck? I wouldn't be able to breathe if he had. I tried to tell myself it was going to be one of the things we'd laugh about in the future. When Indie was pregnant with our kid and we'd be barbecuing in someone's backyard. 'Remember the time you almost broke my neck?' Ha. Ha. Well, shit. I really did need rehab.

"Don't call an ambulance," I grunted, finally wiping his saliva from my face. "I deserve at least an hour more of sulking on the floor. But do me a favor and bring me my fags, yeah?"

He walked off and slammed the door behind him.

I started laughing.

Hysterically.

Madly.

Illogically.

The beast had a reason to wake up tomorrow morning. That was, if he'd ever make it to it.

Chapter Thirty

Indie

Three days after Alex got back to Los Angeles, I got a visit.

It wasn't from him. He still didn't know where I was—with Clara, at her Santa Monica home. It was Jenna, Blake, Lucas, and Hudson.

Jenna had a small baby bump that made my heart burst and ache at the same time. Blake looked like he'd won the lottery when he held her hand in his, barely containing a grin he knew he needed to wipe off—my situation wasn't as great as his. Lucas looked like Lucas, and Hudson...in short, Hudson looked like the fourth lost Jonas brother who'd had too many discount vouchers to the tanning salon. Clara, who was upstairs in bed, told me I could treat this as my own house, so I did, and made them tea with milk and cookies. We all sat in her living room.

"Nice place," Jenna said coldly, rubbing her little bump, an addition to her otherwise slender figure. She was wearing a crisp, white suit, blazer and all. Blake grinned at her like she was the sun, and again, I found myself aching to be looked at that way. Alex didn't really count. He was a full-blown drug addict at this point, so who knew if what he felt for me was genuine.

"Thank you." I tucked my hands between my thighs. "Why are you here?"

They told me they were there because of the whole Fallon thing. They wanted Craig and me to know she would be tried for her crime. I thanked them—and I meant it—I was seriously relieved to know that Lankford would see justice. At the same time, I didn't have it in me to actually be happy.

"Also, we're pregnant," Blake announced.

I smiled. "I knew."

"You did?"

"Yup."

"Why didn't you tell me?" Blake's cheeks pinked. He looked like a child himself in that moment.

"Lies kept the tour running, right?" I took a sip of my tea. "Letters from the Liars. That's what this tour should have been called."

"Also, I'm gay." Lucas tried to lighten up the mood by raising his arm and wiggling his fingers.

"I know that, too."

"Alex?" Lucas sighed.

I shook my head. "I saw the way you looked at him in Paris. It was the same way I looked at him. Like I would kill for him. I knew you would, too."

And wasn't it the ultimate irony? The idea that I would have killed for the man who was connected to my parents' deaths? I decided not to think about it that way. I'd been given a gift—the rare gift of loving wholly and entirely—and it had been good while it had lasted.

"I'm gay, too." Hudson mimicked Lucas' raised hand, and we all burst out laughing. Then Blake asked everyone if we could have a moment, and we walked out to Clara's patio. We stood in front of the perennial shrubs when he opened his blazer and produced an envelope from an inner pocket.

"Your check."

"I've already gotten paid." I scrunched my nose. Fully, actually. Even though I bailed on them three weeks before the tour was over. Though no one could blame me, for obvious reasons.

"Yeah. That's a bonus for suffering through the madness." He smirked.

"You mean, it's silence money so I won't talk to the press about

Alex's connection in the case." I smiled sweetly back. Somewhere along the way during this tour, I'd become a bit of a cynic. Craig said it was a good thing. He said I'd needed that in order to grow.

Blake tilted his head, furrowing his brows. "Not at all. He never spoke a word to me about it, and he talks about you all the time. You should know one thing, Blue. He loves you. In his own, fucked-up, dysfunctional way. He does. This tour changed him. He looked more present than he did the entire seven years since he got big. And I'm not here to make you change your mind—hell, I'm not even sure you should. He is a drug addict and a screwed-up soul beneath it all. But don't regret a moment of what happened there. It was the real deal, Indie. It was what great albums are made of."

I told him I couldn't accept the check.

Then I told him I thought he was going to make a great dad, and he blushed—Blake actually blushed—and told me quietly that he'd bought a ring. I smiled. They were going to make one beautiful, highly functional, extremely put-together family.

I hugged everyone—especially Hudson, time and time again—before they left.

When Lucas squeezed me, he whispered into my ear, "I know I can't have him, so I don't mind if you do. But if you ever take him back, please make him happy."

I told him I would never take Alex back, and Lucas dragged his index finger from his eye to his mouth, like he was sad about it. I was, too.

After they left I picked up my phone—my new phone, not the cracked one, I couldn't look at anything broken anymore without thinking about Alex—and called Craig. I'd been meaning to do it for a long time, but the visit from the guys made me resolute.

"Hello?" Craig coughed into the phone.

"Alex is back in Los Angeles." I drew in a shaky breath. Craig had been asleep when Alex had come to see me three days ago, and I'd asked Nat not to tell him, but her loyalty was with him. Always with him.

"I know. The air already stinks of self-indulgent cockiness."

"Don't do anything stupid," I warned.

"Too late. Did you really think I wasn't going to seek him out? He hurt me just as much as he hurt you, and Nat knew I deserved to know."

He was wrong, but arguing this point was futile.

"Jesus, Craig. What did you do?"

"Messed him up a little. Don't worry, your lover boy will still survive. Why are you calling me, Indie?" He sounded cold. All business. I blinked away my tears, looking up, at the patio, at the shrubs, at the beauty in the world. *I am doing this for you, Craig. And you just made my decision a whole lot easier.* "Pack a bag. You're going to rehab first thing Monday morning."

"Says who?" He snorted, but didn't argue. I knew he was toying with the idea. Nat told me. But I also knew Craig needed me to make him. Needed to rebel against me, just for the sake of it.

"Says the girl who's going to kick you out of the apartment she will stop paying for if you don't get cleaned up. Me."

Alex

I did wake up that morning.

I woke up, and instead of hating the world, and my life, and the Suits, and even Indie for not being with me, I forced myself to say a little thank you—inwardly. In-fucking-wardly, of course—and called a cab to get me to the airport on my way to Bloomington, Indiana.

I was waiting by the locked iron gates of the fancy-schmancy condo with my Wayfarers and scowl intact when I saw him. Simply Steven: blogger, fashion-icon, and the bane of my existence. He loitered outside, hands shoved deep in his pockets, looking worried, anxious, and guilty.

I didn't know why he'd be the latter. Last I checked, I was the one who'd planted a fist in his face. In my defense, his face looked better that way, and not because he was ugly, but because he was smug.

You know, the kind of smug that warranted a punch in the face. Really, I was doing some kind of public service. I didn't ask for a thank you, but the arrest was a stretch.

Contrary to general belief and *Us Weekly*, what had prompted me to lose my shite on Simply Steven wasn't, in fact, because he'd asked me how it felt to have my fiancée shagged by my best friend. No. It was afterward, when he yelled at me that my last album was depressing and that 'music is supposed to be fun.'

On what planet was music supposed to be fun? He sounded like MTV after the Suits killed it and made it a reality TV channel for pimply teenagers. Music is supposed to be overwhelming and defeating and bone-crushingly moving.

So I punched him. Now he hates me. Which begs the eternal question—what the fuck?

"The Botox clinic is down the road." I gathered phlegm in my throat and spat it on the ground. My back still felt naked and too light without Tania. How the hell was I going to face rehab without her?

"Ha-ha. I'm here for you." He shifted a little and kicked a rock that clashed against my boot.

"Yay me," I said flatly, putting a fag in my mouth and lighting up. "What do you want?"

"My sponsor says I owe you an apology."

"You have a sponsor? What did you get addicted to, eyelash extensions?"

"Always the funny guy, Winslow. And, yeah. I was. It…was… heroin."

I did not expect to hear that. Didn't matter, though. This entire city was built on powder and coats upon coats of makeup. Nothing surprised me anymore, other than the sheer surprise of finding someone who still had their soul intact, like Indie. I tapped my cigarette with my finger, looking sideways. *Where's that cab?*

"Apology accepted," I said.

"You don't know what I'm apologizing for," he countered, sticking his head between the bars of the gate like a dumb puppy. As if that wasn't enough, his eyes were sad. His malnourished body and too shiny hair and veneer teeth depressed me, and I wondered if I looked the same. Perfectly pathetic.

"What are you apologizing for?" Seriously, where was that cab?

"Hey, did someone beat you up?" He squinted at the blue and purple staining my face, then rattled the gate like a prisoner. I halted for a moment before opening the gateway and letting him in. Perhaps I was the one who'd had his arse kicked, but he was the one looking pitiful.

"None of your business."

"You look rough, man." He stepped inside the premises.

"Well, let's just say Karma is a nasty bitch, and her brother, Fate, is not much better," I muttered.

"Anyway." He ran his fingers through his sunshine hair. It was obvious we were making conversation—maybe even an important conversation—but we were both locked inside our worlds. "The alcohol you had sent to your rooms…that was me. I hated you, Winslow. Still do. You humiliated me in front of the entire world and made me look like a pussy. Getting back at you was almost easy. Hotel staff would do anything for money. But, it was wrong, and I'm sorry."

I finally stepped out of my own head, from my misery and doubt and worry over everything Stardust-related, to attend the shitshow in front of me. I turned around to face him.

"You sent the alcohol?" My head was pounding. I'd been so certain it was Will. Turned out, it wasn't his doing, either. So what was Will responsible for, really, in terms of ruining my life? Just for taking Fallon. And even that had been a huge favor.

"I did. I wanted you to relapse." He rubbed the back of his neck, sighing. "I wanted you sad. Like me."

"You little…"

The cab arrived just then, the driver honking outside of the gate. I grabbed my duffel bag and slung it over my shoulder. "Fuck you." I shoved my index finger to his chest, then left.

"Alex…" he called after me.

I would forgive him, later. Not today.

I rang Blake on my way to the airport, knowing he'd fill Alfie and Lucas in.

"We should probably report him to the police," Blake said. "That's what he did to you."

"Nah. I'm better than the shithead," I said, and at that time, it wasn't true yet. But I knew I needed to be better than him, and better than most people, to redeem myself.

So I did.

The second time in rehab was different. I knew it was different because this time, I paid attention. Not that I'd had any reason not to give it an honest shot the first time around. I was simply too self-absorbed and full of words like 'integrity' and 'artistic process' and 'Iggy Pop.' The first time I'd had absolutely nothing to distract me. My last album had flopped harder than a Lindsey Lohan movie, Fallon was with Will, Blake and Jenna were putting out all of the fires I'd left behind, and all I'd been asked—literally, the only thing I was expected to do—was to come out of there in one piece.

This time, I had a huge album in my hands, my greatest master-piece, waiting to be produced and released, and I just had to sit on it. I had a girl to win—Stardust—and the uncertainty of second-guessing whether she'd even hear me out consumed every millisecond of my day. Still, I knew rehab was important.

So I listened.

I went to every class.

I held hands with strangers. With suburban mummies who'd

gotten addicted to prescription pills, and a preacher's son who'd fallen into the arms of heroin, and a Russian oligarch's daughter who, like me, had snorted pounds and pounds of cocaine to numb the feeling that the world was closing in on you from all angles. I wrote letters to my family and friends. Angry letters. Apologetic letters. Funny letters. Then I burned them all. I couldn't write Stardust shite, though. Everything I had to say to her—every single groveling word—had to be said in person.

I took the extended rehab program—I call it the I-truly-give-a-shit program—despite my urge to win Indie—but also *because* of it—even though I knew every day I wasn't releasing my new album, I was losing money, and sponsorships, and listeners, and fandom, and who the fuck knows what else.

Three months passed. I came out of rehab.

Blake wanted to pick me up, but I didn't want to rehash the last time I'd gotten out. I thought it'd jinx the whole process, which, in itself, was a ridiculous thought, but I indulged myself anyway. I took a cab straight to the airport. I landed in New York a few hours later. Ate a gas station sandwich—because some things never change—then crashed for fifteen hours. I slept like I'd never slept in my life. Like I'd worked the entire three months in a fucking cornfield. Then I woke up, took the subway just to feel human again, pulling my beanie and hoodie all the way down, and showed up at the recording studio.

Two months passed. I recorded an album.

Another three months of promotions, and interviews, and magazine covers, and *The Comeback of the Year!* headlines. *Alexander Winslow: An Artist, a Poet, and a New Man.* And, *Guess Who's Back?* And, *Will Bushell, Who?*

I felt the time slipping between my hands, but Blake told me it was okay. That she would still remember. That real love never dies. That I needed to prove to her I was actually sober for long enough to make her believe it.

Now, let me tell you something about my album. *Midnight Blue* broke the record for fastest-recording album in the history of that

Williamsburg studio. It took me one week to record and produce twelve songs.

1. The Little Prince
2. Chasing Asteroids
3. Under Darker Skies
4. Maybe It's You
5. Was She Worth It?
6. Perfectly Paranoid
7. Oh, But You Are
8. A Different Kind of Love
9. Seek and Kill
10. Why Now?
11. Fool For You
12. Midnight Blue

Midnight Blue was the first single I dropped. Jenna and Blake flew into New York that weekend to remind my fragile ego and pompous arse that it was a process. That, at first, the radio stations run the song for trial on different hours of the day and see how it goes. That building hype takes time, and patience, and a lot of arse-kissing. But with *Midnight Blue*, I didn't need any of it. The song just sort of exploded, the way my career had when I'd first broken into Billboard when I was twenty-one years old, and took over the charts like they'd been sitting pretty and waiting for me their whole lives.

And it was nice. And reassuring. And completely unimportant in the grand scheme of things. Don't get me wrong—I recorded the album because I wanted to record it. It was a part of a bigger plan, a detailed, persevering, calculated one. I wanted Indie to know what she was to me. She wasn't a dirty fuck, or a pristine secret, or a mistake. She wasn't some roadie I'd climbed on top of every night because she was there and available.

She was my muse.

She was my life.

She was my all.

I took a plane back to Los Angeles nine months after I landed in New York. I was sober, on top of my game, and ready to chase what was mine.

Only Indie had never been mine. She was, in fact, the one thing I couldn't even think about ever claiming, because I didn't deserve her. But I finally understood what Will, Lucas, and Blake had wanted to do. Even more frightening than that—I was happy they'd done it, because if they hadn't thrust her into my life, I would've never given rehab a second chance, I would've never written *Midnight Blue*, and I definitely wouldn't have understood what this thing I made millions upon millions upon—Love—had meant.

"Alex Winslow! Looking mighty fine, dude." An American paparazzo jumped into my face at LAX, followed by a bunch of paparazzi photographers. They all wore ball caps and black clothes and smiles that were a cross between taunting and downright smug.

"Never been better." I smiled. Which was partly right, and partly so, so wrong. I was breezing through security, two nameless bodyguards by my side. I didn't usually use them—I counted on my friends to throw off potential stalkers or overtly aggressive fans—but I needed to do this alone.

I slid into a rental car—I didn't want a driver or anything else remotely fancy—and programmed Indigo's address into my Waze app. I knew she still lived at her old place, even though she'd rented a better one for Craig, Natasha, and Ziggy. Because that's the kind of person she was. Selfless. It'd been so many months, the thought she wouldn't remember me occurred as I pulled out of the massive parking lot and into the constant, never-ending traffic of Los Angeles. It was utterly ridiculous to feel that way. Indie couldn't have forgotten about the first man who'd fucked her—*really fucked her*—the first man she'd given her heart to, the first man who'd broken it without even meaning to, and the first man who'd ruined her life. Those were too many firsts. Good and bad. Fact.

I was all wired up and ready to explode in the car on my way to

her. My foot kept bouncing on the brake pedal, which prompted the
drivers behind and ahead of me to honk their horns and flip me the
bird.

"You can't rush love!" I popped my head out from the window,
forcing myself to laugh.

"Holy shit, Mom! It's Alex Winslow!" a teenybopper yelled from a
Toyota Corolla next to mine amidst the traffic jam.

When I finally took a turn to her neighborhood, my heart started racing insanely fast. I didn't know what the hell was going on, but
I was worried it might be a heart attack. That couldn't be too good.
I already looked like shite. I had bags under my eyes from working
nonstop and my hair needed a cut two months ago, straddling the line
between a tousled mane and an almost man-bun. Not that I would
ever collect my hair in an elastic. That was almost as unacceptable as
making country music. Point was, I looked rough, and now I was also
sweating like a pig. Great.

*Come get it, Indie. A sweaty, ex-druggie with baggy eyes. Every
girl's dream.*

It took me twenty minutes to find a parking space, and I was actually pathetically thankful for that, because it gave me time to stall.
It gave me the chance to think about what I was going to say to her.
You'd think I would've been more prepared, but you'd be wrong, because the conversation I wanted to have with her could go so many
different ways, I constantly changed my mind about how to approach
it.

I parked.

Got out of the car.

Heavy feet. Heavy heart. I climbed up the stairs, feeling irrationally hopeful and soul-crushingly disheartened at the same time. I
knocked on the door. Stared at it for a few seconds, feeling a sweat
drop slithering from my temple all the way into my right eye without
moving an inch. I tried to listen to the sound coming from the inside,
but the place was dead. I knew I would, and could, stay there. In the
hallway. Waiting for her. There was something symbolic about it, too.

But the truth was, I couldn't endure another minute of waiting.

I'd waited for her in rehab.

And I'd waited for her when I recorded *Midnight Blue*.

I'd waited for her on every airplane I took, every interview I'd given, every fan I'd hugged, every hour I'd spent away from her. Every breath I'd taken without knowing what she was doing. I'd paid my dues.

I knocked again. The third time. Then rang the doorbell.

She wasn't there.

I decided to get out of the building and walk around. Maybe she'd gone to the grocery store down the road. Maybe she would meet me halfway, and her big, blue eyes would widen, and she'd run toward me in slow-motion, and we would kiss slow and hard and wouldn't even have to talk about any of the bad shit that had happened between us.

My legs carried me down her street. I passed the grocery, and the Israeli coffee shop, and the Korean nail salon. I knew these places because I may or may not have visited her neighborhood once or twice or twelve times before I'd finally dragged my arse to rehab. I cut a corner and stopped at a junction that kissed a small park with a few benches scattered around some swings and a slide. It was tiny, really, and wouldn't have caught my attention in a million years if it weren't for a bright blue pram parked beside a bench.

A bench on which my very personal Blue, Indie "Stardust" Bellamy, was sitting.

Cooing at the baby inside the pram.

A baby.

Not a toddler like Ziggy. A newborn baby.

She was wearing a big, floaty white dress, and her blue hair was braided and flung over one shoulder the way I liked it. I froze in my spot, unable to take a peek. But she did the job for me by rocking the pram back and forth. When she pulled it away from her, I got a decent look at the little human inside it.

He or she was so tiny.

My heart stopped. Literally stopped—and yes, I know what the word 'literally' means. It was too early in the day, after too many hours on a plane, to do the math. Was it mine? Was it someone else's? God. Fuck. It couldn't have been someone else's. This baby was mine. Jesus Christ. I had a baby. *Indie* had a baby. And she hadn't said anything. Not a phone call. Not a letter. No nothing.

She'd had so many ways of contacting me. I'd made sure my whole staff was available for her. Blake checked on her every week to assure me she was fine. Jenna would accept any message she'd wanted to send me through her with open arms. Especially now, when she was a mother and actually resembled a warm and welcoming human being. Not to mention Indie had both my phone numbers, my email, and my secret Facebook account I'd only given ten people in the entire world. Anger swept through me.

Now I was moving, all right.

Back and forth, pacing on the sidewalk by the busy road like a bloody moron. She hadn't seen me yet, but she would, soon, and what was I going to say? Cheers for letting me know I'm a father? Then again, she had a very good reason to be mad at me…

Fuck. *Fuck.*

We'd deal with it, I decided. We'd deal with the baby. He or she was so small, anyway. They wouldn't even remember I hadn't been present in their lives for the first few months or so. It was fine. We could pick up from where we left things off. If anything, wasn't it an incentive for Indie to give me another chance? I was sober, richer than God, and desperately in love with her. Plus, I'd change diapers and do all the messy shite a lot of blokes shied away from. Hell, I hated that I saw the baby as a way to have leverage over her. I was thinking like high, manipulative Alex again, and I really wanted to leave that bastard behind, in rehab, when I left it.

I took a step into the park at the same time someone else did. But he was faster, not slowed down by the shock and horror at finding out what I just had.

He breezed past me.

Walked over to her.

Wrapped his arm around her shoulder.

Kissed her cheek…

It is scientifically impossible to die of a broken heart. I discovered it in that moment. Because if it was, I'd already be dead. Done. Over. That's how much it had hurt to see them together. I watched them. She smiled at him as he sat down.

She was so beautiful.

He was so…not.

Normal brown hair. Normal clothes. Normal height. Normal weight. Just normal. What the hell did he think? Walking into her life with his normalcy and picking up the pieces—*my* pieces—playing daddy to this baby—*my* baby. I wanted to walk over there and beat the shit out of him. I didn't even care that I had a criminal record, and the last time I got bailed for DUI and insinuating I'd wanted to shag an officer, my lawyer had warned me that the United States of America had just about had enough of my sorry arse, and the next time I got into trouble, I could get deported.

You can't allow yourself to get deported, idiot. You have a baby to think about now.

Fine. I wasn't going to beat the shit out of him. But I was going to do something.

I wish I had the virtue of patience. Then, maybe, I would have thought things through. Taken a few steps away, made a phone call, to Blake or Jenna or even Lucas, and asked them how does one react to the news that his ex—Indie was my ex, for the sake of this argument—had his baby, and moved on with some useless prat. I would maybe even go as far as asking them how—despite all the progress I'd shown—they still couldn't trust my judgment, and had therefore hidden the existence of my baby from me. Because they absolutely knew. They had to know. Blake, Hudson, and Lucas were all in touch with Stardust. I knew that.

But I didn't have anything other than a thousand burning suns in the pit of my stomach, suns that told me I'd be burned alive if I didn't approach them, and so I did.

I light-jogged to them, feeling angry and relieved at the same time.

Indie's head snapped up when I was about three feet away from her, and she dragged her eyes from the baby she cradled and fed, staring back at me.

I stopped, unable to make the rest of the journey. Her eyes paralyzed me, but it was her expression that undid me. She looked like she was...sorry. Like she'd missed me. Like she, too, had a lot of things to say. But she didn't move, either, so we just looked like we were in an old movie that had frozen on a scene. The bastard beside her dragged his gaze up, every muscle in his face lax and happy.

"What's going on? Do you know this guy, Indie?"

This guy?

This guy?

The fucker better not have touched my baby, or I would have to kill him, deportation or not. Besides, what the hell did he mean, 'this guy'? Had she not told him she'd had Alex Winslow's baby? I wasn't some arsehole from the street. Even if he didn't know who I was—fat chance, but some people just have bad taste in music—she still ought to have mentioned I was, in fact, a famous musician of some sort.

"Yeah, I..." she said slowly, still clasping the baby to her chest.

"Don't." I took a step forward, shaking my shock off. "Don't downplay us. Not right now, and especially not after what I'm seeing here."

"And what, exactly, are you seeing here?" She held my gaze. How could she say that? While holding the product of what we were to each other. Did I turn the women in my life into cold bitches, or was I naturally attracted to them and Indie had just been incredibly good at hiding it so far?

"We need to talk." I breathed through my nose slowly, slowly, so fucking slowly, trying to incorporate every single piece of advice I'd been given in rehab. No one had warned me that the outside world I was being sent to had turned upside down while I was sitting in a circle clapping for people who bragged about not drinking their mouthwash to get high when their mother-in-law was in town.

"Maybe it's not a good idea." She sighed. Jesus, *what the fuck?* She didn't even want to talk about it?

"No." Another step forward. "Stardust, you listen to me. I've been through hell the last few months. For you. I'm not asking for a medal, or even for forgiveness—though that'd be really fucking grand, mind you—I'm just asking you kindly, respectfully, *pleadingly*, to listen to me."

She put the formula bottle down on the bench and hugged the baby to her chest. He was cute. Cute, but he did not resemble her, and I was starting to grow incredibly confused. For one thing, he looked closer to a year old than a newborn. Secondly, I wasn't much of a gene expert, but little guy had a head full of raven hair, and both Indie and I had brown hair in different shades. Mine was more chestnut; her original hair color was honey-ish, flirting with blond. I knew that because sometimes she forgot to wax the hair off her p—actually, it didn't really matter how I knew that. I just did.

"Now's not a good time."

Her voice was quiet and guarded, and why in the world had the guy beside her not punched me yet? If this were me sitting beside her, the first fist would have been thrown the moment someone had even approached my girl. *My girl.* Was she his girl? I was going to be sick.

"When's a good time?" I asked, still standing too closely and staring at her too eagerly. She looked left and right, blowing a lock of hair that fell from her braid aside.

"I don't know, eight? Would you still be around?"

Would I still be around? I had no intention of fucking leaving this neighborhood until we had a lengthy talk. I nodded, pointing at the baby. I had to. Even though I knew I was going to hate either answer, though for very different reasons.

"I'll wait outside your door. Just one thing, Indie. Is he mine?"

She looked down at the baby, and smiled at him, and he smiled at her, and oh, fuck, she looked like the perfect, wholesome mum. She opened her mouth and spoke to me, but looked at him.

"No."

Indie

I knew he'd be there, so I stalled.

Alex had never been good at waiting. Everything was given to him quickly, urgently, *easily*. I wanted to see if he had changed. It was stupid, and small, and petty, but also necessary.

I was babysitting Clara's grandson, Grayson. Grayson's dad, Ollie, had gotten back from work early and decided to join us at the park. It wasn't out of character for Ollie to show up, but it was completely unexpected for Alex Winslow to be there.

Shortly after Alex came back to the States and I'd sought refuge somewhere he couldn't find me, Clara called and told me she'd broken her hip and was no longer able to look after Grayson for the upcoming months. She asked if I wanted the job, since I was a friend of the family and got along nicely with her son and his wife, Tiffany, and I immediately said yes. I didn't need the money particularly, but I needed the company, and the temporary accommodation before Alex left for rehab.

I liked my job, but that didn't mean I liked my life.

I hated my life. My life was Alex-less, and that was the worst way to live your life once you'd had a dose of the rocker.

I thought about it as I strolled at the farmer's market, looking, but not touching, all the rows of strawberries, peaches, and jars of homemade jam. It was only two weeks ago that I stopped waking up crying and hating myself for missing him.

Because I did. I missed him every day.

I missed the man who knew, or at the very least had great suspicion that his ex-girlfriend had taken lives that night.

The man who'd covered for his ex-lover's crimes knowingly.

The man who could have saved my mother, maybe, if he had been more persistent, and stubborn, and less jaded, and drunk, and tired of life. Because I knew he hadn't done it out of love for Fallon.

When you love, you want to fix.

When you love, you don't help to destroy.

And wasn't it what Alex was trying to do right now? Fix things between us?

I knew my brother and sister-in-law were not going to fault me for hearing him out. I even knew Alex did everything he could to take care of me. He sent me checks every month. Checks I tore and threw into the trash. Blake called me once a week. Jenna helped Craig get a maintenance job at her office building. The day Craig, Nat, and Ziggy had moved out, Lucas came in to install a new alarm system at the apartment and helped me paint the walls. Hudson would come every other Friday for sushi and *Gossip Girl*.

They all meant well.

Even Fallon hadn't meant any harm, but harm she did, anyway, which was why she was awaiting trial right now. I didn't know what Will thought about the whole thing, and sometimes, when I thought about him, which wasn't often, I'd hurt for him, too.

At seven thirty, I threw in the towel and headed back home. I didn't know what I was going to say to Alex and hadn't decided if I was going to forgive him or not. And that, in itself, was irresponsible and dangerous for my poor heart.

He waited for me in the hallway, his long legs bent in front of my door for lack of space. He was long, and lithe, and completely gorgeous, the way I remembered him. I stopped and squeezed the railing, my knuckles whitening, trying to gather my thoughts.

He noticed me and rose to his feet, and we stood in front of each other, staring, mostly.

"Feels a lot like midnight," he said. I didn't want to smile, but I did, anyway.

"Are you okay?" I whispered.

"Is he really not mine?" His eyes shone.

I shook my head. "No. He's with his dad now," I referred to Grayson.

"Okay." He nodded. "Okay. Have you listened to—"

"I have," I cut through his words. How could I miss the song about me, when it was the most played song in contemporary radio stations all across America?

Two souls collide on a too dark floor in a graveyard for the stars
Funny, when you walked into my life I thought I'd be the one leaving all the scars
There wasn't one moment when I knew you'd be mine
There were pieces of jigsaw, when I looked into your eyes

And at midnight, the sky turned blue
The night belonged to us, it was just me and you
And at midnight, you undressed me from my fears
I devoured your tears
Seconds became illuminated like years
And at midnight, I kissed your skin, your eyes, your lips
You shone so dangerously, my own little personal eclipse
And at midnight, I broke your heart
You broke mine too
We fell apart.

Once upon a time, I wanted to be someone's white knight
One upon a time, I thought I saw the light
Then you burst into my life like cerulean powder falling from above
Teaching me I never knew true love
You took my heart and held it in your teeth
I begged for you to bite it, oh, how I fucking loved your heat

And at midnight, the sky turned blue
You taught me feelings and moves, brand-new
And at midnight, I nipped at your flesh

Your walls crumbled one by one, even though you said you were in
it for the cash
    And at midnight, I fucked your body, your heart, your soul
    Joke's on me, 'cause now I'm the one who needs to crawl
    And at midnight, we broke together
    On the floor
    So fucked forever.

He even used a line I wrote to him.

A line I later saw somewhere else. On the Internet.

"Is that how you see our relationship?" My throat caught. God, I shouldn't have wanted to listen to him, but I couldn't help not to, either.

He nodded. "Not to be a jerk, but I'd rather we have this conversation inside, after you offer me a glass of water, because my mouth is still dry from the notion that baby could've been ours and you were raising it with some random bloke. But just to put it out there, I'm going to raise him as my own if you give me a chance."

Raise him as his own? I frowned, cocking my head to the side, before the penny dropped. Then I started laughing like a maniac. Oh, God. He thought Grayson was ours. *Mine.* That was hilarious, and frightening, and so, completely Alex to jump to such a drastic conclusion. I unlocked my door and pushed it open, and he followed behind me. The tension that was thick in the air evaporated—some of it, anyway—and I took out two bottles of water from the fridge, handing him one. I leaned against the countertop while he stood at the doorway to my small, stuffy kitchen and stared at me.

"I babysit Grayson. He's not mine, or yours. He's Ollie and Tiffany's. Clara's grandson," I clarified.

"Holy fuck, you could have started with that instead of laughing at me." He plastered his forehead to my fridge and smiled. "Thank God. I mean, cute kid. But still. Thank God."

I laughed some more, and he did, too, before we both turned serious again.

"I'm clean now, you know," he said, referring to the time he'd come back to Los Angeles, angry and crazy and so lost, trying to drag me back into his arms, never acknowledging my tragedy but illuminating his. "Just got done with my tour. Nine months sober. I wanted to show up after the month, but couldn't help myself. I was afraid you'd move on."

"I know you're sober." I bit my lower lip, then took a sip of my water just to do something with my hands and mouth. Blake kept me updated—even though I'd told him I didn't want to hear it. I was happy Alex was seeking help. I just didn't want to be in the loop to feed my obsession with him. *Because I hadn't moved on.*

"I'm happy for you, Alex. I am."

He swiveled his body to be aligned with mine, staring me down like the predator I longed to be devoured by. "It was the hardest thing I had to do in my entire life. Not the physical bit. That was a piece of cake, actually. But mentally. Making the conscious decision to never consume another drop of alcohol or a line of cocaine. Being so far away from you, because I knew you wouldn't accept me any other way—but even more alarmingly, maybe you wouldn't accept me even after all the changes I'd made. I'm not here to make promises, because promises are meant to be broken. I'm here to give you the facts, one by one. Fact number one"—he took a deep gulp of air, squeezing his eyes shut before opening them wide like he'd just risen from the bottom of the ocean coming back for air—"I love you, Indigo Bellamy. My love for you is like a studded leather jacket worn inside out. It digs into my chest, eager to produce blood. And I will do anything for you, not because you're my muse or my salvation or my best lay, but because you're inside me, like an organ, like a vital thing I cannot function without. I don't even want you at this point. I *need* you. It's different, and carnal, and completely necessary for my existence. Fact number two." He took a step toward me, and I tried hard not to wince, because it was too soon to touch, even if he'd just swiped my hair off my face. "I recognize, now, that I made your heartbreak about me. I was so consumed with wanting you, I cared more about not losing you than comforting you. I want you to know I'm deeply, wholeheartedly, dreadfully sorry. Regardless of who you are to me—the love of my life or some nameless girl I was never going to meet—I still would have done right by you had I known what was going on when Fallon came home the night of the accident. But I didn't. Not at the time, at least. You have to understand that, Indie, because I won't be able to survive living in this world knowing you think I could have saved your parents but chose not to."

Another step, and the distance between us erased, replaced with body heat and familiarity. The intimacy you couldn't fake in a million years. The one that comes with love. "Fact number three—I didn't know who you were. I didn't see you as a charity case. I thought it was sad that you were an orphan, but no sadder than how I'd lived my life without a family. In my mind, we were two asteroids orbiting around each other. I thought I was the sun and you were earth, but now I see I got it all mixed up. You were always the sun. And even now, when I look at you, I don't see regret and pain and suffering. I see the biggest opportunity, the sweetest promise, the road I should be taking."

We were toe-to-toe now. He put his palms on my cheeks, and my eyes stung, my heart racing wildly. I didn't push him away. Even the pain he gave me was special because it was his. I knew exactly what he'd meant by saying he needed me. I needed him, too. My life felt so hollow without him in it. Most days, I felt like I was merely existing, but nowhere near living.

"Fact number four—it doesn't matter what or who brought us together. But it happened, and we can't undo it. It's there, and we can't go back. When I saw you with a baby this afternoon, the first thing I wanted to do was snatch you both and run away from here with you in tow. Most of all, what scared me was that I wasn't even remotely disturbed by the idea of having a kid with you. And that says a lot. Shit, Stardust, that says everything. You're holding my world together in your delicate, freckled hands, and all I ask is for you not to toss it against the wall and break it to pieces."

His mouth closed in on mine, his lips tracing mine like braille, like he was trying to read the reaction out of me. I sucked in air and opened up for him, and we kissed so slow and so soft I thought I was being drugged into a lull. Eventually, I was the one to suck his tongue into my mouth and moan, trying to peel off his leather jacket. I wanted to believe he was sober and was going to stay that way, because deep inside, I'd already forgiven him.

Alex Winslow made me lose a part of my heart.

But he'd also sewn it back together, in tattered patches, in ugly patches, but it was whole. In its own, imperfect-but-still-working way.

"I love you," I whimpered into his mouth, tearing our kiss apart to say something important. "Before she died, my mother told me that in order to know if you're in love, you need to make a list of all the stupid things you did for that person. I made a list, Alex. It's not pretty. On paper, I'm kind of a fool."

He stared at me for a second, curving one side of his mouth and showing off the perfect row of teeth, like in the movies. His everywhere eyes sparkled with newfound happiness.

We stumbled to my bedroom. I laughed when we tripped over my new sewing machine. He hoisted me up and wrapped me around his waist, his signature move, and we were together again, in Moscow, Poland, Germany, London, and Paris.

He licked my cheek like a dog. "Mine. Claimed it."

"Yours." I licked his stubbled jawline, smiling. "Until the very last note."

Epilogue

Alex

"And the Grammy for Best Album of the Year goes to..." Bella Jordin is stalling, clutching the envelope, a smug smile on her face. I'd like to believe I'm above punching a woman, but the ball of tension blocking my throat begs to differ. Does she think it's cute? Does Bella Jordin think any of the fuckers who sit at the Oscars and Grammys and Emmys and have spent their entire year—fuck that, plural, *years*—working on their albums and movies and shows, really find it adorable, the way she drags it out like a juicy gum? I would like to do the same to her next time she gets checked for an STD.

"Hold it...just a little longer, Bella. Don't you like the anticipation of it all?"

Jenna, squeezing my bicep, throws a glance at my bouncing foot.

Tap. Tap. Tap, tap, tap, tap, tap.

The bloke in front of me—a newbie R&B producer who probably wrote two songs for Justin Bieber and now thinks he's God—turns around and shoots me a death glare. I shoot him an I'm-alive glare. Toothy grin galore.

"And the Grammy goes to...Alex Winslow! 'Harquebus'!" she shrieks into the microphone, and the camera zooms in on me, and I do the usual thing where I feign surprise and point at myself.

I get up and squeeze past Jenna and Blake, who are holding hands. Blake is on his phone—shocker—probably asking the babysitter how their daughter, Cecilia, is doing. Alfie is sitting beside me with his date—some girl from the British *Big Brother*—and Lucas and Hudson are all but making out behind me. On my way to the stage, I tap Will Bushell's shoulder, and he gives me the thumbs-up. This doesn't mean I like him, but I definitely don't hate him anymore. Mostly, I'm relieved he didn't steal the one thing that truly mattered.

Then again, if Fallon were Indie, I wouldn't have fallen so far down in the rabbit hole. I would've stayed above water just in case I needed to save her, too.

I climb up to the stage. There's always this weird notion up there, like the whole world is watching you, waiting for you to cock up. Fall on your arse, burp into the mic, or shit your trousers. The Grammys two years ago was such a disaster. The Prime Minister of England was recorded shaking her head and muttering, "Oh, Christ" when she watched the video of me representing our fine nation. Today, I want to get it over with as soon as possible.

Smiling at Bella and planting the usual, nice-to-see-you-but-please-no-mingling kiss on her cheek, I grab the Grammy and put my lips to the mic. This feels a lot like home. The bumpy metal against my lips. But the only home I'm interested in right now is on the other end of the city, and I'm eager to get back to her.

"Congrats, Alex. I loved your 'Back to Life' tour! My personal favorite." Bella kisses my cheek again. Now I smile my I-heard-your-music-and-I'm-not-sure-whether-to-take-that-as-a-compliment smirk, then turn back to the mic.

"Two years ago, I took this stage and made a fool of myself. I snatched a statue that wasn't mine from someone who deserved it— yeah, mate, guess your album wasn't so bad after all." I shrug and gesture to Will, who laughs softly and shakes his head. His date—a girl he met building a school in Madagascar or something—squeezes his hand as Indie so often squeezes mine. After Fallon finished rehab, she got sentenced to five years of community service, more or less, wrote the Bellamys sincere apology letters, and she is now living with her photographer boyfriend in Georgia and works as a yoga instructor, far away from Hollywood.

"But things have changed since then. For one thing, I checked into rehab." Pause. "Second time is the charm, right?" People clap, snort, some nod knowingly. "The second thing that happened was that I wrote an album I don't deserve the credit for. 'Midnight Blue' doesn't belong to me; it belongs to *her*. And that leads me to the third thing—I met a girl. I fell in love with her, and she fell in love with me. I took her words and her soul and every single original thought and beautiful lyric she gave me, thinking I didn't owe anything back. But this girl, she became my muse for a reason, and she busted my balls for being a selfish arsehole. This girl can't be here today because she's in the delivery room, giving me yet another gift I don't deserve. Only now I'm going to make sure I come close to being enough for her and our baby. I came here to grab this statue because I couldn't make it to the last Grammys—I was too busy groveling and rehabbing in order to win the girl back—but now I need to go back to her. You see, my girl is so selfless, she told me if I never showed up to my own party, then she'd leave me, and I can't let that happen. So, here you go, Stardust." I raise the Grammy in my hand and look at the camera. "Got us another ugly decoration for the bathroom. Can I come back now? I'd really like to save the therapy money for when our kid finds out I was at the Grammys when she was born."

The room fills with more laughter, and everybody gets up and claps, and even though it's nice, I'm done settling for nice. I don't want anyone to pat my ego, and have no need to prove myself to anyone. I jump onto Craig's motorcycle—he is waiting for me, double-parked on the curb behind the arena—and we speed through the traffic jams of L.A. and toward the only thing that matters.

Indie

Poppy has her father's eyes.

Brown flaked with green and gold, they stare back at me with a mixture of mischievousness and curiosity, telling me I'm in for a lot of trouble. She curls her fists and yawns toothlessly before closing her eyes again, and I can't stop looking.

Poppy Elizabeth Winslow is a fresh start. She looks it, she smells it, and she *is* it. We all eventually experience tragedy in our lives—loss of relatives, friends, and things that are important to us—but not all of us are blessed enough to be given great gifts along with our losses.

I am.

I am that blessed.

I've lost my parents and gained a husband and a baby. A family that's not patchy, like The Paris Dress, but resilient, like Alex and me. Every Friday, I invite Nat, Craig, Ziggy, Blake, Jenna, Cecilia, Alfie, Lucas, and Hudson over for dinner. We laugh and eat and play board games like it's 1993 and these people are not rock stars. And to me, they aren't. They're just…people.

And it will probably be a little sad to leave here and move to our new apartment—or rather, *flat*, above the Cambridge Castle. But we love the apartment. It's full of soul, and only five minutes away from the thrift shop I have leased a few months ago and is now getting refurbished.

Alex Winslow asked me to marry him three days after he barged back into my life and into my shitty apartment. I guess I had it coming. After all, everything he does is in spectacular fashion and grand gestures. The proposal happened on the floor of my rundown condo, right after we had kitchen sex. I was letting the cool tiles soothe my sore skin and staring through the window at a tree when he said, "You know, we could be doing the same thing, but on a nicer floor if we just moved in together."

I threw an arm over my face to muffle the sound of my laughter. "Yeah? You think we'll be better off living in some fancy hotel in the middle of traffic-central?"

"I'm thinking somewhere gray and grim in the middle of Camden Town. Close to the tube. Buzzing with people and life and music. A flat with double-glazed windows."

"Why double-glazed?" I whipped my head in his direction. He looked spent, sweaty, and delicious. He ran a hand through his brown locks and hitched one shoulder up. "Don't wanna scare the tourists with your moans."

I swatted his chest, and it was his turn to laugh.

"Seriously, half the time it sounds like I'm attacking you with a chainsaw when we're together. So, what do you say, Stardust?" He rolled to his side, propping his head in his hand. "Move in with me?"

I opened my mouth with the intention of saying yes, because life was too short not to do what you wanted to do, when he beat me to it.

"Actually, forget it. I take it back."

"You take it back?" I blinked, my stomach churning in disbelief.

"Yeah." He crawled to me on his knees. "Moving in is not enough. I want everything. And I want it on fucking paper. Marry me, Indigo 'Stardust' Bellamy. Be my wife. Have my babies. We'll even circumcise them if that's what you want. Well, maybe not the girls. That's a hard limit for me. Or maybe we won't have children. How do you feel about children? Never mind. I don't care. I just want to marry you. Make me a happy bastard, Indie. Say yes."

I didn't say yes. I giggled it.

I also told him that my middle name is Elizabeth, like Poppy's— *not*, in fact, Stardust.

We got married in a rose garden in Kent. The roses were painted blue. I stuffed his private jet with all the people I loved—Natasha, a very sober Craig—who had to take time off from school after enrolling into college—Ziggy, Clara, Tiffany, Ollie, Grayson, and the rest of our tour friends, including Jenna and Hudson. I wore a Bohemian Forest wedding gown, and he wore a shit-eating grin he is still sporting every single day. Getting pregnant wasn't a decision. It was, rather, a moment of insanity. We'd always used condoms, until one night, we didn't. Alex said he'd pull out at the last minute, and he did—I had a stomach covered in semen to prove it—but I guess not enough, because a month later, I started getting violent reactions to the scents of coffee and cigarettes.

I quit the coffee.

He quit the cigarettes.

And now we have Poppy.

"Mate, I'm so happy you had her with someone fit. You really needed some beauty to dilute all the fugliness that's your face. Poppy is gorgeous," Alfie says now, in the hospital suite, staring at Poppy, who is napping in my arms.

Alex awards him with an elbow to the ribs before stretching his arms toward me. I'm still in bed, but I'm feeling better since he helped me take a shower. Poppy is nuzzling into my neck, and my heart is close to bursting from being so full.

"Can I show her off?" He gives me his magnificent shy smirk. It's the kind that only makes a cameo once every few months, so I drink it up.

Three.

Two.

One.

"Of course."

I told you, heart.

We've got this, heart.

Look how far we've come, heart.

It's not the first time he's holding our daughter in his hands and looking down at her like she's a new world he wants to secure and nurture, but it's the first time the realization hits me. We found our planet. Our home. The only place we want to be in.

That's the thing about broken princes. Not all of them have to die. If their soul is whole, they sometimes survive.

Sometimes, they even grow up to be kings.

Mine did.

Loved Indie and Alex?

Sign up for my newsletter for exclusive bonus scenes and news:

http://goo.gl/FwfMzr

Acknowledgements

"Every book has a soul, the soul of the person who wrote it and the soul of those who read it and dream about it" – Carlos Ruiz Zafon, The Angel's Game.

This book is the fruit of a lot of sleepless nights, hectic days, and also the love and attention of the following unicorns:

To my editing team: Tamara Mataya, Paige Smith and Emily A. Lawrence of Lawrence Editing. You ladies are the very best, and your dedication and eye for detail is absolutely amazing.

To Stacey Ryan Blake for the gorgeous formatting, and Letitia Hasser of RBA Designs for the fantastic cover.

To my beta readers: Tijuana Turner, thank you, from the bottom of my heart, for all the love, hours and attention you've given Alex and Indie. You've been my rock for the longest time. Same goes for Amy Halter, who has read this book way too many times. Also read (and re-read, and then re-read again): Jade West, Ava Harrison, Kerry Duke and Paige Jennifer. You are my stars!

To my street team members—how sad and happy I am that I can no longer list all of your names without having to use an entire chapter?—you make all the difference in my career, and I'll continue dedicating all my books to you, one street team member at a time. My rock. My haven. My asteroid.

To my agent, Kimberly Brower. Thank you for your input, expertise, advise, and most of all—for the journey.

To the Sassy Sparrows, my reading group: you push me to grow as an artist with your continued support. So I will. I promise.

To my husband, son, Mom, Dad and best friends, Lin, Sunny and Ella. Hugs.

To all the bloggers who support me—you matter. So, so much.

And to you, my readers.

You're the real deal.

Love you.

L, xoxo.